The Girl In Cell A

About the Author

Vaseem Khan is the author of two crime series set in India: the Baby Ganesh Agency series and the CWA Historical Dagger-winning Malabar House novels set in 1950s Bombay. Vaseem is also the author of the forthcoming series of mystery novels featuring Q, the iconic character from the James Bond franchise. The first in the series, *Quantum of Menace*, will be published in Autumn 2025. Vaseem was born in London but spent a decade working in India. *The Girl in Cell A* is his first standalone thriller.

Also by Vaseem Khan

The Malabar House Series

Midnight at Malabar House
The Dying Day
The Lost Man of Bombay
Death of A Lesser God

The Baby Ganesh Agency Series

The Unexpected Inheritance of Inspector Chopra
The Perplexing Theft of the Jewel in the Crown
The Strange Disappearance of a Bollywood Star
Inspector Chopra and the Million Dollar Motor Car
(Quick Read)
Murder at the Grand Raj Palace
Bad Day at the Vulture Club

The Girl In Cell A

VASEEM KHAN

HODDER &
STOUGHTON

First published in Great Britain in 2025 by Hodder & Stoughton Limited
An Hachette UK company

1

Copyright © Vaseem Khan 2025

The authorised representative in the EEA is Hachette Ireland, 8 Castlecourt Centre, Dublin 15, D15 XTP3, Ireland (email: info@hbgi.ie)

The right of Vaseem Khan to be identified as the Author of the Work has been asserted by him in accordance with the Copyright, Designs and Patents Act 1988.

All rights reserved. No part of this publication may be reproduced, stored in a retrieval system, or transmitted, in any form or by any means without the prior written permission of the publisher, nor be otherwise circulated in any form of binding or cover other than that in which it is published and without a similar condition being imposed on the subsequent purchaser.

All characters in this publication are fictitious and any resemblance to real persons, living or dead, is purely coincidental.

A CIP catalogue record for this title is available from the British Library

Hardback ISBN 978 1 399 70770 1
Trade Paperback ISBN 978 1 399 70771 8
ebook ISBN 978 1 399 70772 5

Typeset in Plantin Light by Hewer Text UK Ltd, Edinburgh
Printed and bound in Great Britain by Clays Ltd, Elcograf S.p.A.

Hodder & Stoughton policy is to use papers that are natural, renewable and recyclable products and made from wood grown in sustainable forests. The logging and manufacturing processes are expected to conform to the environmental regulations of the country of origin.

Hodder & Stoughton Limited
Carmelite House
50 Victoria Embankment
London EC4Y 0DZ

www.hodder.co.uk

To the generous folk of the small American towns I visited last year who were so willing to share their lives with me.

THE WYCLERC FAMILY

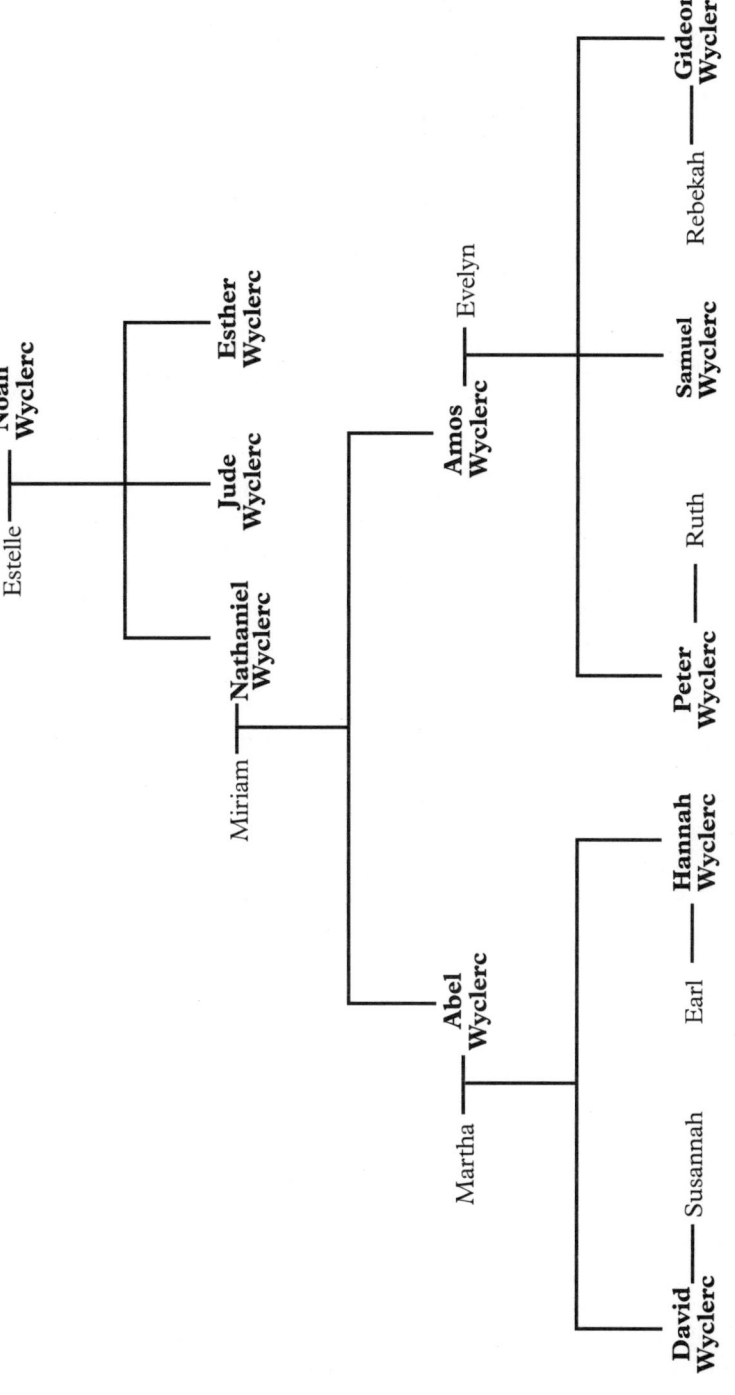

I remember the wolf's head.

Family legend had it that Nathaniel Wyclerc had killed the animal in the town's surrounding forest, mounted the head on a cherrywood medallion, then breathed his own mythos into its gaping mouth. Etched into the plaque, just below the beast's muzzle, the words: *caput lupinum*. Literally: 'wolf's head', but also a medieval English label denoting an outlaw, a dangerous criminal who, having refused the king's summons, might be killed out of hand.

A pariah.

A lone wolf.

I remember dark spots of blood splattered across the underside of its jaws; crimson soaked into fur the colour of faded dreams.

I remember the way light sheared in from the cabin's porthole windows, motes dancing in the beam.

I remember the sound of birdsong in the forest, flies popping on the screen door.

I remember a man's face, or what remained of it, turned up to the ceiling, the unnatural stillness of his body, like a dead horse in a field.

And before that?
Nothing.
A void.
I remember nothing.

1

ANNIE: THEN

I picture her walking along corridors humming with misery and loneliness, the by-products of human confinement. I know that she will be led in here by a man in uniform and left alone with me. Something I insisted on, despite the warnings.

It is my first scheduled session with Orianna, convicted murderer and true-crime celebrity. The Girl in Cell A.

It is not my first time dealing with a killer. But this case is different.

Orianna's application for parole cannot proceed without a thorough psychological evaluation. If she is to be released back into the world, she must pass through me, through the tests I have devised for her. And if she is given her freedom, then, in effect, *I* will be responsible for what happens next.

Where will she go? What will she do? There are no guarantees here. No magic therapy pill that can make a person in Orianna's situation entirely stable, entirely safe.

I cannot pretend that I am not nervous.

I check my watch, then dig a compact out of my handbag. No one will come out and say it but, in the therapeutic setting, appearances matter. Patients, like everyone else in the Instagram Age, are overtly influenced by the visual.

What will Orianna see when she enters the room?

A white woman, medium height, athletically built – though thrice-weekly sessions at the gym are now a distant memory. Blonde and blue-eyed, hair platted down to the middle of my back: a single braid, like a Viking's wife. My outfit is formal – navy trouser suit matched with the best shoes I own, a pair of Jimmy Choo flats that Michael bought me with a month's salary when we were still trying to one-up each other in the romantic gestures' stakes.

They've lasted admirably. Which is more than I can say for our marriage.

I consider taking off my jacket, but then decide to leave it on. It might seem a little stiff, forbidding, but the patient-therapist relationship invariably begins by marking out territory.

My only concession to personality is the breast cancer band around my wrist, a pop of colour in a charcoal painting.

Grey light seeps in through a barred window.

Winter is almost here. The locals are bracing themselves for crippling blizzards and eight-feet-high snowdrifts. In the coffee shops and bars, there will be talk of climate change, advocates and naysayers eyeballing each other over lattes and beer.

In the corner of the room, a sluggish radiator sighs in complaint. It's warm enough, but by no means 'toasty', as Leo, my sixteen-year-old, would say.

The Girl In Cell A

The smell of good coffee permeates the space. I brought it with me – enough for us both. It's not exactly regulation, but I know that in a place like this, decent coffee will be in short supply.

A knock sounds from behind me.

I take a deep breath, stash my compact, then turn and face the door.

Barney enters first.

I have met him several times now, in preparation for this first session. A handsome, middle-aged black man. His blue-shirted uniform is pristine; his shoes spotless. In our interactions, he is unfailingly polite, patience personified as I ask my questions. He has prepared me as best as he is able, though I sense a hesitation, an uncertainty at the wisdom of this course of action.

The last time we were together, he told me bluntly, 'Don't underestimate her. We call her the queen of mood swings. A year ago, she broke another woman's fibula. Snapped it clean in two. Do you know where the fibula is?'

'Yes.'

'Not many people do.' The thunderbolt scar at his temple glows. I am tempted to ask him if it had been inflicted in the line of duty.

Today, he says nothing, simply steps aside and ushers in the woman behind him.

She is smaller than I expected; smaller than her courtroom photographs make her appear. Five-three, five-four. The mind makes ogres of those we fear.

Her hair is short, black, falling to her shoulders. The face is oval, her skin a dusky colour – the legacy of her mixed-race, Indian-American ancestry – and as flawless as a Photoshopped cover. The years may have taken their toll, but Orianna is still a beautiful woman. That beauty was one reason the case took hold of the national imagination. The other was the name of the man she had killed.

The Girl in Cell A.

Some tabloid hack gave her that handle, a sly nod to Orianna's celebrity status, a throwaway remark attributed to one of her prison guards. In the dubious pecking order of the penal system, Orianna is an 'A-lister', an orange-suited VIP.

The hokey tag has followed her around, eminently hashtaggable.

She looks at me, a cool, unblinking gaze from deep-set brown eyes.

Unto the breach.

'Hi, Orianna. My name is Annie. Annie Ledet. I'm a forensic psychotherapist. We'll be working together.'

Does she sense that the environment has been carefully modulated? There's nothing here that might be considered threatening, nothing to conjure up dramatic emotions. Plain walls, adorned by a single watercolour – of the lake that sits just beyond the razor wire – and an improving verse in a cheap plastic frame: *1 John 1:9, 'If we confess our sins, He is faithful and just and will forgive us our sins and purify us from all unrighteousness.'*

Several plants rest uneasily in plastic holders. Rubber figs. Kentia palms. A Boston fern in a seagrass basket. Terracotta holders are forbidden, lest they be smashed to fashion lethal shards.

The Girl In Cell A

'So,' she says finally. 'How does this work?'

Her voice is gravelly, startlingly old. Of course, Orianna is no longer a child. She's a woman, one shaped by the vicissitudes of her unique fate.

And it will now be my task to return her to that time, when the storm first came down on her. The journey that we take together in this cramped little room will determine the next chapter in her life. Is she still a danger to the public? To herself? The law doesn't require me to solve all of Orianna's mysteries – just enough to tick the right boxes.

The fact is that most murderers serve their time and are released. A very small percentage go on to kill again. We simply don't have the luxury of locking up killers and throwing away the key. Our prisons are overcrowded to the point of bursting. And so, former murderers walk among us, indistinguishable from anyone else. The chain-smoking neighbour wheezing behind a lawnmower. The old guy in the cubicle two rows down. The woman serving breakfast at the diner.

Our pasts are rarely emblazoned on our exteriors.

I gesture Orianna towards a scarred coffee table and a pair of beaten-up leather chairs.

'No couch?'

I smile. A sense of humour, no matter how caustic, is a good sign, something I can work with.

And there's no doubt in my mind that I have my work cut out for me.

The world may have long ago relegated Orianna to the basement of horrors where America's monsters reside, but the fact remains that she continues, to this day, to protest her innocence. She continues to claim that her memory of the killing is little more than a white-noise soup of imagery.

And in none of those images does she see herself blasting Gideon Wyclerc's head from his shoulders.

2

ORIANNA: NOW

The road dips just on the threshold of town.

I pull over onto the grass verge and step out into the steaming afternoon heat.

A hundred yards ahead, the blacktop passes below an archway formed by trees, entwined branches reaching out to one another like the arms of arboreal giants. To one side, staked into the soil, stands a painted wooden sign:

EDEN FALLS
Population: 2000

After eighteen years, I am finally back where I started.

I stand in the sizzling silence, my blouse glued to my back, sweat shimmering along my arms.

The migraine strikes me as it always does, like a fire in the mind, a red-hot wire thrust into my ear until all I can see is a flat, white sheet shimmering with random, terrifying images: a ballpoint pen clicking in a darkened office, the shape of my mother dissolving into droplets, the shadow of a wolf slipping through a wooded gloaming.

I fumble the pill bottle from my pocket, down a couple, wait for the violent jag to pass. And then I get back in my car. The beat-up Chevy cost five hundred bucks; a hundred thousand miles on the clock with a rattle like a smoker's cough each time I turn the ignition. I drive through the centre of town, a deliberate act.

Do I want them to see me, to know that I'm here?

In prison, I made little effort to follow the town's fortunes. Why would I? They'd cut me off, cast me out, damaged me in a way they couldn't possibly know.

When my mother, Christine, died, my last link to Eden Falls was severed.

Before the trial, I asked her, just once, why no one had come to see me.

'Because the Wyclercs have forbidden it. Because we're pariahs.'

I push the memory to the back of my thoughts, focus instead on Eden Falls' civic heart: the town hall, blazing white under its summer coat of paint; Sal Pitman's ice cream parlour; Olsen's hardware store; the First National bank; the fire station; the laundromat. The church, with its double-spired roof and stained-glass windows. My mother had always crossed herself twice: once at the threshold – because we were Catholic and the church was determinedly not – and once before the splayed Jesus above the altar.

A row of pickups and semis make a line outside the Wolf & Boar Saloon; the early shift, complete with flag decals on the fenders.

How little things have changed. The layout of the streets, the aspect of the houses and stores, the shambling shapes out in the suffocating heat.

The Girl In Cell A

I feel the anger rising. A rage that has simmered inside me for eighteen long years.

I am back. Not for *them*, but for myself. The need to prove that I am the victim of a miscarriage of justice lives inside me like a wild animal. Because the simple truth is that, in among the jumble of memories I retain of *that* day, I still cannot find a clear and damning version of my guilt.

3

ORIANNA: NOW

The dirt road snakes through the trees, eventually opening up into a wide turning circle, at the centre of which stands a timber-framed cottage, clad in horizontal white boards, a burst of bougainvillea around the door.

Behind the cottage, the trees thin and I catch a glimpse of the lake, sunlight flaring from its surface.

I slide the key into the lock, turn and push back the door.

The space is larger than I remember.

Wooden trusses stretch across the ceiling, a riot of cobwebs between the beams. The walls are a serviceable white; on one, above a pine sideboard, hovers a small frame enclosing pressed flowers like mutated alien heads. A bowed fabric couch sits before a scuffed coffee table. A bookcase houses paperbacks with cracked spines: thrillers and a handful of recipe books, their authors long dead or faded from glory. There is no TV.

A door leads to the cottage's single bedroom.

The bed – and wardrobes – are wood-framed, wide and sturdy. A four-paned casement window is overlaid with a lace curtain, drilled through by moths. A crack spiders across one pane, bubbles visible in the glass.

A door leads to the bathroom – a clean, white space, with a standalone tub, a coiled shower cable attached to the tap and just the faintest mould in the grouting.

I catch sight of myself in the mirror.

Short black hair pushed back around my ears. Muscular shoulders, skin the colour of sun-darkened wheat. My mother's brown eyes, an expression in them of a woman older than the one gazing back at me.

I walk back out, cross the living room and walk through an open archway into the kitchen.

Here, I discover a fridge, a cast-iron stove, a pine table and chairs, and a sink. It's a relief when the water runs clear.

The pantry is a haven for dead flies. A drum of stale flour lurks in a corner. Ancient bottles of peach brandy line the shelves, together with stacks of handmade soaps, canned figs and glass jars housing God only knows what. Elvira Trueblood – once my mother's oldest friend in Eden Falls – was nothing less than a witch when it came to homegrown tinctures.

I remember visits to the cottage, Elvira fussing over me in a way my own mother never did. Elvira is still here in a way, pressed into the grains of the furniture, hovering in the corners like a beneficent ghost.

It's a blessing the place is so isolated. If prison has taught me anything, it's that my notoriety is a curse that I will never shake off. *The Girl in Cell A.* Princess of the Freaks.

And they *will* come for me, of that I'm sure. They'll track me down, once word gets out that I am back in Eden—

The sound of an approaching vehicle shatters the silence.

4

ORIANNA: NOW

I walk outside, stiffen as a black Ford truck pulls up beside the Chevy. Tinted windows, dust on the tyres.

The door swings open and the driver emerges.

Shock thunders through me.

The man who faces me is tall, blond, clean-shaven, dressed in a white cotton shirt with a black tie, sleeves rolled up to the elbows. He is the same age as me – I find it impossible not to superimpose the face of the boy I had known onto the man in his mid-thirties standing before me.

My breathing shallows as his grey eyes focus on me.

'Ori.'

My heart slams around inside my chest. 'What are you doing here, Luke?'

'You were seen. In town. Headed this way. Only thing out here is Elvira's cottage.'

He balances on the edge of saying more, but then just stands there.

'It's good to see you,' he manages eventually.

A tornado of feeling chokes off my reply.

He stirs the dirt at his feet with a wingtip brogue set on a welted rubber sole. 'Are you ready for—? What I mean is, there'll be plenty who won't like it.'

'You mean the Wyclercs won't like it.'

His expression folds into pain. 'Ori. You must know that I never really believed that you . . .' A stutter. 'I should have visited you. I was sorry to hear about your mother.'

I hold his gaze until he is forced to look away. In my mind's eye: an image of Luke on the stand, unable to meet my eyes as he answers the district attorney's questions; softly spoken, cheeks flushed, his delivery endearingly halting; the jury craning forward, hanging on every word.

I remember one of the jurors – an overweight, middle-aged woman with the slack jowls of a bullfrog – casting icy glances my way throughout Luke's testimony. A little in love with him, his beauty making gospel of his words.

I take a deep breath. 'Get the fuck out of here, Luke.'

His eyes widen a fraction. The little-boy-lost expression that so beguiled that fat juror. He stares at me, then reaches into his pants, takes out a wallet. A card appears in his hand. 'You can reach me on these numbers.'

I make no move to take it.

'I'll leave it inside.'

He walks past me, into the cottage, sets the card on the kitchen table, then makes his way back out.

The truck shudders to life, the sound of the engine startling in the strained silence.

He drapes an arm out the window, ripples his fingers on the paintwork.

'Don't hate me, Ori.'

The Girl In Cell A

His words hang in the steaming air as I watch him power away.

Something goes slack inside me.

I have spent a long time planning my return, establishing a clarity of vision years in the making.

And now, within hours of my arrival, I can feel myself unravelling.

For Luke Wyclerc is the one blind spot in my mission here; an emotional cypher with the potential to derail everything. I knew that I would have to face him at some point, but now I realise how unprepared I was for the emotions that such a confrontation could unleash.

What else am I unprepared for?

5

ANNIE: THEN

I had told Orianna that I was a forensic psychotherapist.

There is a little more to it than that.

My specialty – the reason I am here at all – is in dealing with repressed memories, specifically those associated with a condition known as dissociative amnesia. Because of this I have, of late, been dragged into the 'memory wars', a debate in psychological circles that has become increasingly bitter in recent years.

A textbook case of 'the more you know, the less you understand'.

On one side of the divide are those who believe that human memory is rarely faithful to objective facts, that, indeed, false memories can be auto-generated or even implanted through suggestion. Sometimes, even during the process of therapy.

They point to famous instances of alleged childhood abuse – memories often 'recovered' during therapy – which later turn out to be false. Yet, the victim remains utterly convinced of their veracity, refusing to let go of their version of events even when presented with concrete evidence to the contrary.

And on the other side? Those of us who believe that the mind is capable of both inventing and losing memories – something experimentally proven, time and again. We believe that though the brain – and the human mind – remain, in greater part, twin enigmas, there is also another truth: that human beings who undergo trauma often retreat into themselves, hiding away the past behind closed doors, until even basic facts vanish from view.

In Orianna's case, the facts are well established. There can't be many people in the country, even now, who don't remember the case; with its heady concoction of sex, race, and scandal, it had gripped the airwaves for months.

On the day of the murder, seventeen-year-old Orianna Negi had been found unconscious in a hunting cabin on the sprawling Wyclerc family estate at the northern edge of the town of Eden Falls. Inside the cabin, the body of Gideon Wyclerc – scion of the legendary mining dynasty – had been discovered, head all but blown off by a shot fired from a double-barrel shotgun.

The weapon had been found on the floor of the cabin beside Orianna, her fingerprints on the butt, barrel and trigger, gunshot residue on her hands and clothes.

The investigation that followed left little doubt in anyone's mind: Orianna had murdered Gideon Wyclerc in cold blood.

The only question was why?

When that motive came to light, the town had drawn a collective breath, a frisson of scandal that shook the community to its foundations.

As the Wyclercs circled the wagons, America's media machine swung into action, the town irradiated by blanket coverage in the way only small towns can be; picked up, shaken about, turned over. Underbelly exposed for the world to see.

The Wyclercs were a dynastical success story that spoke to America's perception of herself. Not quite the Kennedys, but not far off in terms of wealth, beauty and notoriety. Little wonder that the case generated such a feeding frenzy.

The only snag in the DA's seemingly airtight case was that the principal accused refused to confess her crimes. Despite months of interrogation, Orianna would not admit that she had murdered Gideon.

Instead, she claimed that she could remember nothing of what had happened in that cabin.

Through the long years of her imprisonment, the years of becoming The Girl in Cell A, she has clung to that story, an abiding mystery that has entered the annals of American crime.

I remember following the trial from my dorm room at Princeton. Cameras had been allowed in the courtroom and the coverage captured my imagination – in a way, Orianna's case inspired my desire to specialise in dissociative amnesia. I owe her a debt, crudely speaking.

It was only later – when she began to talk about Grace Wyclerc – that I was called in.

This is a case that continues to tease the imagination – if there's one thing Americans cannot get enough of, it is true-crime porn. But it is also an important case for those of us who work in the field. Dissociative amnesia is a condition still imperfectly understood. Competing theories on causes and treatment engender violent disagreement, even between colleagues. This murkiness makes it difficult to have a sensible conversation about the condition, even with so-called experts, let alone the lay public.

'Orianna, I want to start by thanking you for agreeing to these sessions—'

'How old are you?'

I hesitate. 'Is my age important to you?'

'I tried to find out online – they give us an hour of supervised internet time twice a week for legal research into our cases. But it doesn't say anywhere.'

'I'm forty-six.'

She seems momentarily taken aback by the fact that I have answered.

'You don't look it.'

I wait.

'You know, they gave me a whole bunch of names. For therapists, I mean. Mainly guys. All drooling at the thought of breaking me apart so they can examine the pieces. But I picked you. Do you know why?'

'No.'

'I read somewhere that you chose not to go to your prom night. I didn't go to mine either.'

I shift on my seat. 'Orianna, I'm grateful that you asked for me. But you need to understand that I'm here because I believe I can help.'

'Help *who*, Doctor?'

I keep having to remind myself that when she was convicted, Orianna was little more than a child. Her natural development was, to a great extent, arrested at that instant, the normal buffeting of social intercourse replaced by the closeted, false community of prison. In many ways, her reactions remain those of a child; emotionally immature, subject to jags and lapses. Outwardly, she may now be well into her thirties; but in many ways she remains that lost teenager.

'My priority is to help you recover your memory of . . . that day.'

'The murder, you mean. You can say it.'

'Of the murder.'

'And Grace? What about her?'

Ah. Grace. I hold her gaze as she continues to stare straight at me, fidgeting with the cuff of her uniform.

'Isn't that the real mystery everyone wants the answer to?' Orianna continues. 'What happened to Grace Wyclerc? America's sweetheart.' Bitterness drips from her voice. 'Tell me, do *you* think I killed her? Like the rest of them? That somewhere out there, a seventeen-year-old girl is rotting away in a shallow grave and the only person who knows where she is, is me? Is that why you're really here? To solve the riddle that haunts them all?'

'Orianna, my first, and only, priority is you. *Your* welfare. I am not here to condemn you or to condone your actions, whatever they may or may not have been. Do you believe me?'

She says nothing. We observe each other, a silent battle of wills. I know that she is trying to establish control; many of my patients attempt the same. Ultimately, a futile exercise. The patient-therapist relationship only works when there is a basic foundation of trust.

What lies behind Orianna's gaze?

Can I really trust anything she says?

6

ORIANNA: NOW

I cannot sleep.

Lying on the bed, bare legs prickling against the cheap cotton, I stare sightlessly at the ceiling. My shorts and tank top are soaked through with sweat.

Rising, I walk to the kitchen, take out a bottle of water and press it to my forehead.

Then I walk, barefoot, back into the living room, scoop up my laptop, double back to the kitchen and out the rear door, walking down to the edge of the lake, where I lower myself onto the burnt grass beneath an ancient yew.

I drink greedily from the bottle, the night around me damp and fetid.

A full moon hangs above the trees, low and sulky in a sky dusted with stars.

Memories writhe inside me.

The past is a blur.

A line I'd read in a prison volume, well-thumbed and worn.

But if the past is a blur for the many, then how much more indistinct is it for someone like me, where the most vital moment of my own history, the fulcrum upon which my life tilted, is blocked from view by the eccentricities of human memory?

In court, my lawyer hurled fancy labels at the jury in a bid to convince the twelve wall-eyed members of the public sitting just yards from me of the truth of my claims.

Dissociative amnesia.

I remember now how the DA had leapt upon the term, turned it around and thrust it hard into the soft underbelly of my defence, claiming that it was the very act of committing the crime that had caused the memory loss.

My lawyer, beleaguered, outgunned, the best my mother could afford with the pitiful accumulation of her life savings, had been at sea from the opening day of the trial.

After Luke left earlier, a blind rage overtook me.

Sweeping up the card he'd left behind, I ripped it into a dozen pieces, dumping them in the waste bin.

I lasted a whole five minutes before falling onto my knees to fish them out.

The card tells me that Luke works for the Griffin County District Attorney's Office, Criminal Investigations Division. A legal consultant, whatever that means. I recall that his father, David, was a lawyer; there'd always been Wyclercs occupying positions of influence around the county. Eden Falls, the county seat, is controlled by the clan, always has been, always will be, as long as there's a Wyclerc left to pay a bribe or strong-arm cooperation out of cowed locals.

A part of me had hoped that Luke might have left town by now, found his feet in the world beyond Eden Falls.

The Girl In Cell A

I remember now the thrill of our first touch, our first kiss. Adolescent fumblings in the woods. Feelings I have tried – unsuccessfully – to bury ever since. How many nights, in the jangling darkness of prison, had I held his face between my hands, looked into those grey eyes – wolf's eyes, the mark of the Wyclercs – and asked him for an explanation? A justification for the betrayal that doomed me.

In return, I received only silence.

I shudder away the unhappy memory and change position, sitting cross-legged now and setting the laptop onto my knees.

An image fills the screen: a group photograph, taken in daylight. A formal shot of the Wyclerc family; three generations captured in a single frame. On the wings are the women, for the most part slender and pale. Towards the centre, standing shoulder to shoulder, the Wyclerc men, the sons of Amos and Abel: Gideon, Peter, Samuel and David.

And sat before *them*, in the very centre, upright on a wooden chair, is Amos himself; clan patriarch and heir to Nathaniel Wyclerc's fortune and mantle.

The town's history, hammered into us at school, warms itself anew in my mind.

Nathaniel Wyclerc – Amos and Abel's father – arrived in these woods a century earlier in search of ore, channelling the pioneer spirit that had, once upon a time, tamed the American wilderness. Those had been lean, hard years, buoyed only by Nathaniel's implacable belief that the Good Lord had seen fit to bring him to this place and would, in the fullness of time, unveil his ultimate plan for the Wyclercs.

That destiny was revealed deep in the forested hills, where Nathaniel struck gold – or as close to as made no difference. The mines that founded the town's fortunes transformed the Wyclerc patriarch from a maverick into a figure of legend. Later, he would be remembered as a visionary; others would, rightly or wrongly, label him a tyrant, a ruthless exploiter of opportunity and despoiler of the wooded beauty of the region. Wealth turned Nathaniel into a recluse, his energies refocused on fashioning the perfect Christian community – or his vision of one – deep in this hidden backwater of the state.

He'd christened it *Eden Falls*, after the waterfalls up near the mines that had made his – and the town's – fortune.

By the time the mines were bled dry some two generations later, Wyclerc Industries had diversified: mines across the country, steel refineries, ore processing plants, a timber-logging operation, sawmills, chemical factories.

Despite the company's relentless expansion, the business remained family-owned and the Wyclerc clan true to their founder's vision. The company seat stayed in Eden Falls, and those that ran it – Wyclercs to a man – and woman – remained close-lipped and guarded.

Growing up, I had known it as a place where secrets festered, for no one was ever brave enough to openly voice their thoughts, particularly where the town's ruling dynasty was concerned.

7

ORIANNA: NOW

I have viewed the photograph a thousand times, but each time it is as if I am looking at it anew; each time I find my eyes drawn to Amos.

Amos the lawgiver. Amos, from whom all things flowed.

Even seated, he is an imposing presence. A tall man, straight-backed in his early sixties – as he must have been at the time the photo was taken – with long arms and large, spade-like hands, hands that are wrapped, in the picture, around the hook of a pearl-handled walking cane topped by a wolf's head. An affectation. The Amos I remember never needed a cane. Dark hair, streaked with iron grey, sweeps back from a high, permanently furrowed forehead. Thick eyebrows shade those same Wyclerc eyes, wolf's eyes, the smoky grey of mountain mist; they burn from the image, a searing look containing – to my mind, at least – a mixture of arrogance, malevolence and knowledge of one's own power that characterises the man who'd come to dominate the clan upon the untimely death of his older brother, Abel.

I'd grown up on the Wyclerc estate, but rarely met Amos. He was a passing presence, a voice behind a half-open door, a shadow in the corridors of the Big House, where my mother sometimes took me during the summer months when school was out and there was no one else to watch me for the day.

My gaze jumps to the margins of the picture.

There, ranged in a line, are the staff of the Big House; my mother at their head, dressed in her black uniform, white at the collars and cuffs, nylon stockings and white pumps.

I have spent hours examining my mother's face, the intensity of her expression.

Who is she staring at?

To me, it seems that my mother is looking directly at Amos's sons, Gideon, Samuel and Peter. In Eden Falls, they had been known as the Three Horsemen. I'd never understood whether this was flattering or the opposite. Whether they even knew of it, and cared if they did.

My mother once wondered out loud: '*What must it feel like to have so much?*' There had been a hunger in Christine's eyes that I had been too young to understand. Later, I'd come to the truth; namely, that my mother was a cold and calculating woman, fiercely ambitious, frustrated by fate's design and willing to go to great lengths to change that fact.

My eyes linger on Gideon Wyclerc.

In the photograph, he seems younger than his age, somewhere in his early forties. He has his father's high forehead and lustrous hair, with the same thick eyebrows and smoky eyes. As handsome as a movie star.

Each time I stare at the photograph, I find my heart squeezed between invisible claws. The world says I killed this man. In cold blood.

The Girl In Cell A

What is truth and what is lie?
From Gideon, I trace a line down to *her*.
To Grace.
For so long, I was unable to talk about Grace.

Gideon's daughter is sixteen at the time this picture was taken, wearing a black dress with buckled shoes. Her hair is dark, like her father's, and falls to just below her shoulders. She is extraordinarily beautiful, her expression one of distilled innocence.

A year after the photograph, Grace would be crowned Eden Falls Forest Princess, paraded through the town on a float, a living symbol of the Wyclerc clan's genetic vitality.

That same day – the day Gideon was murdered – she vanished, never to be seen again.

The world claims I did something to Grace too.

A clew of emotion clogs my throat. My eyes blur.

Something inside tells me that in this photograph lies the answer to all my mysteries.

And yet the key to the lock remains out of reach.

8

ORIANNA: NOW

The shrill call of a night bird shatters the silence.

In the ringing echoes that follow, I hear another noise, at odds with the natural sounds of the forest.

I shut the laptop and walk back inside the cottage.

Grabbing the smallest of my suitcases, I set it on the bed, take out a padded cloth bag, then reach in and draw out the object inside.

The semi-automatic compact pistol, a Ruger, set me back almost a thousand dollars. I bought it from an unlicensed source, a friend of a friend made in prison. If I am found with the gun, I'll be back inside so fast my feet won't touch the floor.

I walk out the front door and stand in the clearing.

'Who's there?'

The gun feels dense and slippery in my hand.

'Luke? Is that you?'

For years now, I have had the prickling feeling of being watched. My parole officer told me when I was released – to begin my mandatory, monitored four-year parole, a parole I had to serve out before I could return to Eden Falls – that this is a common reaction for those who have spent as much time in prison as I have.

Paranoia.

But I have never been able to shake the feeling that it is something more.

'Show yourself, goddammit!'

I feel the familiar itch, the crawl of spiders along the naked surface of my brain. An image flashes into my head: Gideon smiling, blood leaking from his forehead down into his mouth, a mouth so wide light seems to vanish inside.

I turn and walk back inside. I grab the gun bag, then go to the pantry. Locating the drum of flour I discovered earlier, I scoop out a hollow, put the gun back in its bag, then set the bag into the drum, palming flour over it until it vanishes from view.

Returning to the living room, I lay back on the sheets, waiting for my heartbeat to flatten.

I know that tomorrow I will have to go into town. The thought of venturing into Eden Falls fills me with a mixture of dread and anger. It's a wonder they haven't turned up by now, with their pitchforks, ready to drive me out.

Hatred.

Like cancer, or a wildfire, it can die back, only to return in a more virulent form. In a community like Eden Falls, hatred festers and becomes communicable; over time, it fossilises into collective memory. *That* was the lesson I learned at my trial.

And that is why I have come back.

Because I know, deep down in my gut, that someone in this godforsaken place knows exactly what happened that day. Someone knows who killed Gideon Wyclerc. Someone knows what happened to Grace.

My notebook is open beside me.

I turn to a clean white page.

Picking up a pen, I write the words I have written a thousand times since leaving prison, words that serve as the driving force for everything I have planned since, everything I am now doing.

I did not kill Gideon.
I did not kill Grace.
I am innocent.

9

ANNIE: THEN

'Your memory is locked.'

The smell of coffee mingles with the scent of my perfume. I note that Orianna hasn't objected to me bringing coffee along for these sessions. Creature comforts in this place are few and far between.

This is our third meeting, staggered over two months. The encounters are erratic, far from ideal. But I have no ability to compel Orianna, and neither would I do so even if I had.

My initial impression is nebulous. I can't get a read on her. Her notoriety precedes her, and she seems all too aware of this fact. *The Girl in Cell A.* A fatuous label, trite and reductive, playing to the Gen Z-ers. But Orianna is a real person; a living, breathing entity, warped by her circumstances, her unique journey.

She watches me from over her polystyrene cup.

I wonder at her initial impression of *me*. In our last session, she asked me, in a roundabout way, why I chose to do what I did. She already knows about women – and men – who find notorious killers irresistible. The letters had started arriving not long after she'd stepped through the gates of her first prison.

I hesitated before answering. There is a fine line between honesty and oversharing in a therapeutic setting. You want your patients to believe that you trust them enough to tell them a little about yourself; at the same time, you need distance if you are to function effectively in your role. The danger of crossing boundaries is ever-present. Orianna is a convicted murderer. I know of a number of cases where colleagues have lost sight of such things.

'The law is predicated on the right of everyone to receive a proper defence. I believe that the same sense of fairness should extend *post*-conviction. Society tries to sweep criminality under the carpet, refusing to take the blame for what are often complicated causal reasons for offending. We put people in prison, lock the gates and turn our backs, forgetting that the vast majority of prisoners have to return to the outside world at some point. We make almost no real effort at rehabilitation. Why? Because the punishment rhetoric is the one that wins votes. Statistics show us just how terrible we are at reintegrating ex-convicts into society. And the blame for that lies with *all* of us.'

Today, I want to focus on the exact nature of Orianna's problem.

'Think of your mind as the black box of a downed airplane. Our job is to recover that black box and access those memories.'

She seems to like the analogy.

'How are you sleeping now?'

'Fine. Better.'

'Any recurring dreams?'

'I don't dream.'

'Everyone dreams, Orianna. You've undergone great trauma. That leaves an imprint deep in our psyche. Sometimes it comes out in ways we don't expect, ways beyond our conscious control.'

I pick up a plastic folder from the table, a ballpoint pen in my hand. I click it three times, an unconscious ritual. 'At our last meeting, I told you that I felt it would be helpful for us to begin talking about the events that led to your conviction. Are you ready to do that?'

'I told you, I can't remember much about that day.'

'I know. But that's why we need to begin chipping away at it. You're a young woman, Orianna. You still have a long life ahead of you. But I believe that if we don't get to the truth of what happened that day, a shadow will remain over you. It will prevent you from living a normal life, should you be released. You've consistently maintained that you cannot remember the actual killing. In court, you pleaded not guilty. I believe that it's critical for you to know for sure, either way. And the only way we can do that is if we unlock that black box in your head.'

Conflicting emotions swirl across her face.

I tap the folder with a fingernail. 'I've read the trial transcript. According to your testimony, your last coherent memory is approaching the cabin where the murder took place. Why did you go to the cabin, Orianna?'

'I don't remember.'

'Did you go there to confront Gideon Wyclerc?'

'I don't remember.'

I set down the folder. Perhaps I shouldn't have started there. This sort of therapy – when it is done right – is an exercise in restraint, in gradually building up a picture of the patient, brick by brick, session by session. If I want to find out why Orianna killed Gideon Wyclerc, why she acted in the way she did, I need to understand her history.

'OK. Let's move backwards in time. I'd like to talk about your past, growing up in Eden Falls, the people around you. Are you ready to share those details with me?'

She says nothing for a moment.

And then she dips her head.

10

ORIANNA: NOW

The Eden Falls Community Library had once been a haven for me when I needed to hide away from the world.

In previous incarnations, the library had served as the town hall and the courthouse, although it had originally been built to house back-office operations for the Wyclerc mining business. As a consequence, the three-storey building had been pampered and coddled, renovated on multiple occasions, briefly neglected when the business operations were moved to grander, modern premises, then revived as a municipal hub following the war.

That period lasted a good four decades before a story broke in the mid-nineties that permanently tarnished the library's reputation. A newspaper in the neighbouring town of Barrier claimed that a black man by the name of Edgar Myers – a local activist – had been lynched on the premises back in the thirties, hung by the neck from a decorative yardarm protruding from the building's façade. The body had been left to swing for two days.

Though the revelation was furiously denied by the town elders – and an ongoing feud established with Barrier – the stink chased the courthouse out to a purpose-built building overlooking the nearby town square, and the town-hall functions to a less imposing but more practical home directly opposite the new courthouse.

Walking up the spiral staircase, I pass an older-looking white man in grubby denim overalls polishing the brass railing. I have the feeling that I know him, that he might be Tommy Quinn, once a local football star, then an equally notorious drunk. Now he looks to be a veteran of the brigade of ill-fated Eden Falls men who perform menial chores for minimum wage for the various municipal institutions that run the town. Quinn, as I remember him, is the sort of good old boy common to these parts, the kind who would have leered at my mother's beauty while looking down on her because of the colour of her skin.

The first floor is taken up by row upon row of old-fashioned wooden shelving, laden with books both purpose-bought and donated from the barely thumbed collections of genteel – and now expired – southern gentlemen.

There is a hush about the place that is stultifying.

I find Gertrude – Gerty – in the back row, squatting on the floor, placing books on the bottommost shelf from a handcart.

I stand there, waiting silently, until my presence twitches the hairs on the back of her neck. She twists around and looks up at me, then takes the spectacles dangling on a chain around her neck and places them on her nose.

A long moment passes.

'Well, damn it all to hell, child.'

11

ORIANNA: NOW

'What are you doing here, Ori?'

'I didn't kill him.'

We are sitting in Gerty's office, a poky, sweltering room on the second floor. The windows are flung open, the place cluttered as if a storm just blew through it. On the tiny desk is a computer that looks like a relic from the vacuum-tube era.

Gerty, a slender woman, nevertheless fills out the space. She is white, blonde, her wide-hipped figure dressed in floral print. Her hard chin and blue eyes give her the aura of cerebral warmth and stubborn strength that I have always associated with her.

For almost two decades, Gerty served as a minor functionary in the county courthouse, filing and retrieving documents for the arbiters of justice that parade through the place, men – or their much younger, and invariably female, paralegals – who barely deigned to throw her a second glance while barking orders, as if the great wheels of American jurisprudence might grind to a halt should their demands not instantly be met.

Gerty's tenure ended when one such eminence picked a fight on the wrong day.

I press on. 'You were friends with my mother.'

I remember this, but precious little else about their relationship.

Gerty picks up a hand towel, wipes her throat. Her hair is still thick and plaited behind her head. 'I heard about it on the news, the day they released you. Figured you'd find your way back here one day.'

'I need your help, Gerty.'

'You can't rewrite the past, child. Even if you could, do you really think *they'd* stand for it? The Wyclercs?'

I lean forward, eyes blazing. 'I didn't kill him. You *know* me, Gerty.'

A hollow laugh. 'No one knows what's inside another person's heart, child. No one knows what anyone is truly capable of.'

I reach across and place a hand over hers. Gerty's eyes widen, but she doesn't pull away. 'The truth is, I can't remember what happened that day. There's a hole, a hole in my memories. That's why I'm back. My life vanished down that hole. Am I really capable of the things they say I did? I don't believe so. But I intend to find out, one way or the other.'

12

ORIANNA: NOW

'So tell me the plan,' Gerty says.

'I need to find out exactly what happened that day,' I say. 'I need to piece it all together, fill in the blanks in my memory. And I need – I *have* to know what really happened to Grace.'

'Grace is dead.'

'*I* didn't kill her.'

Gerty sighs, picks up a ballpoint pen, starts clicking it. The gesture arrests me, takes me back to Annie Ledet and the therapy room. 'What makes you think you can do what all those cops, all those high-and-mighty investigators, couldn't?'

'*They* weren't looking, Gerty. They had me and that's all they needed.'

She seems unconvinced.

'I have to try.'

Her truculent expression dissolves. 'I guess you do. Leastways, I don't think I can stop you . . . They're not going to make it easy for you, you know that, right? The Wyclercs aren't the forgiving kind.'

My mind whips backwards in time to an image of the

Wyclercs sitting in a row at the trial, dressed in funereal tones, grim-faced. Writ large across their brows is that fanatical sense of Puritanism that had defined them ever since Nathaniel Wyclerc had unveiled his creed for the town. I'd sensed their hatred, a palpable thing, reaching out to envelop me, extending outwards to engulf the town, such that every living thing was infected and changed by it.

'I want to start there. The Wyclercs. I need to know everything about them. Do you have records here? At the library? Anything that can give me a feel for the family. I've looked online. There's not much there.'

'That's because if there's one thing the Wyclercs are good at, it's keeping secrets. But, sure, I can dig something up for you. Hell, it's *their* library.'

Gerty sets me up at a reading desk on the second floor.

The space is deserted, save for a studious-looking young man in one corner who glances up from behind a textbook fort at the sudden commotion.

He is too young to remember. Too young to know who it is that is now sitting just yards from him. Perhaps later, when the news reaches him, his eyes will widen in shock, and his memory will refashion our non-encounter into something more: *the day I met a murderer.*

Gerty slams down the tomes she's hauled up with her. 'What you have there is the library's collected works on the history of Eden Falls. The earliest – and, in my humble opinion, the best – is by a local, a Randall McGovern. Town pastor for fifty years – until the mid-seventies, when cancer got him by the balls. I mean that literally. The other two were written by outsiders after the—Well, after what happened. Sensationalist claptrap, if you ask me.'

I brush one of the books with a fingertip. I've seen it before. The glossy, attention-grabbing cover thrust at me while browsing the web, a result, no doubt, of my accumulated search history. I had ignored it, just as I'd ignored the handful of other books that followed in the wake of my conviction, shrilly proclaiming answers to the questions that still plague both the townsfolk of Eden Falls and conspiracy theorists up and down the country. Collectively, they aren't worth the paper they are printed on.

The mystery of Grace Wyclerc's disappearance remains unsolved.

13

ORIANNA: NOW

Gerty leaves me to it, returning fifteen minutes later with a glass of lemonade.

She stands there, watching me work. 'I remember the first time I set eyes on your mother. Practically saw her step off the bus into town. By rights, I should have hated her. An outsider, looking the way she did. But I saw something in her that day. The way she walked. The way she refused to look away. She was dirt poor, but she had *attitude*. She knew she was worth more than the world had given her. Made me feel the same way too, I guess.'

I feel the churn of a familiar emotion: uncertainty – about who my mother had truly been. Throughout my childhood, Christine remained a figure both close and distant, a woman whose priorities were never clear – at least not to me. My mother held on to a past that predated her arrival in Eden Falls. That she harboured secrets was something that only became apparent at the very end of innocence.

'Why didn't you fight Uncle Howard for access to your son?'

If Gerty is taken aback by the question, she hides it well. 'I tried. For a while. But Howard had all the cards. He showed the judge what a shining future our son would have with *him*. Proved what a bad mother I'd been. Neglectful. Too busy being a career superwoman. In the end, I had to make a decision. Watch my son being torn apart, or let him go.'

'You don't miss him?'

'I don't have to. He calls me often enough. He's living in Washington, interning at the White House, if you can believe that.'

'And you never thought about . . . ?'

'Getting back in the saddle? Oh, there *have* been others, child. None that stayed.'

I look down at the book open before me. It details the earliest days of the mining operation that had made the town's fortune, a miniature gold rush that brought men from all over the country to the town. Several photographs show them lined up outside the mine, in plaid work shirts and work boots, sideburned and dirt-faced, ghostly eyes fixed on the future. Other shots depict the growing town. Cheap, timber-framed and cedar-shingled homes, giving way, as the town prospered, to grand municipal buildings, streets lined with shops, each with its own little cross above the lintel. A Christian conurbation growing out into the surrounding forest.

'What is it like here? Haven't things changed at all?'

'You know that old saying? "The more things change, the more they stay the same". Well, that's Eden Falls in a nutshell. The Wyclercs still rule the roost – Amos and his sons are the only authority around here that matters . . .

'No, that's not quite true. Something *has* changed. Gideon's murder changed us. The Wyclercs won't let us forget it, leastways not until Grace's body is found. This much I'll say: that girl deserves a Christian burial.' Her eyes meet mine. 'The truth doesn't always set you free, child. Are you prepared for that?'

How can I explain to Gerty that I have lived with that nameless terror for eighteen long years? That it is a part of me now, the constant fear that the temple of innocence I have erected in my imagination might crumble in the wake of revelation. But what else can I do, except cling to hope? To let go would be to spiral down into the fathomless depths.

'How did my mother die?'

A momentary fear flaps its way through Gerty's eyes. She is saved from answering by footsteps echoing across the library floor.

I look up to see two men approaching, both in the uniforms of the Griffin County Sheriff's Office.

A needle note of fear pierces my ribcage.

The two men stop, and for a moment, there is an uncomfortable silence, the only noise the sound of the fan clicking above.

I realise that I recognise the older of the two: Abner Pence, a fixture in the town's police department since I was a child. A third-generation cop, twitchy and soft-spoken and wholly unsuited – it had always seemed to me – to the profession that fate had picked for him.

Beside him is a much younger colleague, with the build of a linebacker, shoulders practically bursting out of his uniform. His face glows with an obvious love of the job, a zeal I find disturbing.

Pence touches his brim. 'Gerty.'

'How can I help you, Abner?' Gerty's voice is stiff, confrontational.

'Apologies for the intrusion, but we're here for Orianna.' He directs his gaze in my direction. 'Ma'am, I need you to accompany us to the station house.'

14

ANNIE: THEN

The call comes just before I go into my next session with Orianna.

It is Michael, and he is pissed.

'You said you would be there.'

'I'm sorry. I don't know what to say. I double-booked myself.'

'If that's the case, tell me why our son gets second billing?'

My stomach hollows out. I want to hit back, but control myself. 'That's unfair, and you know it.'

'Is it, Annie? If I were a psychologist, I'd say it's all part of a pattern.' His voice drips with angry sarcasm.

Michael. Once, my big, beautiful husband. Now a man who not only cannot stand the sight of me, but would willingly tie me to a stake and light the pyre himself.

'I'm walking into a patient session. I'll call you later.'

He begins a protest, but I shut the phone on him, knowing it will just make things worse.

For a moment, I hold the phone against my cheek, eyes squeezed shut. Then I continue down the corridor and enter the therapy room.

It's been three weeks since last we met.

I know it's bad form to go into a session upset, but Michael has that effect on me.

You'd think by now we might have worked it out.

Physician, heal thyself.

The door opens, and Barney enters, with Orianna trailing him.

'Miss Annie.'

I return his greeting, then watch him leave.

Orianna doesn't immediately sit down. She seems jittery, wanders about the room, stops in front of the framed verse, reads aloud. '"If we confess our sins, He is faithful and just and will forgive us our sins and purify us from all unrighteousness."'

'Do you think I'm going to confess to you? And if I do, will you "purify" me?'

'That's not my role here.'

'Oh no? Are you telling me the DA – whoever it is now – won't be thrilled if you come out of here with a signed confession? The Girl in Cell A finally comes clean. Closure. For the justice system, for America. You'll get to write a book, do the talk-show circuit. On the sofa with Oprah.'

'Would you like to sit down? So that we can continue our chat?'

She flashes me a look I cannot quite interpret, then walks over and falls into her seat.

I pick up my notebook and pen. 'We began to talk about Eden Falls, your life growing up there. If you had to frame that time into a few words, what words would you use?'

The Girl In Cell A

Her eyes are fixed on the barred window. When she eventually looks back at me, something flares deep in her irises.

'Prejudice. Loneliness. Pain.' She stops. Then, 'Outsider.'

15

ORIANNA: NOW

The Griffin County Sheriff's Office is headquartered in Eden Falls, housed in a tall whitewashed building with little of the library's historical presence. The presiding aesthetic is functional, with only the odd detail hinting at a personality: a cantilevered concrete awning above the entrance; an engraved wolf's head above the front door; and a lunette in the upper elevation, like a witching eye, at odds with the rectangular sash windows that line up in rows over the rest of the south-facing façade.

Inside, I discover a hot hush, like the atmosphere inside a reptile tank.

The reception is cramped, with a couple of worn benches shoved against the walls, a bulletin board overcrowded with so much paper it looks like an art installation, and a low counter, behind which sits a red-haired, youngish man in uniform, feet kicked up on the counter, a phone trapped between shoulder and chin, thumbing a sports magazine.

As we enter, his eyes widen. He jumps up, presses the phone to his chest. 'You got her?' He seems incredulous, as if his colleagues have apprehended the number one pick on the FBI's Most Wanted list.

'Is Hank still in his office?' asks Pence.

'Yes, sir.'

I am led down a corridor to a frosted glass door.

Stencilled on the glass: *Sheriff H.W. Faulkes.*

Pence knocks diffidently, waits for a reply, then leads me inside.

The office is large, with a well-set window that lets in natural light.

Behind a cluttered desk sits the sheriff of Griffin County, Henry Faulkes.

A wild energy races through me. I have to hold myself back from charging at him.

Eighteen years ago, Faulkes had been chief deputy; even then he'd been the real power in the sheriff's office, old Don Gantry having already announced his decision to retire at the end of his latest four-year term. In most counties around the country, sheriffs are elected officers and owe at least some measure of allegiance to the people they serve. In Griffin County, the appointment is made by the county's municipal leaders. In effect, this means that the sheriff is a Wyclerc family puppet.

Faulkes had been the man who'd arrested me. The manner in which he'd conducted himself remains raw in my memory.

The sheriff is a big man, fleshy, like a warthog, in a half-sleeve khaki dress shirt, out of which poke burly arms covered in a mat of coarse, peppery hair. His head resembles a statue carved by primitive man: square, with a heavy chin, a greying buzz cut and a thick moustache that someone, long ago, must have told him gave him either gravitas or sex appeal. It does neither.

'Leave us.'

Pence and his young partner depart, the door clicking shut softly behind them.

Faulkes scrutinises me from deep-set eyes. The rub of age, combined with the rigours of small-town policing, have worn him down. My eyes drift to a triptych photo frame on the desk, images of an unattractive woman and two equally unattractive children.

It is a shock to imagine Faulkes as a married man, a father.

I watch as he reaches into a drawer, takes out a shallow tin, pulls off the lid with thick fingers, and extracts a cheroot. He fishes a lighter from his pocket, strikes it twice, three times, until the flame catches.

'You look like her,' he says eventually. 'Christine.' His voice rasps like sandpaper against tree bark.

My mother's name in this man's mouth incites a reckless anger. I bite down hard on my tongue.

He waves me into the seat before his desk.

I hesitate, then, reluctantly, sit.

'It was a mistake coming back here,' Faulkes begins.

'So everyone keeps telling me.'

'Tell me why I shouldn't have Abner put you back in his patrol car and scoot you right out of town?'

'I'd come right back.'

'Do you really want me to arrest you?'

'On what charge?'

'I'm sure we can find something. The thing about

ex-cons is that it don't take much to make people believe they'd cross the line again.'

I feel pressure building against the inside of my skull.

'Did your mother ever tell you about me? No?' His mouth turns up in a parody of a smile. 'I remember it as if it was yesterday. A summer's night, not long after she got here. She'd been out – she was a real party gal, Christine – ran herself into a ditch up near the Duckett place. I happened to be passing by on my way home. She was so drunk her eyeballs were floating. I *was* going to let her off with a citation, but she decided to take a swing at me. Assaulting a sheriff's deputy ...' He kisses his teeth. 'If I'd have hauled her in, the judge would have thrown the book at her. Might have cost her that fancy position up at the Big House. And without that, who was she? Just another out-of-towner with a great ass and no money.' He blows a jet of smoke sideways. 'Sobered up right quick, I'll give her that. Begged me to go easy on her. Offered to fellate me. Right there, by the side of the road.' He blinks in the smoke. 'When I heard what happened to her, I damned near cried.'

My hands close around the sides of my chair with such force I think I might crush the wood to powder. Hank Faulkes had been one of those who had never let my mother and I forget that we were different. That we weren't genteel enough – nor white enough – to deserve his respect.

Don't let him get to you.

He grinds the cheroot into a plastic ashtray, then leans forward. 'You coming back here is a provocation. You think the Wyclercs are going to sit on their hands while you parade yourself under their noses?'

'I don't much care what anyone thinks.'

'You ought to. This town is no bigger than when you left it.' He waves a hand at a bulletin board. Behind the glass is a picture of Grace Wyclerc, the word *MISSING* prominent at the top of the yellowing flier. 'You being here is an insult to her memory.'

I want nothing more than to be away from this place, away from this man. But I haven't come back here to hide. 'I spent years in a place I wouldn't send my worst enemy. You can't intimidate me.'

16

ORIANNA: NOW

They do it by the book.

The search takes me back to my earliest days in prison, hands fumbling over my body, hot breath in my ear, whispered sniggers: '*You like that, baby girl?*'

The red-haired officer from out front approaches cautiously, as if reaching for a wild stallion. 'Ma'am, do you have any sharp objects secreted about your person? Needles, razor blades, that sort of thing?'

'No.'

'Anything in your hair?'

'No.'

He looks at my arm, the regimented hatching of scars, but hasn't the courage to ask.

I endure the unendurable by sending my mind away.

When I return, I am in a tiny whitewashed cell, behind a locked door. A barred window high on one wall lets in a syrupy light. There is no ceiling fan; the heat transforms the six-by-eight room into a sweltering pit.

It reminds me of my first cell.

During those early years, I was moved around the system, finally ending up at a place designed for people like me. My cell became, with the passing of the years, a place where my myth grew and reality faded. I was a bona fide celebrity. Precious few of us in the penal system. The news hacks – and the army of crazies keeping me alive in the outside world – needed a name for their captive princess.

And so I became The Girl in Cell A.

I became their fantasy.

I ask for my obligatory phone call. They drag their heels for an hour, then give it to me, grudgingly.

Now, I lie back on the wafer-thin mattress and wait.

A hoop of panic tightens around my chest. Lightning flares at my temples.

My mind flashes involuntarily to the image of Grace Wyclerc, smiling behind glass in Faulkes's office. Grace's face blurs, reforms, blurs again and stretches in odd ways, as if being pulled apart by unseen hands. Whenever I think of her now, a white noise fills my head, rising to a crescendo until it drowns out rational thought.

We had practically grown up together, Amos Wyclerc's granddaughter and the child of the woman who'd served his household. Fate had not meant for us to be friends, and yet, friendship – of a kind – sprang up between us.

17

ANNIE: THEN

'I want to focus on Grace today.'

Orianna twitches, but says nothing. Her usually quick eyes seem dull and I wonder if it's the effect of her medication. One of the first things I did when I took the case was check her drug regime. In cases of extreme dissociative amnesia, drug-based interventions are common – I have colleagues who swear by the holy magic of the pill bottle.

Personally, I think the jury is still out. The condition is so complex, with a multiplicity of factors in play, that it seems absurdly reductive to believe that drugs can solve the problem.

'Grace,' she murmurs, in such a way that I am almost tempted to abandon the session there and then. To make progress, I need Orianna to be lucid.

Perhaps she senses my trepidation, and snaps to. 'What do you want to know?'

The sudden transformation momentarily wrong-foots me. I look down at my notes, hiding my reaction. When I look back up, I see Orianna staring at me. Is there a wry smile on her lips? Or am I imagining things? Barney's warning chimes in my head: '*We call her the queen of mood swings.*'

'You've stated that you and Grace grew up on the Wyclerc estate. You were both the same age. You went to the same school.'

'People used to say that Grace and I looked alike. That we could have been sisters. Aside from the fact that I was several shades darker, of course.' Her mouth twists. 'But the truth is, Grace grew up with every privilege you can think of. Whereas *I* was her servant's daughter.'

The bitterness in her voice is evident.

'Tell me about the first meaningful encounter with her that you can remember.'

She says nothing for a moment, head half-cocked, as if listening to an inner voice.

And then she begins to speak, transporting us both back to her youth.

> *The sound of music floats up from the lower half of the house, punctuated occasionally by laughter and the voice of Amos Wyclerc barrelling out from the dining room.*
>
> *Orianna stands at the top of the stairwell, hoping she might catch a glimpse of her mother.*
>
> *Christine has banished her upstairs, told her not to come down again until she is called. Her mother rarely allows her young daughter to accompany her to the Big House; on this occasion, Orianna pestered her until she relented. Christine had let slip that Amos's Thanksgiving dinner included, on its guest list, a prominent and absurdly handsome young actor that every girl at school is in love with, even if, like Orianna, they feigned indifference.*

The Girl In Cell A

She toys with the idea of ignoring her mother's edict and sneaking down to peek into the dining room. But the thought of being caught in the headlamps of all those fine folk ...

She turns and walks disconsolately back along the corridor, winding her way further into the house's upper storey. She has rarely been up here. A maze of forbidding portraiture, pile carpeting and stained doors.

A dull thumping stops her in her tracks. She listens, then follows the sound around the corner until she stands before an oaken door.

'Hello?'

The thumping stops. 'Who is that?'

'It's Orianna.' A beat. 'Grace, is that you?'

'Yes. Is there a key in the lock?'

'Yeah.'

A silence. 'Well, are you going to open the door, or just stand there?'

She hesitates, then reaches out and unlocks the door, pushes it open to reveal Grace, in a shimmering white dress, hair styled up, face flushed with heat and a heavy layer of make-up.

'What are you doing in here?'

'What does it look like I'm doing?' Anger squirms beneath her words. She walks back into the bedroom, sits down on the edge of the bed.

'Who locked you in here?'

'My mother.'

Orianna takes a few tentative steps into the room. 'Why?'

Grace says nothing. Orianna allows her eyes to wander around the bedroom, with its pink floral wallpaper, floor-to-ceiling wardrobes, and mirrored dresser.

She watches as Grace pulls something from her pocket. A packet of cigarettes. She lights one, then holds out the pack.

Orianna shakes her head.

'Suit yourself.' She holds the cigarette the way an actress might, delicately posed between two fingers. 'Well, you're dying to know, so I'll tell you. My daddy introduced me to that actor. He sure is handsome. He asked me to come over and talk to him. Whispered something sweet in my ear. I spilled root beer onto his crotch. Amos didn't take kindly to that.'

Her tone is insouciant, but Orianna senses the hard edge to her words.

'Is he still here?' Grace continues.

'I think so. My mother won't let me downstairs.'

'He's not as young as he makes out. Not up close.'

Orianna cannot help but think how beautiful Grace looks, so much older than her years. The make-up and the cigarette give her the pouty look of an adult.

They've never really spoken before, on the rare occasions they've bumped into each other around the estate or at school.

Grace stands up, walks to the dresser, sets the cigarette down, then unpins her hair. She picks up a hairbrush and holds it up. 'Brush out my hair?'

Orianna pads over as Grace settles onto the stool.

Taking the brush, she begins to gently smooth out the curls from Grace's cascade of long, dark hair.

She sees that Grace is looking at her in the mirror.

'You're pretty.'

Is she? Her own hair falls down below her shoulders; she has her mother's dusky complexion, her warm brown eyes, her fine bones.

'Thanks.'

The Girl In Cell A

'We look a little alike.'
She can't see it.
'You wanna know what that actor said to me?'
'No ... Yes.'
Grace bares her teeth. 'Well, let me tell you, then ...'

18

ORIANNA: NOW

A knock on the door.

I shift on my cot, swing my feet to the floor and stand.

Luke enters first, followed closely by the roustabout figure of Sheriff Hank Faulkes.

Luke stands there a moment, a lean figure in a pristine white shirt, shiny shoes and a belt buckle in the shape of a guitar. His blond hair glistens, brushed back from a clean forehead. Our eyes meet. My heart gives a little stutter; a reflex instinct that makes me hate myself.

His jaw tightens. 'Get her out of here.'

Faulkes frowns. 'Have you spoken to Amos about this?'

The younger man turns. 'I said release her. Now.'

Faulkes holds his gaze, then decides the pissing contest isn't worth the trouble. He is a Wyclerc man, bought and paid for. Going up against Luke is pointless.

In the lobby, the redhead goggles at me, then reluctantly returns my bag.

I check the contents, take back my wallet and phone, then turn and make for the door, Luke a step behind me.

'I hear you've taken up over at Elvira's old place,' Sheriff Faulkes calls after us.

I twist my neck around to look at him leaning against the counter.

'Pretty isolated out there. Best be careful. Folks round here are likely to rile themselves up knowing there's a convicted murderer living close by.'

'Are you threatening her?' Luke's voice is even, but I hear the undercurrent.

Faulkes reaches into his pocket, takes out another cheroot, lights it.

We turn a corner, walk a hundred yards and out into the town square.

I stop, surveying a scene that has lived inside my head for the past eighteen years, a postcard image of Eden Falls: a handful of civic buildings – the town hall, council offices, the old brick post office, the courthouse with its gable clock – clustered around a cobbled plaza, at the centre of which stands the great statue of Nathaniel and the Wolf.

The sight of the enormous bronze jolts something inside me.

I see, with new eyes, just how dramatically outsized the wolf is, reared up on its paws like a bear, mouth agape, fangs the size of bowie knives. Faced with the animal's naked aggression, Nathaniel Wyclerc remains stoic, caught in a boxer's stance, balanced lightly on the balls of his feet, right hand clasped around a hunter's blade.

The town's founding myth, cast in metal, glows dully in the sunlight.

I wonder how much truth there is to the story, how much the embellishment of legend . . . How big had the wolf really been? Had Nathaniel really fought it with nothing more than a knife?

The past is malleable; like molten steel, it can be cast in any shape, made to tell any tale depending on the whim – or bias – of the storyteller.

My own truth is the same, sunk deep in the tar pit of my own mind.

19

ORIANNA: NOW

I had known it as Jim Ackerman's place, but now it is Harvey's Diner; a time machine stuck in the fifties, with red canvas booths, chequerboard tiles and a digital jukebox in the corner.

The interior is air-conditioned – a welcome relief from the punishing heat.

There is hardly anyone in the place.

Luke leads us to a booth at the rear, giant menu cards stuck under sheet glass overlaying the pressboard table.

We have barely sat before a heavy-legged waitress with a lopsided beehive hairdo wobbles over, brandishing a notebook in one hand, a pitcher of cold water in the other. She doesn't bother to waste a glance as she takes our order.

I study Luke's face: the dark roots beneath his thatch of blond hair; the smooth planes of his high-cut cheeks; the sweat cooling on his long neck.

He meets my gaze head-on. 'What did you think would happen?'

'They're not going to scare me away.'

'I can't be with you all the time, Ori.'

'I don't need a babysitter.'

'Then why did you call me?'

Because I needed to see you. A throttle of anger erases the thought. 'It seemed the quickest way to get out of that cell.'

'What were you doing with Gerty?'

I say nothing.

'You're not listening to me.'

'I listened to you once before. And look what that got me.'

It was as if I had struck him. 'That's not fair.'

'You want to talk to *me* about fair?'

Behind the counter, I hear the waitress chatting to the short-order cook.

'What's she like?'

Confusion clouds his eyes.

'Your wife. What's she like?'

He blinks, momentarily blindsided. I motion towards his hand. 'You took off the ring. But there's still a tan line.'

The waitress arrives with our order, sets the plates down with a clatter. 'Here you go, folks. Enjoy.'

Luke doesn't move. And then he sticks a hand into the pocket of his pants, returns with a ring, and slips it onto his finger.

'Her name's Abigail. She's thirty-two, a lawyer from Beatty.' Beatty. The second largest town in Griffin County, after Barrier. Eden Falls is third on the list.

The machinery of my throat has rusted. 'Kids?' I manage.

'No. I mean, there's one on the way. But we still have some time.'

I pick up a fork, push fries around my plate.

'Ori—'

'I meant what I said. I'm not going anywhere.' I cannot let him speak, say the things he wants to say. What good would it do either of us? 'I'm staying right here until I figure out what happened that day. To me, to Gideon, to Grace.'

'And what if you find something you don't want to find?'

'I know myself, Luke. That's all I've got. And if *I* didn't kill Gideon, then someone else did ... You know what burns me? That the killer might still be here, living in this godforsaken town. A wolf in the fold.'

The door chime sounds behind me. Footsteps. The expression on Luke's face changes. 'Shit.'

I turn and stiffen as I see the figure approach. A tall, slim-shouldered woman, supple-figured, dressed in a sweat top and hot pants, as if she's just walked out of the gym. Her hair is worn in blonde ringlets, currently plastered to a high, handsome forehead. Wrinkles at the corners of her cobalt-blue eyes betray her age, but she could easily pass for a woman a decade younger than her years.

Rebekah Wyclerc. Gideon's wife. Grace's mother.

I stand to face her, senses crackling like live wires. Behind me, I hear Luke scrabble to his feet.

Rebekah stops a yard from me, eyes twitching over my face, as if unable to believe what they are seeing.

The sounds of the diner fade away.

The last time I faced this woman had been in a courtroom, following the verdict.

The slap, when it comes, blindsides me.

I gasp, stumble sideways, cheek stinging, the burn of humiliation sweeping through me.

'Rebekah!'

Luke's voice sounds muffled in my ringing ears.

'How could you let *her* back in?' A cry of pain and rage.

'She's served her time. The law says she's free to go where she pleases. There's not a thing I – or anyone else – can do to stop her.'

Rebekah's crazed stare threatens to split him in two. She turns back to me. 'Where's my daughter? What did you do to her?'

There is little point in responding. There is nothing I can say to this woman that will make a damned bit of difference.

Luke moves between us. 'Rebekah, please. You have to go.'

'*Where'd you bury her, you murdering bitch?*' The shriek is torn from somewhere deep inside her.

Luke spreads his arms, then half pushes, half leads her outside.

I watch them talking animatedly, until finally Rebekah spins on her heel and stalks away.

Luke puts his hands on his hips, looks down at the floor, closes his eyes.

When he opens them again, he fishes his phone out of his pocket. The call lasts only moments.

The diner has become a diorama, all the actors frozen in place.

When Luke comes back in, he says simply: 'Amos wants to see you.'

20

ANNIE: THEN

What makes a person who they are?

Sooner or later, every patient asks the question, though the exact formulation can come in a hundred guises.

I take a moment to compose my thoughts.

Clearly, the thought has been on Orianna's mind since last we spoke. That discussion gave me an insight into her beginnings with Grace Wyclerc, how the dynamic between them impacted Orianna. I need more information, of course, and a part of me wants to race in. But experience has taught me to proceed cautiously. The work I do is akin to piecing together a jigsaw, where each piece must first be fished from the soup of my patients' uncooperative memories.

And with each piece, I have a judgement call to make. How much of what Orianna is telling me actually happened, how much does she *believe* happened, and how much is an outright lie?

Because I can't discount that possibility. That Orianna is playing games; that she considers me an adversary to be outwitted.

Of course, if she isn't lying, if it *is* true that she didn't kill Gideon, then somewhere out there, a killer is roaming free, ignored by the authorities ... A fanciful notion. I have read the trial notes, the case transcript. Orianna was convicted by a jury of her peers and with good reason. I must not allow myself to be beguiled by her glamour.

The Girl in Cell A.

'Would it surprise you if I said that I haven't the faintest idea? People expect psychiatrists to have some sort of magic window onto the human soul. It doesn't work like that. Each of us is a product of our genetic inheritance, our upbringing, our environment, the circumstances and events that shape us over many years. The smallest thing can affect us in significant ways.' I lock eyes with her. 'Orianna, I can't tell you if you were born to commit the act of violence you were convicted of. Frankly speaking, such a search would be pointless. The truth is that all of us have the capacity to commit violence, given the right circumstances.'

She silently absorbs this.

I shift in my seat. 'Orianna, I want to talk a little more about what it is we're trying to achieve with these sessions. Your mind has been affected deeply by what happened to you. Your memory has closed in on itself. The result of this is that the reality you remember may not be the reality that actually happened. Do you understand?'

Her brow furrows. 'Are you saying I'm lying? That I lied about everything?'

'No. I'm simply saying that trauma has a way of distorting things that appear certain to us. Our goal is to peer through those distortions to the truth.'

The Girl In Cell A

Her face gives nothing away. Yet I can sense her anger. Once again, I remember her guard, Barney's, warning.

There is nothing in the literature that positively correlates violence and dissociative amnesia. While it may be true that mental health can compromise the ability to regulate emotions and that *this* can lead to violence, the vast majority of people with mental illness are not violent. When they are, it is often the result of other factors: substance abuse, adverse childhood experiences, and the impact of their immediate environment.

I pick up a folder and fish out a sheaf of papers. Drawings. Maps.

'You drew these. Barney says you threw them away. I hope you don't mind that I had a look at them?'

She says nothing. I choose to take this as assent.

'I take it this is Eden Falls?'

'Yes.'

'You seem to have retained a very detailed memory of the town.'

'I grew up there. It's home. In a way, I'm still there. I never left.'

The light catches her eyes, making them shine disconcertingly.

'I'm going to use a word-association technique now,' I say. 'I want you to relax and simply respond with the first word that comes into your head.'

'I've seen this in the movies. Do you really think it will help?'

I ignore the scorn in her voice. 'It helps to close your eyes. Respond as quickly as you can, without overthinking things.'

'You're the boss.'
I pause, then: 'Home.'
'Eden Falls.'
'Mother.'
'Gone.'
'Gideon.'
'Dead.'
'Amos.'
A silence.
'Amos,' I repeat.
'Wolf.'

21

ORIANNA: NOW

The Big House comes into view gradually.

I follow Luke in my Chevy. Having made it three-quarters of a mile past the estate's main gate and then through a second gate in the inner wall surrounding the Big House, I find my foot slipping off the gas and slowing the car to a crawl, my thoughts running ahead of me like water racing along cracks in the sidewalk.

I have imagined this moment more times than I can count: a return to the estate that had been my home for half my life before the darkness came for me.

The house, built in the Greek-revivalist antebellum style, is spread out over two storeys, with a rectangular central block abutted on both sides by front-gabled H-shaped wings. A Doric-columned portico fronts the central portion of the house, roofing a deep stone porch. A great pond situated in front of the porch absorbs the sun's light into its tobacco-coloured depths; lily pads float atop the water, where a scarred and pitted statue of Venus rises from its centre.

I pull up behind Luke's Ford until our bumpers are almost touching.

Disembarking, I stand for a moment and look up at the Big House, allowing my gaze to rove over the temple-like pediment, the walls thick with ivy, the grand passage below the porch set with cane furniture where the house's residents congregated on soft summer evenings to sip on mint juleps served in old-fashioned pewter cups as they'd done in taverns up and down the state back in the early 1800s.

A shiver moves up my spine and gathers in a knot between my shoulders.

An intense flare of pain suddenly arcs across the front of my brain, almost driving me to my knees. I am confronted, once again, by a wall of blinding white. The white resolves into images, a film reel of memories.

I am with my mother on what she called 'party nights' up at the Big House; nights when the rich and powerful came to pay homage to Amos Wyclerc. To kiss the ring and court the maker of kings.

Although I grew up on the estate, my mother always kept me at a distance from the Wyclerc family. She told me nothing about them and warned me to stay out of their way. Her attitude confused me. I understood that they were her employers and we modern-day serfs living on their land, but this wasn't the nineteenth century.

It wasn't until the end, and everything that happened, that I finally understood why she had kept me in the dark.

As I grew older, she would surprise me, on occasion, when, in the grip of a desperate shortage of hands, she would take me onto the house staff for party nights. I used these opportunities to explore the vastness of the house, the wealth sunk into ancient furniture that smelled of beeswax, the looming portraits, the fine trappings of people who lived in a manner I could barely comprehend. Something dark would rise inside me, a knife-edged anger at the unfairness of it. At times, it was all I could do not to rip off my uniform and stomp on out of there.

The front door swings back and a black man in a white shirt and tie walks out into the heavy afternoon light.

Cletus Barnes. Amos's PA and valet.

Cletus appears to have stepped directly out of my memories – a striking, upright presence, with square, set-back shoulders, clean-shaven and handsome. Immaculate, down to the sheen on his buffed shoes. He must be in his early fifties now, yet there is barely a glimmer of grey in his hair.

He fastens upon me with his liquid eyes. For a moment, I see something flash in them, an acknowledgement, perhaps, of the years that I grew up beneath his sober gaze, and then he turns to Luke. 'He's waiting for you in the study.'

22

ORIANNA: NOW

We follow Cletus across a grand entranceway and up an imperial staircase, carpeted in deep olive, with teak bannisters and wolf-head finials.

Cletus walks with such a light step he seems to float above the floor.

I recall the patience with which he always addressed himself to my mother; a man of few words but of infinite knowledge and impenetrable nature.

We stop outside a door. Cletus knocks gently.

'Come.'

The grand study is at least ten thousand square feet in dimension. One wall is dominated by floor-to-ceiling bookshelves, crammed with soft-spined volumes. On the far side, a suite of maroon buttoned-leather couches sit by a portable drinks cabinet, facing a giant TV screen. To either side of the TV, floating on the walls, are lithographs of the Eden Falls mines.

A twin-pedestal desk of burled oak floats in the centre of the room.

Behind the desk, seven-foot windows trimmed in granite look out onto the rear of the mansion; manicured grounds that lead down to a high concrete wall, topped by iron spikes.

Beyond the wall, about a half mile back, lies a dark tangle of forest.

Standing behind the desk, tumbler in hand, is Amos Wyclerc.

He is taller than I remember, a broad, thick-shouldered man. Even at this late age, there is a raw strength about him that is instantly intimidating. His thick hair, combed straight back, has whitened, and contrasts with his dark brow and shaven, raw-boned cheeks. He is immaculately dressed: pressed cotton pants, a crisp pale shirt and a buttoned blazer with a faintly nautical flourish. The watch at his wrist glints in the light falling in from the window.

For an instant, only silence reigns in the room.

I have imagined this moment for eighteen long years, but now that it is here, my jaw has welded shut.

'Luke, leave us.'

I see Luke start, a protest fly to his lips. But Amos forestalls it by waving his tumbler at him. 'You can wait downstairs for her.'

Luke glances at me, troubled. Finally, he nods.

I watch Cletus lead him out.

Taking a deep breath, I turn back to Amos, patriarch of the Wyclerc clan, father to Gideon, and grandfather of Grace Wyclerc.

After all these years, he is a creature that has receded almost into myth.

He spreads an expansive hand towards the couch arrangement. 'Shall we sit?'

I watch him walk over and lower himself gingerly into a wing seat, favouring his right side.

Willing my own limbs into motion, I move across the room and sink onto the couch facing him. On the ornate glass coffee table separating us is a silver tray set with a decanter, a bucket of ice and several cut-glass tumblers.

'Bourbon?'

I don't trust myself to speak.

He picks up the decanter and pours me a glass, holds it out. It shakes gently, revealing an infirmity in his grip. I stare at it, then take it from him, raise it to my mouth and feel the whisky light a flame all the way down my throat.

'Thank you for agreeing to visit with me.' His voice has depth and timbre, the resonances of power that I remember. In that respect, and others, time has done little to diminish him.

'Did I have a choice?'

He smiles without mirth. 'I suppose a part of me always knew you'd come back. Or at least, I hoped that you might.'

'Why? So you could finish destroying my life?'

'You were punished by the law, Orianna. Not me.'

I snort angrily. 'Do you really think I could have got an impartial jury in this county?'

He says nothing.

'I didn't kill him.' I practically spit the words at him.

'How do you know? By your own admission, you can't remember what happened that day. Or has the light finally burned its way into that dark vault inside your mind?' He seems genuinely curious, almost hopeful.

I blink. 'No.'

He knuckles his left knee. 'Why *have* you come back?'

'Because . . . because I want to know the truth.'

'And you're willing to put yourself through hell for it?'

I don't bother to reply.

'I can't abide small talk, so let me get straight to the point. I can smell death on me. Cancer. To be frank, the end, when it comes, will be a relief. I want to die before I have to piss in a bag. A most unedifying prospect.' He flashes a louche grin that I find repellent. 'Before I trust my soul to Providence, I want to know what happened to my son. I want to know what happened to my granddaughter. Perhaps, Orianna, our goals are not so far apart.'

My face opens in surprise. This is unexpected. I had assumed Amos has summoned me here to threaten me, to railroad me out of town. The idea that we might have anything in common seems fantastical.

'Eighteen years I've waited for this moment.' His eyes harden. 'There was a time when I thought I might have you killed. Perhaps even inside that prison they sent you to. But what good would that have done? Gideon would still be dead. Grace would still be missing.

'I confess, at first I didn't believe your story. You blow a man's head off, and you can't *remember*?' He clicks his tongue. 'But time has a way of opening up our prejudices.'

He heaves himself to his feet, walks back to his desk, scoops up a set of plastic folders, then returns and sets them down before me.

On the cover of the topmost one, my own name is prominent in stencilled black letters.

Frowning, I pick it up, open it to the first page.

Shock thunders through me. I flick through the folder, pages blurring beneath my gaze, whole passages – my own words, taken from my sessions with Annie Ledet – floating up to meet me.

Finally, I look up. My heart thumps against my ribcage. I feel violated, in a way I cannot reduce into mere words. 'How did you get these?'

'Does it matter?' He shifts in his seat. 'Why did you come back? You could have vanished, started over someplace new. Why *choose* to come back here?'

I don't trust myself to reply.

His face becomes grave. 'I have a proposition for you. Luke tells me you've come back with some notion of reinvestigating what happened all those years ago. All right. I'll take you at your word. I want you to carry on doing what you're doing. But now, you do so with my blessing. And you report to me. Whatever you find, I want to be the first to know.'

I am shaking my head before he has finished. 'No.'

'Hear me out, now. If I should give the word, you won't be able to make it through another day in Eden Falls.' He pulls his lips back from long, yellow teeth. With his Wyclerc eyes, and his thick white hair, he has never looked more like a wolf. 'I want the same thing as you do: to know the truth. We don't have to be friends. Call it a temporary alliance.'

I look past his shoulder. Beyond the window, the darkening sky gains towards the zenith, seems to vibrate.

'How can you be sure I *didn't* kill him? There's a ... a darkness in my mind. Whenever I think of that day.'

'I suppose I can't be sure. Neither of us can. But I'm willing to set my chips on the table, Orianna. It's either this, or you leave town and never come back.'

I breathe in. 'How would it even work? This ... arrangement?'

His eyes quicken, the scent of victory in his nostrils. 'You work through Luke. Anything you need, he'll get you. You need records, doors opening, cash—'

'I don't want your money.'

He gives me a hard look. 'Five years after you were sentenced, I hired a private investigation agency. They raked over everything. And I still haven't a clue what happened to my granddaughter.'

'Which one?' I breathe, the words pulled out of me.

He narrows his eyes. 'I suppose we should address the matter—'

'Don't.'

'Do you think I'm a monster, child? I really can't tell any more. The ordinary rules of civilisation don't apply to men like me, not in a place like Eden Falls.' A beat, as he studies me. 'What is it that you want from me? An acknowledgement? Do you want me to say it out loud?' He leans forward, his breath as ripe as fallen summer fruit. 'Dear Orianna, I hereby acknowledge that you are my flesh and blood. My granddaughter.'

23

ANNIE: THEN

'Patricide.'

The word hangs in the room, a dark hummingbird floating between us.

Orianna continues. 'It was the first word out of the district attorney's mouth, the first word of his opening statement.'

I have taken my time, but now here we are.

Orianna's trial was always going to play a starring role in our sessions together. I know that I have disconcerted her by refusing to proceed in a linear fashion, zigzagging between aspects of her life and the events that sent her to prison – a technique I have used in the past, particularly with complex cases. When you are dealing with those who have suffered trauma, poking directly at the wound doesn't always get results. Sometimes, it is better to approach at an angle, acclimatise the patient to the therapeutic process, and then head towards the smouldering wreck of their memories.

Is Orianna sold on the process?

I catch her, sometimes, staring at me with ancient eyes, picturing me, perhaps, as a high priestess of a cult that might just as easily leave her bloodied on a stone altar as cure her. I have asked her to trust me. But trust is a commodity in short supply in prison, lesser still for a woman who feels betrayed by circumstance in the way Orianna does.

Sitting there, in that tiny room, I ask her to relive for us both the first day of her trial.

The easiest way to do this is to use the official court transcript. I have brought along copies for us both. I hand one to Orianna, wait for her to open it.

She gathers herself, winding back the clock of memory, then begins.

'I remember how packed the public gallery was – the truth is, you could have filled it ten times over. Folk had come from across the county – the trial of Gideon Wyclerc's killer was the hottest ticket in town. Sex and scandal. Wealth and power. And race. We had it all.

'I remember the murderous heat. The way the jurors dabbed sweat from their eyes with blazing-white handkerchiefs. I recognised some of them, corralled onto a wooden platform to my right. My attorney's motion to move the trial to another county had already been dismissed by the judge, Holden Whaley. Whaley had been a circuit-court fixture in the county since before I had been born. That the residents of my hometown might be unfairly prejudiced against me was not an argument he was prepared to entertain, not with the Wyclercs looking over his shoulder.'

'Was your mother there?'

Orianna nods, slowly. 'She was in the front row of the gallery. I remember how drawn her face looked. The abuse that she'd suffered in the months since my arrest had taken something vital from her. From us both.' She stops, momentarily overcome.

I make a note to come back to Christine. These memories of the trial will allow me to explore, in a less confrontational manner, the relationship between mother and daughter.

'Tell me about your lawyer. And the prosecutor.'

'The DA's name was Carl Danziger. A tall, handsome man in his early forties. Hair the colour of autumn leaves. I could see that he was in his element, wallowing in his fifteen minutes of fame. The case had gone national. I remember the way he kept looking over at the row of reporters at the back of the courtroom, like he'd adopt them if he could.

'My own lawyer, Herman Ortega, an out-of-towner, was everything Danziger wasn't. Small, thin-shouldered, buck-toothed, pop-eyed. He looked like a schoolyard dweeb, with bad hair and a birthmark in the shape of a child's hand on his right cheek, as if he'd been slapped and the sting had never gone away. His suits looked like they'd been bought from a thrift store. My mother set against him from the very beginning. It wasn't Ortega's fault – Christine never did like unattractive men.'

'Then why did you hire him?'

'Like we had a choice? Ortega was the only defence attorney willing to take the case. The only one we could afford. It was either Ortega, or the public defender. My mother had been convinced not to take that gamble.'

I shift in my seat. 'How were you feeling? Right then, at the start?'

The Girl In Cell A

A haunted look overtakes her. 'Those last moments before the trial began were almost unbearable. They'd trucked me in from the county jail, where I'd changed out of my prison issues. My mother had insisted I project the appearance of innocence; to her that meant clean clothes and make-up. It was about the only thing Ortega and Christine agreed on.' A grimace. 'When Judge Whaley finally fired the starter pistol, the DA practically ran over to the jury box. I remember every word of his opening statement, I've read it so many times.'

She begins to recite, not bothering to look at the transcript in her lap. I look down at the file in my own hands:

> **DA Danziger:** Patricide. In the Roman republic, it was the only crime for which a civilian might be sentenced to death. Why? Because it is a crime so grotesque, so beyond the pale, that, for most of us, it is simply incomprehensible . . . The facts of this case are straightforward. We intend to prove that, on August thirty-first of last year, the defendant, Orianna Negi, murdered the man who was her biological father, Gideon Wyclerc. We shall show that she did so in a fit of rage, angered that the fact of Gideon's paternity had been kept from her by her mother until that very day, angered that she had been denied her birthright, angered at a lifetime of slights by the very family of which – she had now discovered – she was a member. We shall show that she tracked Gideon down to a hunting cabin on the Wyclerc family estate and shot him dead, killing him with his own shotgun. No doubt the defence will make much of the defendant's age, of

the emotions that led her to act as she did. But I am confident that you will see beyond that. The young woman sat before you today is a cold-blooded killer. The facts will demonstrate this

Orianna wasn't kidding when she said that she'd memorised the DA's opening. I look up and see that she is shaking. These memories are taking her deep into the terrain of her trauma, exposing long-buried emotions.

'Do you need a moment?'

'I'm fine.'

I'm not sure that's true, but I nod. 'What did you think after hearing that opening?'

'I guess, until that exact moment, until Danziger spelled it out, it hadn't seemed real. I remember turning immediately to my lawyer, Ortega. He took his time getting up from his seat. I had the impression the DA's opening had derailed him. A spike of panic jagged inside me as he approached the jury box.'

Orianna pauses, and then looks down at the transcript.

> **Ortega:** Ladies and gentlemen, it is heartening that my colleague has stated that this will be a case that rests on the merits of its facts. Well, here are the facts. Gideon Wyclerc was indeed murdered by a weapon that my client fired that day. Yet, the prosecution cannot produce one witness to testify that they saw her commit this murder. My client was indeed discovered in Gideon's hunting cabin – but, as we shall see, she had gone there merely to speak with the victim. The

prosecution has told you that she went to the cabin in a 'fit of rage'; yet, again, there are no witnesses to testify as to her exact state of mind at the time. The truth is that, having discovered that Gideon Wyclerc, a man she had known all her life, was her father, this confused and vulnerable young woman went in search of him, to verify the accuracy of what she had been told. The fact that my client was knocked out cold and left to take the fall for Gideon Wyclerc's murder – by a party or parties that the State has not looked for – indeed, the existence of which the State has completely ignored – should be all the evidence that you need to acquit. Reasonable doubt, ladies and gentlemen, that's the bar—

She stops.

'Go on,' I murmur.

'That's it. That's when Ortega stopped.'

'Why?'

'There was a commotion at the back of the court. I remember swinging around in my seat to see Amos enter the room and make his way to the front row where the rest of the Wyclercs were seated, directly behind the prosecution table.'

'Why wasn't Amos already there?'

'I don't know. But seeing him there seemed to shift the ground beneath us. I remember how the whole courtroom fell into a hush. Even Judge Whaley, up on his bench, seemed cowed.'

'Did Amos say anything to you?'

'No. But our eyes met for the briefest instant. In the months since my arrest, he hadn't come to see me, hadn't come to ask if I had really killed his son. Or why. He'd cast us out, me *and* my mother. She had lost her position at the Big House. Amos had made sure there were no other openings in town.' A grim smile turns up her lips. 'When I was growing up, I'd hear folk call him the great Wolf of the Wyclercs. Nothing could shake Amos. But, I guess, the loss of his favoured son had blown even Amos out of the water.'

24

ORIANNA: NOW

'Where do you want to start?' Amos locks eyes with me.

'At the beginning. I want to know about the family. *My* family.'

Amos gets up from the armchair, lumbers to the wall of bookshelves and returns with a red-bound album. Lowering himself down beside me, he sets the album down onto the coffee table.

I am acutely aware of his closeness, the woody scent of his aftershave, the sheer fact of his bulk.

He flicks through the album and sticks his finger onto a page. The portrait is sepia, the edges liver-spotted with age. The man in the image wears a buttoned longcoat, calf-high caulk boots and a handlebar moustache. His facial features bear a strong resemblance to Amos, the Wyclerc eyes front and centre.

'Noah Wyclerc – my granddaddy. A man singularly lacking in moral rectitude. Spent the early part of his life moving around the West Coast, riding the rails, working odd jobs. Gill-netter, saloon-hand, lumberjack. He fell into lawless pursuits.

'In 1901, he married Estelle Clayborn, and had three children by her. Nathaniel – my father; and, four years later, Jude and Esther, the twins.

'For a while, Noah settled in Wyoming, worked in the mining business. Ironically, it was *his* vision to found Eden Falls. He'd heard a rumour suggesting there was iron ore just waiting to be found out east. A mine of his very own. He never made it here.' A beat. 'In 1924, Noah was hanged for the crime of murder. The details of it my father would never discuss with me, and I have never had the inclination to find out.' His words are a full stop, forbidding further enquiry. 'A year later, Nathaniel married and set out east with his new bride, Miriam. He left Jude and Esther behind, in the care of a local Quaker couple – this was about the time my father found religion. Once he'd established his mining outpost in the forest, he sent for the twins.'

'They died young, didn't they? I read that somewhere.'

'Yes. In a fire, right here on the estate. Back in the summer of 1934.'

'How old were they?'

'They were both twenty-eight.'

Amos is silent a moment, reliving a past he cannot have known, then jerks to life again, leaning forward and turning several pages. The photograph he lands on is of Jude and Esther Wyclerc, non-identical twins, standing stiffly to attention, dressed in sober clothing, a wooden church building behind them, white-painted cross prominent on the apex of a gabled roof.

'They died in the old chapel. My father never got over it. After Noah's death, he'd taken it upon himself to raise them. They were his younger siblings, but he treated them as if they were his children.'

I absorb this. 'What happened to Noah's wife? Your grandmother?'

'She vanished. Left a week after Noah was hanged. Never looked back.'

'Nathaniel didn't look for her? His own mother?'

'No. My father was not a sentimental man.'

He flicks through the album again.

The next photograph is of two men in their twenties. One is recognisable as a young Amos; the other, his elder brother, Abel, in an infantryman's field uniform.

'My brother, Abel. He died in the Vietnam War.' A beat. 'I prayed that he would.'

I find myself staring.

'Does that shock you? My brother and I hated each other. I was always the smarter one, but he could never lay down with that simple fact. He was older, and so my father anointed him as his successor. I knew that would be a mistake, knew he'd run the firm into the ground. Abel had no head for business, and his arrogance was such that he wouldn't listen to good advice. That's why he went to war. No one could change his mind once an idea got into his head – not even Nathaniel.' A pause. 'His death broke my father. He loved Abel, favoured him over me. I never did understand why.' He picks up his tumbler and takes a sip. 'Abel had two children, David and Hannah. After his death, I raised them as my own. Hannah married outside the family – she left Eden Falls a long time ago, cut herself off from the clan. David . . . Well, David, you already know. Luke's father.'

I did know David. A good and decent man, one of the few among the Wyclercs to have ever treated me with consideration. David had been sent to study corporate law in New York and subsequently served as the family's legal adviser in all business matters. It was he who had found us Herman Ortega, when just about every other defence attorney within reach had turned down the case for fear of inviting Amos Wyclerc's wrath.

As far as I knew, that had remained a secret between David and my mother.

'Why did Hannah leave? Why did she cut herself off?'

He swirls his glass. 'Because some people can't live with the way things are.'

25

ORIANNA: NOW

Amos heaves himself to his feet and leads me to a broad-framed canvas hung above the fireplace.

I want to ask him more about Hannah, why she left the family. There is something here that Amos isn't telling me. But I sense that I will get nothing out of him. At least, not at this moment.

For an instant, my thoughts flashback to my years growing up on the estate, to the way my mother kept me at a remove from the Wyclercs. Gossip, when it came to me, was second-hand; whispers distorted by the mouths they moved through. Over the years, I have spent innumerable hours on the internet, researching the Wyclercs. But all I find are conspiracy theories and conjecture. My *family* has been incredibly successful at holding on to their secrets.

I file Hannah away.

'This is Nathaniel,' he says, crooking a finger at the portrait. 'My father.'

Nathaniel Wyclerc is captured in the guise of a frontiersman – raccoon cap, furs, a rifle cradled in his arms, pearl-handled knife tucked into his belt. His beard is dark, his face rugged, eyes drilling into space.

'When a man becomes a myth, it's hard to know what is truth and what is good old-fashioned bullshit. My father was a hard man, unsparing, unforgiving. A *believer*. He ruled his mining enterprise – and the town that was built on the back of it – with an iron fist. Some might say that without that absolute severity of commitment, Eden Falls might never have made it through the Depression. But Nathaniel wouldn't let his dream die. He was King Midas with a gun. A ruthless captain of industry who, in time, became more concerned with the salvation of our souls than mere lucre.'

'Do you think that was because of what happened with his own father? With Noah?'

'A fair question. Yes, Noah's crime hung over this family. It was never spoken about, but I knew my daddy would have sold his soul to have it expunged from our collective record.'

I look back up at the portrait. 'How did Nathaniel die?'

'Don't you know? Haven't you looked it up?'

'Yes, of course. I want to hear it from you.'

'A hunting accident. Out in the forests around the old mine, up near the abandoned railhead. Someone had dug out a boar pit, staked it like a *trou de loup*. Nathaniel simply fell in. By the time a search party found him, he'd been dead a day, skewered through the heart.'

I suppress a shudder.

'Do you know what *trou de loup* means?'

I say nothing.

'It's French for "wolf hole". Apt, don't you think?'

'What was he doing out there?'

'That, I'm afraid, is where the fabric frays. This much I know: as he got older, my father began abandoning the company of others. He'd taken this town as his warrant; each soul as his charge. It hollowed him out. He told me once that it was a war, the salvation of man's soul. We wage it daily and sometimes, despite our best efforts, we lose.'

His expression broods.

'When did he hand over control of the business to you?'

'Does it matter?'

I recall a piece I had read online about a young Amos, who'd taken over the Wyclerc concern, embarking on five decades of pathological acquisition and expansion before the tide had turned and the primroses faded.

'There was a story about you, from the sixties. An out-of-state mine you'd taken over. A roof collapse. Five men died. A case was brought against you, but you settled out of court. The families were forced to sign a non-disclosure agreement.'

He presses his lips together. 'Mining's a dangerous business.'

'There were rumours, about the decisions you made. That you deliberately delayed sending rescuers in. Because it suited you for those men to die down there, to not come back up and testify against the practices of the firm, practices that led to the accident ... What really happened?'

He nails me with a look of such fury that it is all I can do not to step backwards.

'Now you listen to me, girl. I don't have the time nor the inclination to answer damned fool questions from those who've never picked up a shovel in their lives, who haven't the faintest understanding of what it takes to rip Mother Earth's riches from her. She don't give up nothing without a fight.'

His face has turned ugly. He stomps away, back to the couch.

I count to ten, then join him, wait out an uncomfortable silence.

Finally, he speaks. 'Nathaniel had two sons. Abel, I've just told you about. And me. My father never forgave me for outliving my brother. He was left with no choice but to hand me the reins. He'd lost the appetite to run the firm. In time, he was forced to accept that I knew what I was doing. He stepped aside and let me handle things my way.' A pause. 'And by then, I'd married.'

'Evelyn?'

'Yes. Evelyn Fairchild. She was the grandniece of the state senator. A beautiful woman with the kindest heart. We had three children together. Peter, my oldest. Samuel. And, of course, Gideon. Your father.'

I still cannot hear Gideon's name without a spike of angst.

'Want me to keep going?'

'Yes.'

'Every king has three sons. The smart one, the brave one, the doomed one. Peter was the smart one. Or, at least, he did everything I asked of him. I guess that's why I never took to him.' He looks off into space. 'You don't have children, do you? You can't know what it's like, to not love your own offspring. To not want to be in the same room as them.

'In the end, of course, I had to let Peter run the firm. Like my father before me, I was left with no choice. Samuel ... Samuel was the brave one. He defied me. Caught the Holy Ghost early on; came to me one day and told me he'd decided to join the church. Even I can't compete with God.'

I remembered Samuel. A quiet, contemplative man who had spent years away from Eden Falls, training for his chosen vocation, preaching the gospel in far-flung locations, before returning to take over the Eden Falls parish when Randall McGovern had passed on.

'And that leaves Gideon.'

26

ANNIE: THEN

Orianna fails to show for our next session.

I wait for an hour in case she changes her mind, but eventually, Barney turns up and tells me she will not be coming. I ask him what the problem is, but he says he's not sure. Orianna has simply told him that she doesn't feel well enough.

I wonder if the previous session, when we had begun reliving her trial – touching on the fact that she is Gideon Wyclerc's illegitimate daughter – has affected her more deeply than I had anticipated. Discovering that she was Gideon's child was the inciting event the State claims sparked Orianna's murderous rampage on the day of the killing. As such, we will have to dissect both the event and her prior relationship with Gideon, no matter how difficult the discussion.

Of course, there is no way for me to know which recollections will cause Orianna to stumble, and which will lead us closer towards those memories still veiled by her dissociative amnesia. I am heartened by the progress we have made, but the fact remains that the end goal of the process hasn't changed. Somehow, I must help Orianna to relive the murder for which she has been convicted, to access those lost memories.

The law is clear.

There can be no question of parole until Orianna admits her crime.

And it is my role to help her accept her guilt.

By the time I arrive home, it is well past eight, and the darkness has closed around my building like a fist.

I kick off my shoes as I enter the cramped third-floor apartment – a far cry from the home Michael and I had built together, and which he continues to share with our son.

The place is cold, and I have to thump the boiler to get the heat going.

The apartment is cheap – pretty much all I can afford right now.

The anger flows through me again. I don't deserve this. No one deserves *this*. Broken marriages should not lead to such cruel and unusual punishment. The fates of the involved parties should not be decided on the strength of who can afford the better lawyer.

To give Michael his due, he could have taken more.

And he never used Leo as a pawn. It was Leo's decision to remain with his father. It was Leo's decision not to have regular visitation with me.

The crap piled up in the sink reminds me that I need to eat. I rarely cook, and so it will have to be another Uber Eats: pasta paired with a cheap bottle of white from the fridge. Between the rent for this place and basic costs of living, there isn't much left over for the sort of fine dining Michael and I once enjoyed.

I am curled up on the shitty couch, in woollen socks and an old Princeton sweatshirt, watching *Frasier* reruns on my laptop and forking the last of the pasta into my mouth when my phone rings.

Talk of the devil.

It's unusual for Michael to call during the week. He prefers to keep our interactions to the bare minimum necessary for Leo not to feel as if his father is trying to cut his mother *completely* out of his life. 'Leo wants to talk to you.'

When my son appears on the WhatsApp video, my heart balloons.

He is dressed in his football uniform, helmet tucked under his armpit, black bars smeared across his cheeks. At sixteen, Leo is already almost six and a half feet tall, a natural athlete.

'Hey, Mom.'

'Hey, handsome. Football night? Again?'

'Yeah. Kind of a big game. Coach put me on the starting grid. I thought I'd call. You know, so you can wish me luck.'

'Good luck, my darling.'

He looks uncomfortable, momentarily lost. His unmoored expression pierces me deeply. The internal bleeding that had begun when my son had been wrenched from me has never stopped. Two years and I still cannot get over the fact that I will never again be able to know that I can come home to my child each and every night, know that I can talk to him and love him without fear of what he might be thinking.

We talk for a few minutes, but I can see he is keen to get to the game.

When I finally let him go, Michael comes back on the line.

I feel the tension return.

Whenever I look at Michael, his wholesome, all-American face, his classic dress sense, his my-word-is-my-bond demeanour, I think of our first years together; the seemingly limitless joy of connection, of being fortunate enough to find each other in this big, teeming, confusing world. We were, by common consensus, the most obnoxiously happy couple among our joint circle of friends. When it all imploded, a supernova that consumed all those we loved, before collapsing in on itself to leave us – or at least me – alone in my own dark orbit, it was as if someone had turned out the sun on my world.

'Thanks for taking the call.' His voice is stiff, accusatory, the underlying note of sarcasm – and anger – evident. My crime? I had let him – and our son – down again. I had agreed to be at the game – both parents showing solidarity for a moment important to their child – but had forgotten and scheduled a session with Orianna. Which had turned out to be a bust.

I don't tell Michael this, of course.

'Must be nice up there.'

His brow creases. 'What?'

'On that high horse of yours.'

He stares at me a moment. For an instant, I think he's going to respond, but then he simply says, 'Leo says he'd like to visit you. Let's compare diaries and find a date.'

I am momentarily taken aback. Until now, Leo has shown no interest in coming out here. It is always me who goes to visit him, usually in neutral territory – a coffee shop, the mall, a movie theatre.

We stumble through a few more sentences, then end the call.

Families. What strange institutions they are. Complex and difficult and redeeming and all-consuming.

I wonder for a brief moment if this is another reason Orianna picked me. We have both lost our families.

But the darkness of her loss far outweighs mine.

27

ORIANNA: NOW

'I loved that boy. You're not supposed to play favourites, but, by God, I loved him.'

I notice Amos's hand trembling as he takes another slug of whisky.

'I'm no fool. I know Gideon wasn't blessed with the brains God gave geese. But he was my blind spot, my weakness. He was a free spirit, totally beholden to his nature.'

He stops, shakes his head, as if willing the past away.

'Peter married Ruth Tremaine, a decent woman from Barrier way. Good family, wealthy, connected. They have no kids. Ruth is barren. When they found out, I told him to divorce her and marry again, but he wouldn't hear of it. It's the one thing he's defied me on.'

I stare at him. The blasé way he talks about others' lives, even his own flesh and blood. Every bit the bullying patriarch of legend.

'Samuel has never married. Claims he's wedded to his church. Half the town thinks he's a little light in the loafers. I can barely entertain the notion, let alone confront him with it.' He exhales a bitter laugh. 'Which leaves Gideon. Gideon married Rebekah at the age of twenty-two. Too young and too headstrong for such a commitment.

'He met her out west, on business, in some Vegas casino. She was a croupier, if you can believe it. They were a beautiful couple, I'll give them that. I tried to warn him. Rebekah's the kind of woman you keep as a mistress not a wife. But Gideon wouldn't listen.

'Family was pure trash, of course, a generation out of the swamps. Soon as they found out who their daughter was courting, they were out here, sniffing at my pockets like truffle pigs. I set them straight soon enough. Had a little talk with Rebekah too. Make your choice. Your family or my son. You can't have both. Didn't take her more than a second to decide.' He flashes a skeletal grin. 'That's my daughter-in-law. I wouldn't trust her any more than I'd slip into bed with a rattlesnake. It's turned my stomach these past eighteen years watching her play the grieving widow.'

'Why didn't you drive her out if you hate her so much?'

'Because she gave me Grace.' His breath hitches in his chest. 'Until I found out the truth about you, Grace was my only grandchild. The only bearer of my legacy. She was Gideon's child, and I loved her the more because of it. As beautiful as a bird of paradise. But with Gideon's good nature and adventurous spirit. I doted on her.'

I feel a pang, the idea that this man, who bears as much kin to me as Grace, has never spoken about me in the same way. Fate has decreed an entirely different relationship between us.

He stands and walks to his desk, picks up a sterling silver photo frame. Returning, he hands it to me.

It is a photo of Amos with Grace. She couldn't have been older than ten, even then tall for her age, beaming at the camera with the smile that would one day captivate America.

'I'm a reasonable man. I know that Grace is dead. But the idea that her body is rotting out there in some shallow grave . . . I can't abide that. I can't go to my maker without setting things right. I want— I *must* find her killer. I want to look into his eyes, tell him that he's going to burn in hell.'

His gaze burns. And then, without warning, he bends over and begins to cough. His face pales, and his eyes roll back in his head.

'What's wrong?'

He cannot answer. I take his hand; it pulses warmly in my own.

'Goddammit,' he grunts. A line of spit snakes from his mouth onto his chin.

I race downstairs to find Cletus.

28

ORIANNA: NOW

The doctor is grey-haired, wearing a lilac shirt and a scarlet bow tie below a cream linen jacket. A leather doctor's bag swings at his side; a pair of spectacles dangle from a chain around his neck. He sets them on his nose, looks down at Amos. 'My, my. Have you been overexerting yourself again?'

'Yeah. With your wife.'

The doctor takes off his jacket, hands it to Cletus, rolls up his sleeves, then digs into his bag, emerging with a pressure cuff.

Five minutes later, he stands up. 'What's the point of keeping a doctor on the payroll if you won't take his advice? Not a lot I can do for you, except to tell you to rest.'

'Anyone ever tell you that you're about as useful as tits on a boar?'

Clearly, the doctor has heard it all before as he simply rolls down his sleeves, picks up his bag and jacket, nods at us and marches out.

Amos struggles to his feet, waving away Cletus's attempt to help him.

'I think we've gone as far as we can for today,' he says, turning to me. I see that his right eye is flecked with blood. 'Cletus, fetch me the files.'

Cletus walks to the bookshelf and returns carrying a two-by-two cardboard box.

'These are the files from the private investigation I commissioned. There are five more boxes. I want you to take them, study them. Cast a fresh eye over everything. From now on, we'll meet every evening and go over—'

'No.'

He looks at me impassively.

'You don't get to control this. We'll meet when I say we meet.'

He grinds his jaw. 'Fine. But I think you should move in here. It'll make the work easier.'

I offer a hollow laugh.

'It makes sense.'

'And what do you think Rebekah will have to say about that?'

'Last I checked, I'm still the head of this family.'

'I'll take a pass.'

His features reshape themselves into the squint of a mean drunk. He isn't used to hearing the word *no*. 'I hope you can see in the dark, Orianna. Because no matter what I decree, you're going to be in this town's crosshairs. Rebekah is just the tip of the iceberg.'

'No different to being in prison, I guess.'

'We'll have to talk about that someday. You'll have to tell me if you were sodomised by the guards.'

I stiffen, cheeks flushing, the sudden, unexpected vulgarity throwing me.

'Don't make the mistake of thinking we're partners, child. I could crush you like a bug, any time I take a mind to. If I believe for one instant you're holding out on me . . . Are we clear, granddaughter of mine?'

I turn and walk out.

29

ORIANNA: NOW

I catch up with the doctor as he is getting into an aquamarine Mustang Shelby.

'Doctor, how long does he have?'

'My name's Andrews,' he says, setting his black bag into the trunk. 'Warren, to my friends. You can never tell with these things, but, based on the last set of tests, I'd say three to four months, maybe less.'

Shock roots me to the spot.

'There's been nothing in the news,' I eventually manage.

'Amos is a very private man. He's of the old guard. Death should be handled with stoicism and as little fanfare as possible. Besides, there's been more than a little denial. I guess he thought he'd live forever.' He gives a small sad smile. 'You don't remember me, do you? I used to work over at the hospital in Barrier. When you were about, oh, I'd say, two, your mother brought you in with what at first sight looked like a simple fever. Turned out to be meningitis. It was touch-and-go for a while.'

I cannot remember any of that, cannot remember my mother ever mentioning it.

'Formidable woman. Wouldn't take no for an answer from the intern who tried to shoo her away. Made him fetch someone senior – namely, me. Good thing she did, or we wouldn't be having this conversation today.'

'Where shall I put these?'

I turn to find Cletus crunching over the gravel with a hand truck piled high with cardboard boxes.

I fish out my keys and pop the Chevy's trunk.

Turning back to Andrews, I say, 'Is there no possibility of remission?'

'Not unless God intervenes. Given that Amos has refused treatment, I'd say that's highly unlikely.'

'Why? I mean, why did he refuse?'

'You'd have to ask him that.'

30

ORIANNA: NOW

By the time I reach the cottage, the sun is a heavy red ball, hovering low over the treetops.

I park, then, one by one, haul the cardboard boxes inside, set them down by the bookcase.

Peeling off my clothes, I walk into the bathroom and stand under the sputtering showerhead, watching the day's sweat swirl into the drain. After, I dress in shorts and a tank top and walk back into the living room just in time to hear the guttural roar of an engine out front.

Moving outside, I squint into the gathering gloom.

An intense white light blinds me, and I rear back, shielding my eyes with a hand.

A monstrous red pickup bounces around the curve of the gravel track, a row of LED beams affixed to the front of its roof.

Fear jags into my throat and it takes all my reserve to stand my ground, not to run inside and go for my gun.

The behemoth on wheels grinds to a halt in a flurry of churned dirt. The windows are blacked out. My terror grows wings, right hand curling instinctively into a fist.

The driver's side door swings back.

'Nice truck.'

We are back inside, Gerty setting out dinner. She has brought provisions in a picnic hamper nested with pine straw. Cheese, salt ham, a stick of French bread, a bottle of muscadine wine. Dressed in blue dungarees, above a white T-shirt and tennis shoes, blonde hair in a braid, she spends a long minute running her eyes around the cottage.

'It was Howard's. Only thing I got out of the divorce. Think he was compensating much?'

As we eat, I tell her about my trip to the police station, followed by my visit with Amos.

'Once a peckerwood, always a peckerwood,' says Gerty, meaning Sheriff Hank Faulkes, and then: 'I hadn't realised Amos was so close to the end.'

'You knew about the cancer?'

'Everyone knows, child. We just don't talk about it. When the devil dies, there won't be a lot of rejoicing, just in case what comes next is worse.'

I set my half-eaten sandwich down on the plate. 'Tell me about my mother. What really happened to her?'

Gerty picks up the wine and pours herself a glass. She looks at me. In that instant, Gerty reminds me vividly of Dr Annie Ledet, the way Annie had looked at me during our sessions, expectant, infinitely patient. 'After they led you away, the sky came crashing down around Christine's ears. She went through something none of us can truly understand. Her life crumbled around her. The town cut her out, and so she did the same. One by one, she cut us all off – even the ones who still cared for her.

'I still remember the day they found her body. Floating in the lake out back. Elvira was away, out of town with her kids. Coroner said your mother had been drinking. There was an investigation. They ruled it an accidental death.'

'But you're not sure.'

'Nobody really knows, child . . . Why didn't you come to the funeral?'

'I – I couldn't.'

'I tried to see you. But the prison told me you wouldn't authorise the visit.'

'I didn't want to see anyone after the trial. At least, no one from Eden Falls.'

An uncomfortable silence passes.

'Why did she keep it from me? All those years? About Gideon?'

Gerty shrugs. 'I don't know.'

'Did *you* know he was my father? Did Elvira?'

'No. She never told us. Wouldn't.'

'But you must have suspected?'

'You favoured Christine – there was no real resemblance to Gideon. And your mother was adamant your father was a one-night stand she had in Barrier. Made a point of telling everyone. Said he was some worthless salesman she met in a bar, passing through the county like a comet. She was drunk. One thing led to another.'

That was the story my mother had told me, too. Kept my curiosity at bay by denying she had anything in the way of details. Not even a name to go with a sketchy description that could have been any of a thousand guys.

'Why *did* she tell me about Gideon? Why that day?'

'I honestly don't know.'

Neither of us speaks for a moment.

'Why are you helping me, Gerty?'

A thin smile works the corners of her mouth. 'I've watched the Wyclercs bully and undermine and threaten the people of this town for too long. The way they treated you, your mother. It wasn't right. They painted Christine as the town tramp, an outsider, a woman of colour, a she-devil leading Gideon into temptation. I'm not saying your mother was an innocent – heaven knows, she wasn't that – but Gideon was no altar boy. And, for what it's worth, I just don't think you're capable of something like that. Shooting a man down in cold blood.'

I search her face, but see only quiet regard.

I hold out my glass. 'Well, did you bring that wine along to look at?'

31

ORIANNA: NOW

Later, after Gerty leaves, I walk out to the lake.

The water is an inky pool. Fireflies sparkle between the giant pines on the far bank. A silky whisper turns my head: a screech owl flapping low over the water.

I am acutely aware that I am the only person for miles. I value the isolation, but it leaves me dangerously exposed.

Prison had enforced its own form of isolation; loneliness and alienation in the midst of a strictly regimented babel.

And now that I am back among the living, all I have is unanswered questions, leaping at me like wild cats.

What *had* led to my mother finally telling me about Gideon that day? What happened in that cabin? How is Grace's disappearance tied to any of it?

At the very heart of it: the malfunctioning machinery of my own memory.

Why couldn't I remember?

Annie Ledet's face emerges out of the night, hovers before me.

'*Sometimes we don't want to remember. The brain protects us, suppresses terrible things. Sometimes it actively reinvents the past.*'

A silent scream wells inside me, the desire to claw at my skull, to dig bloody and deep for those lost memories.

I walk back inside.

My eyes fall on the boxes I brought over from the Big House.

I consider having at them, but my head is woozy from the wine.

As I clamber into bed, a voice unfurls inside my head. Gerty's or mine, I can barely tell.

'You can't trust any of them. Least of all Amos.

'Don't believe a word he says.'

32

ANNIE: THEN

Orianna appears to be in a good mood.

There is no apology for missing our last session. No explanation.

I decide not to pursue it. What would be the point?

Instead, I comment on how well she looks.

'I love the snow,' she reveals. 'I love the way it blankets everything, makes the world seem innocent again.'

'Can't say I'm partial to it myself. We don't really seem geared up for extreme weather, judging by the way the whole country shuts down as soon as a single snowflake hits a power line.' I glance down at my notebook. 'Orianna, I'd like to pick up on our discussion about your relationship with Grace. You told me you grew up on the Wyclerc estate with her, but, by your own admission, you didn't get to know her well. Can you tell me at what point that changed?'

'You're assuming that it did.'

'Your memories of her seem vivid.'

She is silent, eyes flicking to the side.

'Let me put it another way. By the time of Grace's ... disappearance, how would you characterise your relationship?'

'We were friends.'

'Close friends?'

'I don't know. Growing up, we didn't see much of each other. Occasionally, we'd meet around the estate or in the Big House, but we never really played together.'

'Because she was Amos Wyclerc's granddaughter, and you were the daughter of his housekeeper.'

Heat rises to her cheeks.

'What I mean is,' I continue, 'that at the time, growing up on the estate, you didn't know that Grace was your half-sister. It couldn't have been easy for you.'

'You think I was jealous of Grace?'

'Were you?'

I can sense an instinctive retort pushing at her lips. She swallows it down, allows herself a moment.

I am impressed and consider this a small victory. Orianna may not yet have reached a place of comfort with these sessions, but perhaps she has begun to understand what it is I am trying to achieve. And the fact that she will have to make an effort if she hopes to pierce the veil of her uncooperative memory.

'It was just so easy for her. I saw how they all fawned over her. Anything she wanted. My mother and I had nothing, by comparison. I didn't even know who my father was.'

'How did that make you feel?'

'I guess I resented her.'

'And did you see each other at school?'

'Not really. She had her own friends.'

'And you?'

'Me?'

'Did you have friends?'

The tip of her tongue touches her upper lip. 'I wasn't very good at making friends.'

'Why do you think that was?'

'I wasn't very outgoing. I ... refused to play their games.'

'And yet at some point, something changed. You and Grace *did* become friends.'

'Yes. And no.'

'Would you like to explain what you mean by that?'

She hesitates. 'Something happened that ... Well, I suppose it brought us closer together. Dissolved some of the awkwardness between us.' A beat. 'My mother and I lived on the Wyclerc estate, in a small cottage near the woods, the same woods where ... you know.'

'Where Gideon was killed?'

A nod. 'I'd got into the habit of taking a walk in the evenings, especially if my mother was working late at the Big House—'

'How old were you?'

'Fourteen. That evening I was sitting behind a tree at the edge of the woods, smoking – I'd stolen a pack of my mother's cigarettes. The tree was unusual; an oak with a riven trunk. Halfway up, a gash split the trunk. A portal into the tree's hollow heart. I liked the tree, liked sitting with my back against its base, imagining the rooted labyrinths that lay beneath me. I used it to hide my cigarettes.

'I saw Grace slip by me into the woods. She didn't see me. I followed her.'

'Why?'

'Why did I follow her? I guess I was curious. Amos had

Grace under this ridiculous curfew; she wasn't allowed off the estate unaccompanied after eight. Grace was straight-laced – at least that's how she presented herself at school. I'd never seen her out in the evening before, not on her own, not like this.' A pause. 'I followed her deep into the woods, to the outer wall. There's a gate, out on the southern edge. It's usually locked. I assumed Grace was going to go through it and outside, but I had no idea where she was going to go on foot at this time of night. You have to remember that the Wyclerc estate is a good couple of miles from its nearest neighbour, with nothing but unlit forest in between.

'And that's when I heard the sound of a bike engine.'

33

ANNIE: THEN

Orianna stops. I wait for her to continue, but she says nothing.

I sense a sudden reluctance in her.

'Orianna?'

She ignores my prompt. 'Have the newspapers been in touch yet?'

I rein in my impatience and instead force myself to answer her question. 'There have been some enquiries. And a bunch of emails, mostly from the whacko elements in your fan club. The ones who aren't just convinced that you're innocent, but that there's also a global conspiracy to keep *The Girl in Cell A* locked up.'

'You can't keep a good killer down.'

'I think there's genuine interest in your case. Yes, some of it may be prurient, but the fact that you have never confessed to the murder, the diagnosis of dissociative amnesia – there is clinical interest there.'

'Clinical interest. You make me sound so sexy, Doc.'

I smile.

'Then again. What use is sexy to me? It's not like I'm getting any in here ... What about you? You getting laid,

Doc? Any new stallions in the stable now that your ex is in the rear window?'

I am intensely uncomfortable, but I also realise that this is another test. Orianna's version of quid pro quo. There's no point trotting out that hackneyed line: *This is about you, not me.* This situation is unique and I have to be willing to bend if I am not to lose whatever rapport I have managed to establish. 'No. There's no one. Frankly, I'm too busy. But even if I were not, I was married for eighteen years, and it ended badly. But I'm sure you know that.'

'It's a wonder how much of a person's life is out there, on the internet.'

I offer a brittle smile. 'Shall we continue with your story?'

She tugs at her sleeve, then carries on where she left off. 'I watched Grace open the gate. A boy slipped inside. I recognised him from school. He didn't *go* to our school, he just hung around outside with a couple of his jerk-off friends. His name was Jake Kristofferson. He was older than us – maybe seventeen – big for his age, handsome. He'd been kicked out earlier that year. I don't know what for, but there were all sorts of rumours. The town delinquent.

'I knew from the way Grace greeted him that this must have been the first time they'd met like this. She was hesitant, unsure of herself. I watched them from behind a tree. I couldn't hear exactly what they were saying, but, after a while, Jake moved in and put his arms around her. They began kissing. That went on for a while, then Jake's hands began moving. At first, she didn't say anything, but then I saw her take his hands off her butt. He started pawing at her chest, his other hand trying to work up under her T-shirt. That's when she stepped away.

'I saw the look on his face. He seemed stunned, and then angry. He moved in and tried to kiss her again. She told him no – loud enough so that I could hear. She told him she had to get back. Turned and started to walk away. It all happened quickly after that.

'He spun her around, then pushed her to the ground. Fell on top of her. I saw him pull his jeans down with one hand, all the while grinding away at her. She was struggling to get away, screaming.

'I looked around, picked up a heavy branch from the ground – red pine, knotted at one end. I walked over to them and hit him across the back of the head as hard as I could. He went out like a light.'

She stops, waiting for a reaction, but I say nothing.

'I pulled him off Grace, then helped her to her feet. She was breathing hard, tears in her eyes, snot trailing down her face. She looked at me as if I'd walked out of another dimension. And then she took a deep breath, looked down and kicked Jake as hard as she could, right in the face. She kept kicking him until I pulled her away. There was blood all over her shoe. If he wasn't out cold before, he surely was now.

'We started to walk away, and then she said, "Wait," and turned back. She grabbed Jake by the ankles and started pulling him towards the gate. She looked at me and said, "Help me."

'Together we dragged him out onto the road, out to where his crappy bike was parked. I remember the way moonlight glistened off his pale butt.

'When we'd made it back through the woods, Grace stopped, and said, "I hope we roughed up his dick, dragging him around like that." I laughed. I couldn't help it. The whole thing was surreal. We were flying high on adrenaline.

'I asked if she was OK. She nodded. "You know we can't tell anyone about this?" There was a note of pleading in her voice, desperation almost. "I mean, if Amos finds out, he'll kill him." The way she said it, I didn't doubt her for a minute. Everything I'd heard about Amos convinced me that she was speaking only the literal truth.

'I asked her if she wanted a cigarette.

'We sat by my tree, the riven oak, smoking. We didn't say much.

'She stood up, looked into the cavity, stuck her arm in. "The perfect hiding place," she said. "Sometimes I wish I had a place like this, where I could go and no one could ever find me."

'"Your ass is too fat to get in there."

'She stared at me, then burst out laughing.

'And that was it. After that day, things were different between us. We had a secret. I think she was terrified, for a while, that I would betray her, but once she saw that I'd kept my word, we became, if not exactly friends ... closer.'

34

ORIANNA: NOW

The next morning, I begin by clearing the kitchen table, setting a pot of strong coffee to one side, then heaving in the boxes Amos had given me.

I cut off the duct tape bundled around each box with a paring knife, then set out a dozen binders on the table.

It takes an hour to get a rough sense of the contents.

The bulk of the information is centred on Grace's disappearance. This makes sense. By the time Amos had commissioned his private investigation, Gideon's killer had long since been apprehended, convicted and sent to prison. Namely, me.

The agency that carried out the investigation hails from the big city. Its letterheads are embossed with gold Cyrillic script, and signed by the lead agent, a Bradford Vance. I find a series of invoices. Eye-watering sums, but Amos appears to have paid up without batting an eyelid.

In return, he has received as thorough an investigation as money can buy.

Vance's team started by going through the police investigation into Grace's disappearance. Copies of the relevant documents are included in the boxes, beginning with a profile of the missing girl.

Grace Kathryn Wyclerc: seventeen-year-old daughter of Gideon and Rebekah Wyclerc, granddaughter of Amos. An only child, and, technically, the principal heir to the Wyclerc fortune. No boyfriend at the time of her disappearance, at least none that her friends could confirm. Attended the only high school in town – the inventively named Eden Falls High School. The school was built by the Wyclerc family, the curriculum set on solid religious foundations; a Christian school in a town where that still meant something.

Growing up, Grace had never once been in trouble with the law or been caught truanting up by the falls. She had appeared several times on the front page of the *Eden Falls Picayune* for various high-school achievements: winning gold at the high hurdles in the annual track meet; starring in a school production of *The Scarlet Letter* – where she played Hester Prynne to rave reviews – and being crowned the Eden Falls Forest Princess.

A photograph of her waving from a parade float is accompanied by the headline: *Eden Falls Forest Princess Vanishes Hours After Being Crowned.*

That Grace had vanished on the day of the town's annual festival caused the authorities great consternation. The influx – relatively small though it always was – of out-of-towners muddied the waters. A short-lived theory developed that perhaps one of these outsiders had been a predator passing through the town, perhaps had even come to Eden Falls that day with the express intention of finding a victim while the locals were otherwise occupied.

The Girl In Cell A

But the police – hounded by Amos – had been unusually thorough, tracking down everyone who had been in town that day – via a heavily publicised statewide appeal – some 126 souls – and gradually crossed each one off the suspect list.

I note that Vance's team have been equally painstaking, returning to each of these individuals and reconfirming their stories. The process took over two years.

In the end, the needle returned to its starting point: namely, that Grace's disappearance was linked to the murder of her father – and that the person responsible is the same in both cases: the young woman convicted of Gideon's murder. Again: me. The so-called Girl in Cell A.

The fact that I had long known Grace and had discovered just that day that I was her illegitimate half-sister lent credence to the official theory that I had initiated an argument with Grace following the revelation – an argument that spiralled out of control – murdered her and then tracked down her – *our* – father and shot him dead in his hunting cabin.

That Grace's body has never been found – nor any forensic artefact pertaining to it – did not seem to detract from this theory. The notion that a seventeen-year-old would have the wherewithal to hide a body so effectively that one of the most thorough searches in the history of American law enforcement had failed to find it did not seem to faze those in charge.

They had their killer. It was only a matter of joining the dots.

In the event, the district attorney did not need Grace Wyclerc's body. He had enough to prosecute me for

Gideon's murder. An airtight case. Why get greedy? Why charge me with another crime that might be torn apart by a halfway competent defence lawyer?

Vance's team have drawn up a comprehensive timeline of Grace's final day.

I scan it quickly – much of this is already familiar to me.

Grace awoke early and had breakfast with her mother, Rebekah, at around 8 a.m. in their home on the Wyclerc estate. She was then driven by Gideon's driver to meet with her grandfather, Amos, at the Big House, before going on to Eden Falls High School, where a command centre for the day's Forest Festival parade had been set up.

Here she spent some time in the company of several school friends and the teacher in charge of the operation – a Catherine McGovern – who taught biology when she wasn't heading up the logistics of assembling and scheduling the dozen or so parade floats planned for the festival. Grace was particularly excited at the fact that she had been named among the final four vying for the title of Forest Princess.

Having dutifully listened to instructions from Ms McGovern, Grace, together with the other girls, had dressed for the occasion. Her parade gown – a vision of pink chiffon – had been bought from a big-city boutique. A visiting hairdresser and make-up artist had then arrived to help the contestants finish prepping for the parade.

At around midday, Grace and the girls left the high school to be driven to the festival's starting point: the town square.

The Girl In Cell A

At precisely 1 p.m., the mayor of Eden Falls, sixty-seven-year-old Walter Willis, a retired dentist, ascended the makeshift stage erected at the northern edge of the square.

The square, and the surrounding streets, were thronged with festival goers, the lampposts and electrical poles strung with bunting and speakers for the PA system, through which Willis's voice boomed, welcoming all to the festivities, detailing, at considerable length, the town's proud heritage, and explaining the plan for the day. His delivery was interlaced with clumsy attempts at humour – jokes that clanged dully.

I remember being in the crowd, listening to Willis. I remember my mother telling Elvira Trueblood that Willis had made a pass at her while she'd been sitting in the dental chair in his office with a steel pick in her mouth.

Following the opening, the festival proper had begun.

First up: the crowning of the Forest Princess. The cynics in the audience rolled their eyes: the competition was a sham. For the first time ever, a Wyclerc was competing for the title. It was a foregone conclusion that Grace would win. Her parents – and, more importantly, her doting grandfather – had driven down for the ceremony. The possibility that anyone other than Grace might be crowned seemed laughable.

At 2.25 p.m., after each of the girls had given breathless auditions and the judges had gone away to play out the charade of deciding on the merits of each contestant's attributes, the anticipated verdict was returned.

Grace Wyclerc was named Eden Falls Forest Princess.

A beaming mayor placed a sterling silver crown atop her head and handed her his ceremonial mace.

Grace ascended the lead float, and the parade, accompanied by the high school's brass band, proceeded on its way through the town, winding from the town square out towards Main Street, down Maple Avenue, and then along Jackson Drive to the high school's softball diamond, where a travelling fair had been set up, with carnival booths, a shooting gallery, a coconut shy, dodgems and a pie-eating contest.

Grace spent some time at the fair, then, at around 4 p.m., got into her car to be driven back to the high school. Here she changed into blue jeans, an olive-coloured halter top, and brand-new Converse canvas shoes – the outfit in which she would last be seen alive. She then returned to the town centre, where she hung out briefly with friends.

At 5.30 p.m., Grace was seen passing behind the town church – alone – by a Kenneth Noon, an out-of-towner who suggested that she seemed distressed, walking purposefully with her head down. That was the last verifiable sighting.

Grace Wyclerc was never seen again.

35

ORIANNA: NOW

I work late into the evening, stopping only when the words on the page before me begin to dance and blur.

Massaging the corners of my eyes, I walk to the kitchen, fix myself a salt beef sandwich, grab a beer and drift out to the lake.

I check my phone and see six missed calls from Amos. I consider calling back, but then I remember the dismissive way he'd treated me at the Big House. His overweening manner. Amos can wait.

Gradually, the sky darkens to the colour of a bruised plum. Night birds and bullfrogs call to each other under a bright moon.

Noise in prison has an altogether different texture. Every sound holds the potential for threat. And then there are the other noises: whimpers, prayers, the refrains of misery. The sound of hope dying slowly in the dark.

My fingers brush my phone.

Why hasn't Luke called? Why hasn't he visited?

A cracking sound snaps my head around.

I am on my feet, heart racing.

Someone is out there.

'Who are you!' I hear myself shout. 'What do you want?'

I head back inside. The echo in my ears becomes the baying of a wolf. But I know that's not possible. There are no wolves left in these woods.

My mind crashes and booms.

I should have expected this. I am, after all, a figure of hate in Eden Falls.

But why are they *watching* me? Why not come out and confront me?

Cowards.

I stagger to bed, but cannot close my eyes as another epic migraine chases sleep away.

36

ANNIE: THEN

At our last session, I noticed a change in Orianna when she began talking about Grace. She became animated; her manner suggested genuine engagement.

I want to harness that energy, use it as a way to guide her towards the key memories I am interested in – the locked memories of Gideon's murder.

'Orianna, in our first session, you asked me a question regarding Grace.' I look down at my notes. 'You said: "Isn't *that* the real mystery everyone wants the answer to? What happened to Grace?"' I look back up. 'What do *you* think happened to her?'

'You mean, assuming *I* didn't kill her?'

There is no point replying to this.

Her jaw writhes a moment, and then she sits up straight in her chair. 'OK. I'll humour you, Doc . . . I've had a lot of time to think about this. Spent a lot of time on the internet, digging. There are several possibilities.' She ticks off points on her fingers. 'First: Grace simply ran away. Tens of thousands of teens do it every year in America. The problem with this scenario is that Grace had it all. A happy life, every desire, every whim catered to. Popular at school. A rich, pretty teen. Living the dream.'

Orianna cannot help the bitterness that has seeped into her voice. I decide not to pick her up on it.

'The other issue is that if Grace *did* run away, and she's still out there somewhere, how in the hell has she survived all these years undetected? Small-town kids don't just vanish off the face of the Earth. Grace isn't some ex-marine trained to live off the land, or some conspiracy nut with an off-grid bunker.'

She ticks off another finger. 'Second possibility: Grace killed herself. But, again, Grace had no reason to throw herself off the falls or under a train. Besides, her body would have been found by now.

'Which brings us to scenario three: an accident. Maybe someone mowed her down, and then, in a panic, bundled her body into the trunk, drove out of town and disposed of her later?' She is shaking her head even as she lays out the theory. 'Of course, there's no evidence to support this. The roads in and around town were searched. There was nothing to suggest any sort of accident had taken place.

'So that leaves us with the last possibility: namely, that Grace was the victim of foul play. An abduction, perhaps? But the police quickly discarded the kidnap scenario when no ransom demand came forward. What would be the point of kidnapping a Wyclerc if you don't ask for a boatload of cash?' She pauses. 'Which leaves . . . murder.'

37

ORIANNA: NOW

For the next few days, I settle into a routine, working through till the afternoon each day, stopping for lunch, then continuing until the evening, going through each of the binders, making notes as I go.

On the third day, at around two, with a blazing sun high overhead, I drive into town to stock up on supplies.

I stop at the library where I find Gerty bent over with her hands on her knees, talking to a child. The boy, eyes as round as apples, listens solemnly, then wanders off.

'You're the talk of the town,' Gerty says, heaving herself upright. 'Word has come down from the Big House. You're to be left alone. Not that certain factions will pay any mind. Amos isn't quite the force he once was.'

I tell Gerty about the almost-encounter from a few nights ago. The noise in the woods.

'Sumbitches.' Gerty frowns. 'You should report it.'

'To Faulkes? What good would that do? Gerty . . . are there wolves in the forest?'

Gerty stares at me.

'I thought I heard wolves howling.'

'There are no more wolves in Eden Falls, child. You know that.'

I am silent a moment, then, 'What does the town think happened to Grace? I mean, those who haven't been brainwashed into believing *I* killed her.'

'That's just it, child. There were never any real suspects. And once they threw you to the wolves, they just stopped looking.' She sighs. 'I don't think you should stay out there. It's too isolated. Come stay with me.'

'I can look after myself.'

Gerty's face becomes serious. 'Amos's edict don't mean a thing to some. Not with Rebekah set against you. There's trouble brewing. Watch your back, child.' She points at my forearm. 'Did doing that to yourself help?'

I glance down at the cross-hatching of scars. 'It relieves the pressure. Inside my head. Or did, for a while.'

Gerty waits.

'I can't explain to you what it was like, Gerty. Being trapped inside those walls, knowing that I was innocent – or believing it, at any rate – but never truly being sure.'

'And what do you see now when you think back? To that day?'

'That's just it. Sometimes I see flashing images. Me. Gideon. The cabin. Sometimes, all I see is blinding white light. It's like snakes writhing around inside my head, snakes that someone set on fire.'

38

ORIANNA: NOW

By the end of the fifth day, I have compiled a series of questions that will shape the next stage in my investigation. Some of these I have set aside for Amos, others require me to widen the scope of my enquiries.

I had made a few calls, trying to set up meetings with Gideon's brothers, Peter and Samuel Wyclerc.

Samuel, I am told, is out of town. Peter refuses to take my calls.

I have also noted down the details of the man who led the original investigations into both Gideon's murder and Grace's disappearance, a Detective Richard Hogan.

I remember him well: a big guy, paunchy and brusque, with a moustache as stiff as wire, and a manner to match. Hogan interviewed me several times. I recall the casually insulting way he'd spoken about me and my mother. Hogan had come into those interviews with one objective: to prove my guilt. His mind was too small to allow for any other possibility. It didn't help that he wore his prejudices on his sleeve.

It was something my mother and I had talked about – whether my heritage, the colour of my skin, had played some part in the way I was treated. In Eden Falls, my mother had never felt overtly ostracised. Her beauty diffused hate. Or invited run-of-the-mill jealousy. But when my trial hit the nightly news, race became a part of the dialogue.

Did bigotry play a role in my conviction? I want to believe not, but how can I? The world has never seemed more divided. Then, and now.

Amos continued to call me during the week, the frequency of his calls tailing away as I made it clear I had no intention of responding. A savage, momentary satisfaction, tempered by the fact that I knew that, ultimately, I would have to return to the Big House.

Evening has fallen. Weary of going through the dozens upon dozens of witness statements, I step away from the kitchen table.

I consider fixing dinner, but the ache in my legs convinces me to first take a walk. In prison, the lack of physical exercise bothered me, until I learned that even within a six-by-eight box, there are ways to train the body.

I set off along the edge of the lake, moonlight picking a path for me through the trees. Around me, the chorus of night sounds is muted, as if the heat has sapped even the cicadas and bullfrogs.

I reflect on the nature of the witness statements I have spent the past week reading.

Memory, as I know only too well, is a fickle mistress. Witnesses are prone to error; they embellish, they fabricate – not by intent, but because of the vagaries of the human mind. The passage of time only makes factual inaccuracy more pronounced.

The Girl In Cell A

I realise, with a sense of disappointment verging on despair, that attempting to interview those witnesses again would be an exercise in futility.

Dry leaves crackle underfoot. Near the water's edge, where birches bow down to the mirror-dark surface, leaves and mud combine to form a mulch that coats my sneakers.

I press on, my clothes pasted to my skin with sweat.

My eye is caught by something to the right.

I turn into the woods, arrive at the base of an abandoned fire tower. The structure, stretching vertically into the canopy, resembles the derrick of an old-fashioned oil rig, with thick wooden legs and a wooden ladder bolted to the skeleton, leading upwards to a platform at the very top.

The ladder is missing several rungs.

I begin to climb, hesitantly at first, and then with increased assurance.

Reaching the underside of the platform, I push against the trapdoor and feel it lift with a creak.

I clamber onto the platform.

I am standing above the canopy, with an unhindered view for miles around; a blanket of primeval green, still and silent in the superheated night. From my vantage point, I can see the break in the trees where Elvira's cottage stands. My eyes rove over the lake, aglow with the light of a thousand stars.

A protective rail runs around the wooden dais; a section has broken off and gapes like a missing tooth.

Looking down, I think how simple it would be to take another step, to float on the thermals rising from the earth below, to leave my body behind and travel to the distant reaches of the cosmos on the wings of my own mind.

Once again, I am overcome by the prickling sensation of being watched.

I clamber back down and set off for home, resisting the urge to look over my shoulder every few yards.

When I arrive, I find Luke waiting patiently out front, back set against his truck.

As he straightens, the moon catches his hair. 'I tried to stay away. I couldn't.'

I want to meet him halfway, but something rebels. 'Have you been following me? Were you out here last night, spying on me?'

'No. Of course not. I ... I wanted to see you. And I have a message from Amos.'

'So you're here as Amos's errand boy?'

He looks pained. 'I'm here because I want to be. But yes, Amos wants to talk to you. He ... requests that you visit with him.'

'Requests, huh?'

'He's not the man you think he is.'

'Why? Because he's dying?'

His eyes widen. 'He told you about that?'

Weariness drops on me. 'What do you want, Luke?'

'I just want to talk.'

'You want to talk. Amos wants to talk. Everyone wants to talk. But when *I* talked, no one wanted to listen.' My bitterness is a shriek in the night. 'OK. Here's what *I* want. I want to meet your wife.'

He blinks rapidly. 'Ori—'

'Take it or leave it.' I turn, head back to the door of my cottage, light leaking through the old timbers.

'I've gone over that day a thousand times—'

I spin around, eyes blazing. 'Don't.'

'Ori—'

'Let it alone.'

I want to say more, but with a supreme effort of will, simply turn and carry on walking back to the cottage.

'Fine. Let's go.'

39

ANNIE: THEN

I am running low on wine, and so I stop at Sammy's All Night Mart.

Sammy isn't the owner's real name. The mart is run by an Indian family, the Guptas. They take it in turns behind the counter; it's usually one of the sons who gets the night shift. Tonight, it's Rohan's turn.

I like him. He's young – eighteen – and taking a year out before he heads off to college. A bachelor's in zoology. He has plans to become a vet. He says the idea horrifies his parents. That a good Hindu boy is going to spend his life with his hand stuck up the rear ends of horses.

I can tell he has a crush on me, wants to impress me a little. I get a lot of that in the classes I teach twice weekly at a local college. I say local, but it's an hour's drive each way.

Four months ago, the mart was raided. Thankfully, no one was hurt, but since then they've installed a Plexiglas barrier so thick you could probably fire a rocket launcher at it and not make a dent. There's a tiny airlock to push cash through. I am reminded of the prisons I have visited over the years. The thought makes me suddenly uncomfortable.

Rohan's voice comes through an intercom. 'That'll be twenty-six dollars.'

Back in my flat, I kick off my clothes, take a hot shower, and slip into warm pyjamas.

Dinner is practically civilised this evening. I take the time to cook, my laptop running in the background. I listen to the news awhile – more war, death, hatred – and then switch to something a little less depressing.

When I am done cooking, I scoop the paella into a plate, pour myself a glass of red, then head to the sofa.

I make myself comfortable and take stock of the day as I eat.

The session with Orianna went as well as I might have hoped. She was willing to talk, to engage. She held nothing back. I turn the pages of my notebook with one hand as I eat.

Orianna's analysis of Grace's disappearance shows a logical and structured thought process. She has pieced together the details as she sees them into a highly ordered scenario, arriving at a conclusion that makes sense to her: namely, that Grace *was* murdered. She has put herself outside of this conjecture, while acknowledging that others in this scenario believe *her* to be Grace's killer.

I dwell on her words, rising from the pages of my notebook.

'Most murders of women are carried out by men who knew them: a boyfriend, a husband, a family member. A lustful, frustrated acquaintance. There was no such male in Grace's immediate circle, leastways not one anyone could point to as having a clear motive – or opportunity.'

I had sat and listened as Orianna outlined her internet research into the case. The lurid headlines, the unsubstantiated musings about a serial killer operating in the state; outlandish speculation about Grace's private life and sexual proclivities.

Orianna had talked about the efforts made by the Wyclerc family to find Grace, starting with a bounty for information leading to the missing girl's whereabouts.

'Not that it had any effect. All they got were cranks. Crazies wasting police time with sightings of Grace all over the country. Carson City, Bakersfield, Odessa, Des Moines, as far north as Limestone, Maine, on the Canadian border. Not a single sighting was ever verified.'

I marvel at how detailed Orianna's summation of the situation is. She has clearly spent a lot of time thinking about this. A part of me understands that this is a way for her to avoid having to think about the crime for which she was actually convicted – the murder of her father, of Gideon.

I realise, with a start, that I am beginning to feel genuine empathy for Orianna. Her mind is a maze, with tripwires around every corner.

I admonish myself for the millionth time to be careful.

But herein lies one of the inherent dangers of psychotherapy. Countertransference. The notion that a *therapist's* emotions can be influenced by the person in therapy.

Of course, these days, therapists make a distinction between *good* and *bad* countertransference. The conscious sharing of feelings can actually help the therapeutic relationship – as long as the therapist remains aware of boundaries and doesn't allow self-disclosure to wander into the realms of the inappropriate. It's an ethical minefield and many licencing-board reviews have been initiated because of badly judged attempts at conscious countertransference.

Once again, my thoughts skip ahead to the end point of Orianna's treatment.

If we can make enough progress, and I can help Orianna gain her parole, what will she do with her freedom? The more I talk to her, the more convinced I am that Orianna will head home, to Eden Falls.

I can sense all sorts of wrong in that scenario. But once she is out, once she has completed her parole period, the law can no longer compel her.

She will be free to return, to engage with those she has long left behind, those who probably fear her, hate her, do not want her there.

How will her mind cope then?

40

ORIANNA: NOW

The home of David and Susannah Wyclerc – Luke's home – lies half a mile from the Big House, at the western edge of the Wyclerc estate. An elaborate timber-framed bungalow that David commissioned years ago, with greystone walls, river-rock chimneys and a gabled roof.

I have no idea what sort of greeting awaits me here. Nerves grip me. My heart races.

Inside, the house is cool, or at least cooler than the sweltering night. The décor is a riot of walnut wainscoting, exposed beams, varnished floors and plush, over-sized furniture more suited to a museum. The home is a curious mixture of old and new, its rugged aspects tempered by every modern amenity that money can buy.

I find Susannah in the kitchen, fingers stained with berry juice. 'I'm making cobbler. Dinner isn't going to be fancy. Meatballs and bread.'

Her welcoming manner is disarming.

Susannah Wyclerc, in her early fifties now, remains a woman of grace, and considerable beauty. Blonde bangs straggle from around a hairband, framing an oval face and striking green eyes. A small woman, about the same size as me, with the lissom grace of a trained dancer. I remember that Susannah had studied ballet.

She wears purple slacks, a white cotton blouse with an embroidered hem, and sandals. Twists of beads adorn her wrists. There is more than a little of the hippy to this version of Susannah Wyclerc, a woman who seems to have settled comfortably into herself with age. I cannot imagine my own mother ever having been so calm or satisfied with life.

I watch as she rinses her hands under the sink, then walks towards me and places her palms on the sides of my arms. 'I want to start by apologising. And to ask for your forgiveness. And your mother's. For the way you were treated. I know my son. If *he* believes in you . . . We should have listened to him. We . . . pressured him into testifying. Because of Amos. Because of Gideon. We thought we were helping.'

The apology is eighteen years too late, but a lump forms in my throat. Tears blur my eyes.

Susannah takes a deep breath. 'Welcome to our home. As Luke has no doubt told you, things have changed a little since you were last here. David is . . . he's not well. And Luke is married. I'll soon be welcoming a grandchild.'

Is there a flicker of steel in her eyes, a warning? She knows, of course – the whole town knows – it had come out at the trial – of her son's youthful indiscretions with the girl who'd murdered Gideon. The girl who'd turned out to be Luke's illegitimate cousin.

An extra frisson of salaciousness for the tabloids to sink their teeth into.

But Susannah's face is guileless. In the years *before*, her kindness had never seemed condescending.

41

ORIANNA: NOW

Luke leads me out to the rear porch where his father, David, is sitting in an oak rocker, listening to classical music drifting from a wood-encased retro-design radio, eyes trained out over the lawn. The night pulses with heat and the whirr of cicadas.

I see, instantly, the droop in the left side of his face, the way his body slumps in his chair. His left palm is laid flat on his knee. The right hand fumbles with a briar pipe, the ball of his thumb massaging tobacco into the bowl. His concentration on the task at hand is absolute, and so I wait, in the shadows, standing silently beside Luke.

A dog dozes on its paws at David's feet, a squint-eyed golden retriever with a hoary muzzle.

I watch as David sticks the pipe in his mouth, before crab-handedly pulling a lighter from the chest pocket of his plaid shirt.

'Welcome back,' he says finally, his voice slurred.

He has lost none of the quiet deliberation that had always been a part of his demeanour. A sadness envelops me; that fate has diminished him in this way, this once vigorous man, one of the few who had ever shown me and my mother any consideration.

Once again, I recall the day David came to us with a recommendation for a defence lawyer. Had he truly believed in my innocence? Some part of him must have, though not enough to stop Luke taking the stand against me. But then, David had been raised by Amos following the death of his own father, Amos's brother, Abel. He owed Amos a debt that could not easily be repaid.

I knew that David had served as Wyclerc Industries' chief legal counsel. He'd spent much of his time travelling, advising on the firm's relentless expansion across the country. Luke, an only child, had grown up starved of his father's company; perhaps that was why we had first bonded.

I watch as Luke pulls a handkerchief from the pocket of his jeans and dabs at a line of drool snaking from the side of his father's mouth. David seems not to mind, content to suck on the stem of his pipe.

'He fades away,' Luke says. 'Loses time.'

There is such sadness in his voice that it almost breaks my heart.

In the past week at Elvira's cabin, I have all but become a creature of the woods, hibernating at the heart of the forest. But now, standing here with Luke and David, confronted by the spectre of the past, my brain feels weightless, unmoored inside my skull. A sudden energy, like ball lightning, seizes everything: the house, the trees, the men before me. I see Luke as I had once known him: a handsome boy with a kind heart, a boy I had loved, whose goodness will forever be his defining feature. I sense the conflict that now tears away at his insides, the vastness of his misery, the forlorn guilt of a child that knows they have made a mistake and wants only to be forgiven and allowed back into the lap of love.

But I am not seventeen, any more. I am hardened, like the stone of the wall at my back, the knotted wood of the boards below my feet.

I steel myself. 'I came here to meet your wife.'

42

ORIANNA: NOW

We sit for dinner around a pine table, a maid serving us the meal Susannah prepared.

Luke's wife, Abigail, is a woman with large brown eyes, a fringe of dark hair, and an easy smile, a small-town beauty dressed plainly in a pale cotton frock that prominently displays her growing bulge.

Luke's wife. Luke's child. The idea is monstrous in my mind.

'Luke says you're here to investigate Grace's disappearance.' Abigail's smile is brittle.

I glance at Luke. 'I am.'

'I was only nine when it happened. Over in Beatty. I still remember my parents talking about it at the breakfast table.'

Silence. The clinking of cutlery on plates.

I glance at David, propped like a corpse in his seat. Lost in his own world.

Abigail picks up a wine glass. 'She's dead. You know that, right?'

'Yes.'

'Wouldn't it be easier for you to ... move on? You've lost so much. I can't even begin to imagine.' A beat. 'You could go somewhere, anywhere. Find a partner. Have children. Live your life.'

'Abigail.' Susannah's voice is soft. Her face glows with a smile, but I can see that she is concerned with the combative note of the conversation.

'I'm sorry,' Abigail presses on. 'Luke tried to explain it to me, but I just don't see what you have to gain by coming back here.' Spots of colour ride high on her cheeks.

My mind hums. I suppress the urge to scream, to claw at the face of this woman, replace it with my own.

The sound of a chair scraping back.

It takes a second for me to realise that I am on my feet, moving.

Luke catches up with me on the gravel path that leads from the front door to the low stone wall surrounding the house.

'I'm sorry. I didn't know she'd—' He stops. There is nothing to say. 'I'm sorry.'

He is still standing there as I get into the Chevy and drive away.

43

ORIANNA: NOW

Minutes later, I pass through the gate at the Big House and drive on up the cypress-lined drive.

Lanterns glow in the house's eaves.

I park, then walk up to the portico, my anger reversing in on itself.

Why had I pushed it? What could I possibly have gained by insisting on meeting Luke's wife? There was nothing between me and Luke now, never could be. We had known each other as teenagers; a brief relationship that had itself been lived under a lie.

It isn't Luke I have come back here for. Luke is a distraction.

My traitorous heart cannot be allowed to undermine my real mission.

The door is opened by Cletus Barnes. He is still dressed in his immaculate day suit, even though it is past nine. I don't think I have ever seen him in a state of dishabille, even on his days off.

As we reach the foot of the stairs, a woman appears. Small, in her early fifties, with dyed auburn hair, a small mouth and squint lines at the corners of her eyes.

Recognition blooms.

This is Ruth, Peter Wyclerc's wife, Amos's daughter-in-law.

She stops, looks at me with deer-startled eyes. 'What are *you* doing here?'

'I'm here to see Amos.'

She steps forward, a prim-looking creature dressed in a cream blouse and slacks. 'What makes you think you have the right to come back here? After what you did?'

I sense that it is pointless replying.

'You think this charade you're playing will change anything?' Without warning, she jabs a finger into my chest, once, twice. '*You* murdered Gideon. *You* murdered Grace.'

Anger flares. I bite down on my tongue. There is no point engaging. Ruth has the wild light of a fanatic in her eyes. Nothing that I can say will make a blind bit of difference.

Ruth turns to Cletus. 'I don't want her in my house.'

'But it's not your house, is it?' I say quietly.

She flashes me a look of pure hatred, then turns and stalks back the way she'd come.

44

ORIANNA: NOW

Amos is stretched out on the couch in his study, the light from the TV flickering over his bloodless face. A half-finished glass of whisky sits on the table, alongside a folded newspaper, and a tray with the remains of a simple supper.

Cletus shakes him gently from his doze. The old man breaks wind as he starts awake, a vague panic in his eyes.

A hand clutches at my heart.

Amos Wyclerc had, in my youth – and in my mind during the long years in prison – always been a creature of towering strength, an ogre, a man to be feared and hated. A man with whom I am forever linked by the tyranny of genetics.

His gaze finds me. He focuses, shakes Cletus away, then clambers to his feet, red-faced. He stares at me, gimlet-eyed, lower lip protruding belligerently. 'Would you like some supper?'

'No.'

'I suppose you've eaten over at David's place?'

I guess that Luke must have told him.

'How is he? I don't see much of him any more. They keep him hidden away back there like the family gimp.'

He studies my reaction. 'You think I'm being unkind? I raised him, gave him a home, a career. He stopped talking to me years ago, even before his . . . misfortune.'

'Why?'

'I asked him to step down from the firm. He'd lost his way. You don't have to be ruthless in business, but you do have to be pragmatic. David was always too straight-laced, too concerned about right and wrong. He forgot how grey the world is. I always thought he needed a little more pussy in his life.' His eyes flicker. 'How is that beautiful wife of his? I suppose he's not much use in the sack any more. A lot of lonely nights for our dear Susannah.'

Once again, an instinctive repulsion fights with my need to understand this man, to get inside his mind.

He senses my discomfort. 'Should I temper myself, granddaughter? Why? If there's one upside to impending death, it is that it is extraordinarily . . . liberating.' He nods at Cletus, who bends to sweep up the tray, then leaves the room. 'It wasn't just about the firm. David stopped believing in me. In what I was doing. They all did. Crazy old coot, continuing to look for his dead granddaughter's killer.'

I sit down opposite him, begin to go through my work of the past week.

I know that Amos has read everything in Bradford Vance's files backwards and forwards, but it helps to sift through my own thoughts with the only other person in the world who believes as ardently in my quest as I do. 'I want to hear your own thoughts. About that day.'

He walks to his desk, returns with a cigar.

'Should you be smoking?'

'Thank you, Nurse Ratched – your concern is duly noted.' He fishes a cigar cutter from his pocket, guillotines the end of the Cuban, lights it, takes a long draw, then blows a smoke ring into the air. 'I remember the heat. Crazy fucking heat. Grace came by to see me early that morning, before she went into town. Wanted to make sure I was going to come see her at the festival, and to pick up the pendant I'd bought her. A gold crucifix studded with diamonds. She'd asked for it, to wear at that damned pageant.'

'Why didn't you just pay off the judges? It would have been cheaper.'

He frowns, looks down at the burning tip of his cigar. 'Were you jealous of her? The way the papers made out?'

My mouth becomes a thin line.

'What say we stick to the facts?' he continues. 'I saw her again later that day, in the town square, when she was crowned Forest Princess. She waved to me from up on the stage, beaming like she'd won the goddamned sweepstakes. And that was the last I ever saw of her.'

'You didn't stay for the parade?'

'No. I had business to attend to in Beatty. I didn't make it back till later that day, about an hour before Gideon's body was discovered.'

'When did you realise she was gone?'

'That evening. It's a Wyclerc tradition to gather for dinner at the Big House after the Forest Festival. Fireworks on the lawn. When Grace didn't show, we assumed she was still out with friends. But by then, I was preoccupied, dealing with . . . Gideon.' He stops, reliving the moment when he'd heard that his son had been found dead.

'When was the last time you saw *him*?'

'You know all this.'

I say nothing. He sighs irritably. 'The last time I saw my son was at the festival that same day.'

'That was the last time you spoke to him?'

'We didn't speak. The last time I talked to him was the night before. He'd come over to the Big House for a poker game. Just us Wyclerc boys. Me, Gideon, Peter and David. Samuel was there too, though he doesn't partake.'

'How was Gideon that night?'

'Gideon ... Gideon was drunk on his ass, as usual. Made a mess.'

'How do you mean?'

He waves his cigar around. 'He and Peter had a ... set-to.'

'What about?'

His face becomes maudlin. 'You can ask Peter. It's his tale to tell. Suffice to say, Gideon left in something of a mood.'

'Peter won't take my calls.'

He grunts. 'I'll talk to him.'

I frown. 'Why didn't you say any of this at my trial?'

'Because it's not relevant. It was just boys bickering – family business, in every sense of the word. It had nothing to do with Gideon's death.'

I resist the urge to argue with his blasé assessment. 'Let's go back to the day of the festival. How soon after the police were informed about Grace did they begin searching for her?'

'You have to understand, we were in shock. We'd found Gideon's body earlier that evening. I'd taken Rebekah to the morgue. She wanted to see Gideon. Perhaps I should have stopped her. She fell apart. Once I found out Grace was missing, I took charge, spoke to Faulkes – he was the chief deputy, then. As I recall, Sheriff Gantry was out of town.

'Faulkes put every available man on the case. In the meantime, David got the word out to the mayor and every damned club and society in town; pretty soon, we had hundreds of volunteers, all gathered at the high school. We organised search parties to go out looking that same night.

'The next morning, I called the governor. We had a National Guard unit combing the forest before dusk. We had teams of dogs all the way up to the falls, and inside the old mine. We dredged every lake and waterway for miles. Nothing. She just upped and vanished into thin air.' His voice has fallen to a low rasp. 'I guess that's what bothers me the most, after all these years. The idea that we might never know who killed her. Might never know how she passed her last moments on this earth.'

A stray thought shoots across my bows. 'That pendant you gave her. Was it valuable?'

'It was. And, yes, I've thought about it a thousand times. Did I put a target on her back by giving it to her?' A pained light hovers in his eyes. 'She was the sweetest child, the gentlest nature. Trusting. She couldn't have imagined the wolves that live in the shadows of our world.' He shakes his head. 'She had her whole life ahead of her.'

'So did I.'

The sudden shift catches him by surprise. His look pierces me.

Once again, I am forced to confront the holes in my memory.

At times, the picture painted by my interrogators had seemed so vivid, so real, that I had begun to doubt myself. Yet, the events that had taken place in the cabin remained inaccessible. I can recollect some of what had happened that day, but not what had gone on in those crucial moments, and why, when I had been shaken awake, I was lying on the floor with Gideon dead just yards from me.

And it is precisely this that has convinced me to fight, to refuse to accept the State's version of events.

Amos grinds the cigar out on the table, then sits back, a hoary old walrus, beached and wounded. I note that his face and throat are slick with perspiration.

'Can I get you some water?'

He waves my concern away. 'What are you going to do next?'

'I still have material to go through. After that . . . I'd like to talk to the detective in charge of the investigation.'

'Dick Hogan? He's retired. Runs a bar out Barrier way. There's nothing he can tell you that you won't find in those files.'

I say nothing.

'Fine. I'll make a call.'

A silence. 'Why are you really helping me?'

He gazes into the distance, says nothing.

'You drove my mother out. You made her life a living hell.'

'She made her own bed. Are you going to blame me for making her lie in it?' He stares me out. 'They call me a tyrant. But I know who I am. Whatever I do, have ever done, I've done for this family.'

'And how long will this *family* last once you're gone?'

'All dynasties pass. The only thing that matters is our legacy. Grace... Grace was our redemption. *My* redemption. I've done things I'm not proud of, made decisions I've had to live with—'

'The miners? The ones you allowed to die?'

He averts his eyes. 'I've told you before, I did nothing wrong.'

'So much for truth.'

'The truth? In my experience, few people have the stomach for the truth.'

'Try me.'

'Careful what you wish for, Orianna.' A beat. When he speaks, his voice is the sound of a deep-throated animal in the dark. 'Noah Wyclerc, my grandfather, your great-great-granddaddy, was a paedophile and a murderer. He married a twelve-year-old, stole her away from her family, told everyone she was sixteen. When she became a little too old for his tastes, he abducted a young Native American girl, raped her and murdered her. They caught him and they hung him by the neck until he was dead. Not because they gave a damn about that little girl, but because they were afraid of what he might do next.'

I don't know how to process this information. Noah Wyclerc has never been anything more than a distant flicker. My connection to him is tenebrous, a thread winding through a hazy dream.

'Do you believe in genetic destiny, Orianna? Perhaps there's a gene for violence, and in the Wyclercs, it has found a home to its liking.'

I take a deep breath. 'How did your wife die?'

The sudden change in direction fazes him. It is a moment before he composes himself. 'She caught an infection. Ten years ago. Sepsis. Happened so fast … One minute she was sitting right there, where you are now, prattling on about our anniversary. The next, I was throwing soil into her grave.'

'Do you live alone now?'

'Martha's still here.'

'Abel's wife?'

'Yes. You lived on this estate, you already know she never remarried after Abel died. Raised her kids here, David and Hannah. Then Hannah moved away, and David built his own house, out on the edge of the estate.'

'Why didn't Martha move in with David?'

He examines his drink. 'Because she's a romantic fool. Says she can feel Abel's presence here.' He grunts. 'They say people who spend enough time in prison become institutionalised, can't imagine any other life. Well, that's Martha. She's over eighty now and she'll die here. She's bedridden, but somehow Death keeps turning away at her door. She'll outlive us all.'

'I saw Ruth on my way in.'

'She comes to visit with Martha. Reads the Bible to her. Ruth thinks the Wyclercs have been brought low. God is punishing me for my hubris.' A beat. 'They chip away at you, until you're nothing more than a junkyard dog barking at the end of a very short chain.'

'Most people in Eden Falls are still terrified of you.'

He offers up a deep, dirty laugh. 'Appearances can be deceiving. The Wyclercs are thieves, murderers and rapists. We're as dysfunctional a family as ever walked the Earth. But here's the thing.' He leans forward, eyes blazing. 'They're *my* family. And I'll do anything to protect them. Even from themselves.'

A hacking cough overtakes him, and he bends double over his knees, lungs rattling inside his chest like a stalled carburettor.

I stand over him in concern. My nostrils twitch; I see a stain spreading from his crotch.

'Shall I fetch Cletus?'

'Get out!'

'I—'

'I said get out, damn you!'

45

ORIANNA: NOW

I sit in my car, listening to the night sounds, reliving another bruising day.

And then, propelled by a nameless instinct, I turn the key in the ignition, drive down to the gate, and turn onto the tarmacked road that circles the interior of the forty-acre estate.

The Chevy flows along the track, a rattle from under the hood the only sound in the muggy, starlit dark.

I skirt the southern woods, the same woods where my life had changed irrevocably. A third of a mile into the trees is the cabin where Gideon had been killed.

Sooner or later, I know I will have to go back there, but at this moment, with the night air whistling from between the darkened trees like the breath of a dangerous dog, I cannot bring myself to venture inside.

A half-mile to the east of the Big House, hidden behind a screen of cypresses, is Rebekah Wyclerc's home, once Gideon's home.

Grace's home.

I park, then get out and walk under the trees so that I

can get a look at the house – a two-storey mansion built in a similar plantation-home style as the Big House, with a whitewashed frontage inset with large square windows and a colonnaded porch below a grey hipped roof.

A solitary car is parked out front.

Lights are on in the upper storey.

I wonder if Rebekah is up there.

Who does she live with now? I know that, like Martha, Gideon's wife has never remarried. Yet, surely, she can't have passed these eighteen years alone, rattling around in a house with the ghosts of her dead husband and daughter?

I watch awhile, then get back in my car and carry on around the estate.

I pass another large house, wreathed in shadow: Samuel Wyclerc's designated home. As far as I know, it has rarely been used, Samuel having spent many years abroad, and then, on his return, preferring to stay in a smaller property near his church in the centre of town.

I know, from Gerty, that there is no house on the estate for Peter Wyclerc.

Peter and Ruth had lived in the Big House with Amos, until they'd moved out to a purpose-built home in town when Peter took over as CEO, ostensibly to be near his office.

I sweep my way around the estate in a broad circle, passing several smaller homes that house some of the estate's on-site serving staff. One of these clinker-brick cottages belongs to Cletus Barnes. Growing up, I had always known him to be single, often spoken of as a confirmed bachelor. I wonder if he has married in the years since, had children?

I come, eventually, to the house where my mother and I had once lived.

From the outside, not much has changed.

The house appears to be deserted. Perhaps it has been held in stasis since my mother was kicked out. I know that the Big House no longer maintains a full-time housekeeper – a team of professional cleaners come in during the week, and two shift cooks alternate to ensure the house's last remaining residents are fed and watered.

Besides, Amos stopped entertaining after Gideon's killing. There hasn't been a party at the Big House for eighteen years.

I step out of the car, walk up to the door, place a hand on the wood and feel the day's stored heat radiate into my palm.

The night swells around me. Memories crowd in, jagged and raw: my mother readying me for school each morning, ticking me off for wandering around in my stockings, for picking at my food, for making a fuss about every little thing.

Such as wanting to know who my father was.

My head is pounding again, but the images won't stop coming.

I see my mother getting ready to step out with another unnamed man for the evening, a smear of lipstick on her teeth, telling me I'd have to spend the night at Elvira's.

All these things I can remember, as if they had happened yesterday, but the events I most need to recall remain a cypher.

I walk back to the car, drive on.

46

ORIANNA: NOW

Eventually, I come to the Wyclerc family graveyard, a small plot at the south-western edge of the estate, surrounded by a whitewashed stone wall and abutting the old chapel. The chapel burned down decades ago – the fire that had killed Nathaniel Wyclerc's younger brother and sister – and has been rebuilt. A white cross at its gable glows dully in the moonlight.

I step between the ornate graves with care, following a winding gravel trail past the lichen-stained final resting places of the Wyclerc clan: Nathaniel Wyclerc; his wife, Miriam; his son, Abel; Nathaniel's brother and sister, the twins, Esther and Jude; and Evelyn – Amos's wife.

Finally, I find Gideon's grave.

It is the most elaborate in the plot – three tiers of white stone with a granite angel on its knees, wings enfolding the altar, head in arms, forlorn, a replica of William Wetmore Story's *Angel of Grief* in Rome.

The engraving on the altar reads: *Beloved Son, Husband, and Father. Forever with the Lord.*

The night presses down on my shoulders.

The Girl In Cell A

Standing in the shadow of Gideon's tomb, I feel the spectral presence of all the fathers I had imagined for myself growing up: good men, kind men, men who, had they known of my existence, would surely have welcomed me into their lives.

Gideon Wyclerc had barely registered my presence.

On the rare occasions I bumped into him at the Big House or around the estate, he'd always been polite – unfailingly so, quick with a handsome smile and a few meaningless words of greeting. I was the illegitimate, mixed-race daughter of a servant, no more, no less. There had never been any indication that he *knew* or that my mother had ever told him. If she had, then it made his behaviour even harder to understand.

How could a man fail to acknowledge his own child?

It occurs to me that it was a miracle that Christine had been kept on at the Big House. An unwed mother, in a home that – to the outside world, at least – lived and breathed the morality of the Bible.

Was it Gideon who'd ensured that she stayed?

What did that imply about his relationship with my mother? Why would he have willingly kept her close?

In the wake of the trial and its revelations, the town had painted their liaison as a crude affair; the tawdry, hackneyed tale of a rich man and a beautiful servant. A power dynamic as old as time.

But was there more to the story of Gideon and Christine? Is that why my mother had chosen never to leave? What had she hoped for? That Gideon might one day leave his wife – Rebekah – and choose *her*?

The dreams of a fool.

I remember the way the town came together in collective grief at Gideon's passing.

And yet, when Christine died, those same people insisted she be buried in another town.

Anger, white-hot and wild, blazes through me.

What right did they have to treat us this way?

My mother had spent the best years of her life in Eden Falls. She'd lived in envy and died in hate. Used and cast aside. Betrayed.

And the people who had done that to her, to us both, the good folk of this town who called themselves righteous and decent, who thought of themselves as God-fearing ... What reckoning, if any, awaited *them*?

47

ANNIE: THEN

I arrive early at the college, with a spare couple of hours before I have to head to the lecture theatre.

The faculty has given me an office, even though I am not here all the time. I should be grateful, but the office is tiny – barely room to swing a mouse, let alone a cat. The sash window jams in the cold, looks out onto a bland, badly paved corridor between two grey-faced buildings. Students – and faculty – tend to avoid the alleyway. Occasionally, when I'm working late, I'll see the flashlight of the night guard on her rounds.

I shrug off my coat, connect my laptop to the monitor screen and check a few emails.

The smell of coffee, grabbed from a Starbucks on the way in, wafts around the room. Together with the piping hot radiator, it's almost cosy; cosier than my apartment, at any rate.

I spend some time transferring the scribblings from my notebook to a Word doc. The process allows me to go over the material again. This is an important part of the therapeutic method. Re-examining sessions, conversations, thinking back on body language, other non-verbal cues. All of this can only be done by putting some distance between the sessions themselves.

A thought strikes me, and I walk to a metal filing cabinet. I unlock it and pull out one of the files I had been sent shortly after I accepted Orianna's case: a background profile of my patient. I return to it on occasion, just to refresh context.

The first page in the file consists of a charcoal sketch drawn by a court artist. A three-quarter profile, hair tied back, the corners of Orianna's mouth turned down, eyes downcast. The dominant emotion, if any can be taken from the image, is of someone in grief or shock.

What had been going through that distant girl's mind?

Orianna Negi, principal suspect in the murder of Gideon Wyclerc. Soon to become the notorious Girl in Cell A.

The written profile accompanying the picture begins with a truncated family history.

I read it once again, looking for any clues I might have missed the first time around, and in light of my recent interviews with Orianna.

Orianna's people hail from the Indian subcontinent. Following the emancipation of slaves throughout the British Empire in 1833, a wave of indentured labourers arrived in the West Indies, from India, to work the sugar and cocoa plantations. A grand total of 249 souls travelled aboard the *Whitby* in 1838, followed the next day by a further 165 on the *Hesperus*, a gruelling one-hundred-day voyage from Calcutta. These Indians – or, at least, their peers – had proved themselves in the fields of Mauritius and now, with the withdrawal of slave labour in the Caribbean, they became a cheap alternative for privateers seeking to hold on to their ill-gotten estates.

One such indentured labourer, a descendant of Catholics converted by the Portuguese conquerors of the Indian state of Goa back in the 1500s, founded Orianna's family line. (Her name is a legacy of that Portuguese conversion – Orianna comes from the medieval Oroana, itself derived from Oro, meaning *gold*.) Several generations later, a scion of that original labourer made the short hop north to America, landing in the southern state of South Carolina – a sycamore seed on the wind.

Within a few decades, the family had established shallow roots, as American as any other immigrant subclass in a land of immigrants.

And that is pretty much all there is to say.

There is no one of note within the family lineage, no one who has distinguished themselves in any way. Orianna's folks are – and always had been – dirt poor and ordinary.

Her mother, Christine, was the second of two children born to a John and Miranda Negi. Christine's older brother, born two years before her, died of a rare blood disorder.

John and Miranda, too, passed at relatively early ages; John of lung cancer at just fifty-five, and Miranda of a debilitating bout of malaria.

They were buried side by side in a tiny plot in the local Christian cemetery.

Orianna never met her grandparents – her mother left home at eighteen and never looked back.

Christine travelled around a bit before ending up in the town of Barrier in Griffin County. Here, she settled for a while, establishing a small circle of friends, and finding gainful employment as a secretary at the town's only real estate agency, before applying for a position as a housekeeper on the Wyclerc estate in the neighbouring town of Eden Falls.

Despite having no previous experience, she was hired.

Two years later, having, by all accounts, endeared herself to her employers and following the retirement of the longstanding head of housekeeping, she was promoted to run the small retinue of staff at the so-called Big House.

A photograph of Christine arrests me, as it does each time I encounter it.

Orianna's mother is – was – breathtakingly beautiful. Orianna is the spit of her mother. There is little resemblance to her father, to Gideon, at all, aside from a watering down of her natural skin colour.

I continue to stare at Christine. There is something in her eyes, a sense of anger and disappointment. I am left with no doubt that a woman like that would have found trouble wherever she went.

Or trouble would have found her.

48

ORIANNA: NOW

The following days pass quickly.

I fall into a routine, working through Bradford Vance's remaining files, cross-checking and correlating his meticulous reports with the documents I have brought with me – court transcripts, and copies of investigative write-ups provided to my attorney during the discovery process at my trial. I have read them so often the information has settled into my mind, the way sediment settles to the bottom of a riverbed.

As the years in prison had blurred by, every so often, in the grip of emotions beyond my control – rage, terror, the feeling of having been betrayed by fate, by others, by my own memory – I would pore over them, for something, anything, some detail that my asshole of a lawyer had missed. Hope would scrabble around inside me, a blind creature, lost in darkness, yearning for the light.

Each day, in the early afternoon, with the heat becoming unbearable, I stop for lunch, sometimes driving into town to eat with Gerty at the diner – an hour of conversation during which Gerty listens, prompts, and challenges me, probing away at my uncooperative memory. The experience takes me back to my sessions with Annie Ledet. Gerty has the same genial doggedness; all bustling civility on the outside, jagged teeth on the inside.

I find myself dwelling on Annie, thinking back to how those sessions unfolded; how, over time, our relationship changed. Did she believe me, by the end? I like to think so. After all, I wouldn't be here now without her. And if the worst happens, if my mind caves in on itself again, it is to Annie that I will return.

After lunch, I go back to the cottage to continue working, until around eight, when I stop and stretch the ache from my neck and lower back, before driving across town to the Wyclerc estate to spend a couple of hours with Amos in the Big House, chewing over the day's findings – or lack of them.

I have become attuned to his moods. The way he can flip at any moment into the Amos I remember, the distant and ogre-ish figure who had run the Wyclerc empire – and his family – with an iron fist.

I am never fully sure of myself around him.

At times, he is eager to discuss the case, or politics, or the state of the nation; at other times, he rages around like a hoary old dragon, breathing fire and invective with a glass of bourbon in one hand, a cigar in the other.

I begin to understand the rhythms of his deteriorating health; the cancer is worse than he lets on. He has been housebound for the best part of a year. More than once, I witness the beast of his illness force him to his knees, drenched in sweat, hacking out his lungs onto the polished wooden floor.

The Girl In Cell A

The fact that he is my grandfather still seems astonishing to me.

One evening, as I am about to leave, he reaches out to me from the couch to take my hand in his calloused paw. The gesture surprises me, and I find myself rooted to the spot, staring down at him, not knowing whether to pull away or stay.

'You told your therapist that you don't dream. Is that true?'

I blink, then nod.

'Do you know where my dreams take *me*, Orianna?' His eyes are misty, but I sense something lurking inside his words. 'Back to a golden summer when I was just a boy, an afternoon in the woods with my father. We were crouched in the blind behind a tree, rifles at the ready, stalking a deer. I remember how hot it was. Air like breathing sin. Mosquitoes swarmed around our ears, the noise like the static you get on the radio. It was the first time I ever killed.' His gaze momentarily loses focus. 'Nathaniel had taught me to shoot, but my hands were shaking when I fired at that doe. I winged her, and she bolted. We were forced to follow her through the woods, dark patches of blood soaked into the earth, a trail as bright as neon.

'She had found her way back to her bed. Her young ones, three of them, just born. My father told me to put a bullet in her skull. I knew it was a kindness, but I couldn't do it.' His cheek twitches. 'He hit me so hard he almost knocked me cold. He killed the doe, then made me shoot each of the fawns. I can still see them, looking up at me each time I close my eyes.'

49

ORIANNA: NOW

Almost two weeks after Amos first invited me to the Big House, I make a breakthrough.

I find it in a witness statement, an interview conducted by Bradford Vance's team with one of Grace Wyclerc's closest friends, a Sally Lomax.

I remember Sally. One of a small group of girls who'd made a tight-knit unit with Grace; sycophants and wide-eyed Wyclerc worshippers, ever-hopeful that some of Grace's glamour might rub off. One of the girls who'd been most vocal in condemning me when word began to circulate that I had been arrested.

That was eighteen years ago.

When Vance interviewed her again, years after the incident, Lomax included something that I couldn't remember reading in her earlier testimony.

I dig it up and compare the two.

In the Vance interview, Lomax stated – in response to a question about Grace's state of mind at the time of her disappearance – that, in the months prior, she'd noticed a change in her friend, a certain sadness about her, an inclination to secrecy – periods when Grace would become uncommunicative, others when she seemed exhilarated. During this time, Grace embraced her Christianity in a way she'd never previously done, carrying around a pocket Bible, and regularly beating a path to church.

The remarks seem to have been made in an unguarded moment; Lomax clammed up immediately afterwards, suggesting that she was probably making something out of nothing. Undeterred, Vance obtained corroboration from another of Grace's friends: but the friend couldn't recall whether Grace's sudden Christian zeal had been an affectation, a passing phase, or an indicator of something more meaningful going on in her life.

This is new information.

I consider discussing it with Amos, but then decide that my thoughts are, as yet, too vague.

I need raw data.

This is a lead I must follow up myself.

50

ORIANNA: NOW

I sit in my car, hunkered down in my seat, watching the kids pour through the gate.

How much would they know? What would their parents have told them?

A sudden thumping startles me.

A red-faced man in a checked shirt is gesticulating angrily at me.

I watch him stalk around to the driver's side, banging the hood. 'Get the hell outta here!' The few strands of his remaining hair are plastered to a pink, angry scalp. His eyes wobble behind cheap-framed spectacles. 'I said get the fuck outta here before I call the cops!'

A teenage girl at his shoulder stares with wide eyes at her dad, the maniac. Other parents, other kids, drift over, or stop what they are doing to watch.

I remember the thumping on the side of the police car that had accompanied my journey to court each day. The abuse directed at me and at my mother.

I turn on the ignition, grip the wheel and slip away from the kerb, forcing Angry Dad to jump backwards.

The Girl In Cell A

I watch him dwindle in the rear-view mirror, others congregating around him, the improbable hero.

I don't stop until I am on the edge of town, a quiet dirt access road bordered by trees. My heart feels slippery and hot.

I want to shout at them. *I'm not who you think I am.*

My head drops to the steering wheel. Sound recedes.

A noise jerks me back up.

Grace is sitting beside me, face rotting. A cockroach crawls out of her ear, along her jaw and into her mouth.

You're a liar.

I am paralysed, my back rigid, the muscles of my neck taut as wire. A pulsing ache hammers through my skull. For a moment, I think I might black out.

I blink, and Grace is gone.

It is an hour before I can return to the school.

51

ORIANNA: NOW

I find Sally Lomax alone in a classroom, a pile of exercise books at her elbow, chin resting in the palm of one long-fingered hand. She is in a sleeveless summer dress, paired with dark-framed glasses on a freckled nose. Her shock of red hair is tied back. Her shoulders shimmer with sweat.

'You can't be here.' Her first words, uttered in a near whisper.

'You were interviewed by Amos's private investigator a few years after Grace disappeared. You said that Grace *changed* that summer. That she'd started carrying a Bible around, embraced her Christianity.'

Lomax blinks rapidly. 'I can't talk to you. You're a convicted murderer. This is a school.'

'I didn't kill Gideon. And I had nothing to do with Grace's disappearance. I'm here to find out what really happened to her. I need your help.'

Lomax stares at me, then reaches into a handbag at her feet, fumbles out a packet of cigarettes, lights one and takes a deep drag into her lungs.

'Grace and I were never really friends. She didn't have any friends. Not the way normal people reckon friendship.

She was a Wyclerc; she knew what that meant. She knew the power she had over us.'

'You gave her that power.'

Her mouth twitches. 'You know, the day she vanished, at the festival, I was up for Forest Princess too. No one ever remembers that. We were always also-rans while Grace was around. After she disappeared, it felt as if the rest of us could finally breathe. Does it make me a monster? To say that?'

I say nothing, waiting.

'Grace told me that she needed help. Spiritual guidance. She'd found out something about her parents. Said they were having problems. She knew that her father was sleeping around; she said that *everyone* knew about Gideon's tomcatting, that he'd always been that way, and that she hated him for it. But something had changed ... She thought her mother was having an affair, too.'

'With who?'

A hesitation. 'With Tommy Quinn.'

Quinn. The town drunk. Former high-school quarterback turned handyman.

I struggle to fit the information into my mind. Why would Rebekah give a man like Quinn the time of day?

'Could Grace have been mistaken?'

'I have no idea. I mean, it's not like she showed me pictures.'

'Why didn't you say anything to the police?'

'She swore me to secrecy.' I continue to stare at her. 'What would I have said? That Grace *suspected* her mother of sleeping around? Rebekah Wyclerc? Would I still be here, in this town, if I'd have accused her of something like that? Besides, I always figured they'd find Grace. Or that she'd come back.'

'You thought she might have run away?'

'Grace was always talking about getting out of Eden Falls. Moving to the big city. Another small-town girl with stars in her eyes.' She sniffs. 'For a while, she thought college might be her escape. But she didn't have the brains for it.'

'Was there any specific reason you thought she might have run away?'

'I don't know. Things were messed up at home; she wanted to get away from it all. She knew her folks wouldn't just let her move out when she turned eighteen. She mentioned it a couple of times – running away, I mean. I guess I never really took it seriously. Until she vanished.'

I absorb this, then: 'At the trial, they said Grace didn't have a boyfriend. Was that true?'

She shrugs. 'As far as I know. She dated a couple of guys in school, but nothing serious. I mean, no one *really* wanted to date Grace, right? Not with Amos and Gideon looking over her shoulder the whole time—' She stops.

'What?'

'I don't know if this means anything, but ... that summer, Grace hinted that she *was* seeing someone, someone she wouldn't – couldn't – talk about. She let it slip only once, and then claimed she'd only been joking.'

'Any idea who?'

'No. Like I said, she clammed up. But I sort of could tell. There was something different about her.' Smoke drifts around her eyes.

'Did you really believe I killed Gideon?'

'We were kids. We believed what we were told to believe.'

52

ORIANNA: NOW

I stop off at the library to question Gerty.

'Do you think there's anything to what Sally Lomax said about Rebekah? That Grace thought her mother was having an affair with Tommy Quinn?'

Gerty sighs. 'I don't know, child. There were always rumours about Gideon and Rebekah. After a while, I learned not to pay them any mind. I had my own marriage to worry about. Besides, if Rebekah *had* been sleeping around, who could blame her? Gideon was the kind of man who gave tomcats a bad name. And I don't just mean your mother. There were stories: women he'd pick up over in Barrier, fishing trips where the only fish he caught were the kind that wore high heels and lipstick. He wasn't exactly picky – no offence to Christine. But if Rebekah had a thing with Tommy, they both kept it pretty quiet.'

'Where can I find him?'

'I'm not sure that's a good idea. Tommy can be real ornery.'

'I saw him here at the library.'

'He does odd jobs for me, now and again. What can I say? He's cheap.' Something dark drifts into her eyes. 'There's something I have to show you.'

The Girl In Cell A

Gerty leads me to the counter. A black teenager in a T-shirt with the words NERDS RULE bangs away at a laptop. 'This is Artie. Artie, meet Orianna.'

He stares at me, as if he has just been introduced to Bigfoot.

'Artie is our resident computer genius. He knows all about the social media and whatnot. Show her, Art.'

He goggles a little longer, then bends back to his keyboard. When he flips the screen around, I see that he has pulled up a Facebook page. The Eden Falls Community Group.

My eyes scan the comments.

> I've got kids. How can we allow a murderer to walk the streets?
> I saw her in the diner the other day. Bold as brass.
> She nearly ran over Pat Larson at the school.
> Christ, what must Rebekah be feeling? I can't believe Amos has let that murdering so-and-so stay, just walking around as if she owns the place.
> Girl's plumb crazy coming back here.
> We gotta do something.

'They're not bad people,' Gerty says. 'They've whipped themselves into a frenzy. You can't just walk around town, child. They're fixing to do something stupid. I can feel it.'

I am silent a moment, then: 'How well do you know Tommy Quinn?'

'Tommy's had a rough ride of it. Grew up in a house where the father was a mean drunk and the mother had no answers. A football scholarship was his one chance to get the hell out. Night before the scout game, he gets into it with his old man. An hour later, Tommy crashes his dad's pickup into a wall. Turns up for the game with a black eye and a bum right knee. Maybe he wasn't good enough, maybe he was. I guess we'll never know.'

'You sound sympathetic.'

'People are complicated, child. You should know that better than anyone. Tommy's father died of the drink. That was just about the only thing Tommy inherited from him. He never married. A lot of women tried to fix him, but Tommy's not the kind who wants or needs salvation. He can't control himself when the drink takes him. But he's got a chivalrous side.'

'He's a violent criminal.'

'Under the right circumstances, most of us have the capacity for violence.' Gerty's phone rings. 'I need to take this.' She stands. 'Tommy has a semi-permanent gig over at the junkyard. I suggest you take Luke with you. Or else wait till tomorrow. I'll act as chaperone.'

'Where was Tommy working back then? When Gideon was killed?'

'Try Casey's Autoshop.'

53

ORIANNA: NOW

The façade of the autoshop has barely changed.

I remember my mother driving her ancient Oldsmobile into its cluttered double bay, hoping against hope that whatever was making that wheezing sound beneath the bonnet wouldn't cost her an arm and a leg.

A slim young black man, with the top half of his overalls rolled down to reveal a vest blackened with grease, lifts his head from under the hood of a Buick. 'Help you?'

'I'm looking for Casey.'

'Out back.'

He turns away, not bothering to look after me as I pick my way through the shop floor to the rear compound, where I find an elderly, puffy-faced white man in blue overalls sitting on a stool in the shade, watching an ancient TV propped on an upended steel drum, hand clawed around a soda can.

He glances at me, shifts his ass a fraction. 'Must be my lucky day,' he rumbles. 'A bona fide celebrity in my little old autoshop. Remind me to take one of them selfies.'

'When Gideon was killed, Rebekah was secretly seeing Tommy Quinn. Quinn was working for you at the time.'

His eyes narrow. 'Well now. That's quite a conversation starter.'

'Is it true?'

He debates some inner quandary. 'She used to come in here with her car. Beautiful little Corvette. Tommy started making eyes at her. She seemed to like the attention. I guess things weren't so peachy at home. Or maybe she was just hankering for something Gideon couldn't give her. Nature took its course, I guess.'

'Why didn't you say anything to the cops?'

He grins, revealing gaping holes in a row of tobacco-stained teeth. 'Nobody asked me.'

I battle the urge to wrap my hands around his throat, pop the eyes from his skull.

'You planning on talking to him? If so, mind where you put your feet. Tommy's a law unto himself. The Wyclercs tried to run him out of town years ago. Maybe they heard about the thing with Rebekah. Didn't appreciate a man like that pissing in their Garden of Eden. Tommy didn't blink. Crazy don't scare easy.' He plucks a shred of tobacco from his bottom lip. 'He did three years over in the county jail in Barrier. Assault. Some jackass thought it would be a good idea to take a swing at him over a girl in a titty bar. Way I heard, Tommy bit his ear off, spat it into his beer.' A grin. 'I had to let him go. He was a good mechanic, great with his hands. But he thought he could make more money selling dope to my customers. Some people just come out corkscrewed from the womb, I guess.'

The Girl In Cell A

He slaps at a mosquito on his neck, examines the smear of blood on his fingers. As I walk away, he hollers out. 'Don't tell Tommy what I said, now. I need that crazy sonofabitch looking for me like I need a dick in my ass.'

54

ORIANNA: NOW

An hour later, I arrive at the Big House.

The trip to the junkyard in search of Tommy Quinn proved a bust. I had been told by the old man in charge that Quinn was out. No idea when he'd be back.

I find Amos in an unusually good mood. Dressed in cream slacks and a sky-blue shirt, he invites me to walk the gardens with him.

The sun has dropped from the face of the sky, staining the horizon a deep red. Sprinklers whir in the grass. As we walk down a tiled path, the sweet smell of honeysuckle, moonflower and gardenia mingle in the gathering dusk.

I tell him about my day.

He stops sharply, fixes his gaze directly on me. He doesn't speak right away. Instead, he lowers himself onto a stone bench. I join him.

'Tommy Quinn,' he says eventually. 'There's a name I haven't heard in a while.'

'Is it true? Did he have an affair with Rebekah?'

'I don't know. There were whispers. But gossip follows beautiful women around like shit on a poor man's shoe.'

'Why did you try and run him out of town?'

'That was Peter's idea. I can't say I disapproved. The man's an ex-con and a drug dealer.'

'*I'm* an ex-con.'

He frowns. 'I'm in no mood for games. If you really think Quinn had something to do with what happened, I suggest you get Luke on the case.'

'No. I want to speak to Quinn myself.'

He snorts. 'Quinn won't give you the time of day.'

'And you think he'll talk to Luke?'

He grunts, looks away.

'Sally Lomax said Grace might have been seeing someone that summer, someone she chose to keep a secret. Have you any idea who?'

'That wasn't the sort of thing Grace shared with her grandfather. I suppose Rebekah might know.'

'She'll never talk to me.'

'That makes two of us. Rebekah seems to have taken against me, ever since I let you back into our lives.' He pulls a cigar from the pocket of his shirt, lights it.

'You really shouldn't.'

'What the hell difference does it make now?' He takes a deep draw, then bursts into a fit of coughing. Cursing, he spits on the floor. 'I'll talk to Rebekah. See if she'll play ball.'

'Did you arrange for me to meet with Dick Hogan? The lead detective on Gideon's murder?'

'I know who Hogan is. I'm dying, not senile.' He reaches into his pocket, hands me a folded slip of paper. 'That's the address of Hogan's bar over Barrier way. He's agreed to see you, but if you want anything more out of him than "Go fuck yourself", you'll need Luke there.'

I hesitate. I haven't spoken to Luke since the visit to his home. 'What do you make of Sally Lomax's conjecture that Grace had suddenly embraced her Christianity? Do you recall that?'

'Faith has always been a strength of this family, this town. I admit, the younger ones have let things slide. But then, the whole country is going to hell in a handbasket. The moral American appears to have made way for a generation of godless consumerists.' He seems more sad than angry. 'But, yes, now that you mention it, Grace did seem to take a renewed interest that summer. It's why I bought her that crucifix. She asked me for it. You should really talk to Samuel about this.'

Samuel. Amos's middle son and the parish pastor.

'He's not in town.'

'No. Every now and again he gets it into his head to take his ministry on the road. He'll be back soon enough.' He sighs. 'My whole life I've tried to navigate a path between faith and progress, told myself that everything I was doing sat square with my principles as a Christian. All those years I occupied myself with money and power. I remember a time I'd sit down to break bread with senators, congressman, titans of industry. I learned early on that the key to everything is people. You have to understand what makes them tick, how to use them to your advantage.

'But the truth is, I despise most human beings. Ever since Cain's brother dashed in his skull, we've known what we are, what we're capable of. Yet we lie to ourselves, hide our true natures away for fear of the horror. But there comes a time when the lies don't sit right and a man has to face up to his failings.' The fading light flickers in his eyes. 'I'm tired, tired beyond reckoning. All I want now is to know what really happened that day. To Gideon. To Grace. And to you.'

55

ANNIE: THEN

A knock behind me.

I set my laptop to sleep, slip my glasses from my nose, and turn just as Frank Simmons pops his head around the door.

He seems to realise he has broken my concentration and mumbles an apology to go with the smile and box of donuts he now brandishes as a peace offering.

'How goes it?'

Frank is my head of department, a professor of psychology, an adjunct professor of law, a former president of the American Psychology–Law Society, and a damned fine forensic psychotherapist in his own right. He doesn't do much in the way of clinical therapy any more, spending most of his time teaching, consulting, editing the AP-LS's bimonthly academic journal, *Law and Human Behavior*, and writing weighty textbooks, at least two of which have become required reading in the field.

Forensic psychotherapy is a relatively small discipline. As a consequence, we gravitate towards the same conferences, read the same papers, argue over the same minutiae. Word quickly gets around.

The Girl In Cell A

Before I took on Orianna's case, I discussed it with Frank.

The pros were obvious. A high-profile patient – the notorious Girl in Cell A – one with as challenging a background as Orianna's? Only a fool would turn it down.

But Frank had helped bring clarity to the cons.

Orianna's case was mired in controversy, the dissociative amnesia diagnosis considered by many – even within the field – as a patent attempt to avoid responsibility, a fiction concocted by a cold-blooded murderer and her shyster lawyer. Any therapist taking on the case would run the gauntlet of both public and professional opinion. And, depending on where the therapy ended up, the therapist might easily become tarred and feathered along with Orianna.

It is something I have thought a lot about since beginning my sessions.

Will I end up as a part of Orianna's story? A coda? A footnote? Or, if Orianna *is* released, and depending on what she does next, an integral part of her ultimate narrative?

Frank and I chat a little about the case. I do not divulge precise details – that would breach the bounds of patient-therapist confidentiality. It's de rigueur to say that the therapy room is as sacred as the confessional. But therapists are human too. Careers have been sunk by careless watercooler chat.

And yet, occasionally, even therapists need counsel, if not counselling.

Frank is *my* counsellor. He helped me through the implosion of my marriage – as a friend – and has always fought my corner when the vicissitudes of the profession threatened to overwhelm me.

Frank's specialty is PTSD. He made his reputation with a body of work that helped transform the way military veterans are compensated for service-connected disability claims. Frank's PTSD work overlaps, on occasion, with dissociative amnesia. PTSD and dissociative amnesia often co-occur. It's no surprise that he has taken a healthy interest in Orianna's case.

'The hardest part for you is going to be untangling earlier stressors in Orianna's life from the direct events of the murder. Both could have impacted on the dissociative amnesia.' He looks down at the half-eaten donut in his hand, decides the diet he's been on for the past three months probably won't forgive him if he eats the whole thing, and sets it back in the box. He licks his fingers, not bothering to stand on ceremony.

'I agree. Getting Orianna to open up about her life in Eden Falls prior to the killing hasn't been easy. I've had to go at it piecemeal, breaking her down bit by bit. But the impression I'm building up is of a confused kid, then an even more confused teen, caught in the middle of something she didn't quite understand until it was too late.'

'Absent-father syndrome.'

Frank is, of course, referring to the fact that an absent father can lead to feelings of abandonment, rejection and low self-worth, all of which can trigger self-destructive behaviour. But what happens when that absent father returns or turns out to have been there all along, hiding behind secrets and lies?

In his usual unassuming way, Frank is nudging me towards his own hypothesis.

Namely, that Orianna's relationship with her father – and the other male role models around her – played the lion's role in her subsequent breakdown. Frank, like most right-thinking clinical therapists that know anything about the case, believes implicitly in Orianna's guilt. His empathy lies in how that guilt came to be, and how we might treat a patient he considers to be a victim of her upbringing.

Freud, though mortally wounded, isn't quite dead in our field.

So far, I am in agreement with Frank. Orianna was convicted of murdering Gideon Wyclerc for good reason. And yet ... There is an intensity in her eyes when she talks about Gideon, about her life in Eden Falls, that almost makes me question myself, question the case against her. Wishful thinking? Most likely. But sometimes, even when we can see the trap, we still fall victim to it. It's that very frailty at the heart of the human condition that makes my work such an imprecise science.

'Is she still talking about Grace?' Frank asks.

'Yes. I'm drawing out more and more detail in each session.'

'Well, I guess that's something.' He checks his watch, heads towards the door. 'Don't forget this evening's seminar. "Artificial Intelligence and the Future of Therapy".' He grins. 'A few more years and we're all going to be obsolete. Patients like Orianna will be cured in mere minutes by Robo-Freud.'

56

ORIANNA: NOW

Two days after the revelations by Sally Lomax – including the fact that Tommy Quinn had been having an affair with Gideon's wife, Rebekah, around the time Gideon was killed – I drive into town to meet with Peter Wyclerc, Amos's words still swirling around my mind.

All I want now is to know what really happened that day. To Gideon. To Grace. And to you.

Does he genuinely believe me to be innocent?

I am beginning to understand that there are layers to Amos that I hadn't anticipated.

He repels and fascinates me. I can't get a fix on him. Is his quest for the truth truly aligned with my own, or is this all an elaborate trap?

At times, staring at him, his eyes wells of shadow, I have to remind myself that here is a man whose ruthlessness is legend, whose spectre has haunted my dreams for longer than I care to remember.

My grandfather.

The headquarters of Wyclerc Industries sit ten minutes from the town square, a purpose-built five-storey office complex that looks like something NASA dropped into the rural landscape by mistake. With blinding white walls that reflect the sun back into the eyes, tinted black windows and steel-fronted doors, the building could easily be mistaken for a Silicon Valley tech giant rather than an old-fashioned mining outfit.

Though 'old-fashioned' is a label that Peter Wyclerc has spent the past decade desperately trying to shed.

Of all the Wyclercs, he is the one I know the least. Growing up, he had spent much of his time away, at first on an extended apprenticeship learning the family business, and then, later, when Amos finally decided it was time to hand over the reins, as his father's successor.

I have read a handful of profile pieces of him over the years. There aren't many.

Peter Wyclerc's relationship with the media is corrosive. Those who understand the world of commerce believe him to be a poor CEO. Several ventures – announced with great fanfare and intended to expand the Wyclerc portfolio – ended in ignominy, collapsing under the weight of misguided ideology, poor management and bad timing. Sometimes, all three.

Peter retreated into a sullen silence to lick his wounds. His last public interview was four years ago.

I am led through the building by a prim secretary in a power suit. I received a call from the same secretary earlier that day, informing me that Peter was available at 2 p.m.

I am ushered into an office the size of a tennis court, with a polished marble floor – inset with a mosaic of the company logo, a stylised wolf's head – and floor-to-ceiling windows overlooking the town. One wall is dominated by abstract art, another by a framed map of the country, little red flags indicating the many and far-flung locations of Wyclerc businesses.

Peter Wyclerc waits beside a large desk by the windows; a tall man, with a runner's physique, impeccable in charcoal-grey pinstripes, the collar points of his shirt so crisp they belong in a West Point passing-out parade.

His face is lightly tanned, hair peppery, mouth cast in a hard line.

I remember my brief encounter with Ruth, Peter's wife, the way she'd hissed at me like an alley cat.

Peter waits for me to approach, then says abruptly, 'I've agreed to meet you at my father's insistence. But please don't make the mistake of thinking that I'm happy to be sitting down with my brother's killer.'

'I didn't kill him.'

'The law says otherwise.' He drops into his seat. 'I'm afraid, Orianna, that you will have to consider me a hostile witness.'

I sit down opposite. 'Did Amos tell you why I'm here? In Eden Falls?'

'He told me about your charade, this little game you're playing.'

Charade. The same word Ruth had used.

'It's not a charade. I had nothing to do with Gideon's murder or Grace's disappearance.'

'It was my impression that your memory is somewhat cloudy on the matter.' Sarcasm drips from his mouth.

'I want to ask you some questions about that summer.'

He purses his lips, then dips his head a fraction.

'Were you close to Grace?'

A frown. 'What is that supposed to mean?'

'I just want to know if you had a close relationship with her. As her uncle.'

A hesitation. 'Not particularly. No.'

'Is that because you and Gideon had never gotten along?'

Indignation drives him back in his seat. 'Who the hell told you that?'

'It's common knowledge. In fact, Amos said that on the evening before Gideon was killed, you had a fight with him. During a card game at the Big House.'

His face purples, and for a moment, I fear that is the end of the interview. But then he picks up a glass of water and sips at it.

'Gideon was a philandering fool. Couldn't keep his dick in his pants if you paid him. For years, I watched him behave like a dog in heat. And my father actually thought he'd be a good choice to take over the reins. Over *me*.'

'Is that why you fought that evening?'

His silence speaks volumes. I wait.

'Gideon was always a sore loser. He'd had too much to drink. I cleaned him out. He took objection. Told me I could keep the few dollars I'd won because that was all I'd ever see once he took over the firm. I had no idea what he was talking about – my whole life I'd been preparing myself to run the business. As the eldest, it was my *right* to succeed my father.' His anger rushes out in a torrent. 'Gideon revealed that our father had led him to believe that *he* was the anointed one. I suppose I knew, deep down, that he'd always been Amos's favourite. His *golden boy*.' He practically spits the words. 'Gideon and I almost came to blows. David had to pull us apart.'

'And the next day Gideon was killed.'

His eyes die. Soft music plays in the silence.

'Be very careful what you say next.'

I allow a beat to pass. 'Does Rebekah know about this fight?'

'Rebekah.' His tone is mocking. 'Some people are addicted to grief, some to wealth. My sister-in-law is guilty on both counts.'

'Did you know that she was having an affair with Tommy Quinn? When Gideon was killed?'

He works through an internal debate. 'I heard an ugly rumour.'

'Did Gideon know?'

'I suspect so.'

'Didn't you think that was worth telling the authorities? Isn't it possible that Tommy Quinn could have—?'

'What? Killed Gideon? A moment ago, you were suggesting *I* might be Gideon's killer. Are you forgetting that *you* were the one found in Gideon's hunting cabin? You're reaching, Orianna.'

'You must have thought Quinn had *something* to do with Gideon's murder, else why did you try and run him out of town?'

'Tommy Quinn brought drugs into our community. He is a reprobate, and a criminal. So, yes, I thought it was judicious to encourage him to go set up someplace else.'

'Yet he's still here.'

'The bigger the roach, the harder to get rid of.'

Frustration buzzes around my thoughts. 'I've read everyone's statements. You told the police that you didn't see Grace on the day she disappeared.'

'No. I was at the office.'

'But the firm was shut. For the Forest Festival.'

'I work hard, Orianna.'

'So you didn't go along to see Grace crowned as Forest Princess?'

'No.'

'Because you knew Gideon would be there?'

He says nothing.

'And you were at the office all day?'

'As I'm sure you've seen in my statement, I left the office to grab lunch.'

'For which you returned home, to the estate. To the Big House.'

'I did.'

'And then you went for a walk.'

He dips his head.

'The Big House is only a twenty-minute walk from the woods where Gideon was killed.'

'The woods where *you* killed him.'

'You were gone an hour. By your own admission. No one else can verify where you were during that hour. Again, by your own admission.'

A fury enters his face, the malevolent anger of a child. 'You have no right to dig up the past. This, this ... *grotesque* thing happened to *our* family. I lost my brother. I lost my niece. It tore us apart. Our ship has never been right since that day. My father has spent eighteen years pursuing his obsession, to the detriment of all else. He refuses to let go of the idea that he'll find Grace's killer one day.' He rises to his feet, points at me with a shaking finger. 'The truth is that *you* killed Gideon. You killed Grace. What you hope to gain by coming back here, God only knows. Take my advice – leave Eden Falls. Go live the rest of your life. And may God judge you on the day of your reckoning.'

I scrape back my chair. 'There's one thing you keep forgetting: I'm a part of this family too. Gideon was my father. Whether you like it or not, I'm a Wyclerc.' I walk to the door, then turn back. 'See you around, Uncle Pete.'

57

ORIANNA: NOW

The meeting with Peter leaves me seething.

The idea that Peter and Gideon had fought the night before Gideon's death, that they had harboured a long-simmering animosity ... At the very least, this had merited investigation. Instead, the family had said nothing. Even if they had, what guarantee was there that the authorities had made any attempt to follow up?

An hour later, unable to contain my swarming anger, I call Luke. 'Amos says Dick Hogan won't talk to me without you there.'

A hesitation, then: 'It's not that Hogan won't talk to you. You just won't get anything useful out of him.'

'Just make it happen.'

Luke's silence breathes down the phone. 'I'm sorry I haven't called. I ... I figured you needed the space. Maybe we both did.'

'You have everything you wanted, Luke. A wife. A kid on the way. The perfect life. I'm happy for you.'

'Ori—'

'I guess Eden Falls turned out to be harder to leave than you thought.'

Amos is in his study, erect at his desk, mobile phone clutched in one liver-spotted hand.

He motions for me to wait.

I stand by the window, looking out over the sweep of the rear lawn, beyond the wall and out to the southern woods. The trees are densely packed, dark and forbidding.

Somewhere in that murk, my life had changed, irrevocably.

What had really happened in those hidden hours?

Amos finishes his call, then lumbers his way over to me, lighting a cigar.

I have almost become used to the smell. Associate it with him now.

'So you met Peter. Suffice to say, you have not endeared yourself to your uncle. A word of advice: if you're going to accuse a man of murder, at least do it with a little subtlety.'

'You *knew*. And you did nothing.'

'What did I know? That my sons didn't always see eye to eye? That they had a minor disagreement the day before Gideon died? Do you think I'd really believe that Peter murdered his own brother? Don't waste my time – or yours – with foolishness.' He gives me the stink eye, then waves the cigar around in a conciliatory fashion. 'You wanted to speak to him and now you have. Sit down and have a drink.'

I continue to glare at him, then feel the wind go out of my sails.

Collapsing onto the couch, I fill a glass and take a large gulp of bourbon.

Amos lowers himself gingerly onto the seat opposite. 'Did you think that just because I've given you my blessing, they'd let you in? They *despise* you. Not just because they believe you killed Gideon. But because of who you are. Trash. Your mother—'

'Don't talk about her. You have no right.'

'I have every right. Way I figure, my son is dead because of her.'

I shoot to my feet. 'Fuck you!' I hurl my glass at the wall, where it strikes a painting of a little girl sat at the top of a stairwell.

'That's a Norman Rockwell,' he says mildly. 'Hell. I'm not saying your mother came into this house fixing to hunt bear. But a woman who looked like that, working as a housekeeper? What was she really doing here? I asked her that once. Right here in this room. She turned those big beautiful eyes on me, made a face like the Blessed Virgin, and told me she wanted to better herself. Well, fucking the boss's son and having his bastard child is one way to better yourself, I suppose.'

'My mother never wanted your money. *I* don't want your money.'

'That's good to know. I'm sure Peter will be reassured. He – among others – is concerned that I might alter my will. In your favour.'

I turn away, clutch at myself, hear him puffing on his cigar.

'Come and sit down.'

Through the window, the sun is a burning red ball, half obscured by the tree-cloaked hills in the middle distance.

I turn and walk stiffly back to the couch.

'Who owns the company?'

'We do. The family. My father was adamant that outsiders should never be able to dictate terms to us, and so, when he died, he ensured that the bulk of the shares went to me. The rest are divided between the others: not just my own sons, but Abel's children too. David and Hannah – though Hannah's never acknowledged it. Martha, Abel's wife – David and Hannah's mother – has a significant holding.'

'And they all have a say in running the company?'

'They have voting rights and, technically, they all sit on the board. But I have the controlling interest. Peter is our chairman and the CEO. He makes the day-to-day decisions.'

'Why haven't you intervened?'

'Intervened?'

'The business has taken a nosedive since Peter took over. He doesn't know what he's doing.'

He sets down the cigar, pours himself a drink. 'Well, that's a mighty bold judgement from a woman who's spent the best part of the past two decades in prison ... The truth? I gave up. Losing Gideon, Grace, it changed me in a way I can't begin to describe. I'd spent my life driving the business forward – for myself, for this town, for my family. I thought I was immune to the misfortunes that afflicted lesser men. I thought I had *control*. I was wrong.' He slurs out a sigh. 'If Peter is a bad leader, it's my fault. I never believed in him. He told you the truth when he said that I wanted Gideon to take over. Gideon was never smart or diligent the way Peter was, and, in the end, his vices got the better of him. But he had bold ideas. We needed them. A leader must have clarity, a vision, and Peter has never had it.

'When I stepped aside for him, he felt the need to make his own mark. Sadly, things haven't panned out for him. It's not all his fault. The mining industry has been hit hard these past two decades. We're not living in the America I grew up in. We're importing a lot of our ore now, making foreigners rich while towns like Eden Falls wither on the vine.'

My phone rings. Luke. 'I spoke with Hogan. We're all set. Eight p.m. tomorrow. I'll pick you up at seven.'

I hesitate. The prospect of journeying out to Barrier with Luke unsettles me. 'Fine.'

After I shut the phone, Amos picks up his cigar again. 'How are you and Luke getting along?'

Has he read my mind? I wouldn't put it past him.

'Fine.'

'He's a good boy. I've come to rely on him a great deal. Ever since David's stroke, he's been a little . . . rudderless. I've tried to do the best I can. With Gideon gone, Luke is the closest thing to a son I have left. Peter shut me out a long time ago, and Samuel . . . Well, Samuel's never really needed anyone except God.' He stops. 'Luke reminds me of him. Of Gideon. One day that boy will realise his true potential. I wanted him to follow his father into the firm, but David had other ideas.'

'He didn't want his son controlled by you.'

His pained look tells me I've hit close to the mark. 'You can think of me what you will. But this family, this town, exists because of the Wyclercs. Without us, without me, there *is* no Eden Falls.'

'I bet the devil says the same thing about hell.'

His mouth twists into a smile. 'Tell me something. How did it feel when you found out Luke was your cousin? To know you'd been fucking your own kin?'

He plugs the cigar into his mouth, looks at me with his cool gaze.

I want nothing more than to smash that knowing look from his face; to pound his skull into a bloody lump.

Instead, I get up and walk away.

58

ANNIE: THEN

My next session with Orianna begins uncomfortably.

I have decided to once again shift the focus, this time to another of the key players in Orianna's life before prison, her life growing up in Eden Falls.

'Orianna, I'd like to start talking a little about Luke Wyclerc.'

Her eyes flash at me; a sudden tension snaps her shoulders into a straight line.

The change in her demeanour takes me by surprise.

In the past months, I have noticed a slow transformation in Orianna's attitude, her body language. Some of her initial hostility has thawed; she no longer enters the room with her guard up. I cannot say for sure that she has accepted the process for what it is, has understood that I am truly here to help, but at the least she seems willing to engage.

But mentioning Luke appears to have been a misstep.

'Orianna?'

She says nothing. Her expression is hunted.

'It's OK if you don't want to talk about him. But your reaction alone tells me that Luke is someone we *need* to talk about. He's important to you. A key player in the events leading up to your conviction.'

Outside, I can hear the sound of a church bell. I know that there is a small chapel on the grounds here, and that they ring out the bell at the canonical hours. Some of those locked away here find the bell, its daily repetition, soothing; a beacon to orient their troubled ship through the maelstrom.

Finally, Orianna speaks. 'What do you want to know?'

'Luke grew up on the Wyclerc estate, as did you. Tell me about an early encounter with him. When you first began to know him.'

She shifts back in her seat. 'There was a moment. On the estate. When we were sixteen. I was walking through the woods, and I saw him, hiding behind a tree. I recognised him instantly, of course. Growing up, I'd seen him around the estate, at school. We'd never really interacted. But he was never stand-offish, not like Grace. He was always willing to exchange a few words, a nod. No more than that. That was the thing about Eden Falls—' She stops.

'Go on.'

'We were told that Nathaniel Wyclerc built the town to create a society where we were all equal under God. Rich and poor. Master and servant. It was a lie. The reality was that like attracted like. The few friends I hung out with weren't the girls Grace would give the time of day. They weren't the girls a boy like Luke might give a second glance.'

'Did you approach Luke? That day in the woods?'

She is silent, and then speaks again, transporting us both to that moment in time.

The Girl In Cell A

A twig cracks under her feet, the sound like a rifle shot. Luke spins around. He blinks, then gradually relaxes.

'Hi.'

'Hi.'

'What are you doing?'

'Nothing.'

She walks towards him. In school, she would have turned and walked the other way. But there is something about him, out here, in her woods, the way he is standing there, the sense of nervousness emanating from him.

She comes right up to him, looks him in the eyes. She has seen eyes like that in the portraits hanging in the Big House.

She peers beyond the tree. 'What were you looking at?'

He says nothing.

And then she sees it. Gideon's hunting cabin. She has always known it was there, of course. Everyone on the estate knew it was out of bounds. Whenever she comes into these woods, she makes sure to give it a wide berth.

'You ever been in there?' he asks.

'No.'

'Never been curious?'

His words whisper along the fine hairs of her ear.

There have been boys, of course. Preening, leering. She's stayed clear. Knuckled down and studied hard. Because that is the only way she's going to make it out of this godforsaken town.

None of those boys had been anything like Luke.

None of them had been a Wyclerc.

'Is he in there now?'

'No.'

She hesitates, and then, before rational thought can get in the way, begins to move.

He catches up to her with a few easy strides.

They reach the cabin, set dead centre in its little clearing.

Fear brakes her to a halt. But she can't chicken out now.

She works her way around to the front, pulls back the screen door, pushes at the wood behind with her fingertips, expecting it to be locked.

It swings back with a soft creak.

She glances at Luke. Sweat shimmers on his brow.

Inside, the space is bigger than she had expected, the walls lined with guns on iron mounts. A batch of rifles stand to attention in a machine-tooled wooden rack.

In a glass case, lined with green velvet, they find an antique revolver.

She watches as Luke takes it out, hefts it in his hand, grins at her. A modern-day Billy the Kid.

'You know how to shoot?' she asks.

'Sure.'

She turns back to the rifle rack. Reaching in, she takes out a gun that looks on the lighter side. It feels strange in her hands.

She holds it to her shoulder, sights along its length at the wolf's head on the wall.

Finally, she turns back to Luke. 'Wanna show me how?'

59

ORIANNA: NOW

The road flows under the tyres of Luke's Ford.

I look out the passenger-side window, thankful for the cool air flowing from the air-conditioning. It is past seven in the evening, yet the humidity outside is suffocating.

'That summer . . . was Grace seeing someone? Someone she wouldn't talk about?'

Luke turns hard into a bend in the road. 'I don't know. We were never really close enough to discuss stuff like that.'

The way he says it turns my head. Something in his tone. Back when we were kids, we never really talked about Grace. She and Luke were the only others of my age on the estate. As cousins, Luke and Grace must have been close, yet Luke had always denied it. Claimed he never really knew Grace, rarely interacted with her.

He speaks while continuing to look straight ahead. 'Who have you been talking to?'

'Sally Lomax.'

He gives me a sidelong glance. 'I haven't bumped into Sally for a while.'

'She also said that Grace told her that Rebekah was having an affair with Tommy Quinn around the time Gideon was killed.'

I hear his intake of breath.

'People in this town . . . Christ. They got nothing better to do but spread gossip. Even if it *is* true, it doesn't mean Quinn had anything to do with Gideon's death.'

'But what if Gideon threatened him? Quinn's a volatile character, by all accounts. It's not inconceivab—'

'You're looking for something that isn't there.'

The edge in his voice surprises me. 'I think it's worth talking to him.'

'Stay away from Quinn. He's dangerous.'

'So I hear.'

'I mean it.'

I turn away, set my gaze on the world blurring by outside.

Being this close to Luke is disconcerting. The car is filled with his cologne, the smell I associate with him, the same cologne he has been wearing since his teenage days, pinched from his daddy's bathroom cabinet.

We are on the county road to Barrier, the neighbouring town, and the largest – by population – in Griffin County. If Eden Falls is the prim older sister, Barrier is the louche younger sibling; a brash, sprawling town that, unlike Eden Falls, long ago hitched up her skirts and stuck up a welcome sign. The town has grown rapidly, relying largely on a seedy tourist economy: day trippers and pleasure seekers, for the most part, working their way through the town's range of juke joints, cathouses and crappy *nouveau cuisine* restaurants. In recent years, cultural refugees and big-city hipsters have moved in – drawn, perhaps, by the cheap living and the rundown but still touristy historic quarter.

Luke breaks the silence. 'A few years ago, Peter tasked Sheriff Faulkes to run Quinn out of town. Quinn was dealing drugs, had a record. Not the kind of stand-up citizen my uncle wanted on the county rolls. Faulkes was too chickenshit to do the deed himself, so he found a couple of guys from Barrier to come over and give Quinn a talking-to.' He pauses. 'Quinn almost took one guy's head off with a length of rebar. Knocked the other guy down, then, while the man watched, caved in his kneecap. Hasn't been able to walk right since. Faulkes couldn't do a thing to him because Quinn got it out of them who'd sent them. Ever since, it's been stalemate.'

I say nothing and go back to looking at the trees as they sweep by on the Barrier road.

60

ORIANNA: NOW

The bar is called, simply, Hogan's.

Inside, barflies, whiskery and sallow-eyed, hunch over long-necked beer bottles, pouring out their grudges against the federal government into the ears of a black barman who looks as if he couldn't be less interested had they been reciting to him from a TiVo manual. A TV above the bar flickers with a football game no one is watching. Bluegrass plays in the background.

Luke introduces himself to the barman.

Moments later, we are led to the rear and parked in a red-Rexined booth. The faux leather is torn in several places, the sticky table surface a postmodernist masterpiece of cigarette burns and battle scars. The booth is located next to the toilets; an electric bug zapper sparks above the door.

A figure approaches. It takes a moment for me to recognise him.

Time is rarely kind to middle-aged white men, but Richard Hogan has changed beyond all recognition. The detective I remember had never been much to look at, but the man bearing down on us looks as if he has swallowed Hogan, with room to spare.

Hogan wears a baseball shirt that drapes over his huge gut like a parachute, untucked from of a pair of heavy-hipped denim slacks. His head is a block of granite, with a cleft chin and a forehead that glistens as if oiled. A grey walrus moustache covers most of his mouth. His skull is shaved and his forearms writhe with tattoos.

Hogan, the former detective, now looks like a shot-caller for a neo-Nazi biker gang.

As he walks towards us, I am once again struck by the electrifying sensation of ball lightning ricocheting around my skull. The past is a wolf, tearing away at me.

Hogan squeezes his enormous bulk into the booth. This simple act brings forth a fresh sheen of sweat.

Finally, he says, 'Hi Orianna. Long time no see.'

I want to spit in his eye.

'How are you, Detective?' Luke says.

He gives Luke a frosty look. 'No one's called me that in a long time. I recall inviting you to my retirement party. You missed a night to remember. They gave me an engraved watch and a framed picture of myself, in case I forgot what I looked like. Thirty years of service. So long, Dick, and don't forget not to write.'

'We're here to—'

'I know why you're here. Amos already told me. How is the old fuck, anyway? Sounded pretty sick on the phone. Hope it's serious.' He turns to me. 'So you're still peddling that whole "I can't remember" line . . . You know why perps can't remember the terrible shit they did? It's either because the crime was so heinous their mind has blanked it out, or it's because if they admit it, even to themselves, they'll have to accept who and what they really are.'

'You agreed to help,' says Luke.

'I agreed to answer a few questions. But it comes at a price.'

'You want money?'

'Look around you, sport. This look like the Copacabana? Retirement hasn't turned out the way I thought it would. But then, not everyone's born with a silver spoon sticking out their ass.' He leans over, wafting the smell of stale sweat. 'You want answers, you pay.'

Luke pulls out his wallet, takes out a billfold and begins counting, but Hogan simply reaches out and plucks the wad from his hand. 'Much obliged.' He twists his bulk on the protesting Rexine to face me. 'So, how can I help you, killer?'

61

ANNIE: THEN

The last session unlocked something.

I am not quite certain what, but I see a difference in Orianna.

Luke is clearly a vulnerable topic for her. I must tread carefully.

But I am glad she has engaged, surprised that she was candid enough to tell me about their earliest teenage encounter and how it led immediately to the hunting cabin in which Gideon's murder took place.

I want to push further, but my intuition tells me to back off and circle back to Luke at a later time.

Instead, I decide to take Orianna back to the trial. It is time to examine the evidence presented by the prosecution. I want to see how she reacts when confronted by cold hard facts.

'"My name is Detective Richard Hogan. I work for the Griffin County District Attorney's Office, Criminal Investigations Division."'

I read these words from the court transcript. Once again, I have brought along copies for us both. It is important for us to keep returning to Orianna's time in court.

Many of the revelations that came out at the trial will form the bedrock for our sessions. But getting Orianna to discuss them directly has proven difficult.

It is a delicate balancing act.

Orianna's dissociative amnesia means that she denies remembering some of the details. By confronting her with them, I am taking the risk that she will withdraw, that the same mechanism that led to the amnesia will be reactivated, building new walls around the past.

There is a very real possibility that the whole process might come to a grinding halt.

But there's no getting around it. If I am to get Orianna to face up to what happened, I need to go on the attack.

Today, I have asked her to take me back to the discovery of Gideon's body and her own arrest. A relatively safe place to start – hours after the actual shooting.

The easiest way to do this is to look at the transcript and the testimony of the key players during those hours, beginning with a Detective Richard Hogan.

I had already spoken on the phone with Hogan. He'd retired from the force some years earlier, to go open a bar in a town neighbouring Eden Falls. On the phone he proved to be surly, rude, arrogant and uncooperative. I got nothing out of him other than an urgent need to shower.

Orianna takes her time before beginning. When she does, her voice slips into that slow, trancelike state that I noted in earlier sessions. To me this is a good sign. It tells me that she is accessing memories in a structured way.

The Girl In Cell A

'I remember watching from the defendant's table as Hogan was sworn in. He wore a crumpled linen suit with a fat-headed paisley tie. His hair had been butchered into a razor cut by a barber who must have been partially sighted, if not outright blind. I hoped he could sense the way I felt about him. If looks could kill, his heart would have stopped on the stand.'

She bends to the transcript.

Detective Hogan: My name is Detective Richard Hogan. I work for the Griffin County District Attorney's Office, Criminal Investigations Division.

DA Danziger: Detective, was it in this capacity that you were called out to the Wyclerc family estate on August 31st last year?

Det. Hogan: Yes. That's correct. In fact, it was the sheriff's office that received the call. I happened to be visiting with Chief Deputy Faulkes at the time, and he suggested that I accompany him.

Danziger: What was the reason for your visit with the chief deputy?

Det. Hogan: It was my weekly meeting with the sheriff's office. Sheriff Gantry was indisposed – out of town, I believe – at the time.

Danziger: And was it in your role as chief investigator for the county that you subsequently became involved in the investigation into the murder of Gideon Wyclerc?

Det. Hogan: Yes. That's correct.

Danziger: And that being the case, is it fair to say you have an overview of the investigation conducted into his murder?

Det. Hogan: Yes.

Danziger: Could you please tell us what you discovered when you arrived at the crime scene?

Det. Hogan: We found Gideon Wyclerc dead in a hunting cabin on the Wyclerc estate. We further discovered the defendant at the scene in the company of Amos Wyclerc; Amos's aide, Cletus Barnes; and two other Wyclerc family employees, Herman Sap and Boris DeWitt.

Danziger: In what capacity are these two gentlemen employed?

Det. Hogan: Sap is the groundskeeper of the Wyclerc estate and DeWitt is his assistant.

Danziger: Who made the call to the sheriff's office?

Det. Hogan: The call came from Cletus Barnes on the instructions of Amos Wyclerc.

Danziger: And could you tell the court the circumstances in which the crime was discovered?

Det. Hogan: Herman Sap and Boris DeWitt were walking through the woods that lie on the southern edge of the Wyclerc estate. They happened to pass by the hunting cabin. They spotted that the door was open. Something about the situation felt off, and so they decided to look inside. They found Gideon's body and the prone body of the defendant on the floor. Herman Sap left Boris DeWitt at the scene and immediately went to the Big House, where he reported the discovery to Cletus Barnes. Cletus reported the same to Amos Wyclerc, who went to ascertain the truth of the matter himself. Shortly thereafter, he instructed Barnes to return to the Big House and call the sheriff's office.

I interrupt: 'Is all of this accurate?'

'It's accurate that Herman and Boris worked at the estate. It's accurate that they say they found me in the cabin, near Gideon's body. But I was out of it. Not that it mattered. The court believed every word that came out of their mouths.' Her voice is thick with emotion; her eyes flash.

She turns back to the transcript, continuing with the DA's questioning.

> **Danziger:** And what was your initial impression of the situation?
>
> **Det. Hogan:** Gideon Wyclerc had been shot dead. A shotgun lay on the floor. Having spoken with those present at the scene, it became clear that the defendant had been found unconscious inside the cabin with the shotgun beside her.
>
> **Danziger:** Had anyone interfered with the crime scene?
>
> **Det. Hogan:** No. Cletus Barnes checked the defendant's pulse, but otherwise did not disturb the scene.
>
> **Danziger:** When did the defendant come to?
>
> **Det. Hogan:** Shortly after the arrival of Amos Wyclerc and Cletus Barnes.
>
> **Danziger:** And did they relate to you anything she said or did upon awakening?
>
> **Det. Hogan:** Yes. They stated that she was uncommunicative. Unwilling to answer questions about what had happened.
>
> **Danziger:** Did you arrest her at this point?
>
> **Det. Hogan:** Yes.

Danziger: Why?

Det. Hogan: Because it was my belief, based on the circumstances, that she had murdered Gideon Wyclerc.

Danziger: And was this belief unequivocal?

Det. Hogan: Yes. Though, of course, many questions remained. But if it looks like a duck and walks like a duck . . .

Danziger: And what did you do at this point, Detective Hogan?

Det. Hogan: I called the state crime lab. Asked for a forensics team to be sent out.

Danziger: We'll look at the forensic evidence in due course, but let me ask you a couple of other questions that may help us determine the exact sequence of events that led to Gideon Wyclerc's murder that day. To begin with: did you determine what Gideon was doing in the cabin at that time?

Det. Hogan: Yes. He'd returned from visiting the Forest Festival earlier that day and had taken lunch at home. This was verified by his wife and their housemaid. He then left his house at around 4 p.m., telling his wife that he intended to spend some time in his hunting cabin before returning that evening for the annual Wyclerc post-festival dinner.

Danziger: For the purpose of clarification, Gideon Wyclerc's wife is Rebekah Wyclerc. Is that correct?

Det. Hogan: Yes, that's correct.

Orianna pauses once more. 'At this point, I remember Danziger stopping for a second so everyone could look over at Rebekah. She was sitting behind the prosecution table, dressed in black, a slouch hat covering her hair. I think she was going for the Jackie Kennedy look.'

'Did she interact with you? Before or during the trial?'

'She barely looked at me.'

Something unspoken moves in her eyes, and then she is back with the transcript:

> **Danziger:** What did Gideon normally do in the shack?
> **Det. Hogan:** He did what men do when they want time to themselves. He listened to the radio. He drank beer. He oiled his guns.
> **Danziger:** Did he keep many guns there?
> **Det. Hogan:** We inventoried the place and found fifteen different weapons. Rifles, shotguns, a couple of automatics and one antique revolver, a Colt Model 1860, shipped to New Orleans in 1861 and used in the Confederate attack on Fort Sumter. All the guns were licenced to Gideon.
> **Danziger:** Would it be fair to say that he was a gun enthusiast?
> **Det. Hogan:** Sure. He was a red-blooded American.
> **Danziger:** Did Gideon usually go to the cabin alone or did he often invite others?
> **Det. Hogan:** Having interviewed the victim's family, it was clear that this was a private bolthole. Gideon had built it for himself years earlier and expected never to be disturbed there. It was strictly off limits.
> **Danziger:** And this was common knowledge?

Det. Hogan: Among the members of the Wyclerc family and those who lived on the Wyclerc estate, yes.

Danziger: So if someone wished to confront Gideon alone, the cabin would be the perfect place to do so? Deep in the woods, far from prying eyes.

Det. Hogan: That would be a fair assessment.

Danziger: Detective Hogan, what did you do next? Once the forensics team had processed the scene?

Det. Hogan: I returned to the sheriff's office to interview the defendant.

Danziger: And how did that initial interview go?

Det. Hogan: The defendant was surly, uncooperative. It was obvious that she'd been drinking—

Danziger: I'm sorry, Detective, but for the sake of clarity, how was it obvious?

Det. Hogan: You could smell it on her breath. Later tests confirmed that she had a substantial amount of alcohol in her system... When questioned, she denied any involvement in Gideon Wyclerc's death. She refused to explain her presence in the cabin, claiming she couldn't remember. She was evasive, fidgety.

Danziger: Detective Hogan, in your opinion, as a man who has conducted innumerable suspect interviews, did you believe that the defendant was being untruthful?

Det. Hogan: I did.

Danziger: And later, when the forensic evidence appeared to bear out your interpretation of events, namely that the defendant had murdered Gideon Wyclerc, did Ms Negi explain her actions?

Det. Hogan: No, sir, she did not.
Danziger: She continued to lie?
Det. Hogan: In my opinion, yes.
Danziger: No further questions at this time. Your witness.

62

ANNIE: THEN

Orianna stops, picks up a glass of water and watches me over the rim as I continue to scribble in my notebook.

I know most of this, of course – I've already read the transcripts. But it is important to the process for me to understand how Orianna views those critical moments when the truth of her narrative was weighed – and found wanting.

I sense the pressure of her gaze and stop.

'Are you OK?'

She nods.

'Can you continue? I think we should.'

Her jaw works silently and then she nods again. Leaning back, she closes her eyes, and resumes. 'I watched as my lawyer, Herman Ortega, stood up. That morning he'd visited me in my cell, together with my mother. He'd carefully explained the workings of the court, the players, what I might expect. I told him I'd seen enough legal thrillers to know what was about to happen. He reminded me that the State had offered a plea bargain – in return for a guilty plea. The plea bargain was still on the table, but would vanish the moment the trial began. We had only hours to accept. He could call the DA now and end this.'

'But you chose *not* to accept.'

'No.'

'Why not?'

'I was angry. Scared. I knew that although the State was willing to set aside a first-degree murder charge, the plea bargain would still see me sent away for a minimum of ten years.'

'But wasn't it your lawyer's belief that, with good behaviour, you could have been out in five, maybe six, years?'

'His optimism was misplaced. I knew the Wyclercs wanted me tried for first-degree murder. I knew Amos wanted the death penalty. It was the DA who had made a judgement call. Based, I was told, on his own political ambitions. Asking for the needle for a teenager in a case where it was going to be difficult to prove malice aforethought was not a horse he saw himself riding to the governor's mansion. In the end, he charged me with second-degree murder. An intentional killing, but not premeditated.'

I nodded. This tallied with what I had read in the trial notes. 'How did your mother feel about you refusing the plea bargain?'

'She wanted me to take the deal. She had convinced herself I had next to no chance. She was afraid they'd send me away for life.'

'Why?'

'She thought the odds were stacked against me. I knew that she blamed herself. If she hadn't told me about

Gideon – about him being my father – perhaps none of this would have happened.'

I pick my next words carefully. 'Orianna, do you think that Christine – perhaps only subconsciously – believed that you *had* killed Gideon?'

Her face becomes fierce. 'No.'

'Are you certain of that?'

Her jaw writhes. 'My memory of those critical moments in Gideon's cabin was hazy. Still is. But I was honest with my mother. I saw myself with a shotgun. I saw myself firing the gun. But who was I firing at? I couldn't see Gideon. And without that clarity, without that internal acknowledgement of guilt, how could I believe that I had murdered him?'

'But Christine didn't believe you. I think you know that, don't you?'

Once again, she reacts with anger. But then it seems to leak out of her. 'All I know is my mother had three thousand dollars in a checking account and pretty soon, as cheap as Herman Ortega was, we would be out of money. I had ruined her, ruined the life she had known.' She stops, looks away. 'But she had ruined me too, by lying to me all those years, and then by telling me the truth.'

63

ANNIE: THEN

I have committed a cardinal sin.

I forgot to turn off my phone before the session, and now it blares into the brief silence, breaking the flow.

'I'm so sorry,' I mumble, grabbing my bag. I stab at my phone and get it to shut up on the second try.

I note that the call is from my ex-husband, Michael.

'Don't mind me,' Orianna says. 'It's just my life.'

'I'm so sorry,' I repeat. 'That was unprofessional.'

'I'm just fucking with you.' Her smile is strained. These are unpleasant memories for Orianna to rehash. But this is a necessary part of the process. Forcing her to confront the past – those bits of the past for which we have a record – will allow me to shine a light on what is real and what is false. At least, that's the plan.

'Please continue,' I say.

Orianna takes a breath. 'After the DA finished questioning Hogan, it was the turn of my lawyer, Herman Ortega.'

She looks back down at the pages in her hands.

Herman Ortega: Detective Hogan, in that initial interview with my client, you stated that she did not admit to involvement in the murder of Gideon Wyclerc.

Det. Hogan: That's right.

Ortega: Did my client ever confess to this crime?

Det. Hogan: No.

Ortega: And yet you interviewed her on several occasions, sometimes for hours at a time. Going over and over the same events.

Det. Hogan: It's standard procedure when a suspect is uncooperative.

Ortega: But this was a seventeen-year-old girl, not some hardened criminal.

Det. Hogan: A girl we suspected of cold-blooded murder.

Ortega: In all that time, across all those interviews, my client continued to maintain her innocence. Isn't that correct?

Det. Hogan: She says she can't remember. That's not the same thing.

Ortega: Detective, did you look into any other suspects for Gideon Wyclerc's murder?

Det. Hogan: We investigated the case thoroughly.

Ortega: Well, in that case, you would have sought out and interviewed other enemies of the victim? Or of the Wyclerc family?

Det. Hogan: As I said, we carried out a thorough investigation. There were no other credible suspects.

Ortega: So what you're saying is that you found no one else predisposed to wish harm to the Wyclercs?

Det. Hogan: No. That's not what I'm saying. What I'm saying is that we found no one else who made a credible suspect for Gideon's murder.

Ortega: Detective, have you heard of the term *confirmation bias*?

Det. Hogan: [Pause] I have.

Ortega: Could you explain to the court what it means when applied to a criminal investigation?

Det. Hogan: It refers to a situation that sometimes arises where investigators determine an early scenario for the circumstances of a crime and then seek evidence to support that scenario.

Ortega: What you mean is that it refers to a situation where investigators decide on the guilty party and seek evidence that points to that party's guilt while ignoring evidence that contradicts their theory. Wouldn't that be a more accurate phrasing, Detective?

Det. Hogan: Some might say that.

Ortega: But not you?

Danziger: Your Honour, Detective Hogan is a decorated law enforcement veteran with no need to prove himself to this court.

Ortega: Withdrawn. The point I was trying to make, Detective, was that you saw what you wanted to see. You drew an early conclusion as to my client's guilt in this matter based on a handful of supposed facts. You never gave her a fair shake. She was seventeen years old, confused. She'd clearly been through a traumatic experience. She told you that her memory was faulty.

[Mr Ortega picks up a manila folder, walks it across to Det. Hogan, introducing it into the record.]

Ortega: Detective, do you recognise this document?
Det. Hogan: Yes.
Ortega: Please tell the court what that is.
Det. Hogan: It's an assessment of the defendant's head injury.
Ortega: And what does it say?
Det. Hogan: That she sustained an injury to the back of her skull.
Ortega: An injury that my client repeatedly told you was inflicted by an unseen attacker, but which the State claims occurred when she fell back and struck her head against the wall of the cabin?
Det. Hogan: Yes.
Ortega: That report also states, does it not, that the potential effects of such a blow – however it may have occurred – might include disorientation and short-term memory loss?

[Witness does not reply.]

Ortega: Detective?
Det. Hogan: Yes.
Ortega: In such a scenario, isn't it entirely possible that this vulnerable young woman, dazed and disoriented, having just lost the man she had only just discovered was her father, believing that she had been attacked, would have been in no fit state to answer your questions? That she would have had every reason to

appear, as you put it, 'uncooperative'? I put it to you, Detective Hogan, that it was your responsibility to seek the truth in this matter, to run down every loose ball. But, instead, you threw a noose around my client's neck and declared her guilty. Would that be an accurate reflection of what transpired during this so-called investigation?

Det. Hogan: An investigation is never a precise business. But if you do this job long enough, you get an instinct for the way things work. The fact is that everything about this case pointed to the defendant. Motive. Means. Opportunity. She hit the jackpot on all three. The forensic evidence backed up our initial theory. There was no evidence to support the idea that anyone other than the defendant had killed Gideon. So, yes, we focused on the defendant. Because there was literally no one else who could have committed the crime.

Orianna lowers the folder.

I can sense her distress. I want to harness it, use it to drill through the mirror. 'What went through your mind at that moment?'

Her mouth twists. 'What went through my mind? I guess the fact that my crummy lawyer wasn't good enough.'

'Was it your lawyer or the evidence?' My voice is gentle but firm. I need Orianna to face the facts here, not to deny them by blaming her attorney.

But she simply closes her eyes and says nothing.

64

ORIANNA: NOW

A woman two booths down stands up and begins yelling. 'You low-life piece-of-shit *asshole.*'

She picks up a glass and hurls the contents in her partner's face. 'I hope she was worth it.'

We watch her stomp off to a succession of catcalls.

'Fun and games on karaoke night,' mutters Hogan. He crooks a finger at a waitress.

'Get me a drink. And something to eat. Chilli dog. What'll you guys have?'

Luke shakes his head. I hesitate, then: 'Shot of bourbon.'

'Well, lookit you. All grown up. Tits and everything.'

He leers.

'Why did you make such a half-assed job of the investigation?'

The grin vanishes. 'What are you talking about?'

I tell him about Tommy Quinn. 'That took me all of five minutes. You had state resources at your disposal.'

The sound of someone kicking the pinball machine in the corner. A shouted 'sumbitch'.

'You look like your mother, anyone tell you that? Fine-looking woman, if a shade on the dark side. Shame she was such a whore.'

I wait. He pulls a crumpled packet of cigarettes from the breast pocket of his shirt, lights one. 'Amos was convinced you'd killed his golden boy. Fact was, all the evidence pointed your way.'

'I've read your investigation reports. I want to know what you *didn't* put in there.'

Our drinks arrive. I watch as Hogan lifts a shot glass to his mouth. 'OK, killer. I'll play along. There *were* a couple of things. Didn't seem relevant at the time, but I guess you might say they been whispering in my ear all these years.'

I feel Luke tense beside me.

'The hunting cabin. You know Gideon didn't just use it for oiling his guns, right?' His grin reveals stained teeth. 'It was a trysting place, a little fuck pad out in the woods. He'd bring women in through the back gate – you know the one I mean?'

Luke leans in. 'Did he have a woman there that day?'

'Not that we found out. But I did get to thinking ... What if Rebekah *knew*? About what went on in that cabin? You know, *she* had no alibi for the time Gideon was killed. Says she was up in her bedroom taking a nap after a busy morning at the Forest Festival. But no one saw her there.'

I speak. 'As I said, she was seeing Tommy Quinn back then.'

His eyes narrow. 'OK. So, yeah, I heard that rumour.'

'Did you interview Quinn?'

'No. Why would I? Are you forgetting that we found

you in that cabin with your prints on the gun, covered in gunshot residue? It's a little thing called evidence. Besides, let's say Rebekah *was* fucking Quinn . . . So what? Can you blame her? Gideon was running around on her for years – why shouldn't she get some?' He leans back. 'What I don't get is why Gideon kept your mother around. Even if she *didn't* tell him, he must have known, on some level, that you were his kid. But he never acknowledged you. How did that feel? When you found out Daddy had been there all along, just didn't give a fuck about you?' His eyes glitter. 'I keep thinking: what if Rebekah found out about *you* that day? Gideon's little lovechild. What would a woman like Rebekah have done? Isn't that what you really came all this way to hear? Well, guess what? I did find something. Rebekah says she was napping when Gideon was killed – but an hour before he died, she was seen in a heated exchange with your mother. And a little after that, your mother told you about Gideon, after all those years of hiding the fact that he was your father . . . What do you think they talked about to make her do that? Your mother said it was nothing important, wouldn't tell us shit. Neither would Rebekah. I never mentioned it in my reports. Why complicate matters, right?'

My body vibrates with anger. I want to reach across and smash the smug off his face.

His chilli dog arrives. I watch him shove the dog into his mouth, dripping sauce onto his chin and shirt.

'What about Grace?'

'What about her?' He speaks while chewing, mouth moving like a cement mixer.

My eyes bore into his.

He sighs, sets down his chilli dog, wipes his mouth with the back of his hand and picks up the cigarette. 'Amos is crazy, you know that, right? Eighteen years he's been at this. Anyone would think he was looking for the Holy Grail.' He jabs the cigarette at me. 'The only person who'll ever know what happened that day is Grace's killer.'

'I didn't kill Grace.'

'You're a fool to come back here. You want my advice? Get the hell out of Eden Falls. Go live your best life.'

I remember him in the interrogation room, the coldness of his manner, the relentlessness. Hour after hour. A hatred had settled into me, deep in the marrow. For him, and for everything he represented.

'How did my mother die?'

He frowns, for the first time unsure of himself. 'Didn't they tell you?'

'They told me she drowned. In the lake behind Elvira Trueblood's cottage. That she was drunk.'

'Sounds about right. She went a little crazy after you did what you did. You gonna blame that on someone else, too?'

'Did you investigate her death?'

'Happened after I quit. You'd have to talk to Faulkes.' His lips curl into a sly smile. 'You wondering if it was an accident or if your mother deliberately walked on into that water? Whether *you* drove her in there?'

When I trust myself to speak again, I say, 'Did you really believe I did it? Killed Gideon?'

He blows smoke across the table. 'What do you want me to tell you? Life ain't fair. Look at me. I was an all-star athlete in high school. Go figure.'

65

ORIANNA: NOW

It is going on eleven by the time we arrive back at the cottage.

Luke rolls the truck to a halt. We had said little to each other on the way back, the tension palpable. I sense his need to talk. But the evening has left a cold rage sloshing around inside me.

'Do you want me to come in?' he says. 'I mean, do you want to talk?'

'No.'

He seems stricken. I notice, for the first time that evening, that his shirt looks new, that he has shaved, that his hair has been trimmed. A dull ache beats inside my chest. I want to take him inside, into the cottage, into my bedroom, into myself.

Instead, I get out.

He gets the message. Nodding sadly, he sets his hands on the wheel, turns the truck around and drives off along the dirt track.

I wait a moment, then turn and begin walking towards home.

Shadows peel away from the side of the cottage.

I gasp, but they are on me before I can react. Two men, masked.

Twisting around, I try to run, but they tackle me to the ground. My forehead bounces off the earth; I taste dirt in my mouth.

I kick out, blindly. A punch finds my kidneys, and I cry out.

Rough hands pull me to my feet. One of the men locks my arms behind me. The other stands in front, breathing heavily. He pulls back a fist; the blow lands in my stomach, doubling me over.

Pain dims conscious thought. Drool leaks from my mouth.

'Get the hell out of Eden Falls. You're not welcome here.'

I straighten slowly, breathing through my nose, stamping down on the pain.

The man before me is tall, wide-shouldered, face hidden by a black balaclava. There is nothing about him that I recognise.

I force myself to a measure of calm.

I recall a similar moment, years ago. Two women in the prison laundry room, one holding me from behind, the other brandishing a fist around which was rolled a length of chain.

Afterwards, with the help of a cellmate, I had taught myself the basics of self-defence, a mixture of naked aggression and prison martial arts, the last hope of the desperate.

I stamp down heavily on the foot of the man behind me. He howls, lets go. I crash an elbow backwards into his stomach, follow up by swinging a foot into the crotch of the man in front.

He goes down, screaming in agony.

I turn and race for the cottage. The keys jangle in my hands. I hear one of my attackers staggering towards me. 'Fucking bitch!'

I have to get to the gun.

My hands shake; the keys slip to the ground.

I duck as he lashes out at me.

Twisting away, I run around the side of the house and into the woods.

66

ORIANNA: NOW

I follow the curve of the lake.

I can hear them close behind, crashing through the woods like a pair of bears.

Fear makes rational thought difficult.

Where can I go? How long can I stay ahead of them?

I run into a clearing, see the abandoned fire tower loom over me.

Without consciously making the decision, I begin to climb.

Clambering through the grate at the top, I walk to the edge of the platform and peer down.

I see them far below, necks craned upwards, two black shapes in the darkness.

I look out over the forest, stretching into the night, all the way up to the old mine.

My heart thunders in my ears.

I fight for calm. Reality seems to ripple around me. Not for the first time, the life I had walked into after leaving prison feels as fragile as gossamer, a veil that might be pierced with the poke of a finger.

I see my mother, Christine, smiling at Gideon, a slow smile that contains unspoken secrets.

My parents vanish, to be replaced by the spectre of Grace, hovering in the darkness.

Liar. You're lying to yourself.

From below, I hear the voices of my attackers.

'What now?'

'I'm not going up there.'

'She's just a girl.'

'You want to stick your head through that grate, be my guest.'

'Bitch nearly broke my balls.'

'Look, we've delivered the message. Let's get the fuck out of here before someone shows up.'

'Who the hell is going to show up? We're in the middle of nowhere.'

'I'm leaving.'

'You're not going anywhere.'

I see the taller man square off against his companion.

The other raises his hands. 'Fine. But I'm still not going up there.'

A moment of silence passes between them. 'Wait here. I have an idea.'

I see the big guy head back into the woods, the sound of dry leaves crackling underfoot.

The remaining man stands at the foot of the ladder, hands on hips.

'Get out of here!' I yell. 'I've called the cops.'

'No, you haven't.' He holds up my mobile phone. 'You dropped it back at the cottage.' He turns and throws it into the trees behind him.

The Girl In Cell A

'Who are you? Why are you doing this?'

'Don't matter who we are. You been warned. Get out of town.'

The second man returns. I see that he is holding something. A jerrycan.

Terror blazes through me.

'What are you doing?' The first guy.

'This tower is old. Wood's like tinder.'

'What are you talking about? We were just supposed to rough her up a bit, scare her. No one said nothing 'bout this.'

'She look scared to you? Now shut the fuck up and help me.'

I watch as he twists the lid off the jerrycan and begins throwing whatever is inside over the ladder and the tower's base posts.

His companion jitters helplessly on the spot. 'This ain't right.'

A chill moves through me. I look around desperately. There is nothing on the wooden platform, nothing I might use as a weapon. And even if there had been, what could I do? Clamber back down and take them both on?

I look back over the edge.

The man with the jerrycan has finished pouring out the gas. He steps back, pulls a lighter from his pocket, looks up.

'Tell us where you buried that dead girl and I promise we'll let you go.'

'Look, I haven't seen your faces. Leave, now, and that'll be the end of it,' I call down.

'Way I see it, there's probably still a hefty reward going for her body.'

'I have no idea where she is.'

'Last chance.'

'Fuck you, you asshole!'

He stiffens, then bends down and casually lights the gas.

Flame whooshes from around his feet, snakes to the tower. An instant later, the base of the tower is aflame.

They reel backwards, as if shocked at the speed with which the fire has caught.

'Come on, let's get out of here.'

I watch them vanish beneath the canopy.

Panic clogs my throat. I can hear the fire crackling its way up the tower's superstructure; smoke billows up towards me, stinging my eyes and forcing me back from the edge.

Think.

I take a deep breath, fight for a centre of calm.

I know that I cannot hope for rescue. The tower is miles from my nearest neighbour. Even if someone sees the flames, by the time they call it in and help arrives, I will be a cinder.

Think.

I look across the clearing. The nearest trees are about ten, twelve feet away.

I sweep my eyes around the platform. How much of a start can I get?

Only one way to find out.

I back away to the edge, set my heels against the trim,

blow out hard, then kick like a long jumper at the start of her run-up, pumping my arms for momentum.

Accelerating to the far edge, I spring, arcing out into the blazing night.

67

ANNIE: THEN

On the drive home, I dwell on Orianna's account of Dick Hogan's testimony.

There is a reason I am asking her to painstakingly relive her time in court, to read through the transcripts with me. I am comparing her recollection to the actual details in the transcripts; I am forcing her to face facts. Literally.

Much of what she recalls is substantially correct. Herein lies the dichotomy at the heart of dissociative amnesia, a contradiction that leads those who have no knowledge of the illness to sometimes accuse those who exhibit it of fakery. Namely, how is it that a person who claims not to be able to recall X can remember Y so clearly?

The answer is deceptively simple. Dissociative amnesia is highly localised. It is usually memories directly surrounding the events that led to the amnesia that are shrouded by the mind. Everything else remains accessible.

In theory, this makes sense. If the dissociative amnesia is the result of a traumatic event or set of events, then it is these that will be buried by the mind in an attempt to protect the patient. Usually, these are memories bookended by a very specific window of time.

This is what I believe has happened to Orianna.

Her testimony regarding Hogan threw up several curious facts.

For one, her own assessment of her lawyer: Orianna clearly feels her defence was less than adequate, adding to her feelings of victimhood. There is the possibility, of course, that her lawyer *was* incompetent. The lawyer himself, Herman Ortega, has refused to speak to me. Moved on, like so many people involved in the case. I read somewhere that he was hounded for years by The Girl in Cell A fanatics, blaming him for her conviction. Perhaps it's not surprising that he wants nothing more to do with the case.

More importantly, I am intrigued by the idea that the police investigation was sketchy, that little effort was made to identify other potential suspects for Gideon's murder.

As a forensic psychotherapist, I am no stranger to bias. It is the reason that two experts in my field can deliver vastly differing profiles of the same suspect in court. I've done it myself, when set against an adversary whose credentials are no less impressive than my own. One woman's murderer is another's martyr.

Maybe Dick Hogan wasn't quite the supercop he made himself out to be.

And if the investigation *was* slipshod, didn't it cast a shade on everything that followed?

Orianna had refused a plea bargain, so certain had she been of her innocence. For a seventeen-year-old facing life imprisonment, that took a resolve I find startling, given that she had no reliable memory to base her self-belief on.

I feel a ramping up of the discomfort I now realise infected me the moment I began to reach behind Orianna's mask. Hogan's testimony only adds to my unease. Orianna was found in a confused and disoriented state in that cabin, carrying a head injury. A girl who had been largely ostracised by the town, a girl who had endured a difficult upbringing. And yet this same girl, when she needed understanding and a sympathetic listener, had, instead, been subjected to days of interrogation by a man who had already decided her guilt.

Did Dick Hogan bully a lost young girl into a corner? Did the town of Eden Falls convict Orianna because, despite being born there, she would never be one of *them*?

Once again, I imagine a possible scenario after my time with Orianna ends: Orianna regaining her freedom and returning to Eden Falls, a misguided attempt to prove to herself that she has been the victim of a miscarriage of justice.

Or worse, a desire to confront those she holds responsible.

If that happens, I fear for both her sanity and her safety.

Because if they did it to her once, they can do it again.

68

ORIANNA: NOW

I fall through the upper branches of the tree.

There is a vivid sense of speed ... and then a jolt as I hit a thick branch, thrash for a grip, then slip to another branch below ... And now I am falling again, ricocheting downwards, a blur of pain and mindless terror.

I hit the ground on my back, breath hammered from my lungs.

I lie there, stunned, unable to move.

Sound goes away.

Moonlight filters through the tree. I blink.

Finally, I lift myself from the earth.

Leaning against the tree's trunk, I fight for equilibrium.

A lancing pain in my left hand. I look down and see a gash, blood seeping from the cut, dripping blackly to the earth below.

Sound returns.

I turn towards the crackling roar of the fire behind me.

The tower is fully engulfed now, the platform I had left only moments before, ablaze.

There is something ancient about the pillar of flame, set against the backdrop of night.

I double over and vomit onto the dirt.

The key is still where I dropped it.

I rest my forehead on the door a moment, then open it, go inside and lock it behind me.

Stumbling to the kitchen, I check that the back door is locked, set a chair under the handle. I move to the flour drum, dig out the cloth bag with the gun, dust it off, slip out the weapon, check that it is still loaded, then set it down on the kitchen table.

I go into the pantry and take out the first aid kit I had brought with me and set it next to the gun.

My clothes stink of smoke from the fire. I strip and kick them to the corner.

I pick up the gun again and pad naked to the bathroom.

Setting the weapon down on the sink with a soft clink, I step into the shower.

The drumming of water is a thunder inside my skull. I stand suspended inside it, watching blood swirl from the cut on my hand into the drain.

I dress in shorts and a T-shirt, then go back into the kitchen, taking the gun with me.

Pulling a long-necked beer from the fridge, I gulp it half down, then sit at the pine table.

My hands are trembling. The gash on my left hand throbs, the edges of the wound pale and crimped after the shower.

I open the first aid kit, take out a bottle of antiseptic and apply it to the cut. Ripping open a white packet with my teeth, I set the waterproof dressing over the cut.

My phone is gone.

I think about going outside to look for it, but fear stays me.

I lift myself from the kitchen table, walk to the couch with the gun, and drop onto it with a thud.

Adrenalin seeps away, to be replaced by exhaustion.

I had known, of course, that something like this might happen. I had returned to Eden Falls knowing they would come for me. But I hadn't expected to come this close to death.

Gerty had warned me. *'Amos's edict don't mean a thing to some. Not with Rebekah set against you. There's trouble brewing. Watch your back, child.'*

Rebekah.

At what point does a mother's loss begin to wane? What line is Rebekah prepared to cross?

I am overcome by an extraordinary fatigue, as if I have been scooped hollow and only a shell remains.

The scars on my arm glow. The world around me shimmers; I see myself back in prison, in my cell, writhing on my cot, my head fit to burst, the pain thundering from me in a violent shriek, tearing down the walls, collapsing time in on itself, until my head is filled, once again, with bright white light, washing away everything, pain and reason and all semblance of rational thought.

I feel the gun go slack in my hand.

Blackness descends.

69

ORIANNA: NOW

I awake with a start.

A moment of disorientation, and then memory jags back in.

A hoop of panic tightens around my chest; my heart thuds in my ears.

I check my watch. Barely an hour has passed since I stumbled back into the cottage, an hour cut out of my life and spirited away in dreamless sleep.

Picking up the gun, I walk to the front door, unlock it and step outside.

My knuckles tighten on the automatic's grip.

I turn in the direction of the fire tower. I can see a thin column of smoke rising above the canopy, a pillar of grey against a charcoal sky.

I am taken by an overwhelming urge to shoot up the dark. But what would that achieve?

My attackers are long gone, of that I am certain.

The futility of my mission falls hard on me.

I had returned to Eden Falls knowing it would take a miracle for me to achieve anything. Eighteen years have passed since that fateful day, eighteen years for the truth to lie undisturbed. So many had advised me to set my face against the past – my parole officer, Annie Ledet – to turn my back on the whole rotten edifice: this town, the people in it, the grotesque thing that happened to me here.

But I had known, on the day I'd walked out of the prison gates, that no matter where I went, no matter the distance, it would never be far enough.

I walk back into the cottage and put the gun down on the kitchen table.

And then I pull away the chair I had stuck under the handle of the rear door, unlock it, pick up the gun and walk outside.

The moon shimmers on the surface of the lake with a luminosity that makes me think of a photograph my cell-mate had kept pinned to the wall of our cell – phosphorescence on waves somewhere in the Pacific, the work of millions of bioluminescent marine organisms.

I strip to the skin and wade into the shallows, toes stirring thick mud beneath the gently lapping surface.

The water is warm, warmer than I had expected. The bruises on my back and ribs ache dully.

I scull towards deeper water, feel my feet leave the bottom.

Twisting around to face the cottage, I tread water, the sound of my breathing loud in my ears. The night closes in. I hear wings flapping in the darkness, the croak of a bullfrog. A pair of eyes glow in the shadows between the trees. Once upon a time, timber wolves roamed these forests, before arriving miners hunted them to extinction.

I imagine a time before man, when this land was the sole preserve of nature and the wild things that lived here. Ancient trees singing to each other in the star-filled night. Creatures that survived on the fertility of the naked earth. A balance, regulated by tooth and claw, blood and sap, and the brutal, unforgiving dynamics of an ever-changing environment. Humans upset that balance, as they do wherever they set their marker. Destruction and appropriation, the end products of the doctrine of manifest destiny.

And yet, I, too, am a product of this land.

Why had my mother come here? Why did she stay?

Christine died in this very lake.

Accident or suicide?

I close my eyes, try to freeze an image of those final moments in my mind: my mother, standing in the warm splash of light spilling from the cottage's rear door, staring sightlessly out at the lake, taking stock of her life, the mistakes she'd made, the wrong turns.

I imagine the light dulling in her eyes, the slow walk into the shallows, the water closing over her, the surrendering of herself to the dark.

Had she felt relief at the end? Or the naked terror of the grave?

Tears mingle with the droplets of water on my cheeks.

70

ORIANNA: NOW

A sound snaps my eyes open.

Luke is standing at the lake's edge.

How long has he been there?

I watch as he unbuttons his shirt.

I know that I must stop him, call out. But I say nothing, do nothing.

He undresses, folds his clothes carefully and places them beneath the old yew tree. A habit I remember from our trysting days in the woods.

He wades into the water, swims powerfully towards me.

When he reaches me, he treads water, blond hair plastered to his scalp, grey eyes shining in the dark. They burn like tiny stars.

He reaches for me; we fall into each other, embracing, skin on skin, as once we had, all those years ago. A circuit is closed. Time bends, and we are back in our woods, trembling in each other's arms, naked and unafraid, oblivious of the world and the obstacles in our path.

I hold my face to his throat, breathe in the smell of him, a smell that receded from me in prison, now as sharp as the musk of a wild animal.

His fingers stroke my back. The muscles of my stomach tighten; I am overcome by a sense of vertigo.

We swim back to the shore and stretch out on the grass.

'I've never stopped loving you,' he whispers.

My heart pops and soars. The heady feeling of being a girl again, remembering every endearment, every promise we made to each other in our youth, promises undone by fate. He was my first love, the boy of the woods, the only man I have known in intimacy. The four years since leaving prison have been barren. I had tried, more than once, driven by my body's need. Picked up strange men in smoke-filled bars. But always, at the last, something intervened.

Luke intervened.

We begin to move, awkwardly at first; and then I gather him in and the rhythm of the past returns. My desire is a flaming thirst, a violence of the mind. His hands travel along the length of my torso, my hips, between my legs; I arch my body to meet him. He kisses my lips, lifts his head to gaze down at me. His eyes hang wraithlike above me in the semi-dark. He kisses me again, then sets his lips to my throat, before moving down until his tongue finds my breast.

When he enters me, I cry out, in pain, in regret, in sorrow for all that I have lost and will never regain.

71

ORIANNA: NOW

An hour later, we are back inside the cottage, dressed, on the couch, my head resting on Luke's thighs.

He strokes my hair, murmurs words that I hear only dimly.

My thoughts are deep in the past.

In the woods, we had loved each other with the carelessness of sprites. It didn't matter that he was a Wyclerc and I the daughter of a woman who served his family. It didn't matter that he was white and I was not quite. We were sheltered by the gods of the woods, our love a rite ordained by nature.

But it had all been a lie.

We had imagined we might deceive the world, but all we'd managed was to deceive ourselves.

'Why did you do it?' I whisper.

At first, he doesn't understand.

'Why did you turn on me?'

I feel him take a deep breath. 'I had no choice.'

I want to tell him that there is *always* a choice. Even in prison, when it seemed that all choice had been taken from me. When all I could do was react, driven to act in ways that at first seemed alien to my nature, until I realised that this, too, was a part of who I am.

A throttling fury rises inside me. How dare Luke tell me that he'd had no choice?

The sense of betrayal howls in my ears; it seeps in from the woods, under the door and into the dark spaces inside my head. And, then, I hear Grace's voice in my ear, a throwaway comment she'd once made, one I had buried deep.

'Luke. Beautiful, beautiful Luke.'

The name crawls over my flesh. A fresh horror, a flame held against my cheek.

Grace. Grace and Luke.

The thought jerks me from Luke's lap.

I stand before him, look down at him with dark wonder.

I remember Luke's longstanding denials that he and Grace had ever been close ... My heart is racing. Is this the answer to the question that has plagued me for so long? I had never been able to fathom why Luke had betrayed me at my trial. Could this be the answer? ... A single thought tolls like a bell in my mind: *I have to let Luke go.*

I can never be with him. I can never trust him.

Luke breaks the silence. 'You can't stay here.'

I return to the moment. 'I don't have anywhere else to go.'

'Amos wants you to come up to the Big House.'

'I won't stay there. I won't live under the same roof as him.'

'They'll come back. Or others like them.'

'This town stole my life once before. I won't let them do it again.'

A silence in which the only sound is the ticking of Luke's watch.

'Where did you get the gun?'

'Does it matter?'

'If you're caught with it, tell them I gave it to you.'

'They said "that dead girl".'

'What?'

'The men who attacked me. They said: "Tell us where you buried that dead girl." Not Grace. That *dead girl*. They were out-of-towners.'

'You can't be sure of that.'

'Weren't you the one who told me that Peter Wyclerc and Sheriff Faulkes once hired out-of-towners to run Tommy Quinn out of Eden Falls?'

'For all you know, it *was* Quinn. You went out to the junkyard looking for him.'

'Why *not* Uncle Pete? He could have done it again,' I persist. 'He was pretty steamed after I spoke to him.'

'You're wrong. Peter wouldn't do that to you.'

His naivety, after all that has happened to me, kindles an elemental fury.

'You have to go. Your wife will be waiting.'

I expect him to deny that Abigail knows he is here, but he says nothing.

Reaching down, I take his face in my hands, look into his wolf's eyes, then kiss him hard on the lips, a brutal act that has nothing to do with affection or joy.

When I straighten, I see the glimmer of tears on his cheeks. In that final kiss, he has understood. Some things cannot be expressed by words – there is no need; the language of the heart decodes all that can be said and understood and felt, down in the chambers of the soul.

As I stand in the doorway and watch him drive away, I become aware of a sense of something vast inside me slipping its moorings, a pain I have held on to for too long.

The dirt of the world soils me; the corruption in men's hearts.

And my helplessness in the face of it.

72

ANNIE: THEN

The kids are boisterous today.

The lecture theatre is packed. Even those usually absent have decided to put in an appearance.

I am teaching an introductory class: Psychological Disorders 101. I usually begin with a general discussion about the history and definitions of common mental disorders. And it's usually not long before someone throws out the word *psychopath*.

Bang on cue, Adrian Scott, a young British student, asks about the nature of *true* psychopathy.

'Let's try a little experiment,' I say. 'How many of you have ever acted on impulse? Rashly, even?'

Nearly everyone puts up their hand.

'How many of you have ever put yourself first on occasion, to hell with everyone else?'

At least half the room admit to that one, though the true number will be higher.

'How many of you have actively avoided responsibility for something you really should have taken ownership of?'

More hands.

'How many of you have lived in the moment, thinking the future will take care of itself?'

A big response to that one.

I smile. 'Congratulations. Those of you who answered yes to at least three of those are exhibiting strong indicators of sociopathy.'

A buzz goes up and down the tiered seats.

'Confused? Don't be. The fact is that almost three per cent of any given human population can be diagnosed as exhibiting strong sociopathic tendencies. That's around ten million Americans. Of course, most sociopathy is, relatively speaking, benign. Not counting politicians and the narcissists on Wall Street.'

That gets a laugh, as ever.

Of course, I know *why* I have such an attentive audience today.

I wonder who will be the first to mention it. Yani, perhaps? Sitting there in his North Face T-shirt and hipster denim checked pants.

'Well, is anyone going to ask me about the elephant in the room?'

They exchange glances, wait a reverential minute, and then a tentative hand goes up. It's Priya Darshani, a student from Connecticut.

'What is she like?'

'You mean is she a slobbering, eye-rolling loony?' I smile.

The *New York Times* piece on my treatment of Orianna has attracted a lot of attention. I have already received a dozen calls and emails, mainly media requests, together with several academic enquiries, and more than a few cranks. There are, as I discovered early on, legions of sweaty obsessives congregating on online forums dedicated to proving Orianna's innocence, jerking off into wadded tissues as they leer at school photos of the beautiful teen killer.

I am now their saviour, as much as Orianna's.

For once, I am glad of the tight security here. College shootings have made armed officers on campus a common sight. But this is the land of the free and home of the brave. It wouldn't be difficult to track me down.

It is natural for my students to be curious. Suddenly, their boring old lecturer is famous. Or infamous. It makes no difference. Fame is the only currency this generation understands, regardless of its hue.

There is very little I can tell them, of course. Not that this tempers their curiosity. After all, they are now one degree of separation away from one of the most famous cases in the field they hope to one day practise in. The fact that I am taking a crack at 'fixing' The Girl in Cell A, at recovering her lost memories, makes the case real for them, lifting it from the dry pages of their textbooks.

We go back and forth for a while. I allow them to air their theories, the outlandish to the plausible. We briefly discuss dissociative amnesia, though we won't be going into the topic in depth until much later in the course. Yani, tongue firmly in cheek, suggests a field trip to visit Orianna. The class erupts in nervous laughter. I can tell they're not entirely sure how to deal with the idea that I am treating one of the country's most notorious murderers, a girl who killed back when she was roughly the same age as they are now.

What I keep to myself: that, ever since my last session with Orianna, a sliver of doubt has crept into me. So much about the way the original investigation was handled now feels ... shaky. My proximity to the material, to Orianna, has moved the needle, at least on my own perspective of the case.

How will I feel if I continue on this path?

No way to find out except to go there.

73

ORIANNA: NOW

The junkyard comes up on my right, gates wide open.

I park beside the wreck of an old Caddy.

The old man in charge of the place is sitting on a metal stool playing checkers with the Invisible Man, the board set on a wooden crate. He wears denim bib overalls above a plaid shirt. As rooted to the junkyard as a geological feature, the only things missing are a banjo and rotting teeth.

'Is Tommy here?'

He squints at me, jerks a thumb over his shoulder. 'Go down a piece, then take a right by the rain barrel.'

That morning, I had walked back to the fire tower, found it reduced to smouldering fragments, the base charred black, radiating heat.

It took twenty minutes to find my phone.

Still in working order.

Small mercies.

Returning to the cottage, I considered my options.

The night before, I had given short shrift to Luke, but the fact was, I'd escaped death by a hair's breadth. Whoever set those men on me is unlikely to relent, not until they have hounded me out of town. Or worse.

Yet . . . how can I leave?

My investigation has thrown up anomalies that cannot be ignored.

The fact that Gideon's wife, Rebekah, had been having an affair with the town hoodlum, Tommy Quinn. The fact that Gideon's brother, Peter, fought with him the night before his death. The fact that Grace's behaviour had changed that summer; the possibility that Grace had found a lover, one she had felt the need to keep a secret from her friends and family.

Something hovers at the edges of memory, something about Grace. Something I once saw, catching Grace in an unguarded moment . . . A fin flashes in the murky waters of my mind, and then is gone.

I almost scream in frustration.

I focus on Luke, recall the dumb hurt in his face as he had left the night before.

Pain twists inside me like glass. The rawness of my need had overtaken me in the lake, but now, in the cold light of day, I know that we made a mistake.

The fact that Luke is my cousin holds no reckoning for me. How can it be a crime to love the person fate has set in your path? No. What bothers me is the notion that I may have returned to Eden Falls *because* of him.

To remain here means making a choice.

I made that choice last night. To pursue truth – the truth of what happened to me all those years ago – I have to let Luke go. Last night, the thought I had tried so hard to suppress through all the years of my imprisonment found its way in. The sense that Luke knows more than he is telling me. That Luke and Grace had . . . what? The idea that Luke cheated on me, that, perhaps, *that* was why he'd lied on the stand . . . Each time I skate near the thought, fire scorches my brain; horror curdles my guts.

Luke. Beautiful, beautiful Luke.

74

ORIANNA: NOW

I move through a canyon of junk: eviscerated cars, household appliances, scrap metal shimmering under a burning sky.

The rain barrel cowers under a leaning tower of worn tyres, filled with stagnant bottle-green liquid, insect corpses floating in the murk.

Taking a right, I walk a ways further, until I come face to face with a mechanical crusher. A man is hunched in the cabin, operating the controls.

Tommy Quinn.

I wait until his eyes find me. For an instant, his posture registers surprise – or is it guilt? If he *is* one of the men from last night, then he won't have expected me to have survived, let alone turn up here.

He cuts the crusher's engine, climbs down from the cab.

A tall man, intimidatingly muscular, he is dressed in filthy blue overalls and has the sort of haggard face made intriguing by its myriad imperfections. Hair the colour of late-autumn corn, streaked with grey, plastered to a corrugated forehead.

'Hear you been looking for me.'

His voice. *Could he be one of the attackers?* I realise that things happened too quickly last night for me to be sure of anything.

'I want to talk to you about Gideon. And Rebekah.'

A wariness enters his eyes. 'Well, now,' he says finally. 'That sounds like a serious conversation. Mind if I spruce up a little?'

He doesn't wait for an answer. Instead, he turns on his heel and stalks off.

I follow him around a couple of corners to a dirt clearing. To one side, a grey-painted trailer is set on cinder blocks. An awning stretches out from the roof, below which sits a plastic table, coupled with a pair of chairs. An old painted corkboard sign hangs from a nail on the side of the trailer: TRESSPASSERS WILL BE FUCKED UP.

A jerry-rigged shower cubicle is located yards away, a hosepipe standing in for a showerhead.

He ducks inside the trailer, returns with a towel, a denim shirt, and a pair of blue jeans.

He strips, all the while looking right at me.

I turn away, hear him walk to the shower cubicle, then a gush of water from the hosepipe.

75

ORIANNA: NOW

Ten minutes later, Quinn ushers me into one of the plastic chairs beneath the awning, sets a couple of sweating beers on the table.

He smells of pine. His hair sticks up like spun glass.

I ignore the beer.

'Come on, now. Ain't polite to accost a man in his own home then turn down his liquor. Especially not a fellow con.'

Blood rushes to my face. 'When Gideon was killed, you were having an affair with Rebekah . . . Did Gideon know?'

He freezes, then picks up his beer, sucks the liquid through his teeth. 'When I heard you were back in town, I thought to myself: now there's a gal with brass balls . . . You think you can rewrite the past? You think you can make any of these people change what they *know*?'

'I just want the truth.'

'The truth? The truth is, your mother had a great ass and Gideon had his head all the way up it.' There is a repressed ferocity in his voice. 'If I were you, I'd get out of town while I still can. Eden Falls is nothing but a tar pit.'

'Is that why *you* stuck around?'

'Me? I got no choice, baby doll.'

'Because of Rebekah?'

His jaw tightens. 'All right. It's just us here. Two jailbirds shooting the shit . . . Sure, Rebekah and I had a thing way back when. I remember the first time she drove that Corvette of hers into Casey's shop. Blew my hair back. I knew the first time I laid eyes on her that she didn't belong with no Wyclerc. Especially not Gideon – walking around town as if he owned the place, higher than a cat's ass. Rebekah came from dirt, and the thing about dirt . . . it never quite rubs off, no matter how far up the ladder you go.' His gaze drifts back into the past. 'I don't mind admitting I had a hunger for her. Ain't never felt anything like it, before or since. A woman like that, taking up with a man like me? Don't happen too often. I thanked the Lord and didn't ask why.' He locks eyes with me. 'You ever felt a hunger like that?'

Heat rises to my face. Images of Luke from the night before.

'Did Gideon know about you and Rebekah?'

He seems to debate whether to answer. 'Guess it don't matter now . . . Yeah, Gideon found out.'

'How?'

'I told him.'

I blink. 'When?'

'On the day of the Forest Festival.'

My mouth is suddenly dry. 'You confronted Gideon on the day he died?'

'I told him I was fucking his wife. He didn't know whether to shit or wind his watch.'

I swallow. 'Where, where was this?'

'In town. They'd come down to see the pageant.'

'Why? I mean, why did you tell him? Why then?'

He looks off into space. 'Because he didn't deserve her. Because he didn't treat her right. Everyone knew he was screwing around on her. A woman like that? . . . No, sir, he didn't deserve Rebekah. I guess he got what was coming to him.'

I take a deep breath. 'Did you kill him?'

He grins, sips on his beer, sets it down with great deliberation. 'I believe a jury of our peers convicted *you* of that crime.'

What had I expected? A confession? 'Where were you when Gideon was killed?'

'I can't remember where I was last week, let alone eighteen years ago.'

'What about Grace?'

He frowns. 'What about her?'

'Did you talk to her that day?'

His eyes shine darkly. 'No. I did not.'

'I hear Peter Wyclerc tried to run you out of town a few years back.'

He snorts. 'I wouldn't give Peter the sweat off my balls. Sitting up there in his office like a dumb stepchild – he's lucky I didn't put him in the ground for that stunt.'

'Is it true that he and Gideon didn't get along?'

'They hated each other's guts.'

'And Rebekah?'

'What about her?'

'Do you think she could have been involved in Gideon's death?'

He moves faster than I would have expected for such a big man. His chair hits the ground, and he is looming over me, face red.

'You go near Rebekah and I'll gut you like a fish, baby doll.'

I react instinctively. The gun is in my hand and pointing at him before I can even register the fact.

He stares at it, breathing through his nose like a bull.

Finally, he turns, sets the chair right again and sits back down.

'Well, look who went and grew up.'

'Answer my question.'

'Rebekah had nothing to do with Gideon's death. Why would she kill him?'

'Because he was cheating on her. Because she found out about me. Because he'd betrayed her.'

'She ain't built like that.'

Realisation dawns. 'You love her, don't you?'

His eyes flare. 'You stay away from her.'

'Does she feel the same way about you? I'm guessing not. She used you. Used you to get back at her cheating husband. But she didn't anticipate that a low-rent asshole like you might actually fall for her ... I'll ask you again: did you kill Gideon?'

'Go fuck yourself.'

'Did you come after me last night, out at Elvira Trueblood's place?'

His eyes don't move from mine.

'I'm not leaving Eden Falls until I get to the truth.'

I stand, back off, then turn and walk away as fast as I can, resisting the urge to break into a run.

76

ORIANNA: NOW

My hands are still trembling by the time I pull into the dirt yard out front of Olsen's Hardware Store.

I wait a moment in the car, my mind still on the encounter with Quinn.

I recall a discussion with Annie Ledet, during one of our earliest sessions, on the nature of evil. I cannot remember precisely what led us there, but the latter part of the conversation has stayed with me.

Evil, Ledet conjectured, is a function of something more than mere circumstance or learned behaviour. In her long years analysing the very worst that humanity has spawned, she has come to believe that evil is a presence, akin to a spirit or vapour, that resides inside the human body. When it finds a suitable host, it feeds and grows fat, consuming the soul a piece at a time, rendering the host ever more liable to commit acts that might otherwise have been circumscribed by the restrictions of a moral or religious upbringing.

It is the only way she can explain the horrors of the human condition, the big and little evils that men unleash upon one another.

In prison, among murderers and thieves, I had rarely felt the presence of such malevolence.

But in Tommy Quinn's eyes, I glimpsed that gleeful evil spirit look out at me and mark my card.

How much of what he told me can I believe?

Why did he speak to me at all?

I sensed a reservoir of resentment inside him. There is no doubt in my mind that he feels genuine anger towards the Wyclercs. And yet, his infatuation with Rebekah appears to have remained undimmed. A burning fire, part lust, part love – for even creatures such as Tommy Quinn are at the mercy of the heart's riptides. That much prison taught me, surrounded by the brutal and the brutalised, each equally liable to the poetic or the profane.

I get out of the Chevy and crunch over gravel past a pale-blue pickup to the hardware store, built to resemble a nineteenth-century trapper's lodge, with a wooden façade and a pair of crossed axes above the door. A white-hot noonday sun trembles in a sky as blue as baked china.

The store is all but deserted, save a couple of men in work boots and grubby T-shirts conversing at the head of the furthest aisle. They look up as I enter.

I make my way to the rear of the store, where I discover a youngish man in a baseball cap and a T-shirt patched with sweat. He leans on the counter, playing with his phone.

He looks up and begins a smile, which quickly congeals on his pimply, bewhiskered face. Recognition flares in his eyes.

The Girl In Cell A

I have come here because I am convinced that there is someone out there, in the woods around the cottage. Watching. Waiting. Not the guys who attacked me, but someone else, someone monitoring my every act.

It's about time I flushed my secret admirer out.

The plan had come to me as I had sat in the lee of Tommy Quinn's trailer. Acting on it now gives me something concrete to focus on, a way of taking a breath, a moment's respite, following the turbulence of the past days.

I tell the store clerk what I need.

He gulps, caught between acceding to my request and running out the door. Clearly, he recognises me. I doubt there is a soul in town who doesn't by now.

Ten minutes later, I leave the store with the item I came for, 300 dollars lighter, my purchase in a large canvas bag that I stick in the Chevy's trunk.

77

ORIANNA: NOW

I find Gerty in the basement of the library.

It is marginally cooler down here, but not in any way that makes it more pleasant.

The basement once served as a storehouse for the endless train of paperwork generated by the courthouse; now it houses what Gerty calls her 'book surgery', a small room with a scratched parquet floor, a long, polished workbench, a swivel chair, and a saggy two-seater couch that looks as if it was rescued from the dump.

Gerty is busy reattaching the cover to an ancient hardback of *The Call of the Wild*.

She looks at me pointedly over the top of her glasses. 'You look as if your stomach's fit to burst. Got a story for me, Scheherazade?'

The momentary calm I had tried to assert with my half-thought out plan to nail my voyeur, my trip to the hardware store, evaporates. The reality of my situation crashes back in, a flood of frustration and anger in its wake.

It pours out of me. The meeting with Dick Hogan, the men who'd attacked me, the confrontation with Tommy Quinn.

The Girl In Cell A

And Luke.

Gerty listens without interrupting. When I finish, she spreads wide her arms. 'Come to me, child.'

For a moment, I hesitate, and then I dissolve into her. Hot tears squeeze from my eyes. I came back to Eden Falls riding on the back of eighteen years of hurt, a pilot light of rage that I had nursed through anguish few can comprehend. I knew there would be resistance, that the good folk of Eden Falls would deny me, just as they'd turned against me all those years ago. But this?

I think of how much of myself I have obliterated simply to survive. And now here I am again, facing down the invisible furies in the hearts of my fellow citizens.

Before I know it, Gerty is lowering me onto the couch. I curl into a ball, and darkness falls.

78

ANNIE: THEN

'I've started to dream again.'

My next session with Orianna takes place on a beautiful wintry Wednesday, a fortnight after the college lecture. There is no longer any doubt that the season has turned. I left the house this morning dressed like a Cossack.

The therapy room, thankfully, is warm. They have made an effort to get the radiators working properly. The pipes hum and gurgle.

Orianna has just come from the prison yard. The cold has rouged her dusky cheeks.

She seems subdued. It is our first meeting since I asked her to relive Detective Hogan's testimony at her trial. No doubt, the session stirred up bad memories. That is a *good* thing. Activating memories adjacent to the ones that have fallen into a black hole is a tried-and-tested method of treatment in cases of dissociative amnesia.

My plan for today's session is to move on to the next segment of the trial, but Orianna leads me in a different direction. I roll with it. Sometimes, it is important to allow the patient to dictate terms.

'I think that's good news, don't you?' I say, responding to her statement about dreaming.

She says nothing.

'Is there a particular dream you would like to share with me?'

The silence lingers, and then, abruptly, she begins to speak.

'I'm in my cell. It's as hot as an oven and my body is slick with sweat. I'm standing in the corner of the room. My father, Gideon, is sitting on the cot. His head is partly blown away. His lips move. It's grotesque.

'He says, "You disgust me."

'I try to shake my head, but paralysis holds me. Sweat streams into my eyes.

'He says, "Your mother was a whore. You're the daughter of a whore."

'I try to speak, but nothing comes.

'He says, "I gave her what she wanted. You took it all away. *You* killed Christine. *You* killed Grace."

'His ruined face breaks into a wretched smile.

'"You're a killer. A wolf. You always have been, little girl of mine."'

79

ORIANNA: NOW

I am being shaken awake.

I blink up at Gerty. A nervous figure hovers at her shoulder. Artie.

I sit upright on the sofa. 'How long have I been out?'

'About four hours. It's just gone seven.'

'Why didn't you wake me?'

'You were exhausted. Not just physically, but emotionally. Did you really think you'd waltz on back here and this place wouldn't take a toll?' Gerty plops down beside me, takes my hand. 'You gotta ask yourself if this is worth it.'

I say nothing. And then, 'I don't have answers for you, Gerty. All the time I was inside, all I wanted was to get back here, to Eden Falls. I had this fire inside me. I worked with a therapist, a Dr Annie Ledet. She helped me unravel so many things, about myself, about growing up here. But there were some places even Annie couldn't go with me.' I grimace. 'Sometimes I think I'm living inside my own head.'

Gerty pats my hand. 'Artie's got something to show you.'

The Girl In Cell A

I see that the boy is clutching a tablet to his chest like a protective shield.

He holds it out to Gerty, who takes it and hands it to me.

The screen is logged on to the Eden Falls Community Group Facebook page.

An event notice:

7 p.m. – Emergency meeting at the Town Hall
Later today we will be convening at the Town Hall to discuss the unacceptable situation with regards to the convicted murderer now residing in our midst. The individual in question appears to have received the 'sanction' of Amos Wyclerc to not only remain in Eden Falls, but to go about her business unhindered. But others in the Wyclerc household are far from happy with the situation. We cannot allow a killer to remain among us, a danger to our children, a constant fear for every law-abiding citizen. We urge you to attend this meeting.

80

ORIANNA: NOW

By general agreement, the Eden Falls Town Hall is a far cry from the architectural masterpiece that many of the townsfolk had been led to expect when plans for the building were first mooted some half a century earlier.

Occupying the entire northern aspect of the town square, the rectangular, two-storey red-brick building stands directly across from the county library with only the great bronze of Nathaniel and the Wolf in between. Tall, white-trimmed windows make regimented rows up the front elevation; a cheap-looking cornice winds around the top, above white letters reading, simply, TOWN HALL.

Gerty dogs me across the square, all the while urging me to reconsider.

I ignore her, march up the shallow flight of steps fronting the main entrance, through a pair of thick oak doors and into a deserted anteroom.

I charge up a flight of curving marble steps to the first floor.

Here, I am brought to a halt outside the meeting hall by a stentorian voice rolling out from an open doorway.

Through a glass panel, I see a sea of heads on white-painted chairs, all looking up at a stage where a man I don't recognise is holding court. Barrel-shaped, and sweating so hard he looks as if he just walked in from a thunderstorm.

'That's Cal Harris,' whispers Gerty. 'The new mayor. He's a fat piece of shit who'd sell his own mother to human traffickers if he thought it would get him in with the Wyclercs.'

A beat.

'Don't go in there, child. There's nothing you can say to them that will make a whit of difference.'

Behind Harris, sat on a row of chairs, are others that I do recognise. Two women who I am certain served on the jury that convicted me. And Rebekah Wyclerc.

Sitting beside Rebekah, expression stoic: Peter Wyclerc.

'Don't let anger get the better of you,' Gerty says softly. 'You're not yourself. You haven't been yourself for a very long time.'

I look at her. 'Then who am I, Gerty?'

I turn and step into the hall.

The gathering has an electric feel to it; the energy of a religious convention, flushed faces practically glowing with excitement. Here is impotent rage given rein to express itself, the type of rage that once led to torchlit pogroms in these parts and nooses in the dark.

As I walk through the hall, I hear a few gasps. An astonished murmur ripples from the back rows.

I climb onto the stage.

Harris's foaming narrative stutters to a halt. His head wobbles on his neck; his eyes cross themselves.

I swing my gaze over the astonished faces of those seated behind him, and then to the crowd below, who are looking up in bemused horror.

The good folk of Eden Falls.

They are what America tells us we are supposed to be. The kind who spend their lives chasing the American dream: a steady pay cheque, a white-picket-fenced home, pizza parties and cookie bakes for the kids, barbeques and Monday night football for the grown-ups. They wear flannel shirts and seersucker pants and oxblood loafers. They make luncheon meat sandwiches for their kids and send them off to school to learn about George Washington and the Second Amendment and war in places they couldn't find on a map.

By most definitions, they are good people.

But what I see is a roomful of buckle-shoed Puritans in black hats, the inheritors of Salem. They need *this*. A common enemy, someone they can all agree to hate. Only then might they drain the town of its natural toxins, the cruel disappointments and rancid jealousies that feed on their souls.

My voice booms into the silence. 'You think you're righteous, but you have no idea what *right* and *wrong* truly mean. You have no idea of the road I've travelled to get here.' A beat. 'I didn't kill Gideon. Somewhere in this town, a killer has lived free for eighteen years. I'm going to find out what happened, even if I have to burn this place to the ground.'

I turn to look directly at Rebekah. Gideon's widow is stock-still in her chair, face as white as paper.

'You can't get rid of me. You can't do a damn thing to

me that hasn't already been done to me. I'm not afraid of you. *You* should be afraid of me.'

Peter Wyclerc stands. 'This is a God-fearing town. There's no place for you here.'

A retort springs to my lips, but I stop as Rebekah rises and steps towards me. I tense, expecting another physical attack. But a strange expression, half rage, half sorrow, distorts her features. 'Please. Tell me where you buried my daughter. I need to know.'

I blink. Something stabs through my ear and into my brain, a memory, as needle sharp as the blade of a stiletto. Rebekah's outline wavers, becomes fluid. I watch her transform into Grace. Who is grinning at me, blood seeping from the corners of her eyes, pooling in her mouth.

Tell her. Tell her the truth. You know what really happened that day. It's right there, inside you.

I turn and stagger away.

By the time I am halfway to the door, I am running.

81

ORIANNA: NOW

Sheriff Hank Faulkes is waiting for me at the bottom of the town-hall steps.

'Nice speech.'

'What do you want?' My heart is racing. I feel insane.

He hooks his thumbs into his belt. 'Just to talk.'

I hear Gerty come up behind me. 'You let her alone, Hank.'

He tips his hat. 'Gerty.'

Gerty scowls in return. 'Why don't you do your job and go throw a bucket of water over that lynch mob in there?'

'It's a lawful gathering. They have concerns, legitimate ones.'

'They're fixing to get them some vigilante justice and you know it. Last night, two men attacked Orianna out in the woods. It's a miracle she's still alive.'

Faulkes transfers his gaze to me. 'That true?'

I study his face. Eyes as dead as ash. Could Faulkes have been involved in the attack? According to Luke, the sheriff had once hired men to run Tommy Quinn out of town, at Peter Wyclerc's behest.

'It doesn't matter. They're not going to scare me away.'

'So I heard you say.' Faulkes purses his lips. 'I need to ask you some questions.'

'Are you arresting me?'

'I don't think Amos would take too kindly to that. I just want to talk.'

Back in his office, he slips off his hat, sets it down on the windowsill, then turns and drops into his chair, waving me into the seat opposite. He points at a pitcher of lemonade. 'Help yourself.'

My first instinct is to refuse, but then I change my mind, pour a glass, drain it in one gulp.

'They're afraid of you. Not just because you're a convicted murderer. But because you remind them of their own complicity. The truth is, aside from Amos, no one in Eden Falls shed tears for Gideon Wyclerc. The man was a fool and a philanderer. Stuck his dick in places he should have known to leave well enough alone. But you already know all about that.'

I say nothing.

'Amos told them to lay off. I don't know what tale you've spun him, but he's an old man. Way I hear it, he could go at any time. The moment that happens, what do you think is going to happen to *you*? . . . I hear you visited with Tommy Quinn.'

My fingers tighten around the glass. 'Quinn told you that?'

'No. The old frog who runs the junkyard. Lamar.'

'Quinn was having an affair with Rebekah Wyclerc when Gideon was killed. Why didn't that come out at my trial? Earlier today, he told me he'd confronted Gideon on the day he died. Practically shoved the affair down his throat.'

The muscles in Faulkes's throat tense. 'I'm betting if I ask Tommy to confirm that, he'll laugh me right out of that trailer he calls a home.'

I say nothing.

He leans forward. 'Tommy Quinn is dangerous. You're playing with fire.'

'Did you ever check his alibi for the time Gideon was killed?'

'Why would we? He was never a suspect.'

I think about something I once read. How it is impossible to explain the difference between darkness and light to a man born blind.

'You've never been held to account, have you?' I say. 'You knew this town better than Dick Hogan. You must have heard rumours about Rebekah and Quinn. But you did nothing.'

His eyes recede down a long, dark tunnel.

I set down my glass and stand up. 'Thanks for the lemonade.'

82

ORIANNA: NOW

Amos is in his bedroom, a cavernous space that could have billeted a legion of Confederate soldiers during the war. He is on his back on an enormous claw-footed bed, soaked in sweat, eyes closed, lips moving without sound.

Cletus Barnes, as ever, had let me in. 'I'm afraid Amos isn't well.'

'I need to see him.'

'He's not up to taking visitors today.'

I blinked, shoved past him.

A moment of astonished silence, and then he'd fallen in behind me.

Now, he stands at my shoulder. 'Dr Andrews has been and gone. He says the fever should break soon.'

'I'll sit with him awhile.'

'Would you like something to eat?'

I hesitate. 'Yes. That would be fine.'

He nods, then turns and leaves, closing the door gently behind him.

I drag over an ornate Versailles armchair with a gold-painted hardwood frame and satin upholstery.

A mist of perspiration hangs on Amos's forehead. His hair is matted with sweat.

His face contorts: 'God help them! God help them!'

I wait, but he says no more.

Cletus delivers a bowl of broth, chunks of beef floating inside it, a square of bread on the side. 'When you've eaten, Martha would like to see you.'

The request takes me by surprise.

'She's at the end of the hall.'

83

ANNIE: THEN

Dreams are important. Ever since Freud put the cat among the pigeons with *The Interpretation of Dreams*, psychoanalysts have sought to use dreams as a sort of Rosetta Stone to decipher their underlying meaning. To Freud, dreams were about wish fulfilment, our unconscious desires expressed through the mechanism of dreams. More importantly, he rooted dreams in *real-world* experiences.

I am discussing Orianna's dream with Frank, my head of department.

We are on a 7 a.m. Amtrak, shuttling to a day-long symposium; a grind of dry papers, academic grandstanding, cheap catering and shitty hotel rooms. If we play our cards right, we can all go out together for an evening meal that fits inside our twenty-dollars-a-head allowance. Domino's Pizza, here we come.

'Well, what do *you* think?'

I smile. The classic therapist's in-joke.

'I think it shows a deep-seated animus towards her father.'

'Stemming from?'

'Rejection.'

'Real or imagined?'

'Well, the rejection was real. In the sense that her father – Gideon – failed to acknowledge her existence, even though she was right there, living on the same estate.'

'We're assuming he knew?'

'That's my working assumption.'

'And have you asked Orianna why *she* thinks he never acknowledged her?'

'I'm working her up to it. Remember, it was the prosecution's assertion that it was the very revelation of Gideon being her father that touched off her "psychotic rampage".'

Frank gives a wry shake of the head.

Psychotic rampage. Hollywood has a lot to answer for.

'Shades of an Electra complex?' he says.

The Electra complex is the female corollary to Freud's by now largely discredited Oedipus complex, the theory that postulates that men have an inbuilt desire to supplant their fathers – harm them, in the extreme version – while harbouring feelings of poorly sublimated desire towards their mothers.

The Electra complex suggests something similar happens with girls – namely, that they fixate on their fathers in a semi-sexual way, resulting in feelings of jealousy and antipathy towards their mothers.

I had considered the theory, of course. Clearly, there were signs that Orianna resented her mother. But she had been convicted of murdering her father. And the Electra complex applies to a father who is *present*, not one who was absent – as a father – for all of Orianna's life up until the day of his death.

Still. There *is* a chance that Orianna had sexually fixated on Gideon – an attractive, wealthy and powerful older man in close proximity during her adolescent years, the son of her mother's employer. Perhaps the internal contradictions set up by such feelings when set against the ultimate revelation that Gideon was her father had caused a catastrophic mental breakdown, resulting in violence.

Not for the first time, I wish I could have been a fly on the wall in Gideon's cabin at the very moment when Orianna had turned up that day.

What had she said to him?

How had he responded?

And what had truly happened next?

My rational self knew that the prosecution's explanation had to be the correct one: an enraged and conflicted Orianna had picked up a weapon and shot Gideon.

But mysteries continued to swirl around that precise instant, questions that no one has satisfactorily answered.

After all, why would a girl who had yearned for a father her whole life shoot him dead on the very day that she found him?

84

ORIANNA: NOW

I find eighty-two-year-old Martha Wyclerc propped up in bed, smoking, eyes glued to a television.

Her wrinkled face broadens into a smile. Picking up a remote control, she turns off the set, then crushes her cigarette into an ashtray balanced on her lap.

'Come in, dear.' She pats the bed.

I pad towards her and sit gingerly down beside her.

'Let me take a look at you.' She peers at me through thick glasses with beaded pink frames. Her wispy grey hair is pulled back; she is comfortable in cotton pyjamas, pink, with a sequinned outline of a bucking horse on the front.

I recall Martha as a somewhat otherworldly presence at the Big House. She is Amos's sister-in-law, his older brother Abel's widow, and Luke's grandmother. I rarely interacted with her back then; know very little about her. She had always seemed to me to be one of those women who kept their own counsel, never made a fuss.

'How's the old buzzard doing?'

'The fever should break soon.'

'And you? How are you doing?'

My breath catches in my throat. A question asked so few times of me in the past eighteen years that it is still a surprise when it is volunteered willingly. 'I'm fine.'

'I hear you've riled up the good folk of Eden Falls ... Do you remember your scripture? Elijah and the prophets of Baal? You're going to have slay every last prophet if you want to get anywhere.'

I am unsure how to take this. 'Amos told me that you're bedridden.'

'Well, I'm not lying here waiting on a lover.' She cackles, face lighting up. 'Did Cletus feed you?'

'Yes.'

'He's a fine man. A fine heart and fine-looking, to boot.'

I stare at her.

'I'm old, girly, not dead. Did Cletus ever tell you how he ended up here?'

I realise that I had never asked. Cletus had always simply been part of the furniture.

'Amos's father, Nathaniel, brought him into the house. Cletus's daddy was a convict, one of those prisoners laying track upstate, chained at the ankle, hammering metal all day long. His mother died during childbirth. Nathaniel was out there, opening up a mine; the rail company wanted to run a railhead right up to the mine's front door.' A pause. 'Cletus's daddy was shot dead by a white foreman – no one really knows what for. The official line is that he tried to escape. We don't know why Nathaniel took an interest in what happened, but, according to Abel, he decided to bring Cletus back here. Call it a whim. And here he's been ever since.'

I have no idea what to say to this. White saviour

narratives don't hold much attraction for me, not after everything that has happened. To me, to my mother.

'Cletus loves Amos like a father. Truth be told, he's been a better son to that old man than any of his real kids. Not that you'll ever hear Amos say it – the man's still pining over his beloved Gideon.'

'You sound as if you didn't think much of him. Gideon, I mean.'

'That boy was dumber than a stump. And the way he carried on with women ... Let's just say, some men, the earth is sucking on their feet soon as they come out their momma's womb.'

'Why did you want to speak to me?'

She picks up her crushed cigarette. 'I thought you could use a friend.'

'I don't need friends. Not in this house.'

'We deserve that. The truth is, I never really believed you did it. Killed Gideon. Or Grace. But I come from a generation of women who are admired but rarely listened to. Amos made the decision for all of us.'

'If that's an apology, you can keep it.'

Martha's face is tinged with sorrow. 'Your mother was a good woman. She knew what she wanted in life and wasn't shy about going after it. She'd talk to me, ask me why I didn't just take what was mine and leave. Sometimes, I wish I'd listened to her.'

I struggle not to let my astonishment show. I had no idea my mother had ever been close to Martha.

'That surprise you? It shouldn't. Christine was a woman of secrets, and she knew how to keep them. Case in point: when she first arrived in this house, she was pregnant. With you. Didn't show, of course – she couldn't have been far in. But *I* knew. Caught her one morning puking up her guts in one of the bathrooms. Tried to pass it off as a stomach bug. I'm guessing that's why Gideon brought her here in the first place. They met in Barrier, when your mother was working there.'

I blink, stunned. Can it be true? What did it mean, if anything?

'What makes you believe I couldn't have hurt Grace?' I say, finally.

'Grace told me you were the only real friend she ever had.'

My surprise is evident. Throughout the time we had known each other, I never had the impression that Grace thought of our relationship as anything more than a lukewarm friendship born of proximity. The idea that she considered me the only true friend of her short life seems preposterous.

Martha reads my thoughts. 'She was a hard girl to like, wasn't she? Self-absorbed. Too beautiful to attract anything but envy and desire. No one took her seriously.' She stops. 'She had a troubled heart. Kinda reminds me of you. Two peas in a pod, the pair of you.'

My eyes rove over Martha's lined face, the way it glows from within, the luminosity of her gaze. My mother once told me that life is a constant test, a series of leaps of faith. You can reside within yourself and never trust anyone. Or you can make that leap.

I tell Martha everything.

When I finish, she plucks a lighter from the nightstand and lights the half-crushed cigarette. She puffs smoke sideways, away from me.

'That's quite a story.'

'Do you think Tommy Quinn could have been involved in Gideon's death?'

'Anything's possible. But I don't know him from Adam. Rumour and gossip aren't exactly hard evidence.'

'What about Rebekah?'

She raises an eyebrow. 'You think Rebekah might have hurt Gideon? Even if that were so, it wouldn't explain what happened to Grace. I don't much like Rebekah, but you're not going to convince me she had anything to do with her own daughter's disappearance. She loved that girl. She just wasn't a very good mother.'

The thought tolls in my mind.

Perhaps that's the reason Grace exaggerated our closeness, at least to herself and to Martha. Grace had never said it out loud, but the fact that Rebekah had been less of a mother than she had desired would have chimed with what Grace knew of my own difficulties with Christine. Perhaps Martha was right. Grace and I were more alike than anyone might have believed possible.

I want to ask Martha if she had ever heard rumours about Grace and Luke, but cannot summon up the words.

Instead, I dredge up something Amos told me, right at the beginning, about Martha's daughter, Hannah. 'Were *you* a good mother?'

She stiffens. 'What's that supposed to mean?'

'Why did Hannah leave the family? Why did you stay on here? At the Big House?'

Martha's eyes become hollow. 'I stayed because ... I feel Abel's presence here. In every brick of this place. By rights, this should have been his. He was a different man to Amos. He had the light of life in his heart. But he was stubborn, so goddamned stubborn.' Tears well in her eyes. 'Hannah just up and packed her bags one day. She was barely eighteen. Moved to New York. I tried to get her to come back, but my daughter is nothing if not resolute.'

'And she never told you why she left?'

'She told me.'

I wait, but Martha simply lifts the cigarette to her lips. 'Not my story to tell.' She hesitates. 'It might even have something to do with—'

'With—?'

'With what you're doing here.'

'What do you mean?'

Martha blinks. 'Nothing. I'm just a crazy old mare. Ignore me.'

'Martha, if there's something you know—?'

'The water's muddy enough for you as it is, child.'

I want to press her, but realise it would be pointless. 'Have you seen her – Hannah – since she left?'

'I tried to visit, at first, when I was still able. She refused to see me. Won't speak to me. Nearly forty years.' She sighs. 'I keep tabs on her, from a distance. I know she married, I know she has children. But I've never met my grandchildren.'

'And she hasn't come to see you, even though you're . . . ?'

'Won't set foot in this house. Wants nothing to do with us. Helluva thing when your own blood can't stand the sight of you.'

'Can you tell me where she lives?'

'They moved to a town in Durham County, about ten years back.' She picks up a pen from the nightstand, scribbles on a notepad. 'I paid a man to find them. That's her address. Never mustered up the courage to go out there myself.'

I slip the paper into my pocket. 'What about David? Do you see much of him?'

'He comes by now and again. It's not easy for him, not after his stroke.' She grimaces. 'Doesn't get any easier, no matter how old they get. Seeing your kids in pain.'

'Are you lonely here?'

Martha's eyes widen in surprise. 'Do you know, you might be the first person who's ever asked me that ... I've been lonely here every single day since I lost Abel. But I get by. Cletus is an angel. And Ruth, Peter's wife, looks in on me. She's a good woman, a good Christian.'

I change direction. 'Is it true that Peter and Gideon never got on?'

Martha huffs. 'They loathed each other. A lot like Abel and Amos. I guess it runs in the blood.'

'Do you think—?'

'That Peter could have killed Gideon?' She snorts. 'Peter's a haircut and a fancy suit. I can't see him picking up a shotgun and shooting his own brother dead.'

85

ORIANNA: NOW

I look in on Amos before I leave. He is awake, a glass of water trembling in his hand.

I walk to the bed, take the glass from him and set it to his mouth.

The simple act exhausts him, and he falls back against his pillows. His body exudes a powerful odour of sweat.

'You were shouting out, "God help them." Who were you talking about?'

He says nothing.

'Was it the miners? The ones who died in the accident?'

His lungs whistle in his chest. 'Age spares no man, Orianna. It's our folly believing that things will be different when it's our turn. You find yourself letting go of all that you once held so dear. Wealth, desire, earthly appetites. Your heart is filled with a new hunger. To know that your time was well spent, that you won't leave as a cypher. That you can lay to rest old ghosts.'

I have no idea what to say to him.

He reaches out and clutches my wrist. His palm is ferociously hot.

'I'm sorry. I'm sorry for the way I treated you and your mother. I believed them; the authorities. I believed everything they told me.'

Tears blur my vision. Heat flows from him until my arm feels molten.

I watch him awhile, until he falls back into the darkness of his dreams, then take his hand from my arm and set it down on the bedspread, get to my feet and quietly leave the room.

86

ORIANNA: NOW

Downstairs, before leaving, I track down Cletus.

He is fiddling in the kitchen, by the double-doored steel fridge.

I hover in the doorway.

The story that Martha had told me, about Cletus's origins, has struck me deeply . . . How had I never thought to ask? Did that not make me as contemptible as the others who'd moved through this home and mistaken Cletus's service for servitude, his complaisance for serfdom?

He must have sensed my presence because he turns his head.

'Is he still awake?'

'No.'

He leans into the fridge. 'Would you like something to drink?'

'No.'

A glassy rattle. 'Did you see Martha?'

'Yes.'

I expect him to ask more, but he says nothing. He emerges from the fridge with a bottle of white wine, pulls a pair of crystal wine glasses from an overhead unit, comes over to the island and fills a glass. He tips the neck of the bottle in my direction. 'Are you sure?'

I hesitate.

He pours a second glass, holds it out. I walk forward and take it, gulp down a large mouthful, set it down on the pecan-coloured granite of the island.

'We've never talked about that day,' I say.

He perches himself on a stool, swirls his glass around.

'Were you here in the house?'

'I was.'

'Did you . . . did you see my mother that day?'

'I did.'

'How did she seem?'

He looks at me. 'Your mother was a complicated person. There were times she found it difficult to make sense of the world. When that happened, she felt compelled to act. She wasn't one of those willing to surrender her fate to a higher authority.'

'I don't know what that means.'

He places a finger on the glass's rim. 'She was a woman constantly at war with herself. I believe she was a good person at heart, but couldn't reconcile that with her desires and her ambition. She wasn't much for perseverance.'

'Why did she tell me about Gideon that day? That he was my father?'

'I don't know.' He hesitates. There's a lightning-shaped scar on his temple, which I don't remember. It reminds me of something, someone else. But before I can place it, he says, 'I saw your mother and Rebekah in conversation through a window just before Gideon's death. I couldn't make out what they were saying, but your mother was visibly upset.'

This was confirmation of what Dick Hogan, the ex-detective who'd investigated Gideon's murder, had told me. He hadn't mentioned that it was Cletus who'd seen my mother and Rebekah arguing.

'Did *you* know? That I was Gideon's daughter?'

'No.'

'But you suspected?'

He says nothing.

'Do you believe I killed him?'

He lifts the glass to his mouth, a strange light in his eyes.

87

ORIANNA: NOW

When I arrive at the cottage, I park, take out the bag from the hardware store and walk out back.

I can feel the fingers of another migraine reaching up from the back of my scalp. The attacks are getting worse, more crippling each time. The pills are having little effect. I realise that I must complete my mission here before I am completely incapacitated.

Starlight spins down onto the lake's surface, quivering it in fleurs-de-lis of silver.

Around me the trees stand tall and still, an enchanted forest.

I listen intently.

Is someone out there?

I turn into the woods and then, without warning, begin to sprint, the bag crashing around my legs.

I run until my lungs catch fire, then duck behind a tree.

My heart thunders in my ears.

I listen intently, but can hear no following runner.

Quickly, I take out the item I had bought at the hardware store.

Five minutes later, I have finished my labours.

I roll up the bag, stick it under my arm. Taking out my pocketknife, I scratch an *X* into the tree.

I wait another moment, ear cocked to the prehistoric night sounds, then turn and head back to the cottage, memorising the route back to the tree.

88

ANNIE: THEN

The bar is a short drive from my apartment; clean, welcoming, and, most importantly, warm.

It has been another long and trying day, and the idea of spending the evening at home, with only my thoughts for company, is about as appealing as an ice pick through the eye. The evenings are beginning to stretch out. As a rule, winter leaves me melancholic; I yearn for company, the sort of company where I can disengage my mind and simply *be*.

The bar backs onto an empty lot that serves as a car park, a duelling ground for drunks, and a pickup point for local working girls. On the other side is a 7-Eleven, showcasing the latest in reinforced-glass windows and graffitied shutters.

Inside, I walk past a pool table, where an overweight man has draped himself over the felt, jeans riding low on his butt, ass crack on display.

I order a beer, and a burger and fries to go with.

While my order arrives, I take out my phone and call Michael.

We talk about Leo, Thanksgiving and Christmas. The conversation leaves me frustrated, as ever. Last year,

Michael had suggested it would be better if I didn't attend the annual gathering at his folks. *Better for who?* I had retorted.

Cliché piled on cliché.

The idea of not being able to celebrate Christmas with Leo tears away at me.

He may not be a kid any more, but those moments of connection between mother and child are inviolable, or so I had always believed.

I order another beer. Thinking about my defunct motherhood takes me back to Orianna and *her* difficult relationship with Christine. It is something we will have to get into at some point. I have already sensed that it might prove a flashpoint. But flashpoints are good. Flashpoints engage deep emotions, and sometimes that is exactly what is needed to move the boulder and open up the cave of memory.

'Buy you a beer?'

I twist around on my stool.

The guy is OK-looking, clean, dressed in everyman shirt and jeans. Stylish – but not outlandish – glasses. No crazy facial hair. A good sign. His expression is neither hopeful grad student nor cocky God's gift to women. He seems . . . decent.

We talk awhile. He is not pushy, waits patiently for me to pronounce verdict.

By the time we get back to my apartment, it is almost ten.

I turn on the heating, pour us wine. Dutch courage.

It has been a long time since I was last with a man.

The truth is that it still stings. The neverness of it. Never again will Michael and I share intimacy. Never again will we confide in each other. Never again will we laugh at each other's silliness, ask after each other's days, console each other in the dead zones that life throws up.

Something about his manner pings my antennae.

'What's the matter?' I ask.

He says nothing, stands there, holding the wine glass awkwardly.

'Changed your mind?'

I hope not. I need this. My body needs this. It's been too long. Deny the body and the mind suffers. Even the ancients knew that.

He reaches up and bounces his glasses on his nose, a telltale sign as loud as an air-raid siren. I cannot guess what's coming, but it won't be anything good.

'I'm sorry. I don't know how to say this—'

'But?'

'But . . . I host an online true-crime group. We've spent years looking at Orianna's case. I tracked you down to ask you to come on a Zoom chat with us.' He stops, then plunges on before I can interrupt. 'We wouldn't ask you to break patient-client confidentiality, obviously. Just talk us through your approach to the case, your background research, why you felt compelled to take it on.'

I stare at him. Whatever I had suspected, it wasn't this. It feels like a shot to the solar plexus. The only reason I'm still standing is because my body hasn't caught up yet.

'I'm sorry. I know this is totally *not* cool. I hadn't intended to let it get this far. It's just – you looked so sad at the bar. And then we got chatting. And—'

'Get out.'

He stumbles to a halt. 'Look. You have every right—'

'Get *the fuck* out of my house!'

My yell frightens him. His pupils contract. And then he is putting down his wine, pulling on his coat, out the door before I can tear him in half.

I slam the door on him, lean against it.

I am empty. Utterly drained. My lungs feel half their normal size.

Later, the thing that stays with me is not his dishonesty or my own gullibility, but his words, the sting of salt rubbed into a wound.

'You looked so sad.'

89

ORIANNA: NOW

The next morning, I receive a call from Cletus.

'Amos asked me to let you know that Samuel is back in town. He'll be at his church later this afternoon.'

'Thank you.' I am standing in the rear doorway, barefoot, in shorts and a tank top, looking out across the lake. 'How is he? Amos, I mean?'

'A lot better. He'd like you to join him for supper this evening. Seven sharp.'

I hesitate, then say, 'I'll be there.'

I finish fixing breakfast – a bowl of cereal into which I shred an apple – then wander outside. The air is hot and dense, the sun turning the motionless water into a silver sheet.

I sit with my back against the yew, spooning around the contents of my bowl without much enthusiasm.

Reconstructing the past is akin to piecing together a shattered mirror. So much of it is unknowable. Slivers of memory that can never be recovered. Each time I delve into *that* day, the white light returns, and with it the pain, like molten lead pouring into the channels of my brain. Sometimes, when I close my eyes, I find snippets playing on the back of my eyelids – but how much of that is fact? How much fiction woven from guesswork?

And now, I have a few new scraps of information to weave into the narrative.

Tommy Quinn. Peter Wyclerc. Rebekah Wyclerc.

Each of them had a reason to wish Gideon harm. But there is nothing definitive, nothing that I can close my fingers around, knowing that I have grasped an essential part of the truth.

Truth.

The one thing you learn in prison is that everyone has a *version* of the truth. Rarely does that truth align with the facts. Over time, remorse gives way to feelings of injustice; guilt softens, blurs, until all that remains is the notion that perhaps, just perhaps, fault lies elsewhere, with others, with the victim, with plain bad luck.

I think of Luke.

I had made the only decision possible, I know that. But letting go of Luke feels akin to abandoning a ship I have spent the past two decades sailing.

My anguish becomes a thrashing beast.

Luke. Golden-haired Luke.

My secret boy of the woods.

Luke, who'd told me he loved me, and then destroyed me on the stand.

90

ORIANNA: NOW

I park directly across from the church.

The Church of Christ the Redeemer. Built in the Georgian style, tall and elegantly double-spired, one spire housing a bronze bell, the other a clock face. Two enormous Tiffany stained-glass windows – each standing twenty-five feet in height and containing seven thousand individual pieces of glass – face the street, depicting scenes from the Bible. On the left, Jesus stands at the prow of a wooden boat, surrounded by disciples as he 'stills the storm'; on the right, Jesus kneels before a grey rock, looking up to a holy light parting the heavens in the Garden of Gethsemane.

Shortly after Nathaniel Wyclerc founded the town, men began to arrive, in trucks, on horseback, on foot, bringing with them various strains of an Anglican faith harking back to America's Third Great Awakening: Methodists and Baptists, Presbyterians and Puritans.

Nathaniel, for his part, did not hold with the sort of overwrought, evangelical piety that relied on pulpit-bashing and penitents writhing on dusty church floors. His was a no-nonsense approach: salvation through labour, moral rectitude and adherence to Jonathan Edwards's central tenets, namely, that man was born a sinner, God was an angry judge, and the path to paradise lay in repentance and atonement. He'd once dragged a visiting revivalist preacher from the steps of the town hall and bullwhipped him halfway to the gates of heaven.

Word soon spread.

Perhaps Nathaniel realised that a hardy faith was the best way to control a swiftly growing population drawn from all parts of the state – and beyond. Men who often had little in common and even less to lose.

The first church he built was a simple thing, constructed from thickly hewed pine logs, some so old they had been around since before white men had set foot on the continent. The second was a backcountry chapel that resembled a tobacco warehouse, with a tacky wooden cross affixed to the roof like a television aerial.

It remained one of the oldest buildings in Eden Falls until Samuel Wyclerc pulled it down and rebuilt it from the ground up.

91

ORIANNA: NOW

Inside the church, a skylight shines a great shaft of opalescent light onto the pulpit, where a youngish man fiddles with a Book of Common Prayer.

He watches me approach, a wariness crossing his clean-cut, boy-band features.

'I'm looking for Samuel.'

'Do you have an appointment?'

'No.'

He struggles with a titanic inner dilemma.

'It's fine, Daniel.'

I twist around to see a tall figure framed in a doorway to the right.

My heart skips a beat.

Samuel Wyclerc, in late middle-age, remains an astonishingly handsome man. He does not resemble his brothers, or his father; his eyes are brown, almond-shaped and liquid, unlike the smoky wolf's eyes of the other males of his clan. His hair is still dark, almost black, barely streaked with grey. In the reflected light of the church, his face takes on the soft splendour of a Byzantine saint.

He beckons me towards him, then turns and vanishes into the room behind.

I follow him into a small office, neatly appointed with a brace of filing cabinets, a desk, a window overlooking the church's rear lawn.

He sits down behind the desk.

'I'm glad you came,' he begins. He is wearing a plain white shirt, open at the neck, above blue jeans. Behind him, a gown hangs from a coat stand.

I remember Sundays with my mother, hiding behind Christine as she set her crypto-Catholicism to one side and flirted shamelessly with Eden Falls' handsome reverend. I remember Samuel leaning down, pressing a bar of candy into my six-year-old hands, winking at me. Of all the Wyclercs, he had somehow remained an enigmatic presence, zealously guarding his privacy, seemingly impervious to the speculation surrounding his personal life, spending long tracts of time out of town, in thrall to neither his fellow townsfolk, nor to the wishes of his father.

Was he gay? A crying shame, if that was the case, or so my mother had said, echoing the general sentiment among the women of Eden Falls; the single ones in lament, the not-so-single ones in wistfulness. To me, their attitude was just another symptom of the small-town prejudice I had come to despise, even before they turned on me.

'Reverend—'

'Please. Call me Samuel. You *are* my niece, after all.'

I see that he is smiling.

I wonder what it must be like, to hold the spiritual well-being of so many in the palm of your hand. To know that you have the capacity to provide solace, but that, equally, in an age of denial, in an increasingly carnivorous society, you might be ignored, deemed redundant, the very precepts of your creed labelled old-fashioned and foolish.

'I wanted to talk to you about Gideon. And Grace.'

He spreads his hands. 'I'll help in any way that I can. My father has told me that he no longer believes that you killed Gideon. For a man like Amos to admit that he was wrong ...' He smiles again, igniting another sunrise inside me.

'What was your relationship like? With Gideon?'

'He was my younger brother, but we were never close. We differed in too many ways. I realised early on that Gideon was not a moral man. But none of us truly are, are we? We're all prone to sin, moments of weakness. I suppose the difference with Gideon was that he never felt an iota of remorse.'

The words feel harsh, judgemental. I am surprised at his candour.

'Did you get on with him?'

'That's a relative term where this family is concerned. We never fought. But then, we had little enough in common to fight about. And once I went away to train as a minister, we saw less and less of each other.'

'I'm told that he and Peter hated each other, that they fought on the night before Gideon was killed.'

Something flashes deep in his irises. 'Am I my brother's keeper?' he whispers softly. I wait. 'Yes. They fought. Peter and Gideon were fire and ice. They disliked each other at a cellular level. It pains me greatly to say that, but it's the truth.'

'Could Peter have hurt Gideon?'

'I pray that isn't the case.'

'But it's possible?'

'I'm his brother. Would you have me testify against him?'

'If he's guilty, then yes.'

He sighs. 'I'm not going to condemn Peter – or anyone else, for that matter – without proof. We did that once already, and we'll spend the rest of our lives begging for your forgiveness.'

There is something comfortingly antiquated in his manner, his adherence to values that became superfluous to me in the realpolitik of prison, a moral goodness that harks back to an earlier age.

I tack in another direction. 'At the beginning of that summer, Grace suddenly became interested in her faith. She began carrying a Bible around, started attending church regularly. Did she speak with you about what brought on this sudden rash of piety?'

His face assumes a thoughtful expression. 'Grace was undergoing what I can only call a crisis of the spirit. It was more than adolescent despair. I never really knew her well until that summer; for that, I must accept my share of the blame. When she first came to see me, I was taken aback by her . . . intensity. Her home life was troubled, that much was obvious, though she was reluctant to discuss the details with me – and *I* equally reluctant to talk about the matter with Gideon. In fact, she extracted a promise from me that I wouldn't. I think she was simply looking for a safe harbour where she might work out her own answers.'

'She didn't reveal *why* she'd sought the solace of the church? It seems an unusual step for a seventeen-year-old.'

'Not in Eden Falls. Not for a Wyclerc. Is it really so strange that a young person should seek sanctuary in faith? I didn't question it. Perhaps I should have.'

'Did she ever mention someone she was involved with? A secret boyfriend?'

'Our discussions didn't exactly range into such territory. She spent much of her time here hanging out with the choir. She didn't have the voice to meet Mrs Abernathy's rather exacting standards, but she loved the spiritual songs. She'd forever be humming "There is a Balm in Gilead".' He leans forward, smelling of sweat and soap, a piney fragrance. 'The truth is that I failed her. I should have dug deeper. I could sense her unhappiness. I just couldn't penetrate it.'

A grim music vibrates in his throat. I see that he is haunted. Perhaps, like so many others, he blames himself – at least in part – for not saving Grace, and in so doing, rescuing the innocence of a town where fear and bigotry had outgrown love.

'I heard about the town-hall meeting last night.'

I say nothing.

'I can't imagine what it must have been like for you these past eighteen years. I failed *you* too – we all did. This family has a lot to answer for. All I can tell you is that you need fear no more. Do you remember your psalms? Psalm 27? "The Lord is my light and my salvation – whom shall I fear? The Lord is the stronghold of my life – of whom shall I be afraid? When evil men advance against me to devour my flesh, when my enemies and my foes attack me, they will stumble and fall."'

The words move me. I lower my eyes, become momentarily lost. When I speak again, I am forced to clear my throat. 'Before she died, did my mother—?' I stop.

'After your conviction, she stopped coming to church. I don't blame her. I blame myself for not reaching out to her.'

'She drowned in the lake behind Elvira Trueblood's cottage. There may be a chance that she killed herself.'

'You can't be sure of that. No one really knows what happened. The simplest explanation is that your mother drowned by accident.'

'But if she *did*—'

'I believe that God's mercy is infinite, Orianna. He forgives sinners and saints who have sinned. Remember, Christ *died* for our sins. Wherever Gideon and Christine now reside, I am certain neither has any need for absolution.' His eyes are luminous. 'My grandfather, Nathaniel, made the same mistake all men make who seek to recreate the moral innocence of Eden on Earth: he forgot that men will always succumb to their base natures. Even the best of us.'

92

ORIANNA: NOW

Hunger leads me to the diner.

As soon as I enter, I know that something is different.

I am confronted by the waitress who served me the first time I came in here with Luke.

'I'm sorry, honey, but you're going to have to leave. We can't serve you no more.'

I look past the woman and see that the entire place has stopped to listen, burgers, hotdogs and hash browns raised halfway to open mouths.

'Owner's instructions,' says the waitress, in a voice that is almost apologetic.

Almost.

When I get back to my car, I find the hood emblazoned with spray-painted graffiti: *MURDERING BITCH*.

I stop at the library, but Gerty is out. I have a need to talk. I can feel the poison entering my veins. The town's venom, pumping blackly through me. I had tried to explain the feeling to Annie Ledet during our sessions together. How, growing up in Eden Falls, each day I had felt myself diminished, a sapling choked off by a lack of sunlight. They had rejected me long before Gideon's killing. The murder had simply given them a chance to bring their prejudices out into the open.

Why? What had I ever done to them?

I find myself trembling. The old familiar itch, the scars on my arm heating up, until they burn.

There's still an hour to go before the supper with Amos. I make a snap decision.

Everything that has happened to me happened because of those compressed, veiled moments in Gideon's cabin. Ever since my return, I have deliberately put off going there because of fear. The terror of what I might find, what I might unlock.

But I cannot put it off any longer.

Whatever the truth may be, whatever my broken memory might reveal, I must confront my past.

I take out my phone and dial Luke. 'I'm going to the cabin.'

93

ORIANNA: NOW

I enter the estate via the gatehouse, waiting for the solitary guard to make his way out of the booth.

I have gotten to know him, but he still makes a production out of every visit.

His name is P. W. Aimes – he insists on being called P. W. He wears aviator shades and walks with a crabwise limp, as if he sustained a noble wound in a war back when he was young and free and brave.

I drive a quarter mile into the estate until I hit the road that circles its interior, then take a right. To my left, I can just about see, in the distance, the upper storey of the Big House, hovering atop a shallow rise, half-hidden behind its own wall.

I park by the edge of the southern woods, kill the engine, then wait a while in case Luke shows up. I check my watch, look back down the road.

Luke is late.

Once again, I find the unbidden thought returning: *Grace and Luke. Luke and Grace.*

A sickening image of them, entwined, on the forest floor where Luke and I had first found each other.

I shake the thought away. I must not surrender to paranoia. I would have known if Luke had been cheating on me, would have sensed it. Besides, Grace was his cousin... Then again, so was I.

I resist the urge to phone him, instead turn to continue on foot, walk into the muggy warmth beneath the trees.

Within moments, I am cocooned by woodland silence.

I follow an old game trail and the winding path of my own memory.

When I arrive at the clearing, I hang on the edge, looking out across thirty yards of dirt and yellowing grass to the cabin, backlit by a powerful column of sunlight washing down between a break in the canopy. There is something almost holy in the scene.

I approach the cabin as if wading through water, each step a leap into the past.

Anxiety rises inside me; the white noise returns, and for a moment, I lose all semblance of where and when I am. I see, suddenly, Annie Ledet, and the tiny therapy room inside the prison, words curling in the air between us like smoke as, together, we attempt to relive that fateful day. My skull expands and contracts; a searing pain, another sudden migraine like the booming of a cannon, almost drives me to my knees.

I hold my head, taste blood as I bite my lip. The blinding agony leaks away.

I am back in the clearing.

Nothing about the cabin's exterior has changed.

Eighteen years, and it looks exactly as it did on the day I was led away in cuffs by Chief Deputy Sheriff Faulkes.

My heart expands as I reach for the door.

94

ANNIE: THEN

'You changed your hair.'

Orianna is smiling, faintly, in that way of hers.

'Yes.'

'Does this change perchance involve a man?'

I offer my own rueful smile. 'No. Most definitely not.'

She turns away. The topic of men, relationships, is, of course, a no-go zone. By Orianna's own admission, made in court, her only sexual experience, to date, is with Luke Wyclerc. And that was far from an ideal relationship, conducted as it was in secrecy, and ending in the gut-wrenching revelation that Luke was her cousin. I could only imagine the psychological damage.

But today is not the moment to unravel that particular Gordian knot.

Today, I want to take Orianna back to the critical moment in the trial when *hard* facts were presented.

'Orianna, I would like us to discuss the forensic analysis presented at your trial. I think we need to unpick why the prosecution was so convinced that you and you alone had to be Gideon's killer.'

It is a bold opening. No easing into it. But this, too, is a calculated gambit and will tell me something by the way Orianna responds.

For a moment, she is utterly still. Her nostrils dilate. I can feel the tension ripple through her.

When she continues to say nothing, I speak again. 'I know this won't be easy for you. But you've shown great courage so far. We've made progress. I need you to hold fast. We're in this together, Orianna. Every step of the way.'

She blinks, hard. 'No, Annie. We're not in this "together". *I* am in here. *You're* out there.'

I don't challenge her. How can I?

Slowly, her anger melts away. 'OK.'

I take the court transcripts from my bag and set them between us.

'The prosecution's forensic expert was a man named Rupert Langdon. Do you remember him?'

'Yes.'

'Tell me about that day.'

She picks up her copy of the transcript. 'I took a strong dislike to Langdon the moment he walked into the courtroom. My attorney, Ortega, had told me he was some sort of minor celebrity. He looked the part, I'll give him that. Tall, with a thick head of silvery hair, dressed in a ridiculous tweed jacket and a black turtleneck. A crazy get-up in the heat. Ortega said Langdon was a media whore, the go-to man for true-crime documentaries and forensics puff pieces. When he wasn't running the state's crime lab, he was in demand as an expert witness. I saw several of the jury members gape at him in awe; an attractive woman in the front row practically swooned in her seat when he looked in her direction.' She takes a beat. 'The courtroom was packed, the heat suffocating. I remember the smells of summer in the room: pomade, strawberries, sweat. There was a sense of spectacle, excitement. The great theatre of the law, a trial that had gripped the nation.

'I knew that Eden Falls was making the nightly news. Scenic shots of small-town America flashing onto millions of screens. Reporters and TV correspondents crowding around the DA each evening on the courthouse steps, begging for sound bites. Stock footage of me arriving at court in the back of a police car replayed endlessly. Trash tabloids assassinated my character, my mother's hedonistic ways. *Nympho Housemaid's Killer Daughter!*'

She looks down at the transcript. 'I remember the reaction in the court when the DA went through the crime-scene photos. The jurors looking at me, one by one. You didn't need a crystal ball to see what was going on inside their heads. Danziger had wheeled in a screen, so the whole court could get a look in. The first shot of Gideon's body raised a gasp from the gallery. The photo had been taken directly facing the body: Gideon in his chair, legs spread wide, arms hanging by his sides. Blood was visible on the front of his shirt, directly above the heart.' She stops. 'The gunshot had pulverised his face, blasting out one side, an eye gone, cheek a crater of blood.'

She is silent a moment, then looks down at the transcript.

The Girl In Cell A

DA Danziger: Dr Langdon, as the head of the state's crime lab, I'd like your help today to lead us through an overview of the forensic evidence in this case. I'd like to start with the murder weapon. Did your team determine the type of weapon that caused these injuries?

Dr Rupert Langdon: Yes. It was a shotgun.

Danziger: The same weapon that was found at the scene?

Langdon: That's correct.

Danziger: Your Honour, the State would like to enter into the record, Exhibit B.

[Murder weapon is entered into the record and displayed by the DA to the court.]

Danziger: Dr Langdon, is this the weapon used to kill Gideon Wyclerc?

Langdon: It is.

Danziger: What type of weapon are we talking here?

Langdon: A shotgun. A Mossberg.

Danziger: And did you determine who this weapon belonged to?

Langdon: It was registered to Gideon Wyclerc.

Danziger: And where was it usually kept?

Langdon: In his hunting cabin.

Danziger: Was the weapon locked away?

Langdon: No. It was in a gun rack.

Danziger: Was the cabin locked?

Langdon: No. According to the police report, Gideon never kept it locked.

Danziger: Doesn't that seem odd? This gun was one of many in the cabin, was it not? A collection of expensive weapons.

Langdon: The cabin is situated on the Wyclerc estate. The estate is surrounded by a security wall. My understanding is that Gideon never felt the need to lock his cabin.

Danziger: We'll come back to the gun in a second... The coroner's report details the injuries sustained by Gideon. We will hear from the coroner in due course. In his report, he has determined that the cause of death was massive injury caused by the twin shotgun blasts, one to the heart and one to the head... Were you able to determine at what range the gun was fired?

Langdon: We were. Our analysis suggests the gun was fired from approximately five feet away, what we would call an 'intermediate' distance.

Danziger: And how were you able to determine this?

Langdon: Wounds caused by shotgun blasts at such a range produce a distinctive scalloped edge. This is because, as the range increases beyond a close-contact firing, air resistance causes the column of pellets exiting the shotgun to spread. Peripheral pellets are slightly separated from the main pellet mass hitting the skin; they strike the edges of the central wound caused by the main mass. By taking detailed measurements of the central hole, the area and pattern of satellite pellet holes, and the presence or absence of soot staining and powder tattooing, we can determine quite accurately the range of fire.

The Girl In Cell A

[The DA indicates towards the screen, depicting a two-dimensional floor plan of the interior of the hunting cabin. A yellow square marked *1* denotes the spot where Gideon Wyclerc's body was found, in his chair. *2* marks the location of the gun. A *3* marks where the defendant was discovered, unconscious on the floor.]

Danziger: Doctor, this diagram marks where the defendant and murder weapon were found in relation to the victim. From your analysis, you determined that the killer must have been standing approximately five feet from the victim when firing the shots. How far was the defendant found from the victim?
Langdon: Approximately six and a half to seven feet.
Danziger: Can you explain the difference?
Langdon: Yes. It is my opinion that the defendant was forced back by the shotgun blast, tripped, and fell against the wall of the cabin, rendering her unconscious.
Danziger: And how did you determine that the defendant had fired the weapon in question?
Langdon: We found the defendant's fingerprints on the shotgun. We also found GSR – that is, gunshot residue – from the gun on the defendant's hands and clothing.
Danziger: [To the jury] Now, we will later hear that the defendant does not deny firing the weapon that day. The defence's claim is that Ms Negi fired the shotgun earlier that afternoon, then returned it to the cabin, and that it was later used to kill Gideon Wyclerc by another, as yet unidentified, party. The defendant was

then 'framed' for the killing – she was knocked unconscious and the gun placed beside her.

Danziger: [To the witness] Dr Langdon, in the course of your team's ballistics analysis, were you able to determine the angle from which the bullets that killed Gideon Wyclerc were fired?

Langdon: We were.

Danziger: And what did you discover?

Langdon: The fatal shots were fired from a height of just over four and a half feet.

Danziger: And what does that mean?

Langdon: If the shooter held the gun to their shoulder, it implies that they would have been somewhere between five feet three and five feet five inches tall, give or take.

Danziger: Do you happen to know how tall the defendant is?

Langdon: Five feet four inches.

Danziger: Dr Langdon, did you employ any other method to determine the killer's height?

Langdon: We can also estimate it by examining the blood spatter.

Danziger: Could you please explain?

Langdon: Blood spatter analysis is the field of forensic science that examines bloodstains at crime scenes with the purpose of drawing conclusions about the nature of the crime and to aid in crime scene reconstruction.

Danziger: Did your crime lab use a blood spatter expert to examine the scene?

Langdon: As a matter of fact, I did it myself. It's my forensic specialty and the subject of my PhD thesis at Yale.

The Girl In Cell A

Danziger: And what did you conclude?

Langdon: Two things. First, the victim was seated when he was shot dead. It wasn't a case of Gideon being in a standing position and then falling into his seat after being shot. Second, given that he was seated, the analysis of the spatter again leads to the conclusion that his killer was short, in the range of five foot three or four.'

Danziger: One final question, Dr Langdon . . . Did you discover any injuries to the victim's hands?

Langdon: No. There were no defensive wounds.

Danziger: You mean to tell this court that Gideon Wyclerc didn't even raise his hands to ward off the shots when they came?

Langdon: He did not.

Danziger: In your opinion, as an expert in forensic analysis with three decades of experience, what does that suggest to you?

Langdon: That Gideon knew his killer. That he didn't anticipate the threat. He simply sat there, and then the killer shot him.

Danziger: Your witness.

95

ANNIE: THEN

Orianna stops. Her expression is strained, her distress evident.

But we haven't finished yet. I need her to see this through, to work with me as we examine her own lawyer's attempts to dismantle the evidence presented by the prosecution.

'Do you want to take a short break before we continue?'

She considers this, then shakes her head.

'OK. In that case, why don't you carry on where you left off?'

She takes a shallow breath, then begins again.

'After the DA finished questioning Langdon, the judge ordered a brief recess. I conferred with Ortega, who, to my eyes, looked deflated. He'd already explained to me – and to my mother – that the State's case relied on the physical evidence. Means and opportunity were a slam dunk – I mean, I was found in the cabin with the murder weapon beside me. But motive was still weak. Danziger knew that and so he'd gone to town on the forensic evidence.'

'Did that give you some confidence? The fact that motive was weak?'

'Not much. When Rupert Langdon retook the stand, he looked bored, as if he knew he'd already said enough to convict me. Throughout his testimony, he'd barely glanced in my direction.'

'Did that bother you?'

'Not as much as watching my lawyer approach the box. He actually pulled up short, looked down at his shoes, as if maybe he'd stepped in shit. He looked completely out of his depth.'

She returns to the transcript.

Herman Ortega: Dr Langdon, I'd like to start with the fingerprints on the gun. They were analysed by an expert from your crime lab. Is that correct?

Dr Rupert Langdon: Yes. That's correct.

Ortega: According to the report, my client's prints were discovered on the trigger, the barrel and the stock.

Langdon: Yes.

Ortega: But isn't it true that some of those prints were smudged?

Langdon: That's correct. But we were able to match the victim's prints on the basis of partials.

Ortega: We're not disputing that my client's prints were on the gun, Dr Langdon. She has already admitted that she fired the gun earlier that day. What I'm suggesting to you is that the fact that many of those prints were smudged indicates that someone else handled that gun after she'd fired it.

Langdon: If that were the case, then we would have found another person's prints on the weapon.

Ortega: Not if the true killer wore gloves. In such a case, the gloves would have smudged my client's prints. Is that not so?

Langdon: The scenario is preposterous.

Ortega: But theoretically possible?

Langdon: Yes. I suppose so.

Ortega: Let's turn to the ballistics and your analysis of the blood spatter. You've harped on quite a bit about the killer's estimated height. But isn't it true to say that you can't be certain exactly how tall the killer is?

Langdon: That's what the word *estimate* means.

Ortega: My point is that there are a great many people in this county who might fit the description of 'between five-three and five-five' – and that's merely your estimate. It might just as well be five-two or five-six. And what if the killer didn't hold the gun to their shoulder? What if they shot from the waist? Or the hip? That would render your calculations completely invalid, would it not?

Langdon: You're forgetting the blood spatter analysis. It points to the same conclusion.

Ortega: Dr Langdon, do you recall a man named Sean Carmichaels?

[Witness does not reply.]

Ortega: Dr Langdon?

Langdon: Yes. I recall Carmichaels.

Ortega: Would you care to explain to the court your interaction with Mr Carmichaels?

Langdon: Carmichaels was convicted some sixteen years ago of the murder of his wife and child in the town of Turow. I was called as an expert forensic witness at his trial.

Ortega: Five years into his sentence, Carmichaels died in an altercation with another prisoner. Is that correct?

Langdon: That's what I heard.

Ortega: Three months ago, analysis of DNA evidence found at the scene exonerated Carmichaels, following an investigation launched by the Innocence Project. Is that correct?

DA Danziger: Objection! Where is the relevance, Your Honour?

Ortega: Speaks to professional competence.

Danziger: Dr Langdon's competence has been well and truly established. He's not on trial here.

Judge Whaley: I'll allow it.

Ortega: Dr Langdon?

Langdon: Yes, that's correct.

Ortega: No more questions.

Danziger: Dr Langdon, did you find evidence of anyone other than the victim and the defendant at the crime scene?

Langdon: No, we did not.

Danziger: Did you find any irrefutable evidence that anyone else fired the murder weapon?

Langdon: No, we did not.

Danziger: In your expert opinion, is there any scenario other than the defendant killing Gideon Wyclerc in that cabin that day that fits the established facts?

Langdon: No, there is not.

Danziger: No more questions, Your Honour.

96

ANNIE: THEN

The sound of Orianna's voice dies away. In the silence, I hear the ringing of the chapel bell.

I allow myself a moment to process the session.

We have gone through the forensic evidence essentially as the prosecution laid it out.

And the fact is, it's damning.

How do I confront Orianna with this without alienating her? The key in challenging a patient in this way is to not be judgemental or reprimanding. To highlight inconsistencies, but to always remain aware that the patient may have built a fortress of self-delusion, inside which they remain on a state of constant alert, ready to pour boiling oil on anyone who dares to charge the ramparts.

Empathy is paramount, the grease that oils the wheels of the psychiatric professions.

But empathy isn't always easy, particularly when you are dealing with those who have committed terrible crimes. No therapist will come out and say it, but, sometimes, in the small hours of the night, we cannot help but question our loyalties. *Do killers and rapists and child abusers truly deserve our empathy?*

'Orianna, thank you for being so open to discussing this very important moment from your past. How did it feel to go back like this?'

She didn't expect me to start there and takes a moment. 'I don't know. Not great.'

'Do you feel anger? Towards the State? The DA? Dr Langdon?'

'Yes.'

'Even though they were simply presenting the facts as they saw them?'

'They *spun* the facts.'

'Would you agree that that is their job? Just as it was your lawyer's job to spin the facts to best enable your defence?'

A vein pulses at her throat.

'I've reviewed the evidence submissions,' I continue. 'I'm no expert, but, based on what was presented in court, I would like you to try a little thought experiment. Let's say you were not on the stand, but that you were just someone in the gallery, looking on. If you saw this evidence – the gunshot residue, the prints, finding you at the scene, the blood spatter pinpointing the assailant's height – what would *you* think?'

Her eyes burn into me.

'I'm not asking you to admit your guilt. I'm merely asking you to place yourself outside of your own bubble and examine the situation dispassionately.'

'How can I be dispassionate about *this*?'

'I agree. It seems impossible. But sometimes a mental block such as yours can be lifted simply by conceding ground. The mind no longer has to tie itself into knots lying to itself and so it relents.'

'So you're saying I've been lying to myself? That I murdered Gideon?' Her voice is heated.

'I'm saying that the truth is locked up inside your head. And to spring the lock, I would like you to consider approaching the evidence in a new way.'

'You want me to doubt myself.' She leans forward. 'You don't get it, do you? When they do eventually let me out of here, I *will* go back. I know I didn't kill Gideon. Which means someone else did. I'm going to go back and find the sonofabitch who stole my life.'

Her eyes blaze.

An uncomfortable silence falls on us. I resist the urge to fill it.

Finally, her anger leaks away. She gets up, paces around the room.

Suddenly, she turns and looks at me. I can see something pushing against her lips.

'What is it that you want to say, Orianna? This is a safe space.'

A tremble, so slight as to be almost invisible, passes through her. 'I threatened to kill him. I threatened to kill my father.'

97

ORIANNA: NOW

A sound behind me snaps me around.

I turn to see Luke approaching across the clearing. The sight of him, here, back in the woods where we first found each other, startles me.

'Ori. Are you all right?'

'Yes. I'm fine.'

He hesitates. 'Why did you come here?'

The sound of my own breathing is loud in my ears. I turn away from him, reaching, once again, for the screen door.

We step inside. The wood creaks softly underfoot. I hear a beetle scurrying along the wall. Dead flies lie in the corners and on the windowsill.

The cabin is bare.

The guns are long gone, as is Gideon's seat, his bench and the wolf's head, removed for forensic analysis. A hollow shell remains, fogged with the dark weight of memories.

I feel time unwinding, the collision of past and present.

Luke is standing directly behind me. I feel the closeness of him, the distinctive scent of his cologne. It stings my nose, transporting me back to our days in the forest.

'Do you remember?' he whispers.

'I remember everything.'

98

ANNIE: THEN

I am stunned. I can feel the slow thud of my heart, a building excitement.

Orianna has made a critical admission.

'I threatened to kill him. I threatened to kill my father.'

This is a key moment in her therapy. An admission that she threatened to kill Gideon might prove a precursor to her gradually accepting her guilt, thus paving the way to a full-blown confession. My gambit of leading her through her trial appears to have worked better than I could possibly have hoped.

But I have to be careful. I can sense her reluctance to speak.

If I push too hard, she may withdraw.

And so I do nothing.

She waits, and then, of her own volition, walks back to her seat.

I allow us both time to settle, silently admonishing myself for my recent doubts, my fanciful idea that perhaps, just perhaps, there was a small chance that Orianna *was* innocent. That a slipshod initial investigation had left room for error.

I was wrong. How could a *feeling* counter the weight of forensic evidence? This wasn't a TV show where gut instinct prevailed over common sense and policecraft, no matter how biased the investigation might have been.

'Would you like to talk about it?'

She nods, a small gesture. Her cheeks are red. 'It's one of the things I remember vividly. Luke and I had started meeting regularly. I told you that we'd first started getting to know each other when I caught him hanging around outside Gideon's cabin. Do you remember?'

'I remember.'

'The cabin became our meeting place. Luke told me that his uncle Gideon never went to the cabin in the mornings. Gideon was usually hungover till noon. He went into the office in the afternoons. He only ever came out to the cabin late in the day or Sundays, after church. And so Luke and I hooked up in the mornings or Saturdays, the day that Gideon was always absent from Eden Falls, in Barrier or Beatty or Turow or any of the half-a-dozen other towns in the county where the beer was cheap and the women were accommodating and there was no Amos looking over his shoulder.' She pauses. 'I remember a day that Luke and I were in the cabin . . .'

'You know he brings women back to this cabin, don't you?'

Luke looks at her slyly.

Orianna has heard rumours about Gideon's wandering eye. 'Does Grace know?' It isn't something she and Grace have ever talked about – on the rare occasions they talk.

'They all know,' Luke says. 'I once heard my father and mother talking about Gideon's tomcatting. My father said it

caused a rift in the family, years ago, before we were born. Apparently, it all got covered up. Not that it changed anything. Gideon can't keep his dick in his pants.'

She turns away from him, doesn't want him to see her blush at that word coming from his handsome mouth.

He had promised to teach her to shoot. It was as good an excuse as any they could come up with to keep meeting like this, telling no one. Each time, they would take a rifle from Gideon's gun rack and wander deep into the woods. Half a mile to the east, they found a glade, a place of tall trees silhouetted against a sky as blue as the eye of a Norse god. There, beneath the arms of a willow, beside a chattering stream, in a place as outside of time as the Garden of Eden, they had discovered each other.

Luke would press close against her, helping her aim the rifle at a tree across the water or an empty beer bottle set on a fallen log. The smell of his cologne. His breath hot in her ear. A faint electricity flowing from him to her and back again.

She remembers the day she had lowered the rifle, turned and looked up into his summer-tanned face, his wolf's eyes, then stretched onto her toes and planted her lips against his.

The first time they made love, on the grass beside the stream, there'd been a rightness to it, at one with the shrine they had made, a place where they were free from the dumb hurts and expectations forced on them by the lives into which they had been born.

They'd dreamed of an impossible future.

'I'm going to leave this town,' she told him. 'That's about the only thing I'm sure of.'

'We'll leave together.' But she'd heard the tremor in his voice. He was a Wyclerc, as deeply rooted in this forest, in this land as the trees pushing up from the earth around them. He would never be able to break from his family. She had sensed it; known it in some vital inner chamber.

That day, in the cabin, as she picks out a rifle, he turns to her: 'Aren't you curious about your father? Wouldn't you like to find him?'

'Why? He's never tried to find me.'

'Maybe he doesn't know.'

'He knows. He just chose never to look back.'

'You can't be sure of that.'

How can she explain to him that, in recent years, she has come to believe that her mother, despite her protestations, does know who her father is. The look in her eye when she is confronted by the question; the tension in her shoulders as she turns away; a tremble in her voice. And a moment, a year earlier, when, in a drunken stupor, she'd mumbled something that was as close to an admission as Orianna would ever get. That, not only did Christine know, but that her father knew too.

And yet he had chosen against them. Against her.

Anger bubbles like lava in her veins.

She raises the rifle and points it at Gideon's chair. 'If he was here, my father, sitting right there, I'd probably kill him.'

99

ORIANNA: NOW

Amos is waiting in the gazebo out by the old peach orchard, on the western edge of the Big House's grounds.

I follow Luke in my Chevy, park beside him on a square of tarmac, crowded by a row of other cars. To the west, a blood-red sun is sinking behind the green-coated hills, the sky veined with fire, the light dying.

I feel sweat across my back, rolling down the narrow valley of my spine.

Being with Luke in the cabin has thrown me. I cannot get rid of the tapeworm that has settled in my guts, the notion that perhaps Luke and Grace had had ... I cannot finish the thought, cannot give it shape and presence.

I realise that I am late for Amos's supper invite.

A scatter of redwood picnic tables has been set up under the gazebo, lights strung along the eaves, attracting clouds of early-evening insects. The tables are set with white cloth, candlesticks, silver serving ware and platters of food. Bottles of water, wine, and good Scotch complete the menu.

Amos sits at the head of the table.

Occupying the other seats are the members of the Wyclerc clan: Peter and his wife Ruth; David and his wife Susannah; Samuel; and Martha, sitting in a wheelchair. Luke joins them too; but of Luke's wife – and Rebekah – there is no sign, and for that I am grateful.

Cletus Barnes sits at Amos's right hand.

A jag of lightning flares in my eyes. The sky seems to blacken in the distance. I see the faces ranged before me as a tableau of grinning skulls; a jury of the damned. My breathing shallows. A crack opens in the earth before me; on one side, the reality of the now; on the far side, the distant past, the members of the Wyclerc clan in the courtroom where I had been tried – the last time I had seen them together like this.

I force back the impending explosion in my skull, return to the moment and register the shock descending on the group.

A gummy smile breaks open Martha's wizened face.

I look directly at Amos. I know that I have been ambushed, as have the Wyclercs sitting at the table; my every instinct tells me to turn around and walk away.

Amos puts a cigar to his mouth, his expression enigmatic.

'What the hell are you doing here?' Peter has shot to his feet, face white. He is wearing a lavender golf shirt with cream slacks and loafers, as if out for a spritzers-and-hors-d'oeuvres night at the country club.

'*I* invited her,' Amos says. 'Come along, Orianna. It's about time I introduced you to your family.'

'Is this a joke? If you think I'm going to sit through a meal with her—'

Amos thumps the table, startles us all. A wine glass crashes to the earth. 'Sit down!'

'I will not. I'm—'

'You will sit down, or I'll fucking disinherit you!'

Peter looks as if he has been slapped. His mouth flaps open, and then snaps shut. He stands there a moment, face purpling, then gingerly lowers himself back into his chair. Beside him, his wife, Ruth, attempts to place a placating hand on his shoulder, but he shrugs it angrily away.

Amos picks up a shot glass and bolts it. 'Where's Rebekah?' He turns to Cletus. 'Did you tell her?'

'I did. She said she'd be here.'

Amos looks back at me. 'Well, sit down, granddaughter.'

I catch Peter wincing at the word.

I reluctantly walk around to an empty chair by Martha and sit. I feel Martha's warm hand on my forearm. A gentle squeeze.

'I can't remember the last time the Wyclercs gathered under one roof,' says Amos dryly. 'Allow me to make the introductions.' He points at Peter. 'Peter, the captain of our ship. If I give him enough rope, he may yet sink us all.'

I see Peter flinch, knuckles whitening around his glass.

Amos swings his gaze to Samuel. 'And the good reverend, who may or may not be a fruit. But we're all God's creatures, aren't we? One big happy menagerie.'

'Amos—' David begins.

'Ah, he speaks! Saint David. David the Righteous. David, my nephew, who I raised as my own son and who now won't even look me in the eye.'

'Let him alone, Amos.'

I twist in my seat to see Martha frowning at Amos.

In the silence, the sound of a car pulling up. Moments later, Rebekah walks into the gazebo. She freezes as she catches sight of me.

'Yes,' rumbles Amos. 'She's here and here she stays. Sit down.'

Rebekah's eyes blaze. Her jaw writhes as words struggle to emerge from her mouth, but then she simply turns and begins to walk away.

'I'd stop right there, if I were you.'

Rebekah ignores him, keeps walking.

Amos pulls out a revolver and fires it into the sky, the sound astonishingly loud in the twilight. And then he points the revolver at Rebekah.

100

ORIANNA: NOW

'Jesus Christ!' Peter is back on his feet.

Rebekah spins around. 'Have you lost your mind?'

Amos waves the revolver around like a wand. 'I'd strongly advise you to sit down.'

I look at Luke, see that his face is impassive. Had he known that Amos was going to do this?

Rebekah is frozen in place. And then, with a monumental effort, she forces herself to move forward and stumble into a seat. Fury boils from her in waves hot enough to sear the tablecloth.

'There's a reason you're all here today,' Amos says. 'I have an announcement. But before we get to that . . . You all know by now why Orianna has come back. She claims she didn't kill Gideon. Now, you can believe her or not; frankly, I couldn't give a damn. But in her time here, she's made some intriguing discoveries, and tonight, we are going to drag the past into the light.' His eyes darken. 'Gideon was killed right here, on the grounds of this estate. I have never voiced the thought before, but I am certain I'm not the only one whose mind it has crossed in all these years . . . If Orianna didn't kill him, then Gideon's killer might well be sitting here at this table. Or at least may know *who* killed him.'

'That's preposterous,' Peter begins. 'Surely, you can't believe *her*?'

'Here's what I think,' continues Amos, ignoring him. 'I think you're waiting for me to drop dead. All of you. You think my death will free you in some way, of guilt, of responsibility. But Gideon, for all his faults, was my son, and I refuse to go to my grave not knowing what really happened to him.'

David tries again. 'Amos—'

'Shut up, David.'

I see Luke flinch. Susannah places a hand on her husband's shoulder. David gazes off into space.

Amos turns to Rebekah. 'Orianna tells me you were fucking Tommy Quinn when Gideon was killed. Is that true?'

Rebekah's face turns scarlet. 'I don't have to listen to this—'

'Oh, you'll listen all right. High up there on your cross. Well, pity party's over, daughter-in-law of mine. Now . . . answer the goddamned question.'

'You have no right—'

'He was my *son*! I loved him. And I will have a fucking answer!'

Her eyes blaze. 'You think I didn't love him? Is that it? You think I married him for his money? Whatever happened between Gideon and me, it was as much his doing as mine. If he hadn't been out there screwing everything in a dress, maybe I wouldn't have gone looking for a Tommy Quinn.'

The words strike Amos with the force of a blow. 'Well, the truth has put its boots on today.' A silence passes. 'Very well, truth is what I asked for and truth is what we shall have. You're right. Gideon was a bad husband. And I was a bad father. But the one thing I know, the one thing I'm certain of, is that *I* had nothing to do with his death. I can no longer say the same about everyone sat at this table... Who is Tommy Quinn to you?'

Rebekah looks like an animal caught in a trap. Finally, she says, 'Tommy and I had a... We had something.'

'And Gideon found out?'

'Tommy told him. On the day of the festival. Just came right up and told him.'

'Told him what?'

'That he was in love with me. That Gideon didn't deserve me.'

'And you? Were you in love with him?'

Colour climbs into her face. 'Tommy was everything Gideon was not. He made me feel as if I was the only thing that mattered.'

Amos picks up the revolver and taps the butt of it gently on the table. 'You fell in love with a low-life junkie degenerate. Tommy Quinn may well have killed my son.'

Her head snaps up. 'Tommy didn't do it! He's not... He's not like that. He's not the brute people make him out to be.'

'He spent three years in prison. He's a drug dealer.' It is Peter who has spoken.

Rebekah flashes him a look of pure hatred. 'And what about you, Peter? You hated Gideon. You knew Amos was going to put him in charge of the business. Gideon's death gave you everything you wanted.'

Peter's eyes burn into her. 'As God is my witness, I had nothing to do with Gideon's killing.'

Rebekah snorts. 'I wouldn't invoke God if I were you. Not at this table.'

I see Ruth flinch. I remember Amos telling me that Ruth is a religious freak.

Amos's smile is a facsimile of mirth. 'That's the first sensible thing you've said in eighteen years. The truth is, God abandoned this house a long time ago.' His roving gaze settles on Samuel. 'Yesterday, I found out that a girl over in Turow, about Grace's age, was doused in gasoline by her father and set alight. For no more reason than she wouldn't fetch him his supper. Tell me, Padre, how do you reconcile your faith with *that*?'

Samuel clears his throat softly. 'Man sins because God ordained it so. But God gave us the capacity to perform penance for our sins. To be forgiven. No man's soul is unredeemable.'

'Evil has an odour,' Amos responds. 'And by God, I smell that odour on us. I hear the serpent slithering in the Garden of Eden that Nathaniel built. The Wyclercs! ... Let me tell you about *my* father. Nathaniel's hands were steeped in blood. For a start, he murdered his brother and sister.'

101

ORIANNA: NOW

The revelation silences the table, hangs over us like a guillotine.

I see the others stare at Amos, the day's dying light frozen in their eyes like shards of mirrored glass.

'My father left his younger siblings – the twins, Esther and Jude – behind when he first came to Eden Falls. They had no one else except each other. They became close, closer than nature or God ever intended for a brother and sister. When they finally got to Eden Falls, and my father found out, he locked them in the chapel and set it alight. They burned to death.'

Something dark and wet stirs inside my guts.

'Nathaniel spent his life trying to understand the nature of evil,' Amos continues. 'The monster inside himself that had made him commit such a terrible act. He never could. In the end, he believed he had no choice but to carry out the ultimate act of penance. He threw himself into that boar pit. He told me he was going to do it, the night before he died. I didn't believe him.' A shudder trembles his shoulders. 'That's who we are. The blood pumping through your veins.'

'That isn't true. It simply isn't,' Peter says eventually. 'You're drunk.'

Amos swings his gaze around the table. 'This family is a lie. This whole goddamned town is a lie.' He picks up the revolver. 'So tell me, my pantheon of the Philistines, why *shouldn't* I believe that one of you killed Gideon?'

'Amos. What are you doing?' David's voice cuts across the table. 'This isn't going to bring Gideon back.'

His words, spoken so quietly, hum with a power that gives Amos pause. His hand trembles. His eyes lose focus. For an instant, I see him as he is: an old man nearing death, bleary-headed with fatigue, grief, and its close cousin, remorse. The angel of darkness hovers at his shoulder; a dead light glimmers in his gaze.

Susannah stands, put her hands on David's wheelchair. 'I'm taking him home.'

We watch as she begins pushing him away.

'Wait.' Amos's voice is a croak. 'I called you here because I want you to know – I want *all* of you to know – that I'll be changing my will. My controlling stake in Wyclerc Industries will pass to Orianna.'

A gasp is pulled from Peter's throat. His chair clatters back as he storms to his feet. 'What the hell are you talking about?'

'Did I stutter, Peter?'

'You can't— you can't do that.'

'I assure you, I can.'

'This is insane.' His hands ball helplessly at his sides. But Amos is looking at David.

For a long moment, David says nothing, and then he nods.

After they leave, I turn to Luke. His face is unreadable.

I hear Rebekah rise to her feet. Without a word, she turns and walks away.

Peter remains rooted to the spot, white-faced, staring at his father as if at an escaped lunatic. Beside him, Ruth wipes her lips with a napkin and stands. Samuel joins them. 'I'm heading back to the church. Mrs Abernathy is hosting an evening recital. Peter, perhaps we should take our leave?'

His brother ignores him. Instead, he points a shaking finger at me. 'You won't see a dime of that money. I'll go to my grave before I let you get your murdering hands on it.'

'I don't want the money. I never asked for it.'

Peter swings his finger towards Amos. 'You're out of your mind if you think I'm going to let you do this. I'll fight you with everything I've got.'

'What *have* you got, Peter? *I* own the controlling stake in Wyclerc Industries. *I* made you CEO. I can just as easily take it away from you.'

'You wouldn't.' The full horror of the situation is dawning on him. He puts a hand on his wife's shoulder to steady himself. 'You can't.'

'Come on, Peter.' Samuel slips a hand through his brother's arm, then gently leads him away.

'Well,' says Martha as the sound of their engines fades, 'that was enormous fun. I should get out of bed more often.'

I pick up my glass and drain it. The whisky is smoky and warm and leaves a dark taste in my throat. I look at Amos. 'Why?'

'If you live long enough, you can learn to stomach anything. Except mendacity.'

'This was pointless. I didn't come back to Eden Falls for your money.'

'My fortune, what's left of it, is better off in your hands than theirs.'

'You really have lost your mind.'

'Perhaps . . . there was another reason I asked you over.' He nods at Cletus.

I watch as Cletus walks to a side table, removes the cover from a steel cloche, and returns with a cake, filled with white cream and ribbons of strawberry jam. He bends over it and lights three candles bunched in the centre.

'Happy birthday,' Amos says.

Something indescribable wells inside me. My mother almost always forgot my birthday, running around at the last instant – a haphazard affair, at best. There were no friends to invite over, no gifts worth the name.

I glance at Luke. He offers up a strained smile. Is this his doing?

'I don't need this.'

'Humour a dying man.'

'That's not fair. You think you can make me . . . what? Forgive? Forget? Because you're dying?'

'I don't need your forgiveness. You're my granddaughter. Nothing you or I say can change that. Now, blow out the fucking candles.'

His brow shimmers with perspiration. He looks ready to pass out.

My mouth is suddenly dry. I glance again at Luke. He nods at me. I see Grace hovering at his shoulder. Grace gives a slow smile. Her face blurs, changes, until it is my own face at Luke's shoulder.

I blink. The apparition vanishes.

I stand on unsteady legs, blow out the candles.

102

ORIANNA: NOW

Afterwards, as we dig into crystal bowls of brandy-and-butterscotch ice cream, I tell Amos about the lynch mob at the town hall. He frowns. 'Once upon a time, they wouldn't have dared cross me.' He massages his chest, as if the thought of the coming conflict has given him heartburn.

'How do you feel today?'

'Like a bear ate me up and shat me into a tin can.'

'Why won't you accept treatment?'

'Never fight a battle you know you can't win.' He clasps his hands around his belly. 'What was it like? In prison?'

I want to tell him that he has no right to ask me that. No birthday cake can make up for what he has done to me, to my mother, the years stolen from us both.

He senses my thoughts. 'Forget it. Forget I asked.'

'I met a woman in there. A cellmate. She'd murdered two people. She would tell me about lost light. The light that illuminates the human soul. Each time we commit acts against our better nature, we lose some of that light. But she believed we could get it back. That lost light. All we have to do is turn the dial.'

'Amen to that,' says Martha.

'Why were you so hard on Rebekah?' I ask Amos. 'Do you really think she could have had something to do with Gideon's death?'

'I don't know. A part of me wants her to be guilty. At least I'd have an answer. But then, I think of Grace. Rebekah loved her, doted on her. She's kept her room like a mausoleum, exactly the way it was on the day she vanished. I can't believe that Rebekah had anything to do with whatever happened to Grace.'

I consider his words. 'What if Tommy Quinn killed Gideon, and Grace somehow found out? Perhaps Quinn did something to Grace, to stop her from telling anyone. Perhaps Rebekah doesn't know.'

Luke speaks up. He has been so quiet, I have almost forgotten he is still here. 'That's quite a leap.'

A silence passes.

'Cletus,' Martha says, 'I think you should get Amos back inside. He looks beat.'

I expect Amos to throw a hissy fit at being treated like a child. But he says nothing as Cletus helps him to his feet.

'That stuff about Nathaniel,' I say. 'Why'd you tell us?'

He looks down at me with a greater measure of sadness than I have seen in human eyes in a very long time. 'Because there are some secrets a man cannot take to the grave. There's only one thing I'm certain of any more, Orianna. If there *is* a heaven up there, I will never see it.'

103

ANNIE: THEN

I stop at a gas station about an hour from the town.

My car, a ten-year-old Subaru, is a luxury I can ill afford but cannot do without.

The gas station is resolutely uncharming, a throwback to the era of wild-grass-edged tarmac, dungareed attendants, and a hostility to outsiders that might as well have been painted onto the flaking signboard hanging from the low-slung canopy.

I wander into the office-cum-shop, grab a bottle of water and a bar of chocolate, hand my credit card to the old soak behind the counter. Who looks at it as if I have just handed him a live grenade.

'Can't take plastic. Machine's busted.'

I curse, dig back in my wallet, find just enough bills to cover the charge.

The decision to go to Eden Falls isn't a spur-of-the-moment thing. I have been planning it ever since I took the case, but knew that I would have to get to know Orianna first, otherwise it would simply be an exercise in curiosity. Like a book tourist visiting a place they'd read about in a favourite novel.

The Girl In Cell A

There are some who consider this sort of thing a blurring of professional boundaries.

But there is also a breed of modern psychotherapists who believe in a holistic form of treatment. Like archaeologists, the things we dig up in therapy can only attain meaning when given context. Sometimes, you have to go out and find that context.

Our last session convinced me that the time was now right for a field trip.

Orianna's admission that she once harboured thoughts about killing her father hadn't quite turned out to be the revelation I had hoped for. It was an admission without admitting anything. At that point, she hadn't known who her father was, so her threat meant little. Then again, had such an admission come out in court, it could easily have been used to demonstrate a long-simmering anger, which had finally exploded the day Orianna discovered that Gideon was her father.

Or perhaps Orianna is playing games with me.

Rehashing the trial, the forensic analysis, has shaken her, of that I am sure.

But she remains closed off to me, some inner part of her held back.

How can I get to that hidden part of her?

I need to immerse myself in the environment in which she grew up – the environment that made her, had led her, inexorably, to that moment in the woods, in the cabin, with Gideon.

I need to go to Eden Falls.

104

ORIANNA: NOW

My mind is still whirring when I reach home.

The Scotch, the evening, Amos's gambit in declaring me his heir.

Why did he do that? It isn't as if I need any more enemies.

And yet, somewhere deep inside, the coals of a long-banked fire smoulder.

Wasn't I owed *something* by them?

They had stolen my life, sentencing me to years imprisoned in a six-by-eight concrete box. They had hounded my mother to her death. They *deserved* to pay.

It is all too much to process.

And then I feel it.

I spin around, look back into the darkness. Is there someone out there?

Fear creeps over me. I have to fight for control.

The crescendo of wolves rises once more in my ears. I know it isn't real, but the sound drowns out all rational thought. I clap my hands to my ears and walk to the cottage.

Slipping inside, I go for the gun, then return outside.

The Girl In Cell A

I walk around the cottage and follow the lake shore into the woods.

When I reach the tree I had marked with an *X*, I move around it, treading carefully, before moving on.

I am barely fifty yards further along when I hear a metallic snap, followed by a scream.

I race back, find the figure writhing in the dirt, right leg caught mid-shins in the boar trap. One hand flails at the ground, the other yanks ineffectually at the trap's metal jaws.

I raise the revolver and take careful aim.

105

ANNIE: THEN

I drive into town past a wooden signboard.

EDEN FALLS
Population: 2000

Graffiti is scribbled across the bottom of the board, but I can't make out exactly what it says.

The ride in is short, and before long I am drifting through the centre of town.

I park on a side street off the town square, then wander back in, checking out the cluster of civic buildings – a courthouse, a library, the town hall – and a large bronze statue of a man grappling with a wolf. The plaque on the base reads: *Nathaniel and the Wolf.*

I remember Orianna telling me about Nathaniel, Eden Falls' founder. Amos's father; Gideon's grandfather.

The town appears to be very much as Orianna has described in our sessions, and depicted in maps and drawings that she has made over the years. Clearly, very little has changed here. But then, in my mind, I always imagined Eden Falls as one of those small American towns untouched by the ravages of progress, a little blister of civilisation where time, like in Shangri La, remains forever arrested.

There are few residents out. The promised cold snap has settled in, though there is no snow on the ground. Yet. When it arrives, we are told to be ready for eight-feet-high drifts. Old folk snowed in. The collapse of civilisation as we know it.

I imagine Orianna drawn back here, like a homing pigeon, following the completion of her sentence. More than once she has expressed her determination to return to Eden Falls and figure out who had *really* killed Gideon ... How would she cope, being back in an environment she remembers with such hostility? What terrors of the mind might that unleash? More importantly, how would the locals treat her, bulldozing her way around the place, pointing fingers, throwing around wild accusations?

I have a rough plan for the day.

I start by taking a half hour for coffee and a bite to eat at a local diner, then find my way to the Griffin County Sheriff's Office.

Inside, I ask for Sheriff Hank Faulkes.

A young man with a blond mullet goggles at me, a fantastical creature with the big-city accent and shoes that probably cost more than he makes in a month.

It's a wonder he doesn't say *golly*.

I am led down a corridor and into a cramped but tidy office where Sheriff Faulkes registers surprise at my presence, but not shock. I had called ahead and been rebuffed.

'How can I help you, Miss . . . ?'

'Ledet. Dr Annie Ledet.'

I take a seat without waiting to be asked, forcing him to follow suit. 'I am a forensic psychotherapist, currently engaged in the treatment of Orianna Negi. I'd like to ask you some questions.'

His jaw works silently. Then he gets up, walks to a sideboard, picks up a coffee pot. 'Get you a cup?'

'Sure.'

When we're both settled, he looks at me over his coffee. In his eyes is the wariness of the country boy for the city slicker. Michael's folks had looked at me like that the first time I'd met them on their big ol' Iowa farm.

Faulkes is a small man, lumpy, with a crew cut. Clean-shaven. He doesn't look much like the man Orianna has described to me. But memory can distort more than material facts; it can reshape those for whom we have strong feelings into altogether transformed creatures that take possession of our minds. I have seen it many times, especially in cases of child abuse; the abuser turned into a giant, a monster residing permanently in the victim's memory.

'Treatment?' he says. 'How exactly do you treat a girl who blew her own daddy's brains onto a wall?'

'Orianna claims she didn't do it.'

'You city folk are all the same. Suckers for a hard-luck story.'

'I didn't say I believed her. The point is that *she* believes it. She cannot remember the killing. My job is to get her to the point where she can access those memories, so that she – and we – can see exactly what happened that day.'

'What happened is that she murdered a man in cold blood. And then lied about losing her memory in the hope the law would go easy on her.'

'You think she's faking? All these years?'

'I do.'

A silence. Faulkes continues to look at me.

'What was she like, growing up?'

'She was a handful. Like her mother. A loner. Always in trouble.'

'Violent?'

'On occasion.'

'Can you name any specific episodes?'

He thinks about this. 'There was one time. She was carrying on with some kid named Jake Kristofferson. Ended up kicking the shit out of the poor boy. Put him in hospital. He didn't press charges, didn't speak about it till years later, after she was convicted of Gideon's murder. Kid was too embarrassed to name her at the time – getting his ass handed to him by a girl.'

I am momentarily blindsided.

Jake Kristofferson is the boy Orianna claimed *Grace* had kicked into unconsciousness after he'd tried to get fresh. But, according to Faulkes, it was Orianna herself who had done that. She had lied to me.

Or rather, lied to herself, so that it was Grace and not her who was the aggressor. Placing herself at a remove from her act of violence.

What else from her past has she subtly redrawn in our sessions together?

'What triggered these violent episodes?'

'She was an angry kid. No father. Mother wasn't around much, too busy peddling her ass all over town. You're the shrink. Do I need to draw you a map?'

'What happened to Orianna is intimately bound up in her relationship with her mother and the fact that Christine kept Gideon's identity as Orianna's father a secret. Did you ever ask Christine about that? About who Orianna's father was?'

'I did. She told me to go fuck myself.'

I hold my tongue, determined to maintain my composure in the face of his hostility.

'What exactly happened to Christine?'

'She lost her mind, is what happened. After the trial, she couldn't find work in Eden Falls – the Wyclercs made sure of that. She had to take a bus out to Barrier every day. She had some friends there. Got herself a position as a hostess at some bar. By then, she'd been kicked out of the Big House. But she was stubborn. Wanted her due. Had this crazy idea she'd sue Amos, get him to hand over a share of his fortune, because Orianna was his grandchild. Of course, no lawyer worth their salt would touch the case, and the one she finally found didn't get very far.' He stops. 'I guess, after a while, everything just became too hard. She gave up, that's about the truth of it.'

'You think she killed herself?'

'Yes, ma'am, I do.'

I change tack. 'I've had a look at the case files, the court transcripts. There wasn't much attempt made to find any other suspects for Gideon's killing.'

'There was no need. All the evidence pointed to Orianna.'

'So you had no doubt? Even though Orianna couldn't remember what had happened?'

He takes a long, slow sip of his coffee. 'None whatsoever.'

106

ORIANNA: NOW

Gerty comes for me two hours after they haul me to the stationhouse and put me back in the cells. They don't charge me, but Sheriff Hank Faulkes gleefully lays out the possibilities: possession of an illegal firearm, and criminal negligence resulting in serious injury. He tells me that the man in my boar trap has been taken to hospital. He doesn't ask me who the man is. I suppose he has already found out, as I did when I asked him while he was screaming in agony, begging me to release him.

Gerty informs me that Luke is waiting outside.

'I asked you not to call him.'

'What did you want me to do, exactly? Use my magic wand to get you out of here?' Gerty's belligerent look is edged with worry.

She waits while they discharge me. Hank Faulkes looks on, expression inscrutable. 'Third strike and you're out.'

Luke is leaning against his truck. He straightens as I approach.

I stop in front of him.

And then I swing a fist, connecting solidly with his jaw.

He falls back, trips and crashes to the ground.

A hand goes, instinctively, to his cheek. He is astonished.

I look down at him, eyes blazing. 'You sonofabitch.'

He lifts himself off the sidewalk, smacks dust off his jeans. His colour is up, nostrils flared. 'It wasn't my idea.'

'Amos?'

He nods, rubbing his jaw.

In that moment, Luke's form seems to waver, flowing into the shape of my mother, then Amos, then Grace, and back again. I am overcome by rage.

I know that my anger, in part, stems from my paranoid fantasy that Luke and Grace might have had something going on, way back when, sneaking around behind my back. And with that comes another thought: *what if I had found out?* The rage I would have felt towards Grace, what would that have made me do?

Is *that* what I have blocked from my memory?

The thought chills me.

Luke pulls me back to the present. 'You could have hurt him badly, Ori. What were you thinking?'

His voice comes from somewhere far away.

'Were you fucking Grace? Back then?'

His eyes widen. 'You're sick, Ori.' He stops, then, 'I mean that your mind is damaged. After what happened, with Gideon . . . No one comes through that unscathed.'

'You think I'm crazy? Is that it?'

'You need help.'

My mind flashes back to my sessions with Annie Ledet.

'*You'll never truly be able to shed the past. The question is whether you can come to terms with it.*'

'Let's go,' I say.

107

ANNIE: THEN

The meeting with Hank Faulkes leaves me frustrated but not exactly surprised.

I am not about to change anyone's mind here.

Frankly, I have no idea why I asked him whether he had doubts as to Orianna's guilt. Going over the forensic evidence – and then learning that Orianna had once fantasised about killing her father – should have been enough to dispel any suspicions I might have had that she was anything but responsible for Gideon's murder.

And yet, being in Eden Falls, breathing the air of a place Orianna has described in such suffocating terms, seeing the hardness in Faulkes's eyes, I cannot suppress the tiny voice in my ear that refuses to remain silent.

There are secrets here. Lies and secrets. Years old and hidden from view.

But even old secrets eventually burst into the light.

The Big House is exactly as Orianna has described to me, the very image of an antebellum plantation home – at least, to my mind. I park by the fountain and make my way to the porch, where I am met by a maid and led through the house.

Having heard so much about it from Orianna, I am slightly spooked by being here. It is almost as if I have walked these corridors before.

Amos Wyclerc is waiting for me in his office. I had called ahead. To my surprise, he had agreed to meet with me.

He is every bit as charismatic as Orianna has described. In the way that, say, Count Dracula is considered charismatic, possessing a dangerous magnetism that pulls me across the room. His eyes, in particular, are wolflike. And waiting.

We shake hands, and then he ushers me to a couch arrangement, offers me a drink. I decline, but watch as he pours himself a bourbon.

I go over my reasons for being here; my time treating Orianna. He listens patiently, then sets down his glass.

'How do you treat madness, Doctor?'

It was an unexpected place to start. 'I don't believe Orianna to be mad.'

'Then how do you explain it? How do you explain a young girl blasting her own daddy's head from his shoulders?'

I shift on the couch. 'She continues to claim she cannot remember the incident. That she didn't do it.'

'She was convicted of murdering my son. Striking him down in cold blood.'

'She's your granddaughter.'

The word momentarily silences him, and then: 'In your sessions, does she talk about me?'

'Yes.'

He looks grim. 'I'm not the ogre she no doubt makes me out to be. I long suspected that Orianna was Gideon's child. My granddaughter. But, given that both Christine and Gideon denied it, I didn't push it. Sometimes, it's better to let sleeping dogs lie.'

'I'm sensing that you changed your opinion at some point?'

His mouth becomes a line. 'For years, I accepted Christine and Orianna's presence on the estate. Gideon had installed Christine here and, after Orianna was born, made it clear they would both stay, despite Christine's unmarried status. He deflected suspicions that he was Orianna's father, brazened it out when questioned. Besides, Christine always insisted that the true father was some stranger she'd shared a one-night stand with.'

'You never told Orianna you thought she might be your granddaughter?'

'No. How could I? It wasn't my place.'

'And any interest in her that you had . . . It all came to an abrupt end after Gideon's murder?'

'Yes. I blamed her. I felt betrayed. I believed Orianna guilty of murdering Gideon, Christine of enabling her. And so I cut them out of my life.' He sighs. 'It has taken me years to finally accept that, even if Orianna *is* my son's killer, there is plenty of blame to go around. The way Gideon treated her was unconscionable. Refusing to acknowledge that he was her father, even though he kept her within touching distance.'

The confession is unexpected. 'If you believe that, why haven't you visited her?'

'What good would that do?'

'It might be crucial in helping me treat her, helping unlock her memories.'

'The Girl in Cell A.' His tone is intended to be mocking, but comes out as sad more than anything else.

'If and when Orianna gets out, I believe she may well return to Eden Falls. How will you react when you have to face her again?'

'Truthfully? I don't know. She murdered my son.'

'And you have no doubt about that?'

He is about to reply, and then hesitates.

'As a purely theoretical exercise ... is it possible that Orianna might be telling the truth? That someone else murdered Gideon and she just happened to find herself in the wrong place at the wrong time?'

'No,' he says. But there is a tremor in his voice.

I decide not to push. 'I'd like to talk about your family. About the Wyclercs. About Peter and Ruth. Martha and David and Susannah. Samuel. Rebekah and Gideon. And about Luke. Everyone who knew Orianna growing up on the estate.'

His long fingers tighten around his glass. Finally, he nods.

I take out my notepad and begin.

An hour later, I lean back, look him squarely in the eyes. 'There's someone else I want to talk to you about. I want to talk to you about Grace.'

108

ORIANNA: NOW

Amos is behind his desk.

When I storm in, he leans back in his chair and sticks a lit cigar in his mouth, battening down the hatches.

'Why did you do it?'

'It was necessary.'

'How long?'

'Does it matter?'

'How *long* was he following me?'

'Didn't *he* tell you?'

I stand there, visibly shaking with rage.

'His name is Rattigan. That boar trap of yours made a mess of his leg. He might have lost a foot. I had a talk with him this morning. He won't be pressing charges.'

'How long?' I practically spit the words.

'Since the day they let you out.'

The floor drops away beneath my feet. The confirmation of my worst suspicions hollows out my stomach. Four years – the years of my mandatory parole – of being spied upon. My every move monitored, even before I made my way back to Eden Falls.

'Why?'

'You know why.'

'I want to hear you say it.'

He sighs. 'Because I wanted to keep tabs on you. Because there was still a tiny possibility that you knew what had happened to Grace, that you might know where she was buried, and that you might go back there. Because you were the last link I had to Gideon's death.'

'All that talk about trusting me? It was all bullshit.'

'I don't believe you killed Gideon, not any more. I don't believe you had anything to do with Grace's death ... What can I say? I hedged my bets.'

'That's how Luke knew where I was on the day I came back to Eden Falls. That's why he showed up at Elvira's place. Rattigan followed me back into town. He *called* Luke.' I glance at Luke in disgust.

Neither man says a thing.

'Was he there every night? At the cottage?'

Luke is shaking his head. 'No. We asked him to cool it once you were back in Eden Falls. It would have been too obvious – this isn't the big city. But after you were attacked, we thought it would be safer for you if he ... if he ...' He falters.

'Spied on me?'

'*Checked in* on you.'

'It was for your own good,' growls Amos. 'If you can't see that without throwing a hissy fit, then there's not much else to be said.'

Fury throbs through my jaw. 'You're going to turn this around on *me*?'

He flaps a hand. 'We've got bigger fish to fry.'

'No. We're *done*.'

'Weren't you paying attention yesterday? I'm making you my heir. I don't have much time left.'

'I don't want a goddamned thing from you.' I turn and stride to the door, stop, look back. 'You're a shitty grandfather.'

'So sue me,' he mutters and plugs the cigar back into his mouth.

Luke catches up with me on the stairs. 'If it hadn't been for Amos, Faulkes would have thrown the book at you for possession of an illegal firearm.' He runs a tired hand through his hair.

'You knew. All this time, you *knew*.'

'You're acting as if it was *my* decision.'

I storm out of the house, hurl myself into the Chevy.

Luke follows me out, stands there, hands on hips, his expression halfway between remorse and exasperation.

My rage is magnified by the blistering heat inside the car.

The idea that for four years I had been silently observed, my most private moments spied on. And Luke had *known* all along.

The walls of the car move inwards, crushing my lungs.

This town. This goddamned town.

I cannot bear it a moment longer. I have to get out. I have to get out *now*.

I turn the ignition, step hard on the gas.

In the rear-view mirror, I see Luke's arms drop to his sides, his head droop forward, sadness push down on his shoulders.

109

ANNIE: THEN

After meeting with Amos, I take a detour – with the help of directions provided by Amos – to visit Gideon's hunting cabin.

The scene of the crime.

My mind is awhirl.

The meeting with Amos has given me much to think on. His descriptions of the estate, what life for Orianna may have been like growing up here. The petty jealousies and rivalries of the Wyclerc family. I have learned, for instance, that Peter and Gideon did not get on. That Hannah Wyclerc – Martha's daughter – Martha being Amos's older brother, Abel's, widow – left the family under a cloud many years earlier. That Amos's grandfather, Noah, was hanged for murder. That Nathaniel, the town's founder and Amos's father, killed himself, possibly out of guilt arising from the arson-murder of his younger brother and sister, Esther and Jude.

Amos is unwilling to reveal all his secrets, but he has told me enough. There are revelations enough here for a team of therapists to dissect. I sensed a need in him to unburden himself. A weakening of his resolve. Perhaps he doesn't quite believe that Orianna might be innocent, but he is willing to concede that there is plenty of blame to go around.

More importantly, he now understands what it is that I am trying to achieve.

He is as eager as I am that we somehow penetrate that dark veil in Orianna's memory and get to the actual truth of what happened that day.

The cabin is a disappointment.

Sitting in an unkempt clearing, it's a large, weather-beaten wooden box; there is nothing that immediately strikes me as out of the ordinary.

Inside, there is little to see. Everything of interest has been removed years ago for forensic analysis following Gideon's murder.

My eyes linger on the wall where a lighter patch indicates the space vacated by the wolf's head Orianna described to me in an early session.

The wolf holds a strong sway over her mind, symbolising as it does the Wyclerc clan.

But she had also described it as a pariah. A lone wolf.

It doesn't take a therapist to realise that the wolf is how she sees herself.

110

ORIANNA: NOW

I barely make it out of town before I am forced to pull over, overcome by nausea and dizziness. My head is in pieces. I look in the mirror. A pale, sweating face, a fever victim, looks back at me.

I walk between the trees, lean over and vomit into a gorse bush.

Drained, I lower myself to the earth, empty my mind of all thought. But a migraine has begun to throb at the base of my skull, hammering nails into my brain.

I am losing myself in this place. Perhaps they were right. Annie Ledet. My parole officer. I should never have come back.

I return to the Chevy, take a bottle of water and wash out my mouth.

The thought of heading back into town is unbearable. I have to get away from Eden Falls, if only for a while.

My mind scrabbles around for a direction, the fingers of a drowning woman against the smooth hull of the boat from which she has fallen . . . I finally land on a task I had given myself after first visiting with Martha Wyclerc, but hadn't yet got around to.

Hannah Wyclerc. Martha and Abel Wyclerc's daughter.

Hannah, who'd quit the family decades ago and never looked back.

Something Martha had said about Hannah's reason for cutting herself off from the rest of the Wyclercs, a veiled hint that it might have some bearing on my own search for answers. I have no idea how that might be the case – I was not even born when Hannah left the family.

But now seems as good a time as any to track her down. Something concrete to focus on. For a short while, I can set aside the feelings of betrayal and shame and suffocation that Amos's actions have left swirling inside me.

I dig out the slip of paper Martha scribbled her daughter's address on, plug it into the satnav on my phone.

Hannah lives in Woolrich, three hours away.

I take the two-lane parish road out of town.

111

ORIANNA: NOW

The house, a two-storey colonial with a flesh-coloured façade and flaking white trim, is fronted by a parched lawn.

A skinny middle-aged white man in a tight white tank top and shorts and raggedy facial hair is hosing down the grass, scrolling a phone with his free hand.

He looks around as I walk across the street towards him.

'I'm looking for Hannah.'

He evaluates me for a moment. 'Nice graffiti.'

I look back at the car where the words *MURDERING BITCH* blaze from the paintwork.

He seems to decide that I am harmless. 'Out back.' He returns to his phone. I catch a flash of porn.

A flagstoned path leads through a side door to the rear of the house.

A woman in leggings and a tan T-shirt is on all fours, face in a vegetable patch, soil baked as hard as ceramic. A steel watering can is on its side by her elbow. I see the heads of turnips, beets. A spool of chicken wire.

The woman registers my presence, twists around to squint up at me from under a wide-brimmed straw hat.

'Hannah?'

'Do I know you?'

'My name is Orianna. Your mother gave me this address.'

We walk through a sunroom, along a cool, dark hallway and into a living room.

Plum-dark drapes, valenced and ruffled, hang beside sash windows. A worn carpet, the colour of boiled cabbage, stretches thinly over a wooden floor. A gilt brass floor lamp stands by a couch that looks like it's been kicked around by mules.

'Can I get you something to drink?'

'No. Thank you.'

'I have a feeling *I'm* going to need one.'

She walks out of the room, returns with two beers, sets them down on the rough-hewn coffee table. Wildflowers stand in a vase.

Hannah's knees click as she lowers herself onto the couch. Her hair is thick, almost entirely grey, stuck to her forehead and the back of her neck in straggling curls.

'I followed your trial. A long time ago now.' She has the Wyclerc eyes. They remain on me as she sips at her beer. 'Why are you here?'

I take a deep breath, then quickly explain my presence.

'You're a glutton for punishment, aren't you? Why the hell did you go back? Nothing you do will make right the things you've lost. Your youth, your innocence, the last eighteen years. Take it from me. The best thing you can do is get as far away from Eden Falls as possible and never look back.'

'Is that what *you* did? Why? What happened to you?'

She sets down the beer and settles her arms around her thin-shouldered frame. The silence stretches. Finally, she says, 'I've been waiting over forty years for someone to ask me that question and mean it.'

'Please. I need to know. Martha hinted it might have something to do with what I'm doing in Eden Falls. Reinvestigating my father's killing, I mean.'

'Your father.' And in the way she says those two words, in the inflection that sinks her voice to a croak, in the light that dies in her eyes, the shape of the past becomes clear. A chill moves through me.

'Gideon raped me. It started when I was seventeen. He kept it up for months until I hit eighteen and left town.' Her T-shirt is dark at the chest. 'I told my mother. I told Amos. No one believed me.'

My insides churn. My voice sounds brittle to my own ears. 'I don't understand. Why wouldn't they believe something like that?'

'Amos was blind when it came to Gideon. And my mother didn't dare cross Amos. She wanted to stay in that house. She wanted to be near my father's ghost.' Her eyes blink rapidly. 'You can't understand a place like Eden Falls until you understand people like Amos and my mother. Morality plays second fiddle to decorum, or at least the appearance of decorum. Besides, it was Gideon's word against mine.'

'But why? Why did Gideon do it?'

'Why do men do the beastly things they do? It was a ... a sickness. He couldn't control himself. I'm not excusing it, of course not. But I've come to believe that some people are born that way. Twisted.'

I feel a great hollowing out. This is the blood in my veins. Gideon's blood. Amos's blood. Noah and Nathaniel Wyclerc's blood. Racists and paedophiles and killers. How many lives had been ruined by the dark chemistry that flowed from one generation of Wyclercs to the next?

'Why didn't you go to the authorities?' I know that I sound desperate, hoping against hope that this woman is lying or exaggerating.

'You have to ask? *You*, of all people?' Hannah picks up her beer. 'That town, those people ... It's a fiefdom and the Wyclercs run it as they goddamned please.'

'You're a Wyclerc.'

'Not for a very long time.' A beat. 'I was a different person then. Easily cowed. Afraid. You can't imagine what it took for me to leave.'

My gaze falls on a family photo on the sideboard. Hannah and a short white man with greying curls and crinkly eyes, a wide, slightly crooked smile; two men flanking the couple, both in their thirties. The family resemblance to the father is strong. One of them is the porn-scrolling deadbeat I saw out front.

'What happened after you left Eden Falls? Where did you go?'

'I stayed with a pen pal I'd made, in New York. I got a job. Eventually, I got my own place. Never looked back.' She follows the direction of my gaze. 'That's

Earl, my husband. He works in retail. The other two are our sons.'

'There's something I have to know.' I hesitate.

'You want to know if Gideon did it to anyone else?' Hannah grimaces. 'I don't know. I cut myself off from my family. They tried to get in touch – at least, my mother did. But I wanted nothing more to do with any of them. I can't ever forgive them for not believing me.'

'What about your brother, David?'

'David was always too much of a Wyclerc to stand up to Amos. And he worshipped Gideon.'

I close my eyes.

This must be what it feels like to have the flesh flayed from your bones. The idea that my father was a rapist. That those who should have helped Hannah had, instead, conspired to cover up Gideon's crime. A wave of nausea shimmers through me.

'Why did you come here, Orianna? What is it that you think I can do for you?'

'Grace,' I whisper.

Hannah seems confused.

'I'm certain *I* didn't hurt her. I couldn't have. But she vanished the day Gideon died. Do you think—' I can barely voice the thought. 'Do you think *he* could have done something to her? She was the same age as you were when Gideon started to . . .' I tail off.

'How would I know? I'd been gone two decades by then.' She seems to sense that I need more. 'Gideon was incorrigible. I believe he had a pathological need to control the women around him, sexually, if he could. I don't believe there was ever a woman near him who could have been safe.' She blinks. 'I followed your trial. If it is true, if you did kill Gideon, I'm glad you did. He was a pig and deserved everything he got.'

112

ORIANNA: NOW

On the way back, I stop at a roadside diner, order pizza and a soda. I haven't eaten all day. What little I had for breakfast I threw up hours ago.

Around me, men, women and children are hunched over burgers and pizza and fries and shakes and super-sized bowls of butter pecan ice cream, the kind of meals that come with shitty little plastic toys that will be turned over in grubby hands for mere minutes before beginning their journey to landfill heaven.

Normality. This is normality.

I could simply keep driving. Never go back.

Invisible insects crawl over my skin.

My father was a rapist. An abuser of women.

My mind races ahead, tumbling into the dark.

What if he *had* abused Grace? Could that explain Grace's sudden change of persona that summer, her taking up of the Bible?

A new reading of that fateful day emerges from the dark well of my thoughts.

What if Grace had been abused by her father and had threatened to tell someone?

Could Gideon have killed her to save himself? Buried her out in the woods?

And if that were so, then might it not be possible that Rebekah had found out? What would a mother do under such circumstances? A woman already disenchanted with her husband's infidelity to the point where she had begun seeing another man in retaliation.

Could Rebekah have killed Gideon? Or, more likely, asked her besotted lover, Tommy Quinn, to kill him? Not for herself, but for her daughter, for Grace.

If that were so, then Rebekah had known all along that it couldn't have been me who had murdered Gideon. She had sat in Judge Whaley's courtroom every day of the trial, knowing that an innocent girl was going to go to jail.

Could it be true?

The horror of it made my head throb.

Grace.

Why hadn't Grace shared her pain with anyone? If it was true, that Gideon had preyed on her ... Grace had always been closed off, always kept her own counsel. But something like *that*? Surely, she'd have needed an outlet for her angst.

And now, the thought that has been pushing for so long at the back of my mind unfurls into the light. The thing I had seen, the thing that Grace had let slip in an unguarded moment, not long before the world ended.

Grace had kept a journal.

That summer.

She had kept a journal.

113

ANNIE: THEN

Whoever says cold showers are good for one's health is a stone-cold psychopath. And that's my professional opinion.

My heating broke down this morning, forcing me to adopt the army method of sixty seconds under a cold showerhead. By the time I arrive to see Orianna, I have all but recovered from the near heart attack.

It has been three weeks since I visited Eden Falls. A combination of a busy period at the college and Orianna being disinclined to see me has meant that this is our first meeting after a lengthy interval.

There is something specific I want to tackle at today's session. Though I have prepped for it, I am not sure how it will go, how Orianna will react.

When she arrives, she seems withdrawn. I note this.

'It's winter. Seasonal affective disorder. I'm SAD.' She smiles grimly.

I decide to break straight in with my visit to Eden Falls.

She listens, stiffening. When I finish, she says nothing for a long moment. I wonder if she considers it a form of betrayal, me going to Eden Falls without discussing it with her first. Talking to the enemy.

But when she finally speaks, it is with surprising calm. 'How was Amos?'

'I believe he has regrets. About the way you were treated. By Gideon. By the Wyclercs.'

'But he still believes I shot my father?'

I hesitate. 'Yes.'

She is silent again. I am surprised. I had expected more questions, some interest in how her hometown might have fared in the years since she left ... Then again, Orianna clearly harbours great resentment towards the good folk of Eden Falls, holds them complicit for the way she was treated, for her conviction.

Perhaps it isn't so surprising that she doesn't want to peel back the scab.

'I've thought about it, of course. What it might be like when I eventually go back there. The town. In my mind, it hasn't changed at all.' She doesn't look at me. I sense a great turmoil inside her. Suddenly, I have connected her – in a real and visceral way – to the place that has imprisoned her mind for so long.

I know I must proceed delicately, but the things I have to talk to her about are anything but gentle.

'Orianna, I spoke with Sheriff Hank Faulkes. He told me something that I'd like to discuss with you ... The incident you mentioned with Jake Kristofferson. According to Faulkes, it was *you* who beat up Jake. It was you that he was involved with.'

Her eyes flare. 'What are you talking about?'

'Why do you think you told me it was Grace who had beaten him?'

She stands abruptly. I think she is going to storm out, but she doesn't move. 'Are you saying I lied to you?'

'I am saying that your memory of the incident is confused. And if we take that as a starting point, then we can assume that other memories might equally be compromised. Our minds are a babel of voices at the best of times. For someone in your situation, it is incredibly difficult to distil the truth from such incoherence.'

She says nothing. I see indecision fly across her features.

'Orianna, please sit.'

She hesitates, then folds back onto her chair.

'Let's go back a bit. I understand that you were involved in a violent incident a month after you arrived here?'

She blinks at the change of direction. 'If you mean that I was attacked, then, yes.'

'The women who attacked you . . . Do you know why they targeted *you*?'

'They wanted to put me in my place. I'd upset a friend of theirs.'

'How?'

'I wanted to be left alone. I refused to play nice.'

I wait for more.

'I was aggressive. I was rude.'

'Is aggression your normal reaction in stressful situations?'

'No. I wouldn't say that.'

'I want to show you something, if I may?' I pick up a folder and hand it to her, open at a typed page.

She runs her eyes over it, recognises it as the analysis that the DA's appointed psychologist, a man named Cozell, had made of her prior to her trial. A passage halfway down the page has been picked out in yellow.

The subject is antisocial and exhibits symptoms of borderline personality disorder. She fears abandonment and harbours aggressive feelings towards her parents, feelings that have been present since childhood due to the absence of her father and the perceived lack of attention from her mother. She admits to a complex and vivid fantasy life. There are precursors of delusional psychosis. She is quick to anger. Violence appears to be second nature.

The words float between us.

'His name is Dr Chester Cozell. I've checked him out.' Her voice is sharp. 'He was an asshole.'

'He's well regarded in the field.'

'Are you saying you agree with him?'

'I'm saying that he's an experienced professional and it would be foolish of us to disregard his analysis, given the nature of the process we're engaged in. I'm saying we should talk about this.'

A flare of light dances in her eyes. I have an image of her hurling the file at me.

And then the fire goes out.

'You had several violent incidents *before* your father's murder,' I continue. 'The incident with Jake Kristofferson was not an isolated one. Fights with other girls. One of them ended in a trip to the sheriff's office. Do you remember that?'

A sullen look.

'Your mother convinced the girl's parents not to take things further. But she was badly hurt. It could have been much worse if others hadn't stepped in to stop you.'

She lowers her eyes to the file in her hand.

Violence appears to be second nature.

I can almost read her thoughts. For years, Orianna has held on to the belief that she simply isn't capable of the act for which she has been imprisoned. She has never regarded herself as an instinctively violent person, possessed of a violent *nature*.

But now, the walls are crumbling around her.

'Why did you attack that girl?'

'She talked trash about my absent father, about my mother's reputation around town, her nights at the Wolf & Boar and what went on there and who she left with and what they did together before she'd come staggering home the next morning, heels in hand, breath stinking of liquor.'

I look through the prism of Cozell's evaluation and see the years of resentment and anger building inside a lonely, isolated girl, a bonfire waiting to be ignited.

'Orianna, it's a myth that we can recreate ourselves in prison. All the work I've done in the penitentiary system only convinces me that, at best, we can learn to adapt. Our great vanity is in believing we have control over ourselves. There are things inside us that are hardwired, all the way back to the cave. In the right circumstances, those atavistic instincts are activated. And there's absolutely nothing we can do about it.'

114

ORIANNA: NOW

I tell the night guard, a congenial black man named Lavell James, that I have come to see Amos up at the Big House. He waves me through, eyes glued to an iPad, excited baseball commentary unfurling into the night. I see his sandwich box on the gatehouse's windowsill. I know that he makes them himself and likes to cut off the crusts.

Turning right at the interior road, I drive east, slowing as I come to Rebekah's house. I park, walk to the screen of cypress trees and look out at the property. The solitary vehicle I had seen out front on my previous visit is gone, the house dark.

I get back in the Chevy, drive a few hundred yards further on, then take the car off-road into the woods, the shot suspension grumbling at the uneven ground.

Getting out, I go to the trunk and rummage in the toolkit I keep there.

It takes me five minutes to walk back to Rebekah's.

I go around back, then climb the waist-high stone wall that surrounds the property.

I walk to the rear porch, skirting a maze of flower beds and a wooden swing seat I recall from my one and only prior visit to the house – on Grace's sixteenth birthday. An awkward occasion; Grace's eyes darting from face to face, never really settling, barely speaking to me, the acute flush of embarrassment when I hand over her present, the cheapest gift in the pile. For a girl who has everything.

Grace. My half-sister.

The one who lucked out in fate's lottery.

Until the day fortune turned against her.

I step onto the porch.

A blue-painted door lets into the back of the house.

A quick glance over my shoulder.

In the distance, the dark velvet of the night sky meets the rising landscape, merging with a shallow band of trees that abut the estate's exterior wall.

I turn back to the door, get down on my knees and peer at the lock.

Looking at the gap between door and frame, I see that it is too narrow for me to use my traveller hook to simply loid the latch.

I will have to pick the lock.

Flipping open the small flat case I took from my toolbox, I take out a flathead screwdriver and a snake rake.

I hear my old cellmate's voice in my ears. *'Might as well teach you something useful while we're in here.'*

I flex my fingers, then stick the screwdriver into the keyway and turn it gently clockwise. I ease the rake in above the screwdriver and begin to scrub the pins inside the lock, continually adjusting the pick until, one by one, the pins have set.

The lock clicks open.

I swing the door back, step quickly inside and shut it behind me.

The hammering sound in my ears is my heart.

I walk through a rear storage room, along a corridor and into the house proper. Darkness swells around me; the lumpy shapes of furniture, a mirror on a wall, carpet underfoot. The house breathes in.

I take out my phone and activate its flashlight.

Stairs leading upwards are bare of a runner; the beam bounces off dark, polished wood.

Halfway up, a board sings out, the sound as loud as a gunshot in the silence.

I freeze, heart pounding, then carry on.

Grace, at the urging of her mother, had given us a reluctant tour of the house on her birthday, ending in her bedroom.

I follow the map in my mind, stop outside the door, grasp the knob, turn. It is unlocked.

Slipping inside, I close the door behind me.

I hesitate, wrestling with myself, and then flick on the light switch. If Rebekah returns, she will come via the front of the house. She won't see the light.

Amos had been right when he'd told me that Rebekah had kept the room unchanged. The bedroom appears to be exactly as I recall it, like a snapshot taken almost two decades earlier. Grace's bed: a king-sized four-poster. Pinewood wardrobes. A prim little writing desk, with a white leather chair. A bean bag in purple corduroy. A Hollywood dresser, the kind Grace probably imagined young starlets ordered the moment they hit LA.

The Girl In Cell A

On one wall is a framed poster. No boy band for Grace. The shot is of New York City, looking down at an angle on a corridor of skyscrapers jostling for space, the Empire State Building dead centre, sun setting in the background. There is something wistful in the image, a hint at Grace's desire to flee the confines of Eden Falls.

This isn't Grace's bedroom. It is her shrine.

How does Rebekah put up with it, living here all alone, with the ghosts of her husband and daughter?

I search the room, meticulously going through all of Grace's clothes, still hanging in her wardrobe, searching the drawers of her desk and dresser, looking under the mattress, poking into every corner.

Finally, I sit back, defeated.

What had I hoped for? That, somehow, *I* might find something that the authorities had missed all these years?

It had been a foolish hope, a fool's errand.

I freeze as a sound comes from somewhere below, in the main body of the house.

115

ORIANNA: NOW

I walk to the door, flick off the light, then open the door, listen.

Footsteps on the stairs.

Panic beats at the inside of my ribcage.

I close the door gently and slip under the bed.

Seconds later, the door swings back, and the light comes on.

For a moment, nothing, and then footsteps enter the room.

I see, from my vantage point, expensive-looking slingback suede pumps. Shapely ankles.

Rebekah.

Seconds tick by. I blink sweat from my eyes, will myself to remain motionless.

Finally, Rebekah walks to the bed and sits down. Springs creak.

Another minute passes, and then the sound of ... weeping.

Shock holds me.

The sound of Rebekah crying, believing herself to be alone, is pitiful.

Something stirs inside me. Who are these tears for? Grace, Gideon, or herself?

The bed creaks as Rebekah stands and leaves the room.

116

ORIANNA: NOW

I count out a full two minutes before slipping out from my hiding place.

Opening the door, I listen, hear the sound of the TV floating up from the stairwell. I imagine Rebekah slumped on the couch, eyes vacant, shoes kicked off, a glass of wine in hand, snail's trails of tears drying on her cheeks.

There is no way back through the house.

I pad to the casement window, gently ease it up.

Looking down, and then to either side, I see a drainpipe just feet from the ledge. It looks sturdy, old-fashioned, cast iron painted black.

The pipe runs through a concrete gutter head three feet below.

I slip onto the ledge, then swing around, lowering myself down until I am hanging from the ledge by both hands. I reach out a leg, try to set a foot on the gutter head, miss, try again and lose my grip, one hand flying off the ledge.

A strangled cry escapes me; pain explodes in my shoulder.

The hand still on the ledge clamps down. I am certain my fingers will leave indents in the wood.

I calm myself, swing my free hand back onto the ledge, then inch along to the very edge and arc my foot out again.

This time I find purchase.

Steadying myself, I let go with my right hand and reach for the drainpipe. My fingers scrabble around it. Barely.

I bite my lip, then let go of the ledge and shove my body along the wall. For a moment, I am sure I have misjudged it, that I will plummet to the ground ... Momentum wins out. I am clinging to the pipe, eyes closed, breathing hard, face slick with sweat.

Twenty minutes later, I am back in the Chevy, head on the steering wheel, cursing my own foolishness.

When my heart has finally settled, I evaluate the situation.

If Grace had wanted to keep her journal secret from prying eyes, she wouldn't have hidden it in her room. That was the first place they'd look.

Where else could she possibly have—?

And then it comes to me.

117

ORIANNA: NOW

I drive back along the loop road to the southern woods, park, then walk fifty yards in from the tree line to the riven oak of my childhood, the oak I had once shown Grace, the oak where I had hidden cigarettes from my mother.

The oak that Grace had agreed made the perfect hiding place.

It hasn't changed. Then again, from the perspective of a tree's life, eighteen years are but the blink of an eye.

I look at the teardrop-shaped gash in the trunk. It seems to breathe, the mouth of an ancient animal.

I lower in my phone, flashlight activated, and wiggle it around, but the angles and the acuteness of the aperture make it difficult to see anything.

Setting the phone down, I stick in my arm, up to the elbow, face set against bark. My fingers grope around blindly.

Something. I tiptoe my fingers over a leathery smoothness.

I stretch out my arm until it feels as if it might pop from its socket. Tweezering whatever it is I have found between two fingers, I gradually pull it back to where I can grab a hold of it, and then draw it out.

Shaking the ache out of my shoulder, I look at what I now hold in my hands.

A leather-bound journal, dated the year Grace vanished.

Time thickens, slows, pools.

I open it.

118

ANNIE: THEN

Orianna and I meet again, several days later.

I'm glad of the shortness of the interval. It's my intention to continue to pull on the thread I began yanking at our last session. Namely, the mechanics of Orianna's memory loss.

When we are settled, I dive straight in. 'Orianna, today I want to discuss repressed memories.'

She blinks, then says, 'I've done my homework. I know that not everyone is convinced repressed memories are even a real thing.'

'Yes. You're correct. The truth is, the jury is still out. Ever since Freud mooted the idea, there's been disagreement. Recently, it's become quite bitter – someone in the media coined it the "memory wars".' I flash a rueful smile. 'Repressed memories are memories we unconsciously block, usually because of a traumatic experience. They can remain blocked for years, and are often only recovered following a trigger or therapy.

'Some researchers claim there is little scientific evidence for them. On the other hand, clinicians say repressed memories are a form of defence mechanism – your mind unconsciously hides traumatic memories because they can be detrimental to your health. But this act of repression takes a toll on the body – in other words, it has what we would call a psychopathological impact. Clinicians see this all the time. Insomnia, anxiety, confusion in certain situations. Sometimes, we invent completely new, fictitious memories to fill in those gaps.'

'Are you talking about . . . delusions?'

'I'm not a fan of that word. It comes from the Latin, and implies defrauding or cheating. I prefer the French *délire*, which suggests a ploughshare jumping out of a furrow, like the way the mind might skip. The truth is that there is no agreed definition of what we mean by delusion. In layman's terms, a patient suffering from delusional psychosis creates a subjective reality, a set of false beliefs that they believe in implicitly, including false or subtly redrawn memories. Of course, these false memories are completely real to the patient.'

She considers my words. 'Do *you* believe repressed memories are real?'

'There's a concept in psychology called phenomenology that is relevant here. In the context of *your* situation, it refers to our attempts to access your subjective understanding of what happened to you, to try to recreate what you think you've experienced.' I stop. 'Orianna, I think that some of the things you believe are false. In fact, I know that they are false.'

'What do you mean?'

'I gave you an example the last time we met. Your memory of the Jake Kristofferson incident. Here is another. You stated that the Wyclercs wanted you tried for first-degree murder, that Amos wanted the death penalty . . . What if I were to tell you that isn't true?'

'That's not possible.'

'I've checked, Orianna. Amos has gone on record saying that he was in agreement with the second-degree charge. He never believed you premeditated Gideon's murder.'

'You're lying.'

I remain impassive, even as I note the defensiveness in her tone, the sudden anger.

With great effort, she brings herself under control. 'Amos lied.'

'Look, I understand that this is a lot to take in. The idea that what you think happened to you may not be the actual version of events in reality. It's hard not to be able to trust one's own memory. But remember, the mind is a living landscape. When it malfunctions, there are consequences. We misremember and we invent things. And the harder we look – for what is *real* – the less we sometimes see. It's like staring at the sun.' I allow this to sink in. 'It will take work to get us to the point where you can accept that. Like I told you at the very beginning, it's a journey, a difficult one, and I'm going to need your help if you truly want to get to the truth.'

119

ORIANNA: NOW

Grace is standing behind me, reflected in the mirror. Light spearing in from the window sets a sheen on her naked shoulders, haloes the wilds of her hair.

'You don't belong here any more.' Grace's voice echoes from the walls.

'Where else would I go?'

'They'll never accept you. You know that, don't you?'

'I can't leave.'

'Yes, you can. Just walk away.'

'They won't let me leave. You won't let me leave.'

A secret smile turns up the corners of her mouth. She leans down, her voice deep and throaty, the growl of a wolf.

'Find me and I'll let you go.'

'And what if I never find you?'

I hear the rasp of my own breathing. I remember the years in prison, Grace coming alive in my mind, the girl preserved in amber.

Light washes around her. Grace's face fades into the brightness, until all that remains is a disembodied voice.

'Accept the truth, Orianna. Accept what you did. Free your mind. Set us both free.'

120

ORIANNA: NOW

I am awoken by the sound of thumping.

For a moment, I lie in a haze of golden light, staring sightlessly at the ceiling. And then the dream evaporates in a mist of flickering images. A hollow opens inside me, a loneliness and a longing akin, I imagine, to falling through empty space.

The thumping becomes urgent.

I lift my naked body from the bed, pull on shorts and a tank top, pad barefoot through the living room to the door.

My heart lurches as Luke crowds the step, framed in a dazzle of sunlight.

Am I still dreaming?

His eyes laser in on the empty bottle of wine on the table. 'It's Quinn,' he says eventually. 'They've found something.'

Blood thrums in my ears.

Sheriff Hank Faulkes makes it clear that he is anything but pleased to see me.

'She's a civilian, Luke. She's got no business here.'

'You want to explain that to Amos?'

Faulkes cracks his jaw. I can practically read his thoughts: to call Luke's bluff or not?

He waves us into seats, picks up a mug of coffee, leans back. On the mug are the words: WORLD'S GREATEST SHERIFF.

'This morning, around dawn, the station house received an anonymous call. Told us to go search Tommy Quinn's trailer. Told us we'd find something linking him to Grace Wyclerc's disappearance. I called up Deputies Pence and Martin and we took a little ride down there.' He breathes through his mouth, gently ruffling his moustache. 'We found this.'

He yanks open a drawer, takes out a clear plastic evidence bag, tosses it on the desk.

I pick it up.

Inside is a diamond-studded crucifix on a length of broken chain.

Grace's crucifix.

My palms tingle. 'Is it really hers?'

'I took it up to Amos. He confirmed it.'

A banked fire in my chest bursts to life. Questions tumble over each other in my mind; I cannot seem to get the words straight in my head to ask them.

Luke's voice: 'Any lead on who made the call?'

'None. The voice was disguised.'

'Have you got him here?' I ask.

Faulkes raises an eyebrow.

'Quinn? Is he in custody?'

The sheriff exchanges glances with Luke. 'You didn't tell her?'

'Tell me what?'

'Quinn's gone. Reckon he heard us coming and lit out. Or someone warned him. Quinn is in the wind.' He pauses. 'But here's the thing. *You* were up at Quinn's trailer just two days ago ... Here's what I'm thinking. Maybe *you* had that pendant all along. Maybe you hid it all those years ago. And now it miraculously turns up in Quinn's trailer, after you pay him a visit.'

'That's horseshit.' Luke has shot to his feet.

'We're not ruling anything out, chief.'

I have the feeling that once again a narrative is being written for me over which I have no control.

'But you've got bigger problems.' A sly smile slips onto Faulkes's face. 'Quinn's out there, somewhere. If he *is* innocent, then he knows the only person who could have planted that crucifix is you. My advice? Get gone while you still can.'

121

ORIANNA: NOW

'You can't stay out there, all by yourself.'

'Where do you suggest I go?'

'Amos wants you safe. Move into the Big House. I'm begging you. Be reasonable.'

The pleading in Luke's voice, the concern, pulls at my heart.

We are sitting in the basement of the library, with Gerty. She says, 'He's right, child. You can't just wait for Tommy to show up on your doorstep.'

'I'm not scared of Quinn.'

'Well, you dang well oughta be!' Gerty's face is puckered into anger. 'This whole lonesome-ranger thing has gone on long enough. Come stay with me. I can make room and you know I'd love to have you.'

I shake my head. My skull is pounding again. I feel feverish.

'Ori. Please.' Luke's eyes beseech me.

'I can't. I was run off once before. I won't let Tommy Quinn or anyone else do that to me again.'

Gerty stands up in a huff, storms off, muttering under her breath.

I turn to Luke. 'There's something I need to show you.'

I take out Grace's journal, set it before him.

Last night, I had skimmed through it. As the blank pages spun before my eyes, disappointment had lodged in my chest.

And then, just when I had begun to think it must be empty: a handful of entries. But they weren't conventional journal entries – accounts of what Grace had been doing, how she'd been feeling, who she'd interacted with. Instead, they read to me as a series of frantic outpourings of emotion, words expressed on a page because they either couldn't be said out loud or were being set down on paper in preparation for a confrontation. In a way, they were messages, addressed to no one, a dozen of them, scattered through the latter half of the journal, on pages dated throughout that summer.

As Luke reads, fragments flash before my eyes.

I love you. It's as simple as that. This is the first time in my life I feel that someone truly sees me, who I am, what I want.

I understand your need for secrecy, but I'm tired of it. I live for our moments together. Have you any idea how hard it is for me to pretend that I'm the same person I was before we fell in love? I want to be able to love you openly. I want us to leave this town. I want us to build a life together, somewhere no one knows us. Please, my love, let's just go. Tell no one. Let's just leave, in the dead of night.

And then, in the later entries, the tone turns sour.

Have I done something wrong? Why are you pushing me away? Is it because of them?

And then the final entry, dated just before Grace vanished, before Gideon was murdered.

Do you think that what we've done is wrong? How can love be wrong? You feel so distant. I can't bear it. I won't let them ruin what we have. I've been thinking about what you said. That you want to end it. I can't go back to being that lost, lonely girl. I won't let you end us. I'll talk to him. I'll talk to my father. I'll tell him everything. I don't care what he thinks. I don't care what he might do. He can't stop us. Remember your psalms, my love. The Lord is my light and my salvation – whom shall I fear?

Luke finishes reading, his face growing still. 'Where did you get this?'

'That's Grace's handwriting. Those are her words.'

His mouth opens and then closes again. I remembered how, a day earlier, I had all but accused Luke of sleeping with Grace . . . *Could these entries be about Luke?* It would make sense. Grace's conflicted feelings about a teenage affair with her cousin. The need for secrecy. Her desire to leave town. Her fear of what her family might think if they found out.

A wave of nausea slices through me.

Luke. Beautiful, beautiful Luke.

'If this is authentic, then this constitutes material evidence,' he says. 'You shouldn't have touched it. We have to hand this in.'

I offer no protest. I have already photographed and saved the pages to my phone. 'This proves that Grace had a secret lover that summer. Someone she couldn't – or wouldn't – tell anyone about. He tried to end it; she wasn't willing to accept that. She wanted to tell her father. Tell Gideon. To drag their affair into the open.'

Luke. Was it you? Could it be?

'I think she was afraid,' I continue. 'Of what her father might do.'

Luke frowns. 'Why would she be afraid of Gideon?'

I tell him about Hannah, watch the colour drain from his cheeks. 'Did you know?' I ask.

He grasps for words. 'I, I heard rumours. But there was nothing concrete. It was all ancient history, before I was born. No one was ever willing to talk about *why* Hannah left. Only that she'd been a wild child and had run away as soon as she was old enough.'

'My father was an animal. It's possible that *he* killed Grace.'

Luke looks stunned. I can see what he is thinking, as if his thoughts are being projected onto a screen. *What would Amos say when confronted by the possibility that his beloved son might have killed his own daughter?*

I suspect Amos will bury his head in the sand, just as he had done when Hannah had told him that Gideon assaulted her all those years ago.

The thought sickens me.

The door to the office swings open.

I turn, expecting to see Gerty, and then stiffen as Rebekah Wyclerc walks in.

122

ANNIE: THEN

I meet Leo a mile from my apartment for brunch.

My son is a mountain. Each time I see him, he appears to have grown several inches. It must be costing Michael a fortune to feed and clothe him.

Good.

We meet in a Chuy's. Leo loves Tex-Mex and the weirdness of Chuy's décor – fifties-era vinyl booths sitting below Elvis and Mexican memorabilia – appeals to him.

The initial awkwardness whenever we get together now is becoming more pronounced. My heart sinks, but I suck it up and grin as if all my Christmases have come at once.

I suppose I can hardly blame him. How is a young boy supposed to react to the revelation that his mother is an adulteress?

Michael had insisted that I be the one to tell him. A deliberate twist of the knife. I suppose I can't blame him. If there was one thing Michael had always been, throughout our marriage, dogged by that Baptist-preacher's-son integrity, was faithful.

But what exactly could I say to Leo? There were no

mitigating circumstances. Michael hadn't pushed me away; our life hadn't become a drudgery. We still had sex. We loved each other.

So why?

As a therapist, I should have been able to analyse it better than I did. But for some things, especially when they are so close to home, there can be no explanation. Human beings are not rational actors. We do crazy things, counter to logic, common sense, and to our own interests. We are capable of destroying our lives for a moment's excitement, for pleasure, out of spite, out of hate, a hundred instinctive emotions that are beyond our reasoning.

We fuck up. It's that simple.

As a defence, it was inadequate.

Did I deserve to lose everything for a handful of meaningless encounters? My home, my husband, my son? The life I had known and adored?

Michael wanted – *needed* – to punish me. I can understand that. But a small part of me had hoped that we might get past it. Other couples did.

I was wrong.

Leo and I chat for a while. He orders a mocktail. I settle for a Coke.

It feels good to immerse myself in his life like this, face to face, and not over the phone or a video call.

Our food arrives and we tuck in.

'Is it true that she blasted her father in the face?'

Leo's question catches me off guard. For a moment, I wonder if his friends have put him up to it. He has never previously shown any interest in my patients. Then again,

The Girl In Cell A

he is a sixteen-year-old boy, with a teenager's nose for blood and gore.

'Yes.'

I expect a follow-up, but he simply looks at me in wonder, then goes back to attacking his plate.

I continue talking to him – about school, football – but images of Orianna intrude.

I imagine what I would do if Leo was in Orianna's place. He is only a year younger than Orianna when she killed Gideon. What if *Leo* were accused of murder, charged, convicted, sentenced to purgatory?

Orianna's mother, Christine, had ended up taking her own life. I cannot imagine doing the same. But who can truly tell until the vice of circumstance clamps itself around our lives?

I think about Orianna and how her life has panned out.

Will she ever be able to lead a *normal* life? The Girl in Cell A. That stupid moniker will follow her wherever she goes. Will she be forced to change her identity? Perhaps she should leave the US entirely, find some corner of the world that has never heard of her.

Who am I kidding? Even if she is released, she will never be free of this. If nothing else, she will remain a magnet for creeps like the online-forum guy who had made it into my apartment, almost into my bed.

And what if she follows through on her plan to return to Eden Falls?

A broken bone can mend completely, but the human mind is rarely so cooperative. We are all dysfunctional, to a greater or lesser degree. But for someone like Orianna, control of the cockpit has been ceded.

I fear that if she returns to Eden Falls, it will precipitate another crash.

Michael calls in the middle of the meal, ostensibly to check on Leo. As if, perhaps, I might be dripping poison into his ear. Or perhaps he thinks I have a van waiting out back, ready to kidnap our six-three, 220-pound gorilla of a son.

I continue to think about Orianna when I shut the phone. Michael would not have approved. During our marriage, he had accused me, more than once, of being obsessive about my work, of caring more about my patients than my family.

In Orianna's case, he may be right. The more I treat her, the more I want to rescue her. Even if it's only from herself.

Perhaps I have been thinking about this in the wrong way.

I have focused on Gideon and the evidence presented at Orianna's trial. On her experiences growing up in Eden Falls.

But the two most influential people in Orianna's life prior to her imprisonment had been her mother, Christine, and Luke Wyclerc, the boy she had loved.

More than anyone, *they* had contributed to her emotional state on the day of Gideon's killing. Both were intimately present in the build-up to the killing, had a part to play in the events of that day.

In a sense, Orianna and I have gradually, inexorably, been moving towards this moment.

To the day of the murder.

123

ORIANNA: NOW

'Shit,' breathes Luke.

A moment of paralysis and then he rises to block the older woman's advance.

'Get out of my way.'

'Please, Rebekah—'

'I said get out of my *fucking* way.'

'Step aside, Luke.'

He looks over his shoulder at me. His lips move soundlessly, and then he turns back to Rebekah. 'OK. But no closer.'

Rebekah's eyes bore into me. 'What did you do? ... Tommy Quinn had nothing to do with Grace's disappearance. He didn't kill Gideon. For eighteen years, no one's seen the crucifix my daughter was wearing the day she went missing. You breeze back into town and suddenly it shows up ... *You* planted it in Tommy's cabin.'

'I had nothing to do with that. You can believe me or not, I really don't care. As for Quinn's innocence ... He was besotted with you. He hated Gideon.'

'Tommy would never have hurt my daughter. Never!' She spits the word.

'Are you sure?' I pick up Grace's journal from the table and hold it out to Rebekah.

'Ori—' Luke begins, but I cut him off with a raised hand. He lapses into silence, looking miserable.

Rebekah blinks rapidly, then takes the journal, flicks through it. Her eyes widen. 'That's ... that's Grace's handwriting.' Her voice is heavy with disbelief. 'Where did you get this?'

I say nothing.

Rebekah's eyes drop back to the open book in her hands. 'Who is Grace talking about? This man she says she ... loves?'

'I don't know.' I hesitate. Luke's name hovers on the tip of my tongue. I swallow it back, then plunge ahead with another thought that has suddenly gripped me. An alternate theory. 'But one possibility is Tommy Quinn. It would explain everything. Quinn seduces your daughter behind your back. When she threatens to tell Gideon, to make their affair public, Quinn kills them both.'

Luke's head snaps around. Rebekah's face goes into meltdown. She seems to gasp for air. 'You've lost your mind.' She takes a deep breath. 'What were you doing in my house?'

It is my turn to feel blindsided.

'The window to Grace's room was open. No one else in this godforsaken town has a reason to be in there. Is *this* what you were looking for?' She flaps the journal at me. 'This, this *fantasy*?'

She throws the diary at me. It bounces off my chest, flutters to the ground like a shot bird.

'If anything happens to Tommy, I'm holding you responsible.'

'You're in love with him, aren't you?' I counter. 'You loved him even then. You thought he felt the same way. But what if he was only leading you on? What if he was busy seducing Grace at the same time? Maybe he used you to get to her.' I take a step towards Rebekah, see Luke tense out of the corner of my eye. 'Maybe that's why he approached Gideon on the day of the Forest Festival. Maybe Grace was set to tell Gideon, as she says in her journal. Maybe that spooked Quinn. And so he made a big production out of telling Gideon about his affair with *you*. Perhaps he hoped Gideon wouldn't believe Grace.

'But he didn't know Gideon. Gideon would never have let it go. The women in his house were *his* property. He couldn't live with the idea of someone like Tommy Quinn soiling *his* goods. Perhaps he asked Quinn to meet him at his cabin, so they could talk it through. Perhaps he had plans for him. All those guns. But Quinn wasn't stupid. Maybe he was just quicker on the draw.'

Rebekah looks ready to claw the skin from my face. Madness wheels in her eyes.

And then she spins on her heel and marches from the room.

124

ORIANNA: NOW

Four hours later, I arrive at the Big House.

Amos has been tied up, unable to see me until late in the afternoon. By then, Luke has gone off on an errand of his own.

I arrive to find a storm blowing in Amos's office, Peter Wyclerc stomping up and down as his father listens from behind his desk.

'I'll fight it, goddammit. I'll challenge it in court.'

'It's my money and I'm of sound mind. There's not a thing you can do about it.'

'You're not competent to make the decision. You're dying. The stress of it.'

'The only one giving me stress is you, Peter.'

'The girl's coerced you, somehow.'

'She didn't do a damn thing.'

'I'm the fucking CEO! You think I'll stay on, knowing *she's* holding most of the stock?'

'You can leave anytime you want.'

Peter looks punch drunk. 'You'd like that, wouldn't you? You never wanted me in charge, did you? I was never good enough. I wasn't *Gideon*.'

Amos grinds his stub angrily into an ashtray. 'I've asked Pruitt to draw up the papers.'

I step further into the room. Peter spins around. His eyes bulge. A look of pure hate threatens to stop my heart where I stand. I see the tension in his shoulders, the corded muscles of his neck. A man reduced to the instinctive reactions of a feral animal.

Could that same fury have exploded over Gideon?

Despite my growing conviction that others – namely Tommy Quinn – may have been behind Gideon's murder, I haven't quite let go of the fact that Peter had loathed his younger brother.

He gains control of himself with a great effort. 'This isn't over.'

I watch him stomp out of the room.

'Peter hates you,' I say.

'Hate is a complicated emotion. It takes many forms. Children tell their parents they hate them. Soldiers are trained to hate their enemy. Sooner or later, we all tell God we hate Him.'

'Why are you doing this? I told you I don't need your money.'

'You don't want it, give it to charity.'

I walk to his desk, hand him my phone.

His brow furrows. 'What's this?'

'I found a journal, Grace's journal. These are the entries she made that summer.'

I wait as he scrolls through, reading the letters, see shadows darken his face. 'Who is she talking about?'

'I don't know. It could be Tommy Quinn.' I explain my theory.

He seems stunned.

'If not Quinn, then perhaps someone else. An older man, perhaps? Someone with everything to lose if it came out. A married man. Perhaps Grace went to the cabin that day to tell Gideon about this man. Perhaps whoever it was followed her, killed them both.'

Amos sits in silence, the only sign of his inner turmoil the clenching and unclenching of his right hand. Finally, he speaks. 'I've been thinking about that day. If what you say is true, then how did Grace get back to the cabin without anyone seeing her? The last time she was seen was in town. How did she get onto the estate without the guard at the gate seeing her?'

'She could have come in via another gate. She'd used them before. Maybe she had a key no one knew about.'

'Grace was no ghost. She didn't just float through town without a soul seeing her.'

A click sounds in my head. White noise fills my thoughts. My brain stutters out of its groove.

'What you're saying,' Amos continues, 'it just isn't plausible.'

My thoughts shimmer. The answer is there. I can feel it, *see* it, the outline of something just beneath the surface of a lake of molten fire. All I need do is plunge my hand into the flaming liquid.

I am gripped, suddenly, by an image of violence: I see Gideon, and Grace. I see a shotgun aimed at Gideon. But the gun isn't in Grace's hands. The gun trembles at my own shoulder. I *feel* the softest pressure on the trigger. A violent blast. Gideon's head vanishes in a cloud of blood.

I return to the moment, see Amos shaking his head. 'Let's say you're right, and that Grace somehow got to the cabin without anyone seeing her ... If she *was* killed there, where's her body?'

Sweat runs down my back. I struggle to regain my bearings. 'The killer buried her.'

'Why?'

'I'm not sure. Possibly to prevent us linking the two killings.'

'I can't see the sense of that.'

He is right, of course. Much of my conjecturing makes sense in only the narrowest way. I came back to Eden Falls looking for simple explanations. All I have found is ever-increasing complexity.

I steel myself. 'I went to see Hannah.' I see him stiffen. 'She told you about Gideon, what he did to her. Why didn't you believe her?'

His face is the colour of baked earth. A long moment passes. 'Hannah was a child.'

'She wasn't lying.'

'Children make things up all the time.'

'You *knew*. You've always known.'

He meets my gaze defiantly.

'If you'd have listened to her then, maybe none of this would have happened. Maybe Gideon and Grace would both still be alive.'

Blood rushes into his face. And then, just as quickly, the fight goes out of him. He slumps in his seat, jaw slack. A choking silence enfolds us. When he speaks again, his voice is low and husky. 'Gideon loved baseball cards. Did I ever tell you that? When I remember him, I remember the boy, never the man. I was never an attentive father. But Gideon brought something out in me. I could never see straight around him.

'They say a bad aura stinks. Like rotten meat. But when I looked at my son, I saw only a sacrament to all that I wanted, all that I knew to be good and right about the world. The lies we tell ourselves are comforting; they give us something to hold on to when darkness falls.' He looks directly at me. 'I can't apologise for the man I was, the things I did. I'm not afraid of being judged. The truth is, none of us knows what lies beyond the veil. What if the throne of God is empty? What if heaven and hell are just dirty little rooms, nothing waiting for us but the dark?'

The room is suddenly too small for us; Amos a creature in a dream; the dream a shadow in the corner of my mind.

I turn and walk out.

I reach the cottage in darkness.

Entering, I discover a folded square of paper, poked under the door.

I look back out into the night, eyes scanning the dark. But there is nothing.

Stooping, I pick up the paper.

Black letters, in capitals, on white.

IF YOU WANT TO KNOW WHAT HAPPENED TO GRACE, COME TO THE OLD CABOOSE AT MIDDAY TOMORROW. BRING AMOS. TELL ANYONE ELSE, AND YOU'LL NEVER KNOW THE TRUTH.

125

ANNIE: THEN

My plan to begin discussing the day of the killing with Orianna is delayed.

Orianna has landed herself in trouble with the authorities. She has been involved in a physical altercation with another woman at the facility and has been confined and will not be available for further sessions for several weeks.

I speak with the people in charge. 'She just went berserk,' her guard, Barney, tells me.

I push down on my anger. Anger is not going to get me what I want.

Besides, a small part of me suspects that *I* may have played a part in this. By bringing Orianna closer and closer to the moment of truth, the traumatic instant that caused her memory loss, I am inciting a storm of emotion inside her.

I have seen such things happen before.

The moment of breakthrough with dissociative amnesia is not always illuminating or cathartic. A reliving of trauma has consequences, side effects, particularly when the patient is confined inside a closed environment.

I have enough experience of such environments to understand the corrosive harm they can do to the human psyche, the build-up of internal pressure. This is the worst place on earth to save a lost soul. Because prisons, of any type, are closed systems, all but cut off from external scrutiny. Inside these walls, there are only predators and prey.

Prison doesn't cure the sociopaths.

It simply gives them victims with nowhere to run.

126

ORIANNA: NOW

'It's a trap.'

Amos is in the garden, sunning himself in a wooden rocker, face turned to a sky the colour of a mountain lake. He reminds me of a lizard basking in the mid-morning heat.

I had awoken early, showered the sweat from my body, dressed, then sat at the kitchen table reading and rereading the note.

Who could have left it? Tommy Quinn? Why? If he really had a story to tell – or an axe to grind – why not just knock on the door?

If not Quinn, then who? Grace's secret lover, perhaps? Assuming that *wasn't* Quinn?

Could it be a hoax? Someone in town running me around, making me chase my own tail?

I had half a mind to ignore it. Tear it up and throw it in the lake.

In the end, I had jumped in the Chevy and driven up to the Big House.

Now, I watch Amos's eyes scan the sheet a second time.

'It has to be Quinn. He wants us up there, alone. Unprotected.'

'If he *did* kill Gideon, if he did kill Grace, he'll know where she's buried.'

His expression changes. The thought that finally, after all this time, he might have an answer.

'I'll go up there alone,' he announces finally.

'No.'

'I've got nothing to lose. Not much you can do to a dying man.'

'First off, the note was for me; you go up there alone, he might not show. Second . . .' I tail off.

He gives me the side-eye. A crafty smile lights up his features. 'Second, you don't want to see me hurt. Is it possible you're developing feelings for your mean old grandpa?'

I turn away, look back at the Big House, golden light in the sky behind, the kind they called 'God light' in some places.

I hear the chair creak as he hauls himself to his feet. 'Fine. We're both going. Come on.'

I follow him into the bowels of the house, down a flight of steps to the basement. We pass through a door with iron facings on the timber into a small room outfitted in burled walnut and racked with guns; for a moment, I am reminded of Gideon's hunting cabin.

'We're not going up there unarmed,' he announces. 'We're not entirely stupid.'

I pick out an automatic, test the weight of it in my hand.

'Cartridges are in the drawers.'

By the time we return upstairs, we are carrying enough guns to start a small war.

Amos has shoved the weapons into an olive-green knapsack. A rifle is slung across his shoulder.

I tuck the automatic into the back of my jeans.

Cletus turns a corner, stops. His eyes widen in alarm. 'Where are you going?'

'Just a little hunting trip.'

His expression remains one of acute and terrible confusion as Amos pulls on a pair of leather-laced field boots.

'Let me come with you.'

'Not this time, Cletus.'

127

ORIANNA: NOW

The road up towards the falls fell into disuse after the mine shut down decades earlier.

It is poorly maintained, the surface pitted and scarred. Trees lean in on either side; branches scrape the Chevy's paintwork.

The old caboose mentioned in the anonymous note is an Eden Falls landmark. It sits near the mine, just yards from the falls.

'You think he means to confess?' Amos says. 'Assuming it *was* Quinn who wrote that note.'

'I don't know.'

A row of long-abandoned shotgun houses flash by, a century old, tumbling down the slope, green-painted storm shutters hanging askew. Miners lived here once, two to a bunk.

The forest is a palette of greens. It is the colour I missed most in prison, the colour I associate with my childhood, the colour of the woods. People talk of heaven being a pearly white, but to my mind, heaven is a mix of blues and greens, sky and trees. Hell is grey. The grey of a cell block; the grey of a prison yard.

Amos shifts in his seat. 'My father showed me the forest. He thought God could be found out here, in the trees and the wild things, in the sap and the scrape of dirt under your fingernails. It was out here that he first told me about the great sin of his life. Killing his brother and sister. He thought he was doing God's work. Punishing them. But the guilt drove him mad. He thought he could find salvation in the woods, in nature. But in the end, he couldn't reconcile what he'd done with what his faith told him was right and just. *Thou shalt not kill.*'

The fan belt squeals as the gradient steepens. The gearstick wobbles in my sweat-slicked palm.

Ten minutes later, we are forced to stop. A tree has fallen into the road, blocking the way.

'We'll have to walk,' I say.

The heat is ferocious, the humidity tropical.

Amos stops every few yards, mops his brow, curses under his breath. He has a walking cane with him, leans hard on it as the slope winds upwards, marine-blue shirt tacked to his back with perspiration.

There is something dreamlike about our progress.

I have the idea that the whole endeavour, returning to Eden Falls, hunting Gideon's true killer, has gained critical mass, and is now tipping away from me at its own uncontrollable speed.

Amos has his back against a tree, breathing heavily. I watch him as he gulps from a water bottle. I had convinced him to leave the knapsack in the car, carry only his rifle, now propped against the tree.

'Are you all right?'

He cocks a grave eye at me. 'Mortality is a wicked mistress.'

Despite his obvious discomfort, I sense that he is enjoying himself. He has purpose again, an adventure.

'It's beautiful, isn't it?' He waves his bottle at the surrounding forest. 'There was a time I'd think nothing of tearing all this down for the sake of a new mine. We're at war with the earth, our principles for sale to the highest bidder. Man's nature becomes ever more rapacious. An insatiable hunger for things we don't need.' His gaze flickers. 'There were wolves here once. We killed them. We killed them all.'

128

ORIANNA: NOW

We arrive at a plateau, denuded of trees.

I feel Amos's hand on my arm, pulling me back. We hang on the edge of the clearing, scanning it for signs of life.

To one side is the abandoned caboose, marking the railhead of the old narrow-gauge track that had once brought men and materiel up the hills to the mine. A hundred yards to the east, a cluster of derelict buildings – a pump house, a forge, an old cistern – bleed into the encroaching forest. Windows are gaping holes; cracked mortar and crumbling brickwork mar the façades; lichen crawls over every surface.

Further along, I spot a gravel track leading up to the mine, a wooden barrier set across the path, a weather-beaten yellow *DANGER!* sign affixed to the barrier.

In the near distance is the low rumble of the falls.

'See anything?'

'No.'

'Come on.'

Amos launches himself onto the narrow plateau, cane thudding into the grassy dirt underfoot.

The caboose looms before us, maroon-painted sides shimmering with heat, seams stained orange with rust. A cupola rises from the centre of the roof, porthole windows still intact. At the rear, a pair of red marker lights make cracked ears.

I watch Amos ascend the rear platform, holding onto the curved grab rail.

He raps with his cane on the door. 'Anyone in there?'

When no reply comes, he pushes the door open and goes inside. I cast a last look over my shoulder, then follow him in.

The caboose is empty, stripped of most of its original furniture. A wooden cot bolted to the floor is all that remains, and a pair of crossed wooden oars screwed to one wall.

Amos checks his watch. 'It's five past midday.'

We wait a while. He lights a cigar.

I hear a soft burble, a pair of doves nesting in the eaves, chicks in a little wicker basket of twigs and leaves.

Heat flows from the walls, making the interior uncomfortably hot.

We wait fifteen, twenty minutes, before Amos has had enough. 'He's not coming. Someone was yanking your chain.'

He lumbers out of the caboose.

I glance again at the nesting chicks – perfect things in an imperfect, alien environment – then follow him out.

Amos drops the cigar onto the ground and snuffs it out beneath his boot.

The sun is a hammer, the air damp and heavy.

'I remember coming up here as a young man. The first time Nathaniel took me down into the mine, I thought it was the grandest thing I'd ever seen. The promise of America, ancient lore passed down from father to son. But the truth is, mining is a hard, brutal business. Most men, first time they go down into the dark, they puke up their guts. A mine swallows courage, bravado. Swallows your soul if you're not ready.'

I think he might say more, but he simply stands there, looking at me, a strange expression, half pity, half cruelty, on his ancient face.

A crack shatters the silence.

Amos falls back, a grunt escaping him. His heavy body thuds against the side of the caboose; the cane flies from his hand, the rifle from his shoulder.

He slides down until his head falls beneath the undercarriage, legs splayed.

Dead.

129

ORIANNA: NOW

For a moment, I am paralysed by shock.

And then I drop to my knees, roll under the caboose.

I squint from beneath the caboose's undercarriage into the trees at the edge of the clearing.

Pulling out my automatic, still flat on the earth, I squeeze off a volley, aiming at where I estimate the shot has come from.

Movement in the trees, the sound of someone running.

I stay motionless for another minute, then squeeze off three more rounds.

Nothing.

I blink sweat out of my eyes, then scoot backwards. Still horizontal, I grab Amos under the shoulders and haul him back, muscles straining, a few inches at a time, until we are both on the far side of the caboose.

Wildly, I examine his face.

His eyelids flutter.

He is still alive.

I sit him upright, see immediately that he has been gutshot, the blood black and frightening.

His eyes are open, brow flexed.

'We have to get back to the car.'

'No point,' he rasps.

'Get up.'

He places a hand on my arm. The coppery smell of blood twitches my nose. 'Orianna. It's OK.'

'I have to go for help.'

'I'll be long gone before you're halfway back. Stay with me. Don't let me die alone.'

Helplessness seizes my throat. I blink back tears.

'Light me a cigar, will you?'

I do as he asks and settle the cigar in his mouth.

'There are worse places to die.' His eyes drift heavenwards. 'I killed them. I killed those boys in the mine. I didn't think they could be saved, no matter what I did. So I delayed the rescue. Just to make sure. I had to save the company. Save the family.' His face drains of light. 'I dream of them, God help me. Their last moments. Down there in the dark.'

He closes his eyes. I grab him by the shoulders, shake them open again.

He smiles at me, the guileless smile of an infant. I see him as he sees himself, a child again, headed into the unknown, the great book open before him, unwritten pages to come.

'"Lord, thou hast been our dwelling place from generation to generation. Before the mountains were brought forth, or ever thou hadst formed the earth and the world, from everlasting to everlasting, thou art God. Thou turnest man to destruction; and sayest, 'Return, ye children of men.' For a thousand years in thy sight are but as yesterday when it is past, and as a watch in the night."'

His voice holds steady as he recites the psalm.

I am weeping now, head bowed, a great unwinding pressure from deep inside pushing everything before it.

His hand touches my cheek. 'Don't waste tears on me, child. God knows I don't deserve them.'

My eyes dart over his face, every seam and wrinkle, committing him to memory. 'Why didn't you give me a chance? Why didn't you believe in me?'

He hovers on the verge of a reply, then says simply, 'I always wanted a daughter.'

I see death drive the light from his eyes.

Something is torn loose from me, and I hear myself moan, burying my face in his shoulder, the smell of him, the sun-burnished skin of his neck, the slickness of sweat, his hair, teeth, sinew.

My mind bucks. Once again, my thoughts are drowned beneath a blizzard of white fire. The world collapses around me, time reverses, until I am back in prison, then back in Eden Falls, a child again, back in the Big House, Amos a great, hovering presence darkening the sky above, a stain of ink in the pool that is my life.

Time passes.

I hear voices. At first, I think they are in my head, and then I push myself to my feet, feel my fractured mind rush back into my skull. I steady myself, then walk around the caboose, gun held out before me.

'Freeze!'

Sheriff Hank Faulkes, flanked by deputies Abner Pence and Garrett Martin, approaches cautiously across the clearing.

The Girl In Cell A

Faulkes and Martin have their weapons out of their holsters and trained on me.

'Freeze,' Faulkes repeats and sights down the barrel of his gun.

130

ORIANNA: NOW

'Where's Amos?' Faulkes says.

'He's dead. Someone shot him.'

Pence stares at me with a startled expression.

'Put the gun down, lay down on the floor, hands behind your head.'

'It wasn't me.'

'I said put the gun down and get on the floor.'

Blood beats at my temples. I see the narrow gullet of the future: Amos lured up here with an anonymous note. Amos's blood on my shirt, my face. The facts won't matter. They didn't matter before.

I begin to back away.

'Stop!'

I keep going.

'I said *stop!*'

I turn and run. The sound of a bullet. A stinging pain high up on my left arm. I stumble, but don't fall, keep running and dive into the tree line behind the caboose.

More shots ring out.

I crash my way through the trees, hear them following.

The Girl In Cell A

I turn and fire up into the canopy, hear them shout out in alarm.

I blunder on, emerge a couple of hundred yards further ahead, at the edge of a shallow cliff.

A hundred yards to my right are the Eden Falls, thundering down onto rocks below.

At my feet is a fifty-foot drop down into the ravine and a narrow churn of swiftly moving water, fresh off the falls.

No time to think.

I step back, then run at the edge of the cliff, hurl myself into the air, dropping like a stone.

I hit the water with a boom, go under, come up spluttering, the gun wrenched from my hand.

The water bears me along in its arms, ducking me under so that I have to fight back up into the light again.

Less than two hundred yards along, the water's fury abates, and I fight my way to a stone ledge, haul myself up and lay there on my back, gasping for breath.

I check my arm. The bullet has grazed me, a flesh wound, slowly leaking blood.

Voices echo down into the canyon.

I look up, see movement at the top of the cliff.

I scrabble behind a rock. Water drips down my face.

If I stay here, they *will* find me.

I consider diving back into the river.

No.

They will see me, know which direction the current will take me, possibly even cut me down in the water.

I look over my shoulder, see a narrow opening in the

cliff face. A thin stream of water dribbles out onto the rock two feet below, where it has worn a bowl in the grey stone.

I move to the opening, hesitate, then slip inside.

131

ANNIE: THEN

'We haven't really talked about your relationship with your mother.'

Orianna's expression is inscrutable. Light falling in from the barred window fills the room. Outside, it is a beautiful day: a high sun, crisp, clean air. A runner's heaven.

Orianna has finally been allowed to continue her therapy. I attempt to engage with her about her recent altercation with a fellow inmate, but she refuses to discuss it.

I am frustrated, as I believe Orianna's anger, if unresolved, will have a detrimental effect on my plan to begin unpicking the day of the murder.

I have no choice but to plunge on.

According to the State, the starting point for the events of that day began with Orianna's mother, Christine, revealing to Orianna that Gideon Wyclerc was her father.

Christine has remained something of an enigma in our sessions together. I had sensed early on that Orianna finds it difficult talking about her. But the inevitable can no longer be put off.

'There's a reason I've left it so long,' I continue. 'I believe your mother is central to the events that led to your father's killing. Your relationship with her was a difficult one. I wanted to give you time to get to know me and to understand how this process works. To build trust. Do you trust me, Orianna?'

The muscles of her face flicker. I wait, and then, finally, she says, 'Yes.'

'Do you think that you trusted your mother? Understood her? Who she was, the things that motivated her, the things that made her happy, or sad?'

'I don't think my mother was ever happy. I don't think she was made that way.'

'Don't you think that's a very shallow assessment of her?'

'My mother was utterly self-involved. She never wanted to be a mother. She never wanted *me*. I was an accident, and she treated me as such my whole life.'

'And yet she raised you. Alone.'

'She had no choice.'

'Isn't that a little unfair?'

A dark flash in her eyes. 'Why are you defending her?'

'It's not my place to defend her. I'm merely asking you to consider the relationship in its full context. Your mother had an affair with her employer. With Gideon. A rich white man in an insular town. She had a child, a child that Gideon did not publicly acknowledge. Your mother kept the fact that he was your father a secret from you, from the world. Why? Instead of leaving town and settling somewhere else, she stayed. Why?'

'I don't know. She was weak. She was an asshole. I wish to God she *had* moved away.'

'Because then none of this would have happened?'

She does not bother to reply.

'I want you to consider another possibility: that your mother staying on in Eden Falls was an act of strength. Could it be that she stayed so that you could remain close to your father, hoping that one day he *would* acknowledge you?'

Her face throbs with sudden anger. 'If my mother stayed, it wasn't for me. It was because one day she thought she could get her hands on Gideon's money. Christine was a conniving, scheming bitch, and I will never forgive her.'

132

ORIANNA: NOW

The passage narrows within ten yards of the opening in the cliff face.

I inch forwards on my elbows, stretch flat, slither through an inch of flowing water. Darkness enfolds me, my body blocking the haze of natural light coming from the tunnel mouth at my feet.

I can feel my phone in my back pocket, but cannot work my arms around to get at it.

The tunnel, a twisting pipe cut through rock by ancient water flow, inclines steadily upwards, twenty yards, fifty, a hundred, until I lose sense of how far I have come. The sound of the falls, thrumming up the shaft, dwindles away.

The passage closes in like a throat. Suddenly, I am stuck, arms pinioned beneath me. I wriggle futilely, but the stone's grip is vice-like.

No way forward. No way back.

Terror explodes at the base of my skull.

I am back in my prison cell, those early days when the walls closed in, inch by inch, crushing bone, driving the breath from my lungs.

I cry out, the sound echoing jaggedly in the tunnel.

Amos's face comes to me then. Not my mother, not Luke, but Amos.

My breath catches. I still myself, calming the hammer beat of my heart.

Turning my skull sideways, I flatten myself, then begin to inch forward by a grim peristalsis, a worm crawling on its belly through the earth.

Fifteen minutes later, I ease my head through an opening eighteen inches high, plopping out like a newborn calf onto stone.

I dig out my phone, switch it on, praying that the water hasn't fried it.

It is fine. I turn on the flashlight, swing it around.

I am in a horizontal, man-made shaft, crouched on a ledge, a foot above inky black water.

A starless river, whispering in the dark.

The flashlight beam is swallowed within yards; there is no indication which way to go.

I choose left, move along the ledge until it ends, then lower myself down into the water. It is warmer than I expect, heated by the earth's geothermal heart. It rises to the level of my chest and I am forced to hold the phone up as I wade forward.

A beep sounds from the phone. I check it. No signal, but the battery is down to 20 per cent.

Shit.

I carry on until I come to what looks like a maintenance shaft in the ceiling, the bottom rungs of a ladder visible in its gaping mouth, the opening surrounded by a ribbon of yellow and black warning paint.

Standing on tiptoe, I can just about reach the ladder.

I stick my phone between my teeth, reach up, grab the lowest rung and haul myself up, then shove the phone back into my jeans.

Halfway up the shaft, I see that the last section of ladder is gone, the notches for the bolts that once tethered it to the rock still evident. The shaft rises vertically for another fifteen feet.

I cannot go back.

I set my back against the wall, plug my feet, one by one, to the far wall.

Slowly, I inch my way up the shaft.

My whole body breaks out in sweat; the effort required to keep myself braced against both sides of the tunnel is astonishing. If I flounder, I will fall forty feet vertically.

The thought tenses my muscles, lends me strength.

Finally, I reach the top, pull myself out into a lateral tunnel running in both directions. The tunnel is dry.

I take out my phone, check it.

Eighteen per cent.

I switch it to power-saver mode, then walk on.

Memory drives a hole through my focus.

A school trip to the mines, part of a 'learn about the history of Eden Falls' week. I recall now that Luke had been there, too. His father, David, who organised the visit on behalf of Wyclerc Industries, had accompanied us, bringing along a man named Baker who'd once supervised operations here, when the mine was still active.

I remember Baker describing the human-made labyrinth beneath the cliff, the men who'd clawed the earth's mineral wealth from the rock, piling it into hoppers, so that the ore could be taken to the surface and begin its journey to power the cities and industries of mankind. He'd told us of the earliest miners, men who had toiled in the baking heat, who had died in rock falls and explosions and flooding. This close to the river, running below it in places, the tunnels were prone to waterlogging. *We have to pump the mine continuously*, David had said. *In the end, it cost more to keep the pumps running than we were making from the mine.*

I pass refuge chambers cut into the sides of the tunnel, fallback sites for when the worst happened.

I come across another ladder, this time bolted to the wall of the tunnel.

I check my phone.

Fifteen per cent.

I begin to climb.

As I near the top, my concentration momentarily wavers.

The heat, my palms slick with a combination of water and sweat.

I lose my grip, fall back ten feet, hit the stone with a thud, the breath blown from my lungs.

Darkness descends.

133

ANNIE: THEN

'Why do you think your mother never told you about your father? For so many years?'

Orianna looks away. I can sense a residual anger following our last session still burning inside her.

'Do you think it might be possible that the reason she kept this from you was because she wanted to protect you?'

'Protect me? From what? The truth?' She shakes her head in disgust.

'No. From rejection.'

She stares at me, blinking hard.

'I want you to consider the possibility that your mother was a victim too. A vulnerable woman, seeking her place in the world, taken advantage of by a wealthy, charismatic man. She had his child. Perhaps she *did* tell Gideon. Perhaps he made it clear to her that if she went public, he would reject you, cast you both out, and use all his considerable powers to deny her, possibly even destroy her.

'On the other hand, if she chose to stay quiet, he would ensure that she – and her illegitimate child – would have a place on the Wyclerc estate for as long as she wanted it.'

'Are you saying my mother made a deal with Gideon?'

'Don't you think it's a possibility? It would explain why she stayed. Why she kept his secret.'

I can almost see her mind baulk at the suggestion. Yet, at the same time, I sense that I am getting through to her.

'Of course, something else might have kept your mother from revealing her secret . . . Love. Have you ever considered the possibility that your mother truly loved Gideon? And that *that* was the reason she stayed, kept his secret? It would explain why she didn't simply leave and take him to court, insist on a DNA test, claim financial support. I think it's a more plausible explanation than Gideon threatening her, don't you?'

'My mother never loved anyone but herself.'

'Is that true? Or is that merely how *you* saw her? Love can make people act in ways that often seem counter to rational decision-making.' I pause. 'In psychology, we talk of something called sublimation, a coping mechanism that helps us deal with pain or anger by finding a productive outlet. Your mother's inability to be with Gideon in a public, healthy relationship no doubt caused her great suffering. Perhaps she sublimated that pain into her role at the estate and into raising you.'

'If that's the case, she made a piss-poor job of it.'

'Do you really have so few good memories of her?'

She says nothing.

'Orianna, I want you to find your most positive memory of your mother. Find it. Fix it in your mind.' I pause, allow a few seconds. 'Now describe it to me.'

For a long moment, I think she will refuse, but then she begins to speak. 'When I was seven, she took me up to the falls by the old mine. We went on foot. I have no idea why she felt the need to do it; she'd never shown any real interest in the town's history before. I remember standing on the edge of the falls with her, holding her hand, looking down at the water churning on the rocks below. There was no one else around. Only the quiet of the woods and the sound of the falls. We must have stood there for half an hour, not speaking. I think it was the only peaceful moment I've ever known in my life.'

I lean forward. 'Orianna, something incited your mother to finally tell you the truth about Gideon. Why *that* day? After so many years of silence? If we can understand what it was that finally cracked her resolve, I believe we can break through the wall in your mind and unravel the events that led to you tracking your father down in his hunting cabin.

'Finally, we might get to the truth.'

134

ORIANNA: NOW

I am surrounded by darkness.

I lie there, swimming in the black.

My mouth tastes of metal and blood. The flesh wound on my arm throbs.

Another violent migraine beats time inside my head.

I have a sudden sense of time flowing around me, of rock taking on the fluidity of water.

Is this how it feels to be buried inside a tomb, a pyramid, a crypt deep in the heart of the world?

I recall a book of Greek myths from the prison library.

Lethe, the river that flows through Hades, from which the souls of the dead drink so that they might forget the living.

Which river had poisoned *my* memory, my life?

And in that silent breath between worlds, a connection sparks somewhere deep inside the matrices of my brain. Something I had read in Grace's journal, connecting with an earlier memory, something I had heard since returning to Eden Falls, words falling from the mouth of a face in shadow . . .

My eyes snap open.

The memory blazes in the dark, then sinks out of sight. I almost cry out in frustration. There was something important there, I can feel it.

But it is gone.

I lift myself up, feel pain flash through the flesh of my back and my skull. I grope for my phone.

The flashlight is still on, the battery running at 4 per cent.

I have lost hours.

Fear cuts through the cloud in my mind.

I have to get moving.

I stand, walk to the ladder, grip it as hard as I can, then begin my ascent.

I proceed upwards, through tunnels and up ladders, until finally I come out into a grand chamber.

Relief floods through me.

I recognise the yellow cage lift on one side of the chamber, up on a mezzanine gantry accessed by a single flight of double-wide steel stairs.

My phone chirps.

One per cent.

I thump up the stairs, the sound echoing like a bell in the man-made cavern.

On the gantry, I pause, swing my phone flashlight to the right, see the beam play over a boxy building, with a semi-cylindrical cross-section, like a Quonset hut. The windows are blacked, the door forbidding. A large map of the mine is bolted to the wall beside the door.

The site office.

I remember Luke's father, David, standing outside the office with the former mine supervisor, Baker, pointing at the map, smiling as he briefed our anxious school tour group before we ventured down into the mine proper. *'Don't worry, no one's died down here for twenty years.'*

Something about the darkness around the hut unsettles me. A feeling of trepidation, of another presence. Could Sheriff Faulkes and his men have made their way down here from the mine's entrance? Had they seen me crawl into that tunnel from the river?

Panic surges inside me. I turn and run to the cage lift.

It is parked at the bottom of an open shaft, a second, empty shaft beside it. I guess that the second lift is at the top of that shaft.

I swing open the door of the cage lift, enter.

The control pad looks simple enough. I press the button marked with an up arrow.

Nothing.

My throat constricts.

There is no power. The cage lift won't work.

My phone beeps again, urgent.

I take my mind back to the school trip, the journey down from the mine entrance far above, a gaggle of us crunched into the lift . . . *How far did we descend?*

Fifty feet, maybe a hundred.

I get out, climb the cage, stand on the roof. A series of rigid cables, clumped together, snake up into the dark.

My phone beeps, dies.

I curse, hold the panic at bay.

I can do this.

I *have* to do this.

I haven't come this far to die in a fucking mine.

I grip the nearest cable, twine my legs around another, and begin to pull my way upwards, hand over steady hand.

The first twenty yards are straightforward. I thank the years I spent in the prison gym, feel the muscles of my arms and back come to life with the effort.

And then my shoulders begin to burn, gradually at first, but, as the lactic acid builds up, the fire becomes a roaring agony.

I am forced to stop, release one arm, shake it out, then repeat the process with the other, holding grimly on with my legs.

I keep going, moving through blackness, the ragged noise of my own breathing the only sound.

My thoughts flutter as the pain reaches a crescendo.

I want to let go, to release the searing agony. To fall and let the darkness embrace me.

I keep going.

Finally, when there is nothing left but a white noise in my head, and I know that the next movement will surely be my last, I arrive at the top of the shaft.

With the last of my strength, I fling myself from the cables to grab the lip of the shaft, almost slipping. I hold on with one hand, my shriek echoing down the vertical tunnel.

Grabbing on with my flailing other hand, I pull myself out and lie on the floor in a sweat-drenched daze.

Eventually, I stand, stumble my way to the end of a long gantry, come to a door, push it back, and find myself in an antechamber leading to the outside world.

Moments later, I exit the mine.

I am out on the gravel track leading down to the caboose.

Dusk has fallen, taking the edge off the heat.

I stand a moment, looking downslope at the surrounding forest.

A blaze of light near the caboose; crime scene tape; a uniformed figure near the mouth of the road leading up to the plateau.

I will have to go through the forest. After the suffocating terror of the mine, the idea of making my way through the woods holds little fear.

My limbs shake with adrenalin, a cocktail of rage and exhaustion.

I imagine the town laid out below me, remember the blast of self-righteous hate as I had walked through the gathering at the town hall, hate ingrained through the repetition of a monstrous lie.

I want to hurt them, the way they had hurt me.

I feel reason slipping from me; the baying of wolves sounds once again, the walls of reality shiver around me.

And, suddenly, the revelation I had experienced in the mine beams brightly back into my mind.

I understand that I have grasped the tail feathers of something that might bring an end to the years of torment, the questions, the not knowing ... I am *almost* there.

I know that I am close to uncovering the truth about Gideon and Grace, about what had happened that day.

I duck low, run swiftly to the timberline, and am swallowed by the shadows.

135

ANNIE: THEN

'Orianna, I want you to recount for me the exact moment when Christine told you that Gideon was your father.'

My voice is even. Now that we have arrived here, I want to ensure that Orianna doesn't run from the memory.

She avoids my eyes, looks down at her hands.

'It's a critical moment in everything that happened. We *must* talk about it.' I stop. 'OK. Let's take this in stages. Let's go back to the start of that day. How did it begin? What did you do that morning?'

She continues to sit in silence, and then, abruptly, jerks into speech.

'I spent the morning in town, at the Forest Festival.'

'And what did you do there?'

'I met Luke. We casually bumped into each other, a whispered moment, no hint of what had been going on between us for months. He was with his friends; I was alone. We agreed to meet at our usual place. Gideon's cabin, back on the estate.'

'And then?'

'And then I watched as Grace was crowned Eden Falls Forest Princess. I waited for the parade to begin winding its way through town, then I slipped away, rode my bicycle back to the Wyclerc estate, and met up with Luke.'

I nod encouragingly. 'Go on.'

She hesitates, then takes us both back to that instant.

Luke is waiting for her in the cabin, having returned from the Forest Festival.

She sees that he is examining the wolf's head on the wall, a gun in his hand. The thick scent of his father's cologne fills her nostrils.

'You know, I sometimes wonder if it's all bullshit,' he says. 'The whole legend of Nathaniel fighting the wolf.'

'At least you have family legends. All I have is lies.'

He turns, walks over. They kiss, then break apart. They both know what will come next, back out in their glade in the woods. Her body vibrates with anticipation. The illicitness of it doesn't frighten her, though the power of her feelings sometimes threatens to overwhelm her. She wonders if he feels the same.

She picks up a shotgun. 'This is new.'

'A shotgun is a man's weapon.' A wicked glint in his eye.

'Fuck you.' The gun is heavy in her hands. The barrel gleams; it looks as if it has never been fired.

Gideon, it turns out, rarely uses his guns. He has no interest in hunting; the cabin is simply a convenient place to bring his fancy women.

The cupboard, nevertheless, is well stocked with ammunition. Luke, through casual investigation, has discovered that it is replenished every few months by the groundskeeper, Herman Sap. Sap must have assumed Gideon stumbled out into the woods on occasion, firing at cut-down stumps and rooting boars.

The fridge, too, is always stocked, with beer, wine, liquor, the occasional bottle of champagne. These, they never touched, knowing that Gideon might well notice.

That day, they break their rule. Luke has something to celebrate. His eighteenth birthday is a week away, and he isn't sure they will be able to meet on the day.

They take a bottle of whisky, and the shotgun, go to their place in the woods.

By the time they finish rolling around in the grass, in between blasting soda cans, the bottle is almost empty.

136

ORIANNA: NOW

I approach Gerty's house from the rear, a single-storey clapboard-and-brick bungalow, surrounded by a cracked and creosoted fence.

The road is empty; it is gone ten in the evening.

It has taken almost two hours to get to Gerty's. Navigating the woods in the dark slowed me down. Faulkes and his men have, no doubt, found my car; I had no choice but to walk back down into town on foot, my mind aflame.

Amos's killing has stunned me. A devastating and unexpected sense of loss fevers through me. Amos, my grandfather, gone. My heart convulses. I am wracked by a feeling of aloneness so crippling it is all I can do to set one foot ahead of the other.

Sheriff Hank Faulkes's face hovers in the dark before me, the grim set of his features as he'd faced me down with a gun in his hand. There had been no doubt in his eyes. Once again, I am caught in the meshing gears of fate. Blamed for a killing I'd had no hand in.

But I won't let them destroy me a second time. I will die before I let them take me back to that grim grey cell that stole half my life.

I clamber over Gerty's fence, drop to the far side.

The tiny backyard is overgrown, wildflowers and weeds running riot.

I walk to the back porch and peer through a lit window into the kitchen.

Empty.

I try the porch door, but it is locked.

Taking a deep breath, I bang on it, hoping I haven't made a fatal error.

Seconds later, the door swings back and there is Gerty, in shorts, a T-shirt and slippers.

Her eyes widen. And then she pulls me into a hug. 'O, thank Jesus! I thought I'd lost you, child, I thought I'd lost you.'

It has been eighteen years since I last set foot in Gerty's place.

A lot has changed. Aside from a single colourful dream-catcher dangling from the kitchen ceiling, the home is modern, sparsely decorated, a vision of clean lines and plain colours.

Gerty notices my expression. 'What can I tell you? I love Marie Kondo.'

'Gerty, have the cops been here?'

'Yes. Busted in here like the Gestapo. Wouldn't believe me when I told them I had no idea where you were.' A pause. 'I heard about Amos. I'm sorry.'

Nausea bubbles up inside me. Amos's face, his dying words.

I stumble into the bathroom, retch, then vomit into the tub.

The Girl In Cell A

Gerty's hands are on my back. 'Let it out, child.'

When my stomach stops heaving, I stay on the tiled floor, back against the tub. My body trembles, until it seems that I might shake myself into a million pieces.

Gerty holds me, soothes me like a wild animal.

Finally, she pulls me up, pushes me towards the shower. 'I'll fetch you some clothes and a clean towel.'

The jet of water dampens the emotions that threaten to derail me. Standing under the showerhead, my mind loosens, my thoughts flowing back in time. I try to grasp the entirety of the situation, to find meaning in the electrical thunderstorm raging inside my head.

I am back in the mine, awakening after having fallen and knocked myself out.

I relive the moment when a connection sparked in my mind, the connection I had made between something written in Grace's journal and something I had heard someone say recently, in Eden Falls. When I had first read the journal entries, the connection had escaped me, but now . . . I clutch at the thought. It is so close . . .

And then, I have it.

Clarity strikes like a hammer on slate.

My mind reels.

The face of Grace's potential killer hovers before my eyes, outlined in the spray ricocheting from my skull.

137

ORIANNA: NOW

After my shower, dressed in a pair of Gerty's jeans, sneakers and a T-shirt with a porcupine printed on the front, I sit at the kitchen table while Gerty fusses over the flesh wound in my arm, patching it up with antiseptic and a cotton bandage.

When she finishes, she fixes us both sandwiches, forcing me to eat. 'So . . . what now?'

Before I can answer, a loud banging sounds on the front door.

'Into the pantry, child.'

I step into the tiny walk-in room, pull shut a flimsy concertina door, leaving it open just a crack.

Moments later, I hear Gerty's voice. 'Hello, Abner. You must stop calling at such unsociable hours. People will talk.'

'May we come in, Gerty?'

'I've already had a visit from the goon squad, thank you.'

'Hank wanted me to come talk to you personally.'

'About what?'

'I'd rather do this inside.'

A pause. 'Well, fine. Don't mind my rights. I suppose you better come in too, Deputy Martin.'

I hear them traipse into the living room.

'So what are you going to do this time? Strip-search me?'

'Gerty, I know you told us that Orianna hasn't been in touch . . . Is that still the case?'

'Yes. Not that I'd tell you if she had.'

'That would be obstructing the law, ma'am.' Martin's voice.

'Would it now? You do know this isn't Nazi Germany, Deputy Martin?'

'Be fair, now, Gerty,' Pence says. 'We've got ourselves a murderer here. It ain't right to protect her.'

'That girl is no more a murderer than you are George Clooney, Abner. Shame on you for regurgitating Hank Faulkes's nonsense.'

'Look, the chances are the girl is dead. We think she drowned in the river. We've got people out there looking for her. But, just in case she didn't, we've got an APB out on her and roadblocks set up. If she's alive, she hasn't a chance in hell of slipping through the net. Her best bet is to give herself up.'

'Why? So your little hanging party can finish the job? It wasn't enough that this town took everything she had; now you're fixing to do it all over again. Well, I won't play any part in it.'

Pence lets out an exasperated sigh.

'Where are *you* going?' Gerty now.

I hear a heavy tread move towards the pantry. I look around the space, step beside a wooden cabinet, flatten myself against the wall, squeezing between the cabinet and a narrow shelf.

'Ma'am, you live alone, don't you?'

'I don't see how that's any business of yours, Deputy Martin.'

'I'm just wondering why there are two plates on your kitchen table.'

A beat. 'I was having a late supper with Desdemona Rawlins. Lives three streets over. Go check with her if you like.'

Martin says nothing. I hear him walk to the back door, swing it open.

I turn my head. Placed casually on the shelf beside me is a holstered handgun. Instinctively, I reach for the weapon, slip it from the holster. My palm feels slick on the grip.

Moments later, Martin's footsteps return. The concertina door is pulled back.

I hear him pull at the chain light. My hand tightens around the gun.

'This light doesn't work, ma'am.'

'Well spotted. That's some Grade A detecting. Perhaps you should apply to the FBI.'

I can feel his eyes sweeping the darkened room. The naked terror of a caged animal pulses through me.

I am capable of anything.

I imagine myself raising the gun, firing directly into Martin's face, watching it vanish in a shower of blood.

138

ORIANNA: NOW

'While you're in there, why don't you fetch me a jar of pickles?' Gerty's voice, cutting through the madness. 'There's some on the shelf at the back.'

Seconds pass. A bead of sweat trickles down my forehead and down the side of my nose.

Martin steps away.

Moments later, I hear them leaving the house.

'What are we going to do, child? I'm afraid that if you try and leave town, they'll shoot first and ask questions later.'

'I'm not leaving, Gerty. Not until I have the answers I came for. I think I know what happened. I think I know who killed Gideon and Grace.'

Gerty stares at me. 'If that's true, you need to tell someone. The authorities.'

'Who should I tell? Hank Faulkes?'

'Luke. Tell Luke. He'll know what to do.'

I shake my head sadly. 'How can I trust Luke? How can I trust anyone?' I take Gerty's hand. 'I need to do this.' Reaching behind me, I take out the gun I had tucked into the seat of my jeans. The light reveals a small frame revolver, a carbon stainless-steel Taurus with a black rubber grip.

'Child, I can't let you walk out of here with that.'

'Do you want me going out to face Gideon's killer unarmed?'

Gerty's eyes roam over my face. 'There's nothing I can say that's going to change your mind, is there?'

'No.'

'In that case, I'm coming with you.'

'No. I've caused you enough trouble.'

'Child—'

'This isn't up for debate, Gerty.'

'If you think I'm going to let you—'

I shove Gerty backwards.

'What are you—?'

Seconds later, I have pushed Gerty into the pantry, locked the door behind her. The door shakes as Gerty hammers madly on the inside.

'I'm sorry.' I lean a moment on the wall beside the door, and then turn and walk into the living room, Gerty still hollering through the door behind me.

I sweep up Gerty's car keys, head for the bay windows, crack the curtains a couple of inches, sweep the road.

Nothing.

I open the door, step into the warm night air.

Gerty's pickup is only yards away.

I duck into it, stick the key in the ignition and start her up.

The passenger door opens and a figure slips into the car, a gun in their hand.

My own hand flies instinctively to the revolver at my back.

'Don't,' says Luke, aiming his automatic at me. 'Please don't, Orianna.'

139

ANNIE: THEN

'"The People call Luke Wyclerc."'

Once again, I am reading from the court transcript. I know that this is a critical moment. I know how traumatic this will be for Orianna. But I am determined to press on.

'Orianna, in our last session you took me to the point in that day where you and Luke met in Gideon's cabin, then went out to the woods. I want to talk about what happened next.' A beat. 'But before we do that, I would like us to talk about *Luke's* version of what happened that day. Are you ready to talk me through Luke's testimony?'

Her face is still. It is an age before she speaks. 'Yes.'

I hand her a copy of the transcript.

Her eyes flicker to the print on the wall, then to me, and then to the folder in her hands.

Finally, she begins. 'After Luke's name was called, I sat in confusion, before turning to my lawyer, Ortega. He explained that Luke had been called as a last-minute witness and that the judge had overruled his objection and allowed it.'

'How did that make you feel?'

'I felt sick. Panicky. I knew that whatever Luke was going to say, he was saying under duress. I could see it in his face. I remember wanting to shout out to him, catch his eye, signal to him in some way, but he avoided looking at me. I hadn't seen him in months. He hadn't visited me in prison, hadn't taken my calls. Ortega told me the police had talked to Luke and that he'd refused to be interviewed. His parents had told the prosecution that he was in no fit state to be questioned, that he'd had some sort of breakdown. When he'd eventually given a statement, he'd said that his memory about that afternoon was hazy.

'All the while Ortega kept telling me he'd be able to convince Luke to testify on my behalf, to at least partly confirm my account of that day, to explain how we'd both been in the woods well before Gideon had been killed, that we'd fired the shotgun that had killed him, and that *that* was how my prints got on the gun and how gunshot residue ended up on my clothes. It made no sense that Luke should now appear for the prosecution.'

She stops. I see something dark fly across her features. I have a sense of what's coming. Orianna knows what lies ahead, as do I. A pit, black as night, one she cannot avoid. A part of me almost baulks at making her relive this.

But it is essential that we do. 'Go on, Orianna,' I prompt.

'I remember that he wore a dark suit,' she says softly. 'I remember the way he sat bolt upright in the stand, as if in church.' Her breathing shallows. She looks down at the transcript.

DA Danziger: Luke, can you tell us how you know the defendant?

Luke Wyclerc: She lives on the estate with her mom. Her mom works up at the Big House. Orianna and I, uh, we go to the same school.

Danziger: Were you close growing up on the Wyclerc estate? What I mean is, did you play together, that sort of thing?

Luke: No.

Danziger: Because she was the daughter of the estate's housekeeper?

Luke: I guess.

Danziger: But things changed last summer? You became closer.

Luke: Yes.

Danziger: Luke, I know this is difficult, but we need the absolute truth here. Did you and Orianna have a relationship? I mean, was she your girlfriend?

Luke: No.

Danziger: But you had carnal relations?

Luke: Wh-what?

Danziger: Luke, did you have sex with the defendant?

Luke: Yes.

Danziger: At the time, did you know she was your uncle Gideon's illegitimate daughter? In effect, your cousin?

Luke: No!

Danziger: Was this a one-off thing?

Luke: We— We were together a bunch of times.

Danziger: And where did these liaisons take place?

Luke: In the woods, on the estate.

Danziger: Anywhere else?

Luke: In my uncle Gideon's hunting cabin.

Danziger: The same cabin in which Gideon was later murdered?

Luke: Yes.

Danziger: Had you ever been in that cabin before you began seeing Orianna?

Luke: No.

Danziger: Why not?

Luke: It was off limits.

Danziger: So it was Orianna who led you to the cabin, encouraged you to break into it?

Luke: [Pauses.] Yes.

Danziger: You used the cabin as a trysting place . . . What else did you find in there?

[Witness does not reply.]

Danziger: Let me be more specific, Luke. Did you find Gideon's gun collection inside his cabin?

Luke: Yes.

Danziger: And did the defendant ask something of you, Luke, in relation to these guns that you found in your uncle's cabin?

Luke: She asked me to teach her to shoot.

Danziger: Luke, this is very important now. I'm going to ask you to go back to the day that Gideon was killed. The defendant has testified to the police that she was with you that afternoon, that you were teaching her how to fire the shotgun that Gideon was killed with. She claims that is how gunshot residue from the murder weapon ended up on her clothes and hands and how her prints ended up on the gun. Luke, is this true? Did you meet with Orianna that afternoon in the woods?

She stops.

I wait, then: 'Orianna?'

Her mouth curls into a smile that has nothing to do with humour. I can sense that she is being torn up from the inside out. This is a critical moment, one she has replayed countless times, but now is being forced to replay with me. The moment that she refers to as 'Luke's betrayal'.

'I remember the way I was suddenly cut loose from it all. It was as if I was floating above the court, looking down on the end of the life I'd known. I knew what Luke was going to say before he spoke.'

'What *did* Luke say?' I want her to acknowledge it. I need her to say it.

'He said: "No."'

140

ORIANNA: NOW

'Did you do it?'

Light falling in from a street lamp yellows Luke's face into a sickly pallor.

I can feel the familiar thunder in my head. Another headache blasting away inside my skull. Instinctively, I reach for my pocket, but the pill bottle isn't there. I bite my cheek, force down the pain.

I am back at my trial, that exact moment when Luke condemned me.

A single word, and time stopped.

Guilt is never binary. That is the fallacy at the heart of our justice system. There are shades to every story, to every truth.

It was true that I came from trash. But it was equally true that I was a Wyclerc.

It was true that *my* truth counted for less because of the mouth it came from. But it was also true that my truth was the only truth that mattered – to me.

In the end, there is no equal music in the house of God. What matters is the manner of presentation. The way in which one *version* of the truth can be painted over another until the original disappears from the world.

In the years to come, trapped in the prison dark of my cell, I would know and understand only one thing.

The boy I loved beyond all reason had betrayed me.

'Did you do it?' Luke repeats. 'Did you kill Amos?'

I think: *There are so many ways I could answer him.* I could talk to him of guilt and innocence. Or of love and how it lingers in the veins like molten gold. How, even when you try to leave it behind, it returns, time and again, in the darkest pit of night.

'No,' I say. 'I didn't kill Amos.'

Something goes out of him; his chest caves.

He lowers the gun, sets his hand on his thigh.

I try not to let him see me breathe out. For one steep second, I had thought the worst, that perhaps my fears about him—

'What happened up there?'

I lay it all out for him: the note, the caboose, Amos's death, Faulkes, the mine.

His gaze becomes hollow. 'Why didn't you tell me? About the note?'

There is nothing I can say that will give him any solace.

'They've brought Amos's body back down,' he says eventually. 'It's in the morgue. I don't think I've ever seen him look so peaceful.'

A beat.

'He never gave up hope. He always thought we'd find an answer, one day. That he'd finally know what really happened to Gideon, to Grace.' He swings around in his seat, brow crinkling. 'How did Faulkes know you were up there?'

'I don't know. But I think whoever sent the note told him. I think they intended him to find our bodies. Or at least, Amos's body.'

'But why? Why kill Amos?'

'To frame me. To stop me. I'm almost there, Luke. I think I know who killed Gideon and why.'

His face trembles. Finally, he slips his automatic back into the holster at his hip. 'Tommy Quinn's still out there. We have an APB out on him too.'

'I don't think it was Quinn up at the mine. I don't think Quinn had anything to do with any of this.'

'Then who, Ori? Who the hell killed them?'

141

ORIANNA: NOW

The house is a relative new build, barely into its fourth decade, constructed with a sense of simplicity in keeping with its sole occupant. Standing on its own gated plot next door to the Church of Christ the Redeemer, its double-storey façade looks down on an olive tree and a concrete fountain of Mary cradling the baby Jesus.

I park the truck directly outside the wrought-iron gates, step out and wait for Luke.

On the short drive over, I had expected to be spotted, stopped, arrested.

But the town is dead, the roads empty.

The idea that two killers – one known – in me – and one potential – in Tommy Quinn – are on the loose has sent the good folk of Eden Falls to ground. The dark days following Gideon's murder all those years ago have returned. It is only a matter of time before the press arrives.

'What are we doing *here*?' Luke sounds like a little boy at the top of stairs leading down into a darkened cellar.

I turn and jab the intercom by the gate.

When a voice comes on the line, I say, 'This is Orianna. Luke's here too. I need to speak with you.'

'Orianna?' Confusion.

'I have Grace's journal.'

Silence drifts from the intercom. The church looms over us. Above, the moon winks out behind a cloud.

The gate clicks open.

He greets us at the door.

142

ANNIE: THEN

We are getting close. I can feel it.

I am certain Orianna must sense it too.

She has become increasingly agitated. Forcing her to confront Luke's 'betrayal' at her trial has also forced her to engage with the fact that his testimony directly conflicts with her own account of that day.

She continues to protest her innocence, but there is no way to square this circle.

Either Luke is lying or she is. Either she met with Luke in the woods that day – and this explains the forensic evidence that led to her conviction – or she didn't. In which case, the only way the gunshot residue on her clothes and her prints on the murder weapon can be explained is if Orianna was in that cabin when the gun was fired. By her.

I lead her gently through this minefield.

'No,' she says. 'Luke lied because he was forced to lie. By his family. By the Wyclercs. By Amos.'

There is a small possibility, of course, that this is true. I cannot verify this one way or the other because Luke continues to refuse to talk to me. He appears to have completely washed his hands of anything to do with the case, with Orianna.

My understanding is that he has married, moved on with his life. He has no desire to revisit the past.

I wonder, briefly, what would happen if Orianna *did* return to Eden Falls after her sentence. How would Luke react? And if he *had* lied, how would he respond when forced to confront that lie?

I know that Orianna believes there were other suspects who should have been investigated for Gideon's murder. Does she include Luke among those suspects? I don't know. She shies away from the notion each time I ask her.

Part of my role is to guide Orianna to the truth. To face up to her own guilt. And that means helping her to some sort of realisation that her alternative-suspect theories have been built on shaky foundations. No parole board in this state will let Orianna free if she continues to maintain that she was somehow framed, that the murder for which she was convicted is someone else's fault.

But here is where things break down, where we encounter the 'innocent prisoner's dilemma'. If Orianna *is* innocent, pleading guilty – finally fessing up – might get her out early. But if she pleads guilty, after all these years of claiming her innocence, how will that affect her mental wellbeing? It is a sad fact that our legal system punishes an innocent person for displaying integrity and rewards the unscrupulous.

The truth is that if I cannot get Orianna to admit her guilt, then *I* will have failed.

And even should she do so, and thus secure early parole, it won't stop her from going back to Eden Falls to 'prove' her innocence, by carrying out her own reinvestigation, something she has threatened to do on several occasions during our sessions.

I cannot put it past her. Orianna displays a fanatic's determination.

'What if—?' She stops. 'What if Luke and Grace were in it together?'

'Grace couldn't have had anything to do with Gideon's murder.'

'Why not?'

'You know why.'

'Because *I* killed Grace. That's what you mean, isn't it?'

'No.'

And now I realise something else.

I realise that Luke's betrayal may well have been the final straw, following on from her father's lifelong failure to acknowledge her, his murder, and being accused of his killing. The blow that later sent Orianna's mind spinning into self-delusion, on the back of her dissociative amnesia.

A blow that she has not – and may never – recover from.

143

ORIANNA: NOW

Samuel Wyclerc looks as if he has aged in the days since I last saw him.

Barefoot, in shorts and a T-shirt, his gaze hops from me to Luke and back again. Then he turns and leads us along a hallway to a living room floored in blazing-white tiles, a pair of mustard couches set to one side.

He sits down. We take the couch opposite.

I take out my phone, find the images I had taken of Grace's journal, and hand the phone to Samuel.

He scans the images. His hand begins to tremble.

I speak: 'Psalm 27. "The Lord is my light and my salvation – whom shall I fear?" Grace wrote that in her journal. You said the same words to me when I came to see you the other day.'

He sets the phone down, then collapses into the couch, legs splayed, head back, as if drained of blood. 'You think of all the ways that you can sin. But you never think it will be love that finally gets you. If you were to ask me how it happened, I couldn't tell you. She came to me that summer. Needed to talk to someone. About her father. Her mother. Their love–hate relationship. Gideon's philandering. Rebekah's affair with Tommy Quinn. She was confused, angry. She wanted to get away. Away from her family, away from Eden Falls.

'She held me up as some sort of hero. I'd escaped. Pursued my own passion. Had grand adventures around the world. Returned on my own terms.' He stops. 'We fell in love. She was ... so much more than a girl. She was intoxicating.'

'She was *your niece*,' I say.

He reacts as if punched.

'I can't explain it. There's an impulse inside us, towards desire; it's similar to our impulse towards death. It has its own reason, its own morality.' He takes a huge breath that shudders the length of his body. 'I can only describe it as a psychotic break. I was outside of myself. I lost all reason when I was with her. I had never really been with a woman, beyond the odd meaningless encounter. For so many years, I was confused. About myself. About what and who I was. Grace ended that confusion. She made me understand myself. She made me whole.'

'You're sick. It's a sickness.'

'It's our curse.' Luke's voice is a whisper. 'The Wyclercs are damned. Ever since Esther and Jude.'

I know that Luke is thinking about *us* too, about that brief summer when two cousins had, unknowingly, become lovers. A silence as dark as the breath from a crypt seeps into the room. I understand then that Samuel has been waiting eighteen years to make his confession.

'*You* killed them,' I say. 'Grace *and* Gideon.'

He is startled. 'No. I wouldn't— I could never have harmed them. I *loved* them.'

My certainty flounders. I had come here believing that finally I had solved the riddle. That Samuel killed his brother to cover up his own illicit relationship with Gideon's daughter.

But now, in the face of his denial, doubt returns. There is the ring of truth to his words. Instead of a killer, I see only a man broken on the wheel of his own shame.

'Where were you when Gideon was killed?'

'I was in the church.'

'Were you alone?'

'Yes. I always shut the church during the Forest Festival.'

'Then why were you there?'

He hesitates. 'Because I'd asked Grace to meet me there, after she'd finished with the pageant.'

'Grace was with you that afternoon?'

'Only for a short while. I wanted to talk to her. I, I told her we couldn't see each other any more. Not in that way.'

'You ended it on the day of the Forest Festival?'

'Yes. I'd been building up to it for a while. Hinting at it. Grace was ... unhappy. She had this idea that we could simply leave town, start somewhere new, together. I knew that was impossible. I knew that I couldn't go through with something like that.'

My mind goes to the entries in Grace's journal, the tone of desperation that had infected her at the very end.

Luke speaks up. 'How did Grace take it?'

'She wouldn't accept it. She wanted to go to Gideon and tell him everything, tell him she didn't care what anyone thought. That she wanted to be with me. She was blind to reason. I can't explain it.'

'That must have terrified you. The thought that your filthy secret would be exposed. That you'd be shown up as a predator.' Luke's disgust could not have been more evident. 'Is that why you killed her? Killed Gideon?'

'No!'

Luke gets to his feet. 'Stand up.'

'I didn't kill them. How could you think that I'd ... ?' He looks between us in wonder. 'I loved Grace. That was my sin. But I had nothing to do with her disappearance.'

'I said stand up.'

Samuel lumbers to his feet.

Luke's fist lashes out.

Samuel grunts, falls back onto the sofa, blood spraying onto his chin and T-shirt.

Luke looks down at him, and then reaches for his gun.

144

ORIANNA: NOW

I sit there, caught off guard, and then spring to my feet, wrapping both arms around Luke's midriff and wrenching him away.

He staggers aside, turns back, breathing hard, a wild look in his eye.

I bend to Samuel.

He lies sprawled on the couch, bleeding from his nose. Blood dots his T-shirt.

I offer him my hand.

He takes it, lurches to his feet.

'Where's the bathroom?' I ask.

I follow him as he walks along a corridor and into a cream-tiled bathroom.

I pull a towel from the rack, hold it out.

He bends to the sink, spits blood into the bowl. Turning on the tap, he wets the towel and holds it to his face.

I want to join him, to run cold water over my face, my scalp. My skull is vibrating with pain, with the shock of revelation. How much more can I withstand?

Sooner or later, I will crack, my mind, my body, disintegrating into a million pieces.

But not now. I must go on.

When the blood has stopped flowing, Samuel turns back to me. 'You can call me a monster for what I did with Grace. But I'm no killer. God knows the truth and only He can judge me.'

The purple shadows under his eyes throb. His massively powerful upper body radiates an angry heat.

My mind loops around, comes back in on itself. I think of all the lies I had heard in prison, lies told so many times even the liars could no longer distinguish them from the truth. But there is always something, if you look hard enough. A hesitation, a look in the eye, a choke in the flow of words.

I see none of this in Samuel.

'They say sin without salvation is meaningless,' Samuel continues. 'I've spent eighteen years paying for my sin. I'm a good man. I don't expect you to believe me, but God sees what is in our hearts. "Blessed is he whose transgressions are forgiven, whose sins are covered. Blessed is the man whose sin the Lord does not count against him and in whose spirit is no deceit."'

I allow the echoes of his words to fade away.

He lowers the towel. 'Is it true that you were with Amos when he died?'

'Yes.'

'Did he . . . did he mention me?'

'No.'

He looks back at the mirror. 'It's a difficult thing to never really know your father. We have that in common.'

'We have nothing in common.'

145

ORIANNA: NOW

Back in the car, Luke sits with stiff shoulders, as if held up by wire. 'If *he* didn't do it, then who?'

'I don't know.'

My certainty has vanished and with it my resolve.

I no longer believe that I will solve the mystery. Time and circumstance have defeated me. I am overcome by an exhaustion so complete it is all I can do not to close my eyes and fall into a thousand-year slumber. My head continues to pound, the pain so acute I want to twist off my skull, to bite off my tongue, swallow it down.

'We have to get you off the streets,' Luke says.

'What's the point? There's nowhere I can go. Nowhere they won't find me.'

'Do you trust me?'

I twist in my seat to stare at him.

'Do you trust me?' he repeats.

I hear the gate swing open, the night guard, Lavell, holler out. 'Evening, Mr Luke.'

'Evening, Lavell.'

'Have they found her yet?'

'No.'

'Did she really kill him? Mr Amos?'

'No, Lavell.'

A beat, and then, 'Gladdens my heart you say that, Mr Luke. I never pegged her for no killer.'

The pickup jerks into motion.

Five minutes later, Luke calls out from the driver's seat. 'OK. You can get out.'

I heave aside the tarpaulin in the back of Gerty's truck, slip out from under it.

Luke parks on the edge of the woods. 'They'll be looking for you up at the Big House. But they won't be expecting you to go to Gideon's cabin.'

I take a deep breath. 'I can't.'

'You've run out of road, Ori. Either you hand yourself in or you hide. There's no other way.' He plucks a cushion from the driver's seat, presumably to make the floor of the cabin a little more accommodating. 'Come on.'

We reach the cabin, still hunkered in its clearing, a revenant as clear in my mind as a pure note struck on a bell.

Opening the door, I step inside.

The interior is a portal to another world, a gaping mouth strung with teeth.

I stand there, the silence banking around me like falling snow. My brain throbs. I feel as if I might melt through the cracks in the floorboards like a candle under a blowtorch.

I think of the wolves that once roamed this land. The wolves I had heard in the night may have been a figment of my fevered imagination, but wolves still lived in Eden Falls – only now they wore the skins of men.

The Girl In Cell A

I become aware of Luke's presence behind me, a pale question mark in the darkness.

The scent of him, his cologne. The smell cuts through the pounding in my head.

A shudder. A jerk.

A blinding white light, accompanied by another shattering fusillade detonating inside my skull.

I am torn through a rip in time, returned to the exact moment I had stood in this place eighteen years earlier, looking down on Gideon's blasted body.

Time wavers, stretches, snaps.

The howling in my ears stops; a ringing silence descends.

I pull out Gerty's revolver and turn to face Luke. 'Give me your gun.'

146

ANNIE: THEN

'Orianna, I know that you are upset. But I believe we have to continue. I think we're very close to a breakthrough.'

She stares at me. Colour has drained from her face. She seems simultaneously exhausted and energised. A warrior at the end of a battle.

'After meeting with Luke in the woods on the day of Gideon's killing, what did you do next?'

It is almost a minute before she responds. When she does, her voice is steady. 'I went back home. I found my mother there.'

'Were you surprised to find Christine there?'

'Yes. She had come back from the Big House. I knew that she was busy supervising preparations for the evening dinner, the annual Wyclerc family gathering after the Forest Festival. I had no idea what she was doing home. But one look at her face told me that something was wrong.' A beat. 'It spilled out of her in a torrent. The secret she'd held on to for so long. She finally told me the name of my father.'

'Gideon?'

'Yes.'
'What exactly did she say?'
'Just that. *"Gideon Wyclerc is your father."*'
'And can you remember how you felt at that exact moment?'
'I remember standing there and staring at her. I remember a numbness. She tried to embrace me. Her face was puckered with sorrow, with regret, with emotions I couldn't guess at.'
'And what did you say?'

I watch her vanish into the past, relive the unbearable intensity of those moments.

'Did he know?'
'Oh, baby.'
'Did he know!'

Her face is haggard. 'I was shouting by then. All those years, the father I had searched for, yearned for, had been right there, an arm's length away. And if Gideon had known – and how could he not have known? – then the fact that he'd never acknowledged me, ignored me, denied me . . .'
'You were angry. You had every right to be. It was a perfectly understandable reaction.'
'I remember a sound like rushing steam inside my head. Rage like I had never felt before. Or since.'

'Where is he?'
'Oh, Ori.'

'I remember my mother reaching for me. I remember knocking her hands away.'

'Tell me where he is.'

147

ORIANNA: NOW

Luke stares at me, uncomprehending.

'Take out your gun and give it to me. Slowly.'

'Ori. What are you doi—?'

'Do it!'

He sets down the cushion he has brought along from the pickup, then slips his automatic from its holster and sets it down on the floor.

'Step back.'

He moves backwards, face wreathed in shadow.

I sweep up the gun, stick it in my belt. I hold his eyes. 'You were there that day. Just before I blacked out. Just before someone struck me.'

He is shaking his head. 'No.'

'Your cologne. I remember now. The smell of it. It's the one thing I remember clearly, the *last* thing I remember, the sharp sting of your cologne, just before I was hit from behind.'

'It wasn't me. Orianna, I lied once before, at your trial. I promised myself I'd never lie to you again. If you want to shoot me for testifying against you, for betraying you, go ahead. I won't stop you. I deserve it.'

I raise the gun.

He doesn't flinch, standing there, framed by the door, as still as a telegraph pole.

An unbearable conflict rages inside me. My skull expands and contracts. The migraine has become an epiphany, a piercing light so bright it washes out the world.

Could I be wrong?

No.

I know Luke's smell. It has lived with me for eighteen years.

Still, I waver.

How is it possible to be so certain and yet also admit the possibility of error?

And then, in a blinding flash, I understand.

The fragmented images merge into a whole.

The world trembles on its axis.

The wreck rises from the water, and finally I see the truth and, with it, the horror.

148

ANNIE: THEN

In physics, there is a concept known as a singularity. A place in space-time where everything breaks down, where the rules we are familiar with no longer apply. Singularities are found at the centres of black holes.

They are also found deep in the dark spaces of our minds.

Will we ever understand what truly happened that day?

A question I ask myself each time I sit with Orianna, each time I review my notes of our meetings.

The last few sessions have brought us closer than ever to finally penetrating Orianna's uncooperative memory. But each time we get to that exact moment, the instant that Gideon was killed, Orianna stops.

The frame freezes. I cannot move her past it.

It has been months – and several sessions – since Orianna told me about the moment her mother revealed to her that Gideon was her father. Since she admitted that she was in a black rage when she went to find him at his cabin.

She remembers arriving at the cabin. She remembers the shotgun. She remembers Gideon in his chair. And one more thing . . . a sense memory. The smell of Luke's cologne, retained on her clothes, she believes, from their earlier encounter in the woods.

And that's it.

The curtain drops.

And, try as I may, I cannot get her to relive the next few seconds, the instant that she shot her father.

Will she *ever* admit the truth to herself?

Most dissociative amnesia patients eventually recover their memories. It can take years, even decades.

But sometimes a patient never recovers.

Never remembers.

149

ORIANNA: NOW

Luke leads us through the silent house, out to the back porch.

We find David sitting in his rocker, facing the lawn and the surrounding plum trees. The scent of the fruit is sickly, warmed by the heat, like molasses on a spoon.

The moon has climbed out of the forest and shines down with a hard, pure light.

David holds a paring knife in his working hand, his long pale fingers curved around the handle. A sliced apple lies on a small plate on his lap.

He sees the gun in my hand, looks at Luke, then back at me.

Something shifts behind his eyes.

In that instant, I know that he understands.

'*You* were in the cabin that day,' I say. 'It was *your* cologne I registered. The same cologne Luke always wore. *You* killed Gideon. *You* killed Grace. Why?'

His head is a void in the night, a space filled with stars. When he speaks, his voice is as coarse as gravel. 'The family had to be protected. *My* family.'

The sound of cicadas threatens to drown out the world. My mind melts into lava; I am living through a fever dream.

I raise the gun. My arm shakes.

'Ori.' Luke's voice is a croak.

'David. Tell me what I want to know, or, as God is my witness, I'll shoot you dead in that fucking chair.'

'Put the gun down.'

I spin around to find Susannah Wyclerc in the doorway, a rifle pointed at me.

A dull sound emerges from Luke's throat. His vocal chords have seized.

'I want the truth,' I say. 'It's either that, or you'll have to kill me.'

Susannah's eyes are chips of glass. 'The truth? Do you think you can bear it?' She advances a step. 'The truth lives in taking the unbearable and *making* it bearable, in living with horror, each and every day, because that's the only choice you have. Horror so dark no imagination could invent it. But you do it, because that's the only way you can save yourself, your family. In the end, that's all that matters. You do what you have to, to protect the ones you love.'

'What did you do? Tell me. Please. Tell me the truth.' My voice is a sob of rage.

For an instant, Susannah wavers, held between implacability and my plea. 'David was away so much of the time. And I was stuck here, on my own. You can't begin to imagine how hard it is. The loneliness of it. To crave affection, a caress, the warmth of another body . . . It was a few days before the Forest Festival. Gideon had come around. We got talking. Perhaps . . . Perhaps I gave him some encouragement. I don't know. But I never wanted—I never . . . Before I knew what was happening, he was . . . on me.'

'Are you saying Gideon assaulted you?'

Her gaze is hollow. 'He *raped* me.'

Silence. Shock.

'Did you tell anyone?'

'No.'

'Why?'

'Because Hannah tried that, and where did it get her? Because I wanted to pretend that it hadn't happened. Because I didn't want to destroy David, my marriage, this family.'

I take a deep breath. 'Did Rebekah know?'

'No. I didn't tell her. Rebekah had enough problems with Gideon. She'd always known about his philandering, how he simply had to have every woman that came within arm's reach of him. In the end, she snapped. She went looking elsewhere. Took up with Tommy Quinn. I don't know if she did it to get back at Gideon or because she . . . needed someone.' Her thumb moves on the shotgun's barrel. 'But then something happened between them. Between her and Tommy. Something she hadn't planned on. They fell hard for each other.

'And so Rebekah decided not to tell Gideon. She didn't want to wreck what she had with Tommy. But Tommy got tired of hiding it. And so he did it for her. On the day of the Forest Festival. Just walked up to Gideon and told him.'

'How do you know all this?'

'Rebekah told me.' A beat. 'It broke Gideon. He was one of those men who excused himself every excess, but when he found out Rebekah had repaid him in kind, it became something monstrous in his mind. And so he lashed out. He wanted to hurt her in the only way he had left. He told her about *you*.'

I feel the heat of the night close in on me.

'Rebekah always suspected you were Gideon's child. That your mother and Gideon were ... whatever they were. But Gideon and Christine always denied it. But now, it was out in the open. Confirmed by Gideon himself.

'*That's* why your mother finally told you that day. Because Rebekah confronted her. After she got back from the Forest Festival, after Gideon told her about you. Rebekah wanted to hear it from Christine's own lips – that you were Gideon's child, I mean.

'And after Rebekah spoke with her, your mother knew it was only a matter of time before Rebekah tracked you down and forced the truth down *your* throat. She didn't want you to find out that way, and so she told you herself.' She shifts on her feet. 'She couldn't have known that you'd go looking for Gideon, that you'd track him down to his cabin. And she couldn't have known that the same afternoon, I'd told David about what Gideon had done. I couldn't face the idea of the family dinner at the Big House that evening, Gideon pretending everything was normal, that he hadn't assaulted me just days earlier. I couldn't have predicted that David would pick up a gun and go looking for Gideon too. I tried to stop him. I begged him. But he was beyond my control. And so I went with him.

'We found Gideon in his cabin, in the woods. We got there just ahead of you.

'David told Gideon that he *knew*. Gideon just stared at him. And then he burst out laughing. That was the worst of it. He'd been drinking. The revelation of Rebekah's affair with Tommy had wounded him and he'd come to the cabin, gone to ground like a wild animal. I saw David's face. I saw what it did to him. His helplessness. He raised the gun. His hands shook.

'But then he lowered it again.

'I knew then that David wouldn't, *couldn't* do anything. He's not made that way. He wasn't going to shoot Gideon. I saw the long, bitter road that lay ahead, of trying to live on that estate with this monstrous thing hanging over us, with Gideon having this hold over us, over David.' Susannah stops. 'I remember . . . a moment of utter clarity. I realised that Gideon's assault – and my telling David of it – had destroyed the only man I'd ever loved.

'I knew then what I had to do.

'I had gloves in my pocket. I'd worn them to the Forest Festival, with my summer dress. White gloves. I pulled them on. I picked up a shotgun from the rack. And then I shot Gideon. In the end, it was no more difficult than putting down a rabid dog.

'I dropped the shotgun and then I pulled David outside.

'That's when we heard footsteps approaching through the woods. I acted on instinct. I dragged David behind the cabin and we waited. He was stunned, in shock.

'I heard your voice, calling out to Gideon. You sounded furious. And then I heard you go into the cabin.' She stops. 'I've thought about what happened next for the past eighteen years. At that moment, I saw the future – a future in which David and I were convicted of murdering Gideon. And then I saw another path, a path to salvation. And I took it.

'I told David what had to be done. I told him there was no time to think. Not if he wanted us to survive, as a unit, as a family. I told him to think about Luke. What would happen to Luke if we were implicated in Gideon's murder?

'David walked back around, stepped into the cabin behind you. You were standing there, in shock, staring at Gideon's body.

'David hit you on the back of the head with the butt of his gun. You fell to the floor, unconscious, right beside the shotgun, where I'd dropped it after killing Gideon.

'We had no idea then that you'd been out in the woods with that same gun *earlier* that day. Luke only told us about you both being out there later, about what had been going on between you for months. That's when we told him he couldn't testify on your behalf. That's when we told him to lie. For the good of the family.

'He wasn't sure, you see. Luke wasn't certain that you *hadn't* killed Gideon. You'd talked so often about what you'd do if you ever found your father . . . We told him that he couldn't allow Gideon's killer to slip through the net. Luke's testimony could go a long way to ensuring that. His first loyalty was to the family. He was a Wyclerc.

'When it came out – that your prints were on the murder weapon, the very gun I'd picked up and killed Gideon with – it was as if fate had conspired in our favour.

The Girl In Cell A

God must have wanted it that way. At least, that's what I told myself.'

I feel my stomach fall away. All these years . . . and now, to have my innocence confirmed. My mind collapses in on itself. The wolves return, howling inside my head. Words choke up through my gullet. 'And Grace?'

Susannah's face freezes. 'Grace . . . Grace was in the woods too. She saw us as we were making our way from the cabin. Our plan had been to hurry back and tell someone that we'd heard shots in the woods. We'd left you unconscious on the cabin floor, arranged with the shotgun beside you. We thought we'd round up someone at the Big House, and go investigate, find you there still stretched out on the floor. Who would have believed you had nothing to do with Gideon's death? At the least, your presence in the cabin would muddy the waters.

'But when we saw Grace coming towards us, we knew that wouldn't work. Grace had *seen* us coming from the cabin. We couldn't just . . . let her go. You can understand that, can't you? She'd seen us. It was just bad luck.'

'*You* killed Grace.' I try to wrap my arms around the monstrousness of it, but find it impossible to make the thought stand up.

Susannah's face remains impassive, her skin waxy under the moon. And then she raises the rifle.

Luke steps directly in front of his mother. 'You're going to have to kill me first.'

'Get out of the way, Luke.'

'Did you kill Grace?'

'We did what had to be done.'

'What about Amos? Was it you up at the mine?'

'Death was already coming for Amos,' says Susannah. 'He'd lost his mind, pursuing Grace's disappearance all these years. Leaving his fortune to Orianna. I had to stop him, stop them both. Don't you see?'

Luke steps towards his mother. 'Put the gun down. It's over.'

'We can't let her walk out of here.'

'Put the fucking gun down! *Now!*'

The rifle trembles in her hands.

'Susannah.' David's voice.

Susannah switches her gaze to her husband.

He stares at her with eyes from another world, a world of such pain and suffering that life itself would be frightened to be conceived. His cheeks are wet with tears.

And then his hand closes around the paring knife at his thigh, and he stabs upwards, plunging the blade into his throat.

The world stops.

Susannah screams. The rifle clatters to the porch.

She runs to David, cradles his head as the blood sprays from his throat.

Luke stands paralysed, stunned, and then a guttural cry escapes him. He rushes to his father, tries to pull his mother away so that he can reach the wound.

But I know that it is too late.

I feel my body go slack, as if my strings have been cut.

Here is a resolution, an ending. But at what cost?

I feel darkness descending; my lungs are full of dirt, thick and choking. A sensation akin to being buried alive.

How can anything survive in the devastation that humans inflict upon one another?

The Girl In Cell A

For if David is a lie and Samuel is a lie and Susannah is a lie, then what of Eden itself? There is no God and no Satan. No garden, no salvation, no white-picket-fenced heaven. The people of the Earth are blind, low-bellied animals writhing in the dirt, battling in the dying light as the storm rages and the cities fall to ruin and the stars shake in their infinite loops.

150

ANNIE: THEN

Music plays softly in my office. It is late in the evening and the campus is quiet. I have a bottle of wine at my elbow, smuggled in, and a plastic glass taken from our kitchen-cum-meeting room.

I have turned down the lights. My laptop screen is a bright glow in the dark.

It has been a month since my last session with Orianna.

A month during which I have been tasked to prepare an interim evaluation report on our progress together.

Time has become fluid. For Orianna, in her narrative. And for me too. Past, present, future all tumble together.

I have all the pieces of the jigsaw. It's all there. In the case files, in my extensive notes from our sessions together. All I have to do is piece it together.

We have not had the breakthrough that I had hoped for. A clear and unequivocal unlocking of Orianna's memory that tells us exactly what happened in Gideon's cabin.

Instead, Orianna insists that she is innocent, that one day she will return to Eden Falls and prove this so.

I am convinced that Orianna must resolve the matter of Grace – in her own mind – before she can resolve herself. She must admit the truth about Grace. To herself, and to me. Only then can she access those hidden memories and discover the truth about Gideon's murder.

Yet I cannot shake the feeling that something is wrong.

What if somewhere in the narrative that Orianna has presented me with during our sessions, there is a grain of truth? Because if that is the case, then somewhere, out there, a killer is still at large.

I shake my head. The wine is fuelling fanciful notions. I must remain professional, not allow my feelings towards Orianna – which, despite that fact that I am barely a decade older than her, have become distinctly maternal – to cloud my judgement.

Tomorrow, I have invited Amos Wyclerc to meet with me. Since visiting him in Eden Falls, he has taken an interest in Orianna's treatment. He has followed my progress – or lack of it. He is an inscrutable man, his motivations hidden from me. I can only assume that he has decided either to determine Orianna's guilt for himself – through me – or is wavering towards the notion that perhaps, just perhaps, she may be innocent.

I explain to him that nothing Orianna says can be taken at face value. Not only are there holes in her memory, but her mind has actively created false memories. Delusions.

In a sense, a duel is taking place inside her head. Between Guilty Orianna and Innocent Orianna. She is being sheared in two. The manifestation of that conflict has made Orianna's treatment a complex process.

I don't know what Amos will make of things as they stand. It has been a difficult journey, fully understanding

Orianna's mind, the narrative she has fashioned. Of her past, of the events of that fateful day. And of the future.

My treatment of her will be assessed and a decision will have to be made.

My phone beeps. It is almost eight.

I must get on and finish the report.

Whatever happens, whatever doubts I may have, I must present my conclusions with a clear mind.

I settle in front of my laptop and begin again.

151

ORIANNA: NOW

Midges dance above the lake. The trees on the far bank rise like leviathans, reaching up into the hazy light of dusk.

'You did it.'

I turn from under the yew tree.

Grace is standing there, hovering inches above the earth, naked, illuminated by the sun's dying light.

'You did it, Orianna. You solved the mystery.'

I want to ask her why she is naked. But my throat is jammed.

'Isn't it astonishing? The cold comfort people take from their own justifications.'

Tears spring to my eyes. I am helpless in Grace's light.

Grace smiles. *'Don't you feel bad for me. Don't you dare.'* Her outline wavers. *'There is one more thing you can do for me ... I'm just a story to them. But I was flesh and blood, once. I was your friend, your sister. Don't let the memory of me rot, Ori. Don't let them take that from me, too. Hold me inside you. Keep me alive.'*

152

ORIANNA: NOW

The service takes place beneath a high sun, a sweltering day as hot as any the town has experienced.

They come in their hundreds, packing out the church, spilling onto the street outside, lining the route that will eventually take Amos back to the Wyclerc estate to be interred in the family graveyard.

If there had been ambivalence towards the old man, you couldn't tell. Death has transformed the ogre into a mythic figure, Eden Falls' larger-than-life paterfamilias, the last true link to the town's founding father, Nathaniel Wyclerc.

I watch them close ranks, bullying out the reporters and the podcasters and the TV correspondents, forcing them outside, where they stand in sulky clumps, brick-jawed and wall-eyed.

The service is led by the elderly Reverend Clarence Blake, invited over from Barrier. Eden Falls' parish priest, Samuel Wyclerc, has vanished. He was seen leaving town; no one knows when he might return.

In the past week, I have sensed the town reorient itself. The realisation that they had sent a girl to prison for a crime she hadn't committed has sobered even the most obstinate. And yet, they cannot admit their wrongness. Because it would diminish them – in their own eyes. Once again, I feel them push me away – courteously, but no less firmly than the last time; a newly grafted limb rejected from the body corpus.

The anger returns, a whiplash of rage that all but blinds me.

Annie Ledet taught me many things, but not how to live with the truth.

'The human mind is a fragile construct, Orianna, full of tripwires. It never truly heals after trauma.'

The Wyclercs, too, have been circumspect. I sense their coldness, their accusation. I walked back into their lives, dragging hell with me.

They expected me to speak at Amos's funeral, knowing that Amos had made good on his threat and left me his fortune. They are beholden to me now. They are *afraid* of me, of what I might do with my newfound power.

I surprised them by declining to speak.

Instead, I asked Peter, to his shock. I think he expected me to banish him from the estate, from the company.

He stands at the lectern now, sombre in a black suit, a tall figure, as patrician as a crane. Marshalling his words, he addresses the crowd, sweating and shuffling in the pews.

He talks of Amos, the titan of industry; Amos, the keeper of Nathaniel Wyclerc's legacy, the town's shepherd, for good or ill.

And then, finally, he talks of Amos, his father. 'My father's death marks the passing of an age. We will not see his like again.'

A lump swells in my throat. An image of Amos behind his chair, cigar in hand, cursing to beat the band.

153

ORIANNA: NOW

Afterwards, at the Big House, we gather beneath the gazebo near the old peach orchard, a small crowd. We eat and drink and remember the dead man, all the while twitching and grimacing at the pall of darkness hanging over the occasion.

I pick up my glass, step out of the gazebo, walk out to where Luke stands by a tree, talking with his wife, Abigail.

They turn as I approach, a strained look taking up residence on Abigail's face.

'Do you mind if I talk to Luke for a moment?'

Abigail glances at her husband, then nods, clearly unhappy, before wandering back to the gazebo.

'How is she?'

'Abigail?' Luke grimaces. 'She's not exactly overjoyed with the way things have turned out. She loved my parents. And the media scrutiny is hardly what the doctor ordered for a heavily pregnant woman.'

'I meant Susannah.'

He sighs. 'She's ... lost. I think she's still in shock at my father's suicide. She's not telling us much, or at least, she talks in fits and starts. She's gone over the day

Gideon died, his killing. The story hasn't changed. She's confirmed, for the record, that she killed Gideon, that David knocked you out cold in Gideon's cabin, that the pair of them arranged it so that it looked as if you'd shot Gideon and then stumbled back and knocked yourself out against the wall of the cabin. They pretty much covered it up together. Frankly, if you hadn't returned to Eden Falls . . .' He falls silent a moment. 'Once you came back and began snooping around – with Amos's blessing – Susannah felt compelled to act. She admits to hiring the two Neanderthals who attacked you out at Elvira's, though she says she told them only to scare you off, not to hurt you. She admits to planting the crucifix in Tommy Quinn's trailer, making the anonymous call to the sheriff's office. Her idea was to implicate Quinn in Grace's disappearance. A backup, in case you got too close to the truth. It was a good idea. Especially given that you'd made it so public about Quinn and Rebekah's affair.'

'Where did she get the crucifix?'

He looks away. 'Presumably from Grace.' He didn't have to add 'after they killed her'.

'But then you spoke to Hannah,' he continues. 'That spooked her. You were getting closer and closer to the truth about Gideon, about the predator that he was. And that brought you one step closer to the truth about Gideon raping Susannah. If that ever came out, it would immediately give her and David a motive to have killed Gideon.'

Luke's voice is toneless as he describes his mother's crimes. I feel momentarily hot and thick-headed, a combination of wine, heat and Luke's proximity. A queasy horror rolls around my guts. Nothing about this is right.

'She admits to writing the note that lured you and Amos up to the mine, admits to shooting him. I think she was reacting in panic, by then. She had some crazy notion that she'd kill Amos and get everyone blaming you all over again.

'There was also the fact that Amos had made it clear he intended to leave his share of the estate to you. I don't think it was about the money. I think my mother felt the money, the inheritance, would give you more reason to stay in Eden Falls, and the resources to get to the bottom of what happened to Gideon and Grace. She didn't know – none of us did – that Amos had actually gone ahead and carried out his threat. He had already signed the new will by the time she shot him. Killing him made no difference.' His voice cracks. I see the effort it is taking for him to speak about his family in this way, those he loved, now dead, or lost to him. How is he handling his father's death? I am afraid to ask, given the revelations of David's complicity in Gideon's and Grace's fates.

Perhaps he has read my mind because next he says: 'The one thing my mother won't tell us is where she and my father buried Grace.'

The sun makes prisms on the surface of the wine in my glass. 'What will they do to her? To Susannah?'

'The DA is assessing the case. It'll go to court. She'll be convicted of Amos's murder – we found the rifle she used to kill him in our house. But when it comes to Gideon's death . . . there's no physical evidence to go on, not after all this time. Just our testimony, yours and mine, about the things she said, confessed to.'

'You said she'd also confessed to the authorities.'

'Yes. But if she changes her mind, claims she confessed under duress . . .'

'Are you saying the DA might not try her for Gideon's and Grace's killings?'

'It's been eighteen years. You know better than anyone that the law doesn't always find its way through the murk.'

We say nothing for a while.

I break the silence. 'When I was young, I always imagined that if I *had* a father, I'd want him to be like David.'

His expression becomes wretched. 'I'm so sorry, Ori—'

'Don't apologise. If I hear one more apology, I'll—' I stop.

I look back, beyond the house, to the rising elevation sweeping to the north.

Beyond the estate, green hills rise to meet the sky.

The dead weight of the past should have lifted from me, but now, gazing out beyond the breakwaters of the present, I sense the black swell of the future racing towards me.

A terrifying loneliness closes in.

Already, Amos is fading, just as my mother has faded. The process of transubstantiation has made wraiths of all those I once loved.

It is a lie that the living find their way in the shadow of death; sometimes the human spirit simply fails to cast enough light to see by.

The Girl In Cell A

I look at Luke and see, perhaps for the first time, the great gulf between us. No gravity can pull us together.

The chains we rattle behind each other will forever drown out the beat of our hearts.

154

ORIANNA: NOW

Later, after they have left, I take a last wander around the house.

My bags are already packed.

I have told no one I am leaving, not even Luke.

My mind is in a tumult.

The migraines have returned. In truth, they never went away. Resolution has not brought with it relief.

Earlier, Gerty had taken me aside.

'You're holding on to something dark inside you, child. Until you let go, you'll never be free.'

I had felt a rage then, a fire of the mind that threatened to overwhelm me. My anger stemmed not from Gerty's words, but from the fact that I knew, at a level below conscious thought, that she was right. The peace that I had anticipated with vindication eludes me. I haven't slept in days. My thoughts grind together like boulders in my head; my stomach is a lake of acid.

Something is wrong, and I have no idea what.

Eighteen years ago, my life was torn apart. Now I have returned to Eden Falls and overturned the great injustice done to me. I have found answers to the questions that

The Girl In Cell A

tormented me throughout the long years in prison. So then . . . why? Why won't peace come?

Gerty had kept at me, coaxing, her knowing eyes never leaving me. In so many ways, she reminds me of Annie Ledet. That same gentle persistence, that same tap, tap, tap, until I feel my skull might implode under the weight of it.

In the end, it became too much. 'Leave me the fuck alone!'

I saw the shock in Gerty's eyes; the truth is, I stunned myself.

Where had that rage come from?

The fact that it is still there, a wolf prowling inside me, only vindicates Gerty's assessment.

I know that Gerty, like Annie before her, only wants the best for me.

Annie had wanted to cure me, to fix me up so that the parole board could stamp me ready for polite society . . . *Why had they let me out?* Would they have let me out if they could have seen inside me?

The truth comes at a heavy price. Looking inwards and seeing the monster inside.

The closer you get to it, the greater the terror.

Perhaps Annie had been wrong, after all.

She had compared my mind to a black box, had sought to pry it open.

But perhaps it should have remained forever closed.

We stand there, facing each other in the courtyard, as Gerty blurs and vanishes into the burning sun.

155

ORIANNA: NOW

On my final walk through the house, the wildfire rages inside me. I want to burn the place down; to leave not a trace of the Wyclercs or my past. Gerty is right. Anger, raw and reckless, dominates my every waking moment.

In Amos's study, I pick up the framed photograph of Amos and Grace.

Something about the image strikes me, and I walk it to the window, look at it in the light. A finger rises to trace Amos's face. A feeling I cannot put into words bubbles up inside me like air rising to the surface of a tar pit.

White light bleeds into the edges of my vision. The room ripples around me.

I focus on Grace.

Regret eats away at me. I cannot help the feeling that I somehow failed my half-sister. I had hoped that Susannah might, by now, have revealed Grace's ultimate fate, what she and David had done with the body. If the bones were recoverable, they might yet be interred in the family plot. But Susannah has said nothing, holding tight to the last of her secrets.

'Were we truly friends?' I hear myself whisper.

Slowly, I become aware of the soft note that has chimed in the subterranean chambers of my mind ever since I returned from the mine, a note so low I had chosen to ignore it, relegating it to the realm of meaningless noise. Now, in the dazzle of the sun, the pane of window glass acting as a prism for memory, it moves into a higher register.

I try to assemble my fractured thoughts ... *What was my subconscious trying to tell me?* ... Something I had heard or seen in the mine as I had climbed up onto the gantry leading to the cage lift ...

A blaze of light blasts through the shadows of my thoughts. A thunderous realisation rocks me. The floor tilts beneath my feet, and I find myself reaching for the windowsill to steady myself.

The monstrous thought that has struck me transforms into a creature stomping through my brain, a furious scream that lays waste to everything but its own insistent narrative.

Moments later, I am on the move.

156

ORIANNA: NOW

The drive up to the mine brings back memories of that last day with Amos.

He had told me about a Roman cult, the worshippers of Mithras, who built their temples underground, in caves and beneath mountains. Amos too had been a god of the underworld, of stone caverns and straight-sided shafts, and the dark spaces that honeycombed the Earth's crust.

I realised then, that, despite the many sins of his life, there was an essential goodness inside him. The truth was that Amos, like so many – like Gideon, like my mother, like myself – had spent the best part of his life fighting the demons that battled for his soul.

The tree that had previously blocked our progress has been shunted aside by the authorities following Amos's death; I am able to drive right up to the old caboose.

I leave the car behind and walk up the gravel track leading to the mine entrance.

A shudder trembles through me as I walk inside.

My mind sings, but the song is garbled, a high-pitched

chorus that makes me think of death and delirium. These migraines will kill me one day. Perhaps this is the moment.

Am I crazy?

Reaching the cage-lift shafts, I locate the control panel embedded in the wall. A switch feeds power to the twin lifts.

Minutes later, I am back on the gantry leading from the base of the lifts.

The gantry stretches into darkness, at its far reach, the prefab hut that had once served as a site office.

I walk with my flashlight held out.

I arrive at the door to the hut, stand a moment, then turn off the flashlight.

It takes a while for my eyes to adjust to the dark.

And there it is.

A thin line, barely visible, at the bottom of the door.

Light.

Light in a place where it has no right to be.

I walk to the door, try the handle. It is locked.

I had expected it to be and have come prepared.

I set my grab bag onto the floor, take out a chisel and hammer, set the chisel to the square base in which the handle is inset, and strike down on it. The sound echoes loudly off the walls of the chamber.

Five blows, and the plate comes away from the door.

Minutes later, I have levered out the lock's innards, enough to be able to push the door back.

I take a deep breath, feel shadows move inside me.

The world around me begins to crack, the cracks racing up through my feet until my body begins to shake.

I walk on trembling legs into a large space, illuminated by a single low-wattage striplight.

A sofa. A bed. A wardrobe. A fridge. A television. A DVD player. A bookcase. A door, half ajar, through which I can see a toilet, a washbasin, a shower cubicle. A portable electrical generator in one corner.

On a table, beside the bed, is a plate. The remains of a simple meal. An empty water bottle.

And on the bed: a woman.

I stumble to the bed, numbed by waves of profound shock. With each step, a rising gale blows through my thoughts. Light glows from the walls, gradually washing out everything except the bed. An intense pain jabs through my skull, almost buckling my knees.

I fight on, grimacing.

I sit down beside the figure, lift an arm and place my fingers at the wrist. The flutter of a butterfly's wings.

Another intense stab of pain, a stake driven deep into my ear.

The white light around me drowns out everything except the face of the woman before me.

I stare down at Grace, a face that is barely recognisable, old before its time.

I am unable to speak. I feel disassociated from the moment, from myself, from the monstrousness of the crime before me.

Grace's eyelids flutter.

I reach under her, bring her to my chest, hold her in a

rigid embrace, tears falling freely. 'It's OK, Grace. I've got you. I've got you now.'

Grace dissolves into my arms. It seems to me, down in the howling dark, that we have become one and the same person.

PSYCHIATRIC EVALUATION REPORT

Prepared by:

(Dr) Annie Ledet

Status: Confidential

Location: Wolfson State Hospital

Patient Number: 85799

Patient Name: Orianna Negi

Age: 35 years, 10 months

Sex: Female

Reason for assessment: Ongoing treatment

157

AMOS: NOW

The meeting takes place in a corner office, behind a heavy oak door. A plaque screwed to the wall states simply: *DIRECTOR*.

Annie Ledet leads me in. Light floods in through expansive bay windows, illuminating the space and highlighting a tall, patrician figure standing behind a desk.

'Mr Wyclerc, thank you for coming in today.' The man – early sixties, by the look of him – extends a hand. 'My name is Charles Hackett. I am the director of this institute.'

We settle ourselves around the desk. Hackett offers refreshments; I decline.

'Mr Wyclerc, you've now had a chance to read Dr Ledet's report. The purpose of today's meeting is to determine how to proceed with Orianna's treatment.'

'That was some account.' Phlegm rattles in my throat.

'If I may be frank: it's spectacular. "The Girl in Cell A" has outdone herself.'

His tone is dry. I don't care for it.

'I suggest we start by going over the material facts. For the record.' Hackett turns towards Annie. 'Dr Ledet, shall we start with your assessment?'

'As delusional pathologies go,' Annie begins, 'it's a curious mixture of fact and fantasy. I've rarely seen anything like it. Quite incredible, actually.'

'Why don't you lead us through what's real and what's not?' says Hackett. 'I'm afraid my memory of the case's minutiae is a little hazy. Despite its notoriety.' A grimace.

Annie glances at me. 'The basic facts are straightforward. Eighteen years ago, Orianna was found unconscious in Gideon Wyclerc's cabin, together with Gideon's body and the murder weapon. She was subsequently tried and convicted of his murder, the forensic evidence being overwhelming. The trial caused a sensation.

'During the case, it came out that Orianna was Gideon's illegitimate daughter and that her mother, Christine, had kept this from her until the day of the murder. The killing happened shortly after Christine finally revealed the truth to Orianna.'

'And yet,' says Hackett, 'Orianna claimed that she couldn't remember anything about the killing itself?'

'Correct. Leading to a diagnosis of dissociative amnesia. And for many years, her story didn't change. She continued to insist on her innocence. Her appeals were denied. She refused therapy. And then, a few years ago, Orianna began to exhibit full-blown schizophrenic delusions. On the advice of her prison counsellor, she was transferred to our facility.' A beat. 'For reasons I'm still not sure of, Orianna agreed to talk to me. The report you're holding is the sum total of the highly complex scenario that she has created in her mind and revealed to me over the course of our sessions. A delusion in which she is released from prison and returns to Eden Falls with the express purpose of working out who *really* killed Gideon Wyclerc.'

'And *Grace* Wyclerc,' says Hackett.

'Yes. Though Grace doesn't exist, of course,' Annie says. 'Or rather, Grace and Orianna are one and the same person. Grace is a construct; the girl Orianna wished that *she* had been – namely, Gideon's *legitimate* daughter, a girl doted upon by her father and her grandfather Amos. A girl raised as part of the Wyclerc family, rather than a girl who grew up on the estate as the illegitimate daughter of the housekeeper.

'It is my belief that Orianna created Grace shortly after murdering Gideon. Grace is a result of the alternate reality that Orianna subconsciously established in order to refute the very obvious fact of her guilt.' Annie turns to me. 'Basically, Grace became Orianna's alter ego. The way that she imagines, in her account, that Eden Falls – and the world at large – responds to Grace's "disappearance" – with sympathy and compassion – is the way Orianna always wished that she had been treated by her – for want of a better word – family, and the community of Eden Falls. It's a classic case of dissociative identity disorder resulting from dissociative amnesia.'

I frown. 'Dissociative identity disorder?'

'What used to be called multiple personality disorder.' She continues: 'Much of Grace is taken from Orianna's own life. For instance, she tells us Grace ran hurdles at school, that she acted in the school play. Orianna did both of these things. She even entered the Forest Princess competition, though didn't make it to the final judging on the day of the festival. She seems to have harboured a grudge, believing that she was being judged unfairly against her peers due to her "lesser" status in the town's hierarchy. I believe she grew up with this feeling of being treated as an outsider, internalising her resentment over many years, contributing to her depiction of Eden Falls as an insular, narrow-minded place, intolerant of people such as her and her mother.

'Ultimately, the Grace that we see in Orianna's account is portrayed as an unhappy young woman, despite being born into privilege. A young woman doomed to a terrible fate.'

A short silence follows, then Hackett says, 'There are usually early markers for the kind of delusional pathology you're describing.'

'Yes. Much of this fits with what we now know about Orianna. She was diagnosed early on – during her teenage years – with borderline personality disorder. Even then, she exhibited symptoms of delusional paranoia, and a very vivid fantasy life. A tendency to violence in confrontational situations. The diagnosis was reconfirmed after Gideon's murder and her arrest.'

'By Dr Chester Cozell?'

Annie nods. 'Her symptoms were sharpened by the dissociative amnesia that followed Gideon's killing. It's my belief that the trauma of the killing sent Orianna over the edge; a darkness settled on her mind. That's when she began to construct these elaborate fantasies about what had actually happened that day. Anything but face up to the truth of her crime.'

Hackett picks up the report again, flicks through it. 'The detail is extraordinary.'

'Much of it is based on reality. As you know, I've been working with the Wyclerc family, through Amos, to determine how much of Orianna's account can be discounted, how much might be taken as truth. I should add that Amos *did* hire an investigative agency to go through the case again – Gideon's murder, that is. This was shortly after I first approached him. It was mentioned on various internet true-crime forums dedicated to Orianna's case, forums that she has been actively following in prison.

'In fact, all the alternative-suspect theories in her narrative have come from such forums, and also from an ongoing dialogue she has maintained with representatives of the Innocence Project who, for obvious reasons, have had a longstanding interest in her case. Speculation about the other Wyclercs, the rumours of an affair between Tommy Quinn and Rebekah Wyclerc – something that was confirmed by Tommy Quinn in an interview he gave to a scandal blog, claiming that he told Gideon about the affair on the day of his death – you can see how Orianna has picked up such details from public forums and woven them into her story. This also explains her speculation that, on the day of his death, Gideon went to Rebekah and told her about Orianna being his illegitimate daughter, after which Rebekah confronted Christine, who then, as we know, told Orianna that Gideon was her father. In fact, Christine also confirmed publicly that this is exactly what happened.' A beat. 'Don't forget that amateur sleuths have been sniffing around Eden Falls ever since Orianna's conviction, digging up information and inventing theories to prove her innocence. Orianna simply used such conjectures in her own narrative.' Another pause. 'I *had* hoped to slowly draw her out of her delusion by confronting her with inconsistences in her account, but my attempts to do so have been met with a wall of disbelief. Even when she shows signs of wavering, Orianna ultimately resets the next time we meet, returning to the same story. Namely, that she's innocent; that many other suspects existed for Gideon's murder; that she was released from prison, "returned" to Eden Falls and discovered the true killer.' She angles herself towards me. 'Orianna's portrayal of Amos is of a hard, severe man, who ultimately becomes more sympathetic as her account progresses. That's pretty close to what really happened between them. Amos does – did – feel great regret over what happened to Orianna. It's one of the reasons he agreed to help when I approached him after I began treating her.'

Hackett now turns to me. 'Is that why you've taken such a keen interest? Because you think you mistreated her?'

Hackett's question is blunt. I can appreciate bluntness.

'I'm dying, Dr Hackett. Cancer. Orianna is my only grandchild.'

'So it's true that you've written her into your will?'

'Yes.'

'Your cancer, the will – these things seem to have made their way into her account.'

Annie cuts in. 'Again, this stuff is all available online.'

'Nothing is sacred, any more,' I rumble.

Hackett looks thoughtful. 'You leave her a fortune – yet she has *you* shot dead in her narrative. Up at this abandoned mine. A little residual anger, wouldn't you say?

Subconscious, perhaps, but potent nonetheless.' He dips back into the report. 'I'd like to check a couple of details, if I may? Nathaniel Wyclerc. Your father. Is it true that he killed himself?'

'Yes. Staked out a boar pit and threw himself into it. The official verdict was accidental death.'

'Do you really believe that your father killed himself because of guilt over murdering his brother and sister, as Orianna claims in her narrative?'

'I believe that. Yes.'

'How would Orianna know that?'

Annie interjects. 'These matters weren't the secrets Orianna treats them as in her narrative. In *her* story, she's the protagonist. It's important for her to demonstrate – to herself, if no one else – that she has *agency*, that she is the one unravelling these secrets leading her closer and closer to the truth – namely to the true killer of Gideon Wyclerc.' She glances my way. 'Amos tells me rumours about his father had been floating around the Wyclerc estate for years. Many people thought that Nathaniel burned the chapel down and killed his own brother and sister because he believed they were in an incestuous relationship.'

'Do *you* believe that your father got away with murder?' Hackett's tone is curious.

'He didn't get away with it,' I respond. 'He was haunted by it. Before he died, he confessed to me, and then he killed himself.'

Hackett shifts in his seat. 'What about Hannah Wyclerc? Her accusation that she was raped by Gideon?'

'That recently came into the public domain,' Annie

says. 'But I also believe Orianna could have picked that up from Luke Wyclerc.'

'Luke? Her cousin? The boy she had a relationship with? Did that actually happen, by the way? I mean, he testified *against* her at trial, didn't he?'

'He did. But the relationship was real. Luke admitted to it on the stand. It happened pretty much as Orianna tells us, beginning with their chance meeting as teenagers in the woods on the Wyclerc estate. But Luke remains adamant that he *didn't* meet up with Orianna on the day of Gideon's killing. Just as he said in court.'

'But in Orianna's version, being with Luke earlier that day, firing that shotgun, explains why her prints were on the weapon and why she had gunshot residue on her?'

'That's correct.'

'Do you think Luke could be lying?'

'He's always stuck to his story. And he has consistently refused to meet with me during my treatment of Orianna. Even Amos couldn't get him to talk to me.'

'Why *would* he lie?' Hackett muses.

'Well, if you follow Orianna's logic, she continues to insist that she caught the scent of Luke's cologne just before she was "knocked out" by an unknown assailant in Gideon's cabin. In her narrative, she eventually discovers that this assailant was David Wyclerc, Luke's father. So – playing devil's advocate for a moment – if we assume Orianna is *not* delusional, at least not about the cologne – then Luke would have a strong motive for lying. He lied to protect his father and, of course, his mother, Susannah, who – according to Orianna – fired the actual shots that killed Gideon.'

'There's no evidence that David or Susannah were in that cabin – according to the police report,' I rumble. 'The real one, I mean.'

'No. No evidence,' Annie says. 'But, as Orianna tells us in her accounts of the trial – which *are* accurate, by the way – they accord with the trial transcript – the police didn't look very hard.'

Hackett strokes his chin. 'Let's go back to Hannah Wyclerc. Was she or was she not sexually assaulted by Gideon?'

I purse my mouth. 'She told me that Gideon raped her. Back when they were kids. I refused to believe her. I stopped her mother, Martha, from believing her. She left home at eighteen and cut herself off from the family. That's all true.'

'And do you believe her now?'

'I do. My understanding is that Hannah has spoken about it since Orianna's trial. One of those MeToo revelations.' He sniffs. 'It's in the public domain, as Annie says. I suppose that's where Orianna got it from.'

'And Susannah Wyclerc? In Orianna's narrative, Susannah tells Orianna that the motive behind her killing of Gideon was that he'd raped her too.'

'Susannah has never said anything to me. But there was an ugly rumour, a few years ago, after David died, and after Hannah went public. Maybe Susannah said something to someone on the estate. Word gets out. Goddamned crazies sniffing around all the time.'

'Perhaps that's how Orianna heard of it, and later built it into her narrative?'

'That would be my guess,' Annie says. 'We have to

remember that there were blank spots in Orianna's memory until I began treating her. Fugue states often exhibit as an inability to recall traumatic events. In Orianna's case, she found herself shaken awake in Gideon's cabin with Gideon's corpse yards from her and no clear memory of what had happened. But it is my belief that, during our therapy, certain things began to come back to her. She patched together those fragmented memories, woven in with an increasingly complex delusion – fuelled by theories she accessed via her regular internet sessions in prison – to create a narrative in which she "solves" Gideon's murder and the disappearance of the girl she had invented to carry her guilt: Grace Wyclerc. But I am convinced that some of what she has managed to recall is fact.'

'Is internet access in prison a routine thing now?' I ask. 'What about the security issues?'

'Most prisons allow supervised access,' Hackett answers. 'Especially when it is for the purposes of legal research into an inmate's own case. For appeals and the like. Also, it is now considered, in liberal circles, cruel and inhumane punishment to deprive the average American of his – or her – God-given right to surf the web. Even behind bars.' He grimaces.

A short silence falls on us.

'Tommy Quinn,' says Hackett suddenly. 'Is *he* real? And if so, do we know how he fits into this grand delusion?'

I stir to life. 'He's real, all right. Another high-school quarterback whose life didn't turn out the way he'd hoped. Quinn fell into drugs. Spent years in prison. It was common knowledge that Rebekah and Tommy had a thing. As Annie said, he later confirmed it publicly.'

'I believe that's the reason Orianna incorporated him into her fantasy,' Annie adds. 'Quinn became another very obvious alternative suspect for Gideon's murder – at least in her mind.'

'And Orianna's account of this crucifix pendant found in Quinn's trailer ... A fabrication, I presume?'

'The crucifix is real,' I say. 'I gave it to Orianna.'

Hackett seems surprised. 'Why would you do that?'

'I was never the ogre Orianna makes out. Like I said, I suspected she was my grandchild long before it became common knowledge. I came to believe that Gideon had met Christine in Barrier, Eden Falls' neighbouring town. It's where he went to pick up women. When Christine became pregnant by him, he gave her a job at the Big House. I don't know why he did that, why she kept the child, why she agreed to work up at the house, why she kept his secret. My guess is money. A home. Security. Maybe Gideon offered it of his own accord, maybe Christine blackmailed it out of him. I guess we'll never know.'

'Why the crucifix?' repeats Hackett.

Annie cuts in. 'Again, this is where fact and fiction meet. Namely in the person of Samuel Wyclerc, Amos's second son, and Eden Falls' pastor. In Orianna's account, Samuel becomes another suspect for Gideon's killing because of an affair with the fictional figure of Grace Wyclerc – his niece. I believe that this affair was Orianna's interpretation of her own real-life affair with Luke, an affair that ended badly with Luke betraying her on the stand – according to *her* account.

'Remember that Luke, ultimately, was revealed as

Orianna's first cousin. That relationship mirrors, to a certain extent, the incestuous nature of Samuel and Grace's relationship.' A beat. 'What *is* fact is that Samuel counselled Orianna during that summer. Her increasingly fraught relationship with her mother, her relationship with Luke and the fact that they had to keep it a secret – Orianna was convinced that should it come out, she and her mother would be booted off the estate. All of this was exacerbated by her lifelong anger at the absence of her father. That summer, Orianna went to Samuel to seek guidance.'

'You've spoken with him?'

'Amos has.'

I speak up. 'Samuel told me that Orianna came to him as a troubled young woman. She always had been. The abandonment by Gideon. Her mother's sexual profligacy. Orianna needed someone to talk to, something to believe in. Samuel directed her towards the church. He told her it had helped him and thought it might help her. She took the advice to heart. I noticed Orianna carrying a Bible around that summer. Her increased interest in her faith. It's why I bought her the crucifix.'

Hackett absorbs this. 'Tell me about Orianna's mother, Christine. Why did she stay on at the Big House all those years? Why hide the fact that Gideon was the father of her child?'

'I think she was in love with him,' Annie answers.

'And yet, he was, by your account, a serial rapist. Are we certain Christine didn't make a devil's bargain with the man? Keep his secret – namely, that she'd had his child – and, in return, as Amos suggests, she receives financial security, a home – on the estate, where he could control her. Reveal it and he'd come for her. A wealthy, powerful white man in a small town.'

'I'm not sure I agree,' Annie says. 'Christine was a strange mixture of vulnerability and strength. I think she got stuck on Gideon, despite knowing the sort of man he was.'

'Strength? She killed herself, didn't she?'

I interject. 'Coroner's verdict was death by accidental drowning.'

'Nevertheless,' Hackett says, 'I find it hard to believe that she would willingly agree to a lifetime without legitimacy. For herself or her child.'

'Gideon was married,' I say. 'Christine must have realised there was no way he would walk away from that. He was a Wyclerc, with the Wyclerc legacy to consider. She was the hired help. A woman of colour—' I stop. 'Christine died two years after Orianna was imprisoned. In that time, she was cut adrift. By me; by the townsfolk of Eden Falls. She hired a lawyer to extract a settlement on the basis that Orianna was my granddaughter. But she didn't get very far, just as Orianna says in that report.'

'I can only imagine how Christine's death exacerbated Orianna's dissociative disorders,' Hackett says.

I clear my throat. 'What does Orianna think actually happened to "Grace"? What I mean is, how did this creation of hers, this Grace, end up imprisoned in the mine for all those years? As I recall, in Orianna's account, Susannah tells her that Grace showed up at the cabin just after Susannah and David murdered Gideon and knocked out Orianna.'

'It's in the report, towards the end,' Annie says. 'After "finding" Grace in the mine, Orianna tells us that Susannah finally "confesses" under police questioning. Susannah explains that after she and David had left the cabin that day, with Gideon dead and Orianna unconscious on the cabin floor, they ran straight into Grace. They had no time to think the situation through; they simply reacted, knowing that if they did nothing, Grace would raise the alarm and place them at the scene of the crime.

'They were in an impossible position. They both knew that if Grace spoke to the authorities, they would likely spend the rest of their days in prison, their lives and family destroyed. Yet neither could they bring themselves to consider the obvious solution – *killing* Grace. And so – according to Orianna – David grabbed her, clamping a hand over her mouth and subduing her. It was David who then came up with a plan.

'He rushed back to their home and drove his car back to the forest. He gagged and tied Grace up and stuck her in the trunk. And that's where she stayed, as the "search" for her raged around Eden Falls. Two days later, when the dogs had finished searching the grand chamber in the mine, David moved Grace to the administrative hut in which Orianna "found" her. David had access to the mine and the hut. That's how it began.

'Later, as days blurred into weeks, weeks into months, and months into years, the horror of the situation faded, became routine. Susannah and David visited regularly, with food, with furnishings, making Grace as comfortable as they could. Whenever they went down there, David would activate the power to the lifts, then cut it again when he left so that anyone poking around the mine wouldn't be able to get down to the hut. For Grace, he installed a portable generator, to power the hut. Their relationship became that of prisoner and guards.'

Hackett absorbs this silently. 'Presumably, the police interviewed David and Susannah after Gideon's murder?'

'They interviewed us all,' I reply.

'David had a stroke several years ago. It put him in a wheelchair,' Annie says. 'And then he killed himself. With a paring knife, just as Orianna tells us. It gripped the news cycle for a couple of days. Because of the link back to The Girl in Cell A.'

Hackett raises an eyebrow. 'I'm guessing he didn't leave a confession behind?'

'Susannah claimed he was depressed about being crippled.'

Hackett shakes his head. 'You have to marvel at the human mind, don't you? To take a few facts, rumours and scraps of conjecture and come up with something this byzantine?' Then, to me: 'I understand that your will is being contested by your son, Peter?'

I frown. 'What has that got to do with anything?'

'Merely an observation. Peter comes across as a rather unpleasant individual . . . Is there any truth to Orianna's suggestion that Peter and Gideon hated each other?'

'They were brothers. They didn't see eye to eye. Brothers often don't.'

'And the fight Orianna says they had the night before Gideon was killed?'

'Yes. They fought. It wasn't the first time.'

'How would Orianna have found out about that?'

'Word spread around the estate, around the town. It wasn't exactly a secret.'

'And there's no possibility that Peter might be *involved* in Gideon's death?'

'You're buying into Orianna's conspiracy theory?'

Hackett looks irritated. 'Of course not.'

Annie speaks in the uncomfortable silence. 'The police still don't believe that anyone other than Orianna had anything to do with Gideon's killing.'

Hackett: 'A couple more things. This Gerty, she seems to have played a central part in Orianna's narrative. Who is she?'

'A local librarian,' Annie says. 'Someone Orianna got to know. But Gerty was never a close friend of Christine's. I believe Orianna's version of Gerty is a representation of me. A sympathetic figure, a counsellor. Orianna even makes her look like me. The real Gerty doesn't.'

'Of course,' says Hackett. 'I should have seen that. And I'm guessing that this Cletus Barnes is none other than our very own Barney?'

Annie nods. 'Yes. She even gives them both the same lightning-shaped scar. There is no real Cletus, of course.'

I recall that Barney is Orianna's regular orderly here at the institute.

Hackett continues: 'And the retired detective she mentions meeting in her account, this Dick Hogan?'

'Very real,' says Annie. 'And just as unpleasant in real life as he is in Orianna's account. His testimony against Orianna was pretty much as she laid out.'

Hackett looks off into the ether. 'I don't suppose anyone actually took a look in that mine? I mean, I know Grace isn't real, but Orianna's account is so vivid, I can't believe that it doesn't reference some prior memory.'

'She visited the mine on school trips as a child,' I say. 'All the kids in Eden Falls do. Orianna recalls it the way it looks.'

Annie says: 'I think the episode in the mine is a representation of Orianna's long imprisonment. She even hints at it. There's a line during her account of being trapped in the mine where she says: "She was back in her prison cell, those early days when the walls closed in, inch by inch, crushing bone, driving the breath from her lungs." I remember it because it was so obvious.'

Hackett nods, looking vaguely embarrassed at not having picked this up himself. 'And Luke? So much of this account circles back to him and Orianna's feelings about their brief relationship.'

'Luke remains an enigma. All we know is that he and Orianna had a relationship that summer, that they kept it a secret, for fear of how his parents and the rest of the Wyclerc family might react. We know they met regularly in Gideon's cabin, that he taught her to shoot. All of that is in line with Orianna's narrative and came out in court.'

I interject. 'Luke told me that he had tried to end the relationship for weeks, finally broke it off the day *before* Gideon's death. He believes this may have contributed to Orianna's feelings of betrayal and anger towards us Wyclercs and that, ultimately, this may have pushed her over the edge the following day, when her mother told her that Gideon was her father.'

Annie speaks: 'The truth is, no one knows for certain what happened between Orianna and Gideon in that cabin. My guess is that Gideon dismissed her, treated her in the same high-handed manner he'd always approached his paternal obligations. Perhaps he laughed at her. Orianna, already unstable, picked up the shotgun and allowed the violent self-expression that underlies her psyche to take over.'

Hackett drums his fingers on the table. 'In forty years of practice, I've never seen anything so elaborate. Quite incredible . . . So tell me, what is it that Orianna thinks is happening *now*? I mean, if she actually believes her delusion, then – according to her – she was released from prison, returned to Eden Falls and solved the mystery of Gideon's killing, thus exonerating herself in the process. At the same time, she delivered this fictitious alter ego of hers – Grace Wyclerc – from her makeshift prison in the mine. But then what? Why does she think she's now locked up in this institute, talking to you?'

'She doesn't believe that this is a prison. She believes that she left Eden Falls after the events that she describes, after solving Gideon's murder, and then, subsequently, found it impossible to move on with her life. She became troubled by bad memories, of everything that had happened, her lost years, the trauma she'd suffered, her mother's death. In the end, she could no longer function and went to see someone about it. They sent her here. Orianna believes that she has checked herself into a therapeutic clinic. To get well.'

'So she's here for therapy?'

'That's what she's chosen to believe.'

Hackett looks thoughtful. 'You said you'd tried confronting her with inconsistencies in her account?'

'Yes. For instance, in Orianna's account, Grace was last seen in town before her disappearance. But Orianna later says that Grace ended up at Gideon's cabin – but she doesn't explain how Grace could have got there without anyone seeing her return to the estate.'

'How did she react when you put this to her?'

'She closed down. The problem is that so much fact has been woven into Orianna's account that it's almost impossible for her to begin untangling what's real and what's not. Take her description of being attacked when she first arrived in prison. That's true. Similarly, the incident she describes where Grace meets with a famous actor at the Big House and is banished upstairs. That actually happened – but to Orianna.

'And yet, other things are clearly fabrications. The man hired by Amos to follow her around after her "release" from prison, spying on her in the woods – he's simply a manifestation of Orianna's paranoia, her belief that the people of her hometown were set against her. The same can be said of her account of being attacked at the fire tower – the attack is a representation of the antipathy she believes her Eden Falls' peers have always felt towards her.

'Orianna suffers from a complex set of disorders. They interact in ways that make them incredibly difficult to treat. Delusional psychosis, dissociative identity disorder, post-traumatic stress. Ordinary people use what we call "autobiographical memories" to create and maintain a coherent, stable self-identity over time. This allows us to reflect on past experiences with insight and thus achieve self-growth. But for Orianna, her ability to recall and process autobiographical memories is faulty. We cannot be sure which of the memories she's recalling are real and which are merely propping up her delusion.'

Hackett blows out his cheeks. 'Orianna is clearly a victim of her own fantasies. She murdered Gideon Wyclerc, and I see nothing here to suggest that she would be anything other than a danger to herself and to others if she were to be let out into the free world.'

'I agree,' says Annie. 'Only . . .' She glances at me. 'This is going to sound completely unscientific, but sometimes, Orianna speaks with such conviction . . .'

Hackett flashes an indulgent smile. 'It happens to the best of us, Annie. As much as we may strive for distance, when you work with someone as long as you have with Orianna, it's impossible not to become . . . involved. Just remember, you're her therapist. Not her confessor or her lawyer. Our job here is to determine what happens next. Based on this evidence, I think it's fair to say we cannot recommend moving forward with parole proceedings. Her stay with us will be extended indefinitely. I'm afraid The Girl in Cell A will have to remain in "Cell A". Do we concur?'

Annie hesitates. 'Yes. I agree.'

Hackett turns to me. 'Mr Wyclerc?'

I hold his gaze, then unfurl from my seat. I look down at them both. 'Keep her here as long as you need to.'

158

AMOS: NOW

Outside, at the entrance, Annie Ledet turns to me. 'I'm sorry not to have better news for you.'

I crab at my pocket, take out a cigar, light it. Drawing in a deep lungful, I blow smoke into the humid afternoon air. 'Is she crazy?'

'That's not a word we use.'

'This place was an institution for the criminally insane.'

'Once upon a time, yes.'

'Level with me. Do you think she'll ever get past this? I mean, can you fix her?'

'I don't know. They say the ocean is the last great unexplored wilderness. But the truth is, the human mind is a far greater unknown.'

I pluck out the cigar, examine it. 'You had doubts. Back there. About Orianna's guilt.'

'I wouldn't exactly say doubts . . .'

I look at her. 'Don't tell me what you think. Tell me what you *feel*.'

She takes a deep breath, teeters on the brink, then brings herself back. 'Orianna murdered her own father, a father she spent her whole life yearning for. She committed a terrible crime that she cannot forgive herself for. And so, she has retreated to the one place where that crime can be erased – into fantasy.' She pauses, waiting for my reaction.

I wait her out.

'It's astonishingly difficult to break down full-blown delusional paranoia,' she continues. 'Orianna believes *she* was the victim; her entire narrative is constructed to reinforce that notion. The fact that so much of that narrative is based *on* facts, however selectively she has chosen to weave those facts into her account, simply reinforces its credibility in her own mind. It may seem fantastical to us, but to her, it is reality. She cannot simply snap out of it. There is no medication we can give her that will wake her up. Her mind is broken, a psychic fracture where she compartmentalises her guilt. And remember, the day she does let go of her fantasy, she will have to face the very painful reality of her crime. Who's to say that won't have an equally devastating effect?'

A car rumbles along the driveway from the gate to the facility.

'But if she really didn't do it?' I persist.

'Then someone framed her, and, somewhere out there, a killer walks free.' She looks away. 'There's something I'd like to ask *you*.' She stops.

'Spit it out.'

'Orianna mentions in her account the miners you ...' She searches for the words. 'I read about the incident online. Did you really let them die?'

I look at her with eyes that feel ancient, then turn and limp away.

159

AMOS: NOW

Instead of going up to the Big House, I turn right and drive to the edge of the southern woods.

Parking up, I walk into the trees, following the map I made in my mind after reading Annie Ledet's report.

I find the riven oak easily enough. It is only a little way in and its distinctive appearance stands it out from the trees surrounding it.

It would be a lie to say that I am haunted by Gideon's death. I have long ago laid my son to rest. What truly haunts me is the need for answers. For truth.

The gash in the tree's trunk draws me in.

I reach in, feeling foolish – the victim of a broken woman's fantasy – scrabble around, until, against all expectation, my fingers find . . . *something*.

I pull out a journal, hold it in my hands, stare at it in astonishment.

I had convinced myself that the notebook was simply another of the details that Orianna has made up, a fabrication created to suit her narrative.

An odd feeling moves through me.

Here is concrete physical evidence that – at least, in part – truth underpins Orianna's delusion.

I open the book – it is barely held together, rain-mildewed and bored by insects over so many years – flip past blank pages to a series of entries at the end.

I love you. It's a simple as that. This is the first time in my life I feel that someone truly sees me, who I am, what I want.

I understand your need for secrecy, but I'm tired of it. I live for our moments together. Have you any idea how hard it is for me to pretend that I'm the same person I was before we fell in love? I want to be able to love you openly. I want us to leave this town. I want us to build a life together, somewhere no one knows us. Please, my love, let's just go. Tell no one. Just leave, in the dead of night.

Have I done something wrong? Why are you pushing me away? Is it because of them?

And then the final entry, dated just before Gideon had been murdered.

Do you think that what we've done is wrong? How can love be wrong? You feel so distant. I can't bear it. I won't let them ruin what we have. I've been thinking about what you said. That you want to end it. I can't go back to being that lost, lonely girl. I won't let you end us. I love you, Luke. I'll never let you go.

The entries are all but identical to the ones Orianna has described in her narrative. The only difference is how she has ended the final entry.

I love you, Luke. I'll never let you go.

My hands are shaking.

The journal seems to bear out Annie Ledet's conjecture that the fictional relationship Orianna described between Samuel and Grace was a corollary of the real affair Orianna had with Luke. In Orianna's delusional narrative, the notebook belonged to her alter ego, Grace. In reality, the notebook is Orianna's and its pages contain a record of her unhappiness at the way things ended with Luke, a precursor of her descent into the rage that would end with Gideon's murder.

I slip the notebook into my pocket and walk back to my car.

160

AMOS: NOW

Susannah stands by the windows behind my desk, nervously fingering a clutch of beads around her throat.

As I enter, she turns to face me.

'Susannah. Thanks for coming.'

She nods. 'The housemaid tells me you went to visit Orianna again. Why?'

I ease onto the couch, wait as Susannah takes the seat opposite.

'Isn't the truth important?'

'Truth? Orianna is in denial. She wants you to believe in this fairy tale of hers. That she was set up. That David was Gideon's killer. Frankly, I'm livid that you've entertained this, this *nonsense* for so long. David always treated her and her mother with consideration, which is more than I can say for others in this family.'

'Orianna doesn't believe that *David* killed Gideon. She believes *you* killed him. Because Gideon raped you. It was David who knocked Orianna unconscious in Gideon's cabin; it was David's cologne that Orianna recalls.'

Susannah is shaking her head. 'Do you realise how ridiculous that sounds? All these years, she's clung to the idea that someone set her up. On the basis of what? A whiff of cologne? Doesn't she understand that it's all in her mind? Aren't her therapists supposed to be able to convince her of what's real and what's not?' Her mouth makes a hard line. 'I'm almost glad David is gone.'

I say nothing. Three years ago, David killed himself, a year after the stroke that put him in a wheelchair. Orianna got that part right. It was widely publicised, of course. Everything about the Wyclercs seems to find itself into the public domain, sooner or later. If our own fame has waned in recent years, Orianna's notoriety ensures that nothing of the family's business remains outside of the spotlight.

'Why did David kill himself, Susannah?'

'We've been through this. He couldn't take living as a cripple. The man was depressed, for Christ's sake.'

'They say guilt can drive a man into an early grave.'

She ignores this.

'Is Luke back?' I ask.

For the past year, Luke has been stationed in Barrier. He's had enough of Eden Falls. For now.

'No. And I'd appreciate you leaving him alone. Luke doesn't need you to keep dragging him back into the past. He's let Orianna go. Moved on with his life. Maybe you should too.'

'Luke is at the heart of Orianna's narrative. His testimony against her, at trial, was instrumental in her conviction. Their affair, back when they were teenagers, has left a deep imprint on Orianna, hence his starring role in her delusion ... He could be helpful in her treatment.'

'I don't give a damn about her treatment!' The anger comes like a squall of rain. She seems to realise that it is out of character, calms herself. 'What I mean is, it's time you let this alone.'

'Why won't Luke talk to me, Susannah?' My voice is a rasp. 'Why is he avoiding me? What are you both hiding?'

Her face hardens. 'Why did you ask me to come here today? As far as I'm concerned – as far as *my* family is concerned – Orianna is in the past.'

'And yet, I've left her a controlling stake in Wyclerc Industries.'

Susannah's cheeks tighten.

'I know what you're all thinking. "Amos has lost his mind. How can he leave his fortune to a murderer?"'

'For God's sake, by your own account, Orianna is crazy, delusional. She invented this whole story about how someone else killed Gideon. Invented a whole other girl – Grace – to carry her guilt. The woman is a *schizo*.'

A ringing silence, and then Susannah stands up. 'I'm afraid I really must get back to the house. I have friends coming over.'

'There's a couple of other things. I never really made the connection before ... You and Orianna are about the same height.'

Her expression pinches into confusion.

'The forensic evidence suggested Gideon's killer was around five-four. You're about five-four.' I dig out the notebook, hold it out to her. 'I found this inside a tree on the estate. Exactly where Orianna said it would be.' I observe her closely, waiting for a reaction. She gives me nothing. 'So much of her delusion is based on facts, small details that, when you examine them, turn out to be accurate. It makes me wonder ... If Orianna *is* telling the truth – or some version of it – and her memory of that cologne is real, then it would mean that David really was there that day. Which would suggest that the rest of her story about what happened in that cabin might, conceivably, also be true.' I stop. 'You know, if you *did* shoot Gideon because he raped you, then maybe he deserved it. He was my son, and I loved him, but I won't defend the indefensible.'

Her face is carved in stone.

'Orianna doesn't deserve to spend her life locked up because of something she may not have done, lost inside a fantasy.'

Nothing.

'They still call her The Girl in Cell A. There are legions out there to whom she is nothing but a cause. Or a cautionary tale. But she's more than that, Susannah. She's Gideon's child. She's a Wyclerc. She's one of us.'

Something unnameable flickers in Susannah's eyes. 'Let it go, Amos,' she says wearily. 'Let it go or you'll never know any peace.'

I watch her as she stands up and walks away.

When she reaches her car, down in the courtyard, she looks back up at the Big House.

I stare down at her from the window behind my desk, imagine the last heat of the day sizzling around her.

Susannah meets my gaze. For the longest moment, we stare at each other.

And then, she smiles, a slow, secret smile that vanishes so quickly I cannot be certain that I saw it at all.

A chill envelops me.

I watch as Susannah ducks into her car and drives away.

THE END

Acknowledgements

It's always frightening doing something new. With this book I've had to do several new things. This is my first book set outside India. It's my first psychological thriller. It's my first book written using first person narrative. It's the first book that has taken me three years to finish. It's the first book where I've had to take a complete draft, and then tear it apart and restructure it. It's the first book where I've wanted to hurl myself off a cliff, several times.

So, all in all, a long, exhilarating, and sometimes painful journey.

The good news? I am incredibly happy with the end result. However the book ultimately fares, as a writer I'm glad I took on the challenge of doing something different. I hope you've enjoyed reading it.

Why small-town America? I have always been fascinated by Americana, both onscreen and on the page, all the way from *To Kill a Mockingbird* to Stephen King. One of my favourite films, which I first saw as a teenager, is *In the Heat of the Night*, starring Sydney Poitier in a seminal role. This film – and others – shaped my vision of such places, places of quiet heartbreak, simmering hostilities, and shattering secrets. Human drama is at its keenest in such settings – and what more could a writer wish for?

I could not have got this far without a whole team behind (and usually in front) of me.

So, thank you to my agent Euan Thorneycroft at A.M. Heath, my editor Jo Dickinson, assistant editor Kate Norman, and my publicist Alainna Hadjigeorgiou.

I would also like to thank the others involved at Hodder, namely, Inayah Sheikh Thomas in production and Dom Gribben in audiobooks. Similar thanks go to Euan's assistant Jessica Lee. And thank you once again to Jack Smyth for another terrific cover.

Thank you also to the many readers, critics, reviewers, bloggers, book-groupers, podcasters, and word-of-mouth enthusiasts who have helped me get to a point in my career where I can take such risks. Your kindness is hugely appreciated.

Special credit to early chapter readers, Tracy Fenton and the TBC (THE Book Club) gang, and Sam Brownley, Kath Middleton and Caroline Maston from the UK Crime Book Club. Your feedback helped me immensely.

And another special thank you to writer Nev March and Pravesh Chatturvedi who drove me around small-town America last year, introduced me to my first po'boy (if you know, you know), and went way beyond the call of duty. Thank you too, to the gang at Malice Domestic who all made me feel so welcome and gave me excellent tips on how to 'write America'.

My gratitude, as ever, to my WhatsApp pals, namely, Abir Mukherjee, Ayisha Malik, Amit Dhand, Imran Mahmood, and Alex Caan. Brilliant writers and even better human beings. For the most part.

And lastly, a thank you to my family. My brothers and

sisters, nephews and nieces, for keeping me grounded; and to my wife, Nirupama, for keeping me sane and healthy. After a couple of medical issues last year, she has not only transformed my diet, but also insists on replacing my 'author wardrobe', for no good reason that I can understand, but which apparently is very necessary for the modern writer.

READ THE HIGHLY ACCLAIMED MALABAR HOUSE SERIES

BOOK 1

BOOK 2

BOOK 3

BOOK 4

BOOK 5

And the fun never stops… Listen to bestselling crime authors Vaseem Khan and Abir Mukherjee on the Red Hot Chilli Writers podcast

A podcast that discusses books and writing, as well as the creative arts, pop culture, risqué humour and Big Fat Asian weddings. The podcast features big name interviews, alongside offering advice, on-air therapy and lashings of cultural anarchy. Listen in on iTunes, Spotify, Spreaker or visit WWW.REDHOTCHILLIWRITERS.COM

You can also keep up to date with Vaseem's work by joining his newsletter. It goes out quarterly and includes:

*Extracts from Vaseem's next book *Exclusive short stories and articles *News of forthcoming events and signings *Competitions – win signed copies of books *Writing advice *Latest forensic and crime science articles *Vaseem's reading recommendations

You can join the newsletter in just a few seconds at Vaseem's website:

WWW.VASEEMKHAN.COM

DISCOVER
VASEEM KHAN'S
charming Baby Ganesh Agency series, combining murder, Mumbai and a baby elephant.

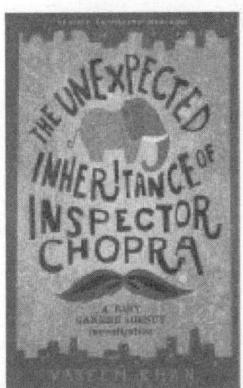